HEAL ME, DADDY

LAYLAH ROBERTS

Laylah Roberts.

Heal Me, Daddy.

Cover Design by: Allycat's Creations

Editing: Celeste Jones

✿ Created with Vellum

LET'S KEEP IN TOUCH!

Don't miss a new release, sign up to my newsletter for sneak peeks, deleted scenes and giveaways: https://landing.mailerlite.com/web-forms/landing/p7l6g0

You can also join my Facebook readers group here: https://www.facebook.com/groups/386830425069911/

BOOKS BY LAYLAH ROBERTS

Doms of Decadence

Just for You, Sir

Forever Yours, Sir

For the Love of Sir

Sinfully Yours, Sir

Make me, Sir

A Taste of Sir

To Save Sir

Sir's Redemption

Reveal Me, Sir

Montana Daddies

Daddy Bear

Daddy's Little Darling

Daddy's Naughty Darling Novella

Daddy's Sweet Girl

Daddy's Lost Love

A Montana Daddies Christmas

Daring Daddy

Warrior Daddy

Daddy's Angel

Heal Me, Daddy

MC Daddy

Motorcycle Daddy

Hero Daddy (coming August 2020)

Haven, Texas Series

Lila's Loves

Laken's Surrender

Saving Savannah

Molly's Man

Saxon's Soul

Mastered by Malone

How West was Won

Cole's Mistake

Men of Orion

Worlds Apart

Cavan Gang

Rectify

Redemption

Redemption Valley

Audra's Awakening

Old-Fashioned Series

An Old-Fashioned Man

Two Old-Fashioned Men

Her Old-Fashioned Husband

Her Old-Fashioned Boss

His Old-Fashioned Love

An Old-Fashioned Christmas

Bad Boys of Wildeside

Wilde

Sinclair

Luke

1

———————

"**Y**ou've gone the wrong damn way."

Archer Miller tightened his hands around the steering wheel of his BMW.

Deep breath. Calm. You cannot kill him. One day you might need him. For a kidney. Or bone marrow. Or ...

Okay, he was out of reasons for why he shouldn't murder his asshole younger brother.

"Isaac—"

"Don't call me that," Isaac muttered back, glaring out the window, his arms crossed over his chest, looking much like he had as a petulant teenager. Except he was now closing in on forty, had bulked up and there were a few grays peeking through his dark-blond hair.

Archer didn't like to think too closely about what had given his brother those gray hairs. Isaac's time spent in the Navy had only hardened his already rough edges, until it was extremely rare to see him smile.

And he couldn't remember the last time he'd heard his brother laugh.

"I'm not calling you Doc," he said with exasperation. It was what everyone on Sanctuary Ranch called him. Living there suited him. A quiet ranch nestled into the Montana landscape. A place where people who enjoyed relationships out of the norm were accepted and embraced.

Sanctuary wasn't the sort of place Archer could live. While he was a Dom, he didn't want a relationship where he was always in charge. Unlike Isaac. He wanted a Little. He liked to always be in control. Unfortunately, he hadn't had a Little in a long time.

Archer worried he'd never take another one.

Living on a ranch in the middle of nowhere wasn't for him. He liked civilization, thank you very much.

Which is why you're driving along a dirt road to spend a long weekend in an isolated cabin? He sighed. The things he did in an attempt to heal the relationship with his brother.

"Why not?"

"Let's see. Because I'm a doctor as well? Because I'm your brother and you have a perfectly good name?"

Isaac grumbled something under his breath. He hated his name, since it was one he shared with his father. To say they weren't on good terms was putting it mildly.

"Would you rather I call you Issy?" he asked, using his child-hood nickname.

"No," Isaac bit back sharply. "Where the fuck are we even headed? Do you know where this place is? Are you sure you can drive in these conditions? No fancy streets down this part of the country."

"Fancy streets? What constitutes fancy? Lights? Pavement? Signs?" Archer asked. It was getting increasingly hard to see. Dusk had hit and it wouldn't be long until it was fully dark. He would rather have been at the cabin by now, but Isaac had insisted they couldn't leave until after lunch. He had a thing about eating out. As in he refused to do it.

Archer had been a psychiatrist for over fifteen years and he'd never come across someone as difficult as Isaac.

Then after his brother had lunch, he'd gotten called away and Archer had ended up visiting with Ari, so they hadn't left Sanctuary until late afternoon.

His brother just grunted. Archer ignored him, concentrating on his driving. "And I'm headed in the direction the GPS told me to take."

"Fancy fucking machines can't replace an actual map."

"Jesus fucking Christ, Isaac," he muttered. His brother could make him lose his patience quicker than anyone else. "You're thirty-nine not ninety-eight. GPS has been around for freaking years. Would it hurt you to at least pretend like you want to be here?"

"Might," Isaac grunted back.

"You're an asshole. This weekend is supposed to be about the two of us—holy fuck!"

He slammed on the brakes, turning the vehicle towards the right as a deer bounded out across the road in front of them. He hadn't been going that fast, but the downpour of rain had turned the dirt road to mud and his tires slid across the surface. Fuck! The vehicle slammed into a tree, making him jolt against the seatbelt.

His breath came in fast pants, adrenaline racing through him. Shit. Shit.

Why hadn't the airbags detonated? This was a rental vehicle, but they should still work. Maybe they'd been going too slow to set them off.

Fuck, Isaac!

He turned to check on his brother. "Isaac, you okay? Isaac?" He undid his seatbelt as his brother let out a low groan. "Isaac!"

His brother shifted around to face him. Archer turned on the overhead light.

"Fuck!" Archer swore. "Your head!"

There was a gash on the right side of the other man's temple. Blood was dripping down his face. "I'll get your bag out of the back."

"It's fine. Just a bit of a scratch."

Bit of a scratch. Right. Archer shook his head as he reached into the back for his jacket, pulling it on then jumping out of the truck. His boots squelched in the mud.

And this is why he stuck to paved roads. Fancy, his ass.

He moved to the back, opening it up and grabbing Isaac's medical bag. He never went anywhere without it. There was probably a first aid kit, but he knew his brother's bag was better stocked. Rain pelted down. Icy cold. He grimaced as he saw the damage to the rental. Fuck. He wondered if roadside assistance would make it out this far. And in this weather. In the growing dark.

Shit. Fuck.

With a sigh, he stomped his way back around to the driver's side door, climbing in. Isaac had his belt off and was pressing the sleeve of his sweater to his head.

"How bad's the damage?" he rumbled, taking a bandage from Archer and pressing it against the wound.

"Don't think we're gonna make it to the cabin tonight. I'll call Murray, see if he knows someone local who can come get us. Might need to leave the rental here overnight until it can get towed." He looked at his brother guiltily. "I'm really sorry. I thought I was going slow enough. I didn't see that deer."

Perhaps he should have let Isaac drive instead of being so damned sure he could handle these conditions.

"Not your fault. Deer came out of nowhere," Isaac muttered, surprising him. He'd thought he would take this opportunity to snipe at him.

Well. All right then.

FUCK.

Doc's head was throbbing. He was trying not to let the pain show but he'd kill for some Tylenol right now. He grabbed his medical bag from Archer as his brother spoke on the phone to his friend, Murray, the guy whose holiday cabin they were meant to be staying at for the weekend.

He tuned out Archer's voice as he grabbed some painkillers and swallowed them dry.

This was probably karma for being such a grumpy asshole. He knew Archer was trying. But he was trying too hard. It just made it more difficult for him to relax. He was here, wasn't he? Wasn't that enough for big bro? Oh no, he had to keep pushing.

Archer didn't get that all he wanted was to be alone. This was the best out of life he could expect. He hardly ever had to leave Sanctuary. Everyone there accepted him as he was.

They didn't try to change him. They definitely didn't try to psychoanalyze him.

He didn't get why Archer couldn't leave well enough alone. Not all brothers had to be super close. They were just different.

Archer liked living in the city. He enjoyed eating at restaurants, going to concerts, dating women with as much personality as a wet rag.

While he...just wanted to be left alone.

He closed his eyes tiredly.

"Hey, don't close your eyes. You can't go to sleep on me," Archer demanded, shaking him lightly. Shit. He must have ended his call.

"Jesus, I'm not falling asleep," he snapped back. "Don't shake me. My head is already fucking throbbing from having my brains knocked around."

"What brains?" Archer joked.

He opened one eye and glared at his brother. "Har-har."

"Sorry," Archer said again. "Just don't want you going unconscious on me."

"Worried I'll die, and you'll have to deal with mom and dad on your own in their old age?"

Archer sighed. "We both know I'll have to deal with them whether you're alive or not."

"Hey, that's not fair. I'm willing to go halves in paying for their retirement home. But I ain't willing to pay off all the nurses the old man tries to feel up."

Archer grimaced. "Christ. Fuck. You think he'll do that?"

"No reason his personality would get better with age."

They both fell silent thinking about their cheating asshole of a father.

"Remember that secretary he used to have?" Archer asked.

"Which one?" he asked dryly.

"The one who would always hug you and press your face right into her big boobs."

"Oh yeah. She was my favorite."

Archer shook his head. "I once walked in on him banging her over his desk. I was nine. Their marriage is so messed up."

"What? The fact the old man tries to bang anyone that moves? Or that mother knows and pays them off, so they don't go to the press?"

"All of it." Archer sighed. "Murray's sending one of his neighbors to get us. He said it's unlikely the guy that runs the garage will come up here tonight. I got an earful about how we should have left earlier."

"Great. Wonder how long we'll have to wait."

"We could always have a talk about why we're here."

"Fun. Talking. My favorite thing."

"Isaac."

"Archer," he repeated. He hated his fucking name. All he could hear was his mother saying it in that disappointed drawl of hers. Nothing he'd ever done had been right. Not like her golden child.

Enough. You have to get past this.

He thought he had. But that was before Evelyn messed him up all over again.

"I want us to have a relationship again. I know you don't believe that I had nothing to do with Evelyn—"

"How about we agree never to talk about her? That would be a good start to mending this shit between us. Also, how about we don't talk at all. About any of it. Just agree to move on. See? We didn't need to come to some cabin in the middle of the woods to chat. I've solved it all. We could have stayed at the ranch."

"You never leave the ranch. And we've solved nothing. You can't just agree to get over everything."

"Why not?" he snapped. "Why can't we do that?"

"Because you still fucking hate me," Archer replied. "And you always will unless you let me explain."

"Maybe I don't want your explanation. Maybe I like things the way they are. Perhaps we're not supposed to be close. We should just agree to send each other fucking Christmas cards and call on our birthdays and leave it at that."

"When's the last time you sent a damn Christmas card?" Archer snarled. "And do you even know when my birthday is?"

Isaac shrugged. "There's no need for any heart to hearts or lies about forgiveness and becoming best bros. Let's just keep the truth between us. We're both completely different and we're never gonna be close and leave it at that."

Archer threw up his hands. "Fine. If that's what you really want. We can go back to being near-strangers."

That should make him happy. But very little made him happy anymore.

He opened his mouth to say something. What, he had no idea.

An apology? To tell his brother he didn't mean it? But then lights shone into the truck and Archer was climbing out.

The moment was gone.

2

Murray owed her big-time.

If he wasn't such a good neighbor, who had helped her out more than once, she wouldn't be here.

Caley knew she shouldn't have answered her phone. Most of the time, she didn't even have it charged. But just her luck, she'd charged it up last night. And so here she was. Rescuing some friends of Murray who'd had a car accident.

Probably a pair of city dwellers, looking for a weekend in the country and unused to driving on these sorts of road.

Her old truck bounced over the ruts. The suspension was shot. She just hoped she had plenty of gas. When was the last time she'd put any in? She should have brought a fuel can with her. Her gas gauge had stopped working at some stage and she'd never gotten it fixed. Come to think of it, when was the last time she'd had it serviced?

Oh well. It still went. That was what counted, right?

She spotted the large vehicle on the side of the road. Looked almost brand new. It seemed they'd skidded off the road and smashed the right side of the vehicle into a large tree. Well, the truck wasn't going anywhere until Mal could get out here and tow it. At least no one was likely to be driving past, and it was pretty much off the road. Beyond this point, there were only holiday homes. Except for Murray's, most of them were empty during the colder months. Murray came out more regularly since he didn't live far away.

She opened her door, wishing she'd remembered to bring her jacket with her. She'd been in such a state over having to leave her house to deal with strangers that she'd completely forgotten it. At least she had rainboots on.

She jumped down, grabbing onto the door as her worn boots slid in the mud. Drat. *Be careful where you walk, Caley.*

Last thing she needed was to land on her ass in the mud.

That would just be the cherry on top of this shitter of a day. Cold wind whipped through her. The rain was still pelting down as she sludged her way towards the truck. The front driver's door opened, and a tall, large figure stepped out. She came to a stop.

Shit. Fuck. She wished she'd been able to ask Murray about exactly who his guests were, but the phone connection had cut out.

Stupid storm.

She just hoped like hell there wasn't going to be any thunder. She shuddered. Thunderstorms were her nemesis.

"Hello?" she called out nervously.

Surely, Murray wouldn't have sent her down to pick up a psycho about to go on a murderous rampage.

Yes, Caley. That's exactly who Murray sent you down to rescue. A mass murderer intent on making you their next victim. Murray is in on it. It's a whole conspiracy. They deliberately crashed their expensive-looking vehicle in order to lure you out of your home and they're going to tie you up in the basement and chop you into tiny pieces...

"Hello? Hello, ma'am? Are you all right?"

"Someone knows where I am!" she yelled, taking a step back, her arms windmilling as she tried to catch her balance. "If I go missing, they'll call the cops."

Two hands grabbed her upper arms, saving her from falling onto her ass in the mud. A handsome face frowned down at her.

"Ma'am? Are you all right?"

No. She was not. Her breath heaved in and out of her lungs.

"You're not a serial killer, are you?" she asked.

"No."

"Rapist?"

His eyes widened. "Definitely not."

"Have you ever had the urge to chop someone into pieces?"

"Well, we had to dissect corpses in medical school. Does that count?"

"Medical school?"

"Um, yes. I'm Doctor Archer Miller. I'm a friend of Murray Wakely's. He lives a few miles from here."

"Yes, I know. I'm his neighbor. He sent me here to get you. Is there someone else with you?"

Or had he chopped them into little pieces?

Calm, Caley. Overactive imagination strikes again.

"Yes. He's hurt his head. I'll go get him. Umm, he's not a murderer, rapist or torturer. Just FYI."

"Good to know," she said, feeling stupid. What kind of person asked someone they'd just met those questions? Well, actually, they were the sort of questions you probably wanted to know the answers to upfront.

No use asking the questions once you were trussed up in the basement of Murray's cabin, having your fingernails plucked off as souvenirs.

"I'll help him over here," Archer told her. "Then I'll move our bags to the back of your truck? Are you able to take us to Murray's place?"

"Yep. Sure. I can do that." She hadn't actually thought about where she would be taking them. But Murray's was definitely a better idea than taking them into town.

Please don't let there be any thunder.

Another man walked towards her. He was holding something against his head. Archer turned towards him then back to her.

"Why don't you get in your truck, ma'am? It's pouring down and freezing, and you don't have a jacket on."

Was that a note of censure in his voice? She shrugged it off. What did he care if she didn't have a jacket on? He didn't know her.

But yeah, getting in the truck wasn't a bad idea. She spun, at the last minute remembering how muddy it was. Thankfully, this time, she managed to keep her balance.

Graceful as always, Caley Jane.

She climbed into her truck and turned the heater on full, aware now of how badly she was shivering. Remembering a jacket would have been smart. Caley knew she was smart. She just didn't have a lot of common sense sometimes.

If Dave had still been alive, he wouldn't have let her go out in the rain without a coat. But then, if he was still here, he'd have come out to get these guys himself.

The familiar pang of sadness hit her. Although it was growing less painful as time went on. Which made her feel guilty. It should hurt just as badly as it did when he was taken from her, right?

It felt wrong that it didn't. Like she wasn't respecting his memory. Like she was starting to love him less when that just wasn't true. She still loved him. It was just that she was so damn lonely.

The door opened and another large man swung himself into the passenger seat. What? Did they grow them huge wherever these two came from? This guy seemed a bit broader across the shoulders. Although it was hard to tell unless she saw him up against the first man. Archer. Cool name. She filed it away to use in a story.

He shut the door. He wore a slicker with the collar turned up. No doubt that kept him nice and dry. She needed to invest in one of those. She stared at him, trying to make out his features. All she could really see was that he seemed to have a short beard.

Hmm. She was a sucker for a beard. A good mountain man should have a beard. And he certainly looked like a mountain man. As though he could wrestle a grizzly bear single-handed then start a fire from scratch, skin a fish and build a shelter without breaking a sweat.

He slumped back in his seat and turned to look at her.

"Looked your fill, girl?"

She blinked at the rude comment. "Excuse me?"

"You're gawking."

Her temper stirred. All right, maybe she had been staring. But he was a stranger in her vehicle. Plus, she didn't meet many new people anymore. Certainly not men who were quite so, umm, masculine.

Good word usage there, Caley. You must be a writer.

"You're in my truck. I came out to rescue you in a storm."

"And that gives you the right to stare at me?"

"Yes."

There was a moment of silence. "Fair enough."

She'd opened her mouth to argue some more when she realized he was agreeing with her. That was unexpected. Archer walked past with the bags and placed them in the truck.

She turned back to the strange guy as he pulled a bit of cloth away from his head, feeling ill at the sight of blood on it.

"You're bleeding."

"Yep," he agreed.

"Do you need a doctor?"

The back-passenger door opened, and Archer climbed in.

"I don't need a doctor," the cranky one grumbled.

"But you're bleeding. It looks bad. It might need stitches."

"It doesn't need stitches."

"How do you know? You can't see it. We should take you to the doctor." It was going to be a painful drive into town, but better that than have this guy die on her. All right, it wasn't bleeding that much. But what if he had a concussion?

"I'm a doctor."

"You're a doctor?" she asked skeptically.

"Yeah. Why's that such a surprise? I don't look like a doctor?"

Not really but that wasn't it...

"Are you a good doctor?"

He turned more fully towards her.

"What? Yes," he said with clear irritation in his voice.

"No need to get grumpy, just seems to me that if you were a decent doctor, you'd want to look at the wound before deciding if you need stitches. But then you did hit your head." She turned to look back at Archer. "Did he lose consciousness?"

"Ahh, no, I don't think he lost consciousness."

"Oh good. 'Cause if he did, you'd need to wake him in the night to make sure he's okay."

"I'm a doctor," Dr. Cranky said loudly. "I know all of that."

"And remember, I'm a doctor too," Archer claimed. "Don't worry, he's in good hands."

The other guy snorted, as though disagreeing. She leaned towards the guy in the front, pointing back towards Archer. "What? He's not very good?"

"He's a psychiatrist."

She straightened. "Ahh. Say no more."

"Hey!" Archer complained from the back.

"So the two of you are doctors? Is that how you met?"

"We're brothers," Archer explained.

"Oh."

"Although sometimes I feel more like his keeper," Archer muttered.

"Can we get moving?" Dr. Cranky asked.

"Sure. No need to get all irritable." She turned off the hazard lights and put her truck in drive. The gears crunched. She really needed that service.

"Are you a good driver?" Dr. Cranky asked.

"Eh, I'm passable," she replied. She suddenly realized she had the urge to smile. When was the last time that happened? Mind you, when was the last time she'd said more than hello to someone? Christ, maybe she should think about getting out more. Or at least buying a pet. Someone to talk to.

"Thank you for coming to get us, ma'am," Archer said, leaning forward as she took off towards Murray's place at a slow pace. She wondered when the last time her brakes had been tested.

"Oh. That's okay. You're lucky Murray got hold of me. There's no one else up here this time of year and I don't always have my cell charged."

"You don't have your cell charged?" Dr. Cranky asked.

"Umm, no," she said slowly, wondering why he sounded so irritated.

"Why did you come? Where's your man?" Dr. Cranky queried.

Archer groaned. "Jesus, Isaac, have you got any manners?"

Isaac? That was far too nice a name for this guy.

"Not that it's any of your business, but I don't have a man."

Isaac, aka Dr. Cranky, let out a low sound. "So you live alone, and you don't keep your phone charged? Is that smart?"

"I don't know. You're a doctor and you don't think a deep cut on your head should be stitched, is that smart?"

Archer let out a small bark of laughter. But Isaac seemed like he was in the mood to scold her.

"Where's your jacket?"

She glanced briefly down at her oversized man's shirt which

was soaked through. Just as well it was dark, or she thought she might be showing off a bit more of her body than she would have liked. Her hair, which was pulled back in a low ponytail, was dripping down her back and even her underwear was wet. Yuck.

She was shivering, the heater in the old truck just not cutting it.

"Umm, ma'am, could you please keep your eyes on the road," Archer said in a strangled voice.

Oh right. She was driving.

She turned her attention back to the road. Her windshield wipers were at full speed but still not doing much. Another thing to have checked.

"I forgot it. And it's Caley."

"You know I'm Archer. This is Isaac."

"Call me Doc," Isaac said.

"Is that a bit confusing when you're both doctors?"

"We're not together that much. Isaac is my father's name," he explained. "We don't get along."

"Oh, I'm sorry."

He just shrugged, but she could tell there was a lot of emotion behind his desire not to share his father's name.

"You came out into a storm without a jacket. And in a truck that looks like it should have been crushed a long time ago. Did you even bring your cell with you?"

"He always like this or is it the hit to the head?" she asked Archer.

"I wish I could say it was the hit to his head," Archer replied dryly.

She sighed and tried to crank the heater up further. Damn it.

"Here, take my jacket." Doc reached for the zipper at the top of his jacket.

"No. I'm fine."

"You're shivering. You're going to get sick and die."

"Is that your professional opinion?"

Doc just grunted.

"I'll be fine. By the time I get your jacket on, we'll be there."

By now, he had his jacket off and was trying to hand it to her. "Take it."

"I can't. I'm driving. I don't want to run off the road."

"What road?" he replied.

"You're gonna need it when you get out."

"Take the damn jacket, Caley," he growled.

Ooh, why did her name have to sound so sexy coming from his lips? That wasn't fair.

"I don't need the jacket. I'm f-fine."

Except her teeth were chattering so badly, she could barely finish that sentence.

"Please take the jacket," Archer urged. "I'd offer mine but then he'll just get grumpy."

"Grumpier than he is now?"

"Yep."

"How is that even possible?" she muttered as she turned the truck around the corner. "I can't take it right now. I need both hands on the wheel."

This truck didn't have power steering and the suspension was so bad she needed both hands to control the wheel. Which is why she didn't drive much. She usually ended up with sore shoulders and a crick in her back when she got out.

"This heap of junk shouldn't even be on the road," Doc muttered.

"Hey!" she protested.

"Jesus, Isaac," Archer muttered. "She's doing us a favor. At least try to be polite."

"It's just the truth. Foolish thing coming out in the dark and a storm to pick up two strangers without a jacket or a cell phone and in a truck that looks like Fred Flintstone used to use his feet to power it."

"Ooh the Flintstones. I loved that as a kid," she said as they turned another corner.

Oh. Crap.

She slowed the vehicle to a stop.

"Fuck," Doc muttered beside her, staring out the window.

"I take it we were supposed to go through that creek," Archer leaned forward between their seats. Staring out at the very flooded creek.

"Yep," she said. "I should've guessed it might be flooded. Your truck might have managed it. Mine definitely won't." Not that they probably would've wanted to drive their fancy truck through that.

"Murray didn't warn us about this," Archer muttered. "Then again, he probably didn't think we would be coming out this late."

Crap. Damn it. What now? She tapped her fingers against her thigh nervously. She really didn't want to drive into town. She was tired. Her shoulders ached from controlling the truck on the rough road and it was late.

But what choice did she have?

"There another way round?" Doc asked.

"Yeah. But it's gonna take you a few hours and you have to go back through town to take it," she told them. "You're better off staying the night there and setting out for the cabin tomorrow."

"Better off just going home," Doc grumbled. "Now put the jacket on."

She sighed but she grabbed the jacket and slid it on. It was huge on her and she had to push the sleeves back off her hands. It immediately started to warm her chilled skin, though. And the scent of pine and sandalwood drifted around her.

"Why isn't your damn seatbelt on, girl?" Doc demanded.

"Oh, it doesn't work."

"It doesn't...it doesn't work?" Archer spluttered from the back while Doc mumbled something under his breath. "That's not even legal."

"Well, can't remember the last time I ever saw a cop up here. Old Arnie doesn't bother himself with coming up these parts just for me."

"She's killing me, Archer," Doc said bizarrely. "Make her stop."

"Stop what?" she asked in confusion.

"Girl, you need a keeper," Doc told her.

"I can take care of myself just fine." But his words sent a pang of longing through her. Okay, she could be slightly forgetful. But she'd survived this far on her own. Just.

She'd once had someone who had watched out for her. And she remembered how nice it felt to have someone there. Someone to share the load.

"How long to get back to town?" Archer asked.

"Dunno. In this weather, maybe about an hour and a half."

"Shit." Doc turned to Archer. "Not having her do a three-hour trip in this weather in a truck that is on its last legs and doesn't have a working seatbelt. Plus she's gonna get pneumonia sitting in those wet clothes."

"Agreed," Archer said. "Too dangerous."

"Didn't your momma teach you two that it's rude to talk about someone like they're not here?" she grumbled.

Archer turned to her, both of them were now staring at her. Which was a little intense. "Caley, I don't suppose we could impose on you for the night?"

"You...you want to stay the night? With me?"

3

If there was any other choice, he wouldn't let her drive.

However, Doc knew he shouldn't be driving right now. Not with the gash in his head. Which likely did need stitches, but now that he'd proclaimed that it didn't, he wasn't going to back down without a fight.

Plus, he didn't know where they were headed, and conditions out here were treacherous enough. But he didn't like that she was driving around in this heap of junk without a seatbelt.

And don't get him started on her lack of jacket and phone. Damn fool woman. What the hell was Murray doing sending out a little bit like her to pick up two strange men? It had been years since Murray had seen Archer. They could have changed in that time. Could be the type of men to take advantage of a woman alone.

Luckily, they weren't.

But still, it made him grumpy thinking about all the ways that Caley could be hurt. Injured. Taken advantage of.

What would cause a young woman to live out here all alone?

Something bad, he was guessing.

Maybe he should insist that Archer drive. But he'd probably just crash again. Doc sighed. He knew that wasn't fair. Knew it wasn't his fault.

But still, he was in a mood.

When aren't you in a mood?

"You want to stay the night at my cabin? With me?"

"Unless you have other suggestions," Archer said gently. That was his 'I'm so reasonable, everyone should listen to me because I know best' voice.

"I, umm, well, I don't mind taking you both into town," she said.

"You're not taking us into town," he barked. He had a roaring headache. It was cold. He was tired. He wanted to lie down. Most of all, he wanted for Caley not to be driving around in these conditions, shivering her ass off. "We're going home with you."

"But...but..." she stumbled out.

"I promise we're not murderers, rapists or torturers," Archer told her easily.

He turned to gape at his older brother. "Why the hell would you put that stuff into her mind?"

"I didn't," Archer told him. "Those were the first questions she asked me."

Doc turned to her. She shrugged. "Can't be too careful, right?"

"Jesus," he muttered. "Girl like you shouldn't be worrying about that."

"A girl like me?" she asked curiously.

"Doesn't matter," he replied, not sure what he was thinking. What did he mean, a girl like her? He didn't even know her. "We're not any of those things. You're safe with us. Now, let's head back to your place so you can take a hot bath and get out of those wet clothes before you make yourself sick."

"What my brother is trying to say is that we would really appreciate it if we could stay the night at your place. Driving long hours in this storm in a truck with a barely working heater and no seatbelt is dangerous and we don't want you putting yourself at risk for us. We promise to keep out of your way and be model house guests."

"I do not promise that," Doc replied. He turned to glare at Archer, holding in a wince as his head throbbed mercilessly. "And don't put words in my mouth."

"We can always drug him," Archer told her. "I'm a doctor. I have the necessary credentials."

"Barely," Doc muttered.

Archer sighed. "We can give you the number of someone you can call to vouch for us if you'd like." Archer dug into his pocket and brought out his cell phone. "I have several other psychiatrists I know or a judge. I even have a television host."

"She doesn't want to talk to one of your ex-girlfriends," he said. Okay, he was being a prick. But he just knew Caley would be bamboozled by Archer's charm. Everyone preferred Archer. He told himself he shouldn't care.

She's not Evelyn. She doesn't mean anything to you. You just met the girl.

"Murray vouched for you. That's enough for me," she muttered. "Judges can be bought off. And a television host? No thanks. You can stay the night, I guess. Don't really trust this weather anyway. Better we hunker down and try in the morning."

"What about psychiatrists? Aren't they trustworthy?" Archer asked as she started turning her big behemoth of a truck around. Damn thing was so ancient it probably didn't even have power steering. How was a little thing like her meant to drive around in this?

She grunted with effort. And he reached over and helped her tug at the steering wheel.

"Psychiatrists are talkers. Like television personalities. Don't trust talkers."

"Good Lord, I'm stuck in a truck with two of them," Archer muttered with exasperation.

"Thanks, I got this," she said to Isaac, panting slightly.

"Just take the help, girl. Ain't no one giving out prizes for doing it all on your own." And he wanted to help her. Normally he avoided meeting new people. Even the people he knew, he kept away from. He looked after everyone on the ranch, but he couldn't say he was particularly close to anyone.

Yet this petite girl who was a combination of spitfire and sweet totally had his attention.

It's just because she came out to help you. You feel responsible for her.

Yeah, that had to be it.

~

ARCHER SAT BACK in the ancient truck, wincing as a spring dug into his ass. This piece of junk should have been retired a long time ago. He'd thought Caley would put up more of a fight. After all, having two strange men stay with you when you lived in the middle of nowhere would be enough to make any woman worry.

And Caley...well, she seemed to have more of an overactive imagination than most.

He'd thought that he'd have to run interference for his brother. Most people could only handle Isaac in small doses.

But to his shock, Caley could give as good as she got. She didn't seem intimidated by Isaac's gruffness. Which gave him an idea...

Nah. That was ridiculous. He didn't know anything about her other than she had some sass. There was no reason to think she was a submissive, let alone a Little. And that's what Isaac needed. Someone that he could focus entirely on. Archer knew that Isaac wouldn't truly be complete without someone to look after. He might have a terrible bedside manner, but he had a deep need to take care of people. And a Little who was his, would give him that. Would help round out his rough edges.

Because underneath the snarly exterior was a man who could be caring and kind. With the right person.

They rattled along in the truck, with Caley bouncing around in her seat. Christ, her ass had to hurt, not to mention her arms and shoulders. No doubt she could do with a good rubdown... maybe he should mention that to Isaac.

He groaned. *Not here to be a matchmaker.*

"You okay back there?" Caley asked, sounding concerned. "You didn't hurt yourself, did you?"

"Oh no. I'm fine, thank you."

"He's probably worried you don't have indoor plumbing," Isaac said.

He'd bite back if they were on their own and he couldn't hear the note of tiredness and pain in his brother's voice. Just how bad was his head? Great. Now, he'd have to convince him to sit down and let him doctor him.

And put up with a hundred and one complaints about how he was doing it wrong.

Why was he trying to mend fences with this asshole again?

Oh yeah. Because he was his brother and he loved him.

He had to keep reminding himself of that.

4

Great.

What had she been thinking? Agreeing to them staying the night? Did she have enough food to feed them? They were big guys. They probably ate a lot. But they'd only be here for dinner and breakfast. Maybe they'd already eaten.

Forget about the food, Caley. What about the mess!

Oh shit. She hadn't even thought about that. She lived alone and she didn't have a lot of stuff, but she wasn't all that fond of picking up after herself either. And without someone riding her ass, reminding her to clean up...

Well...to call it a pigsty was uncharitable but if the shoe fit...

She stopped the truck close to the front door of her cute, three-bedroom log cabin. It had a large porch out the front where she liked to sit and work in summer. Inside was a fairly simple layout. One large room in the middle of the cabin that served as living, dining and kitchen. To the right were two small bedrooms, one of which she used as a study and a bathroom.

On the other side was a larger master suite. It was almost too much room for her on her own.

"Maybe you two should wait here," she said as she turned off the truck. Oh drat. She'd forgotten to turn on the outside porch light. Shouldn't the sensor lights come on? Hmm, when had she last checked that they were working?

"Wait out here?" Doc asked. "Why?"

Did everything he said come out as a demand?

"It's just...umm..."

"Spit it out, girl," Doc told her tiredly.

"Isaac," Archer snapped.

"She's shivering, even with my jacket on. We need to get her warm before she catches pneumonia."

"I didn't think you caught pneumonia from being cold."

"Girl..." Doc warned.

Jeez. Why did he keep calling her that? She was thirty-one years old. Definitely not a girl by any stretch of the imagination.

"I left in a hurry and I wasn't expecting visitors. It's a bit of a mess."

They were both silent for a moment.

"We don't care about a bit of a mess, girl."

"Let's just get inside and get you warm," Archer agreed with his brother. "Isaac needs his head looked at too."

"Oh, yes, of course." What was she thinking keeping them out here when Isaac was injured, and they were likely both cold and hungry?

"The fire should be still going, at least. I might need to get some more wood in." She started pulling off the jacket Doc had given her. "Here, have your—"

"Keep that on," he demanded as he opened his door. "I'll be fine."

He was out before she could say anything more.

"Shoot."

"I'll get the bags, you two head in," Archer called out, before climbing out. Leaving her sitting there.

Why are you just sitting there, Caley? Get a move on.

Sometimes, she was such an idiot.

Doc stepped into the log cabin.

Okay. When she said a mess, he thought she meant that she'd left a few things sitting around. But unless a tornado had somehow hit and only gone through her living room…

His lips twitched with another smile.

Jesus, that was twice in one day. Something of a miracle.

"See. I told you it was a mess." She whipped past him before he could grab at her. Dressed in his dripping jacket which was miles too big on her and her muddy rainboots, she stomped around picking up pieces of clothing that lay strewn over the sectional in front of the stone fireplace. Which was, thankfully, still burning.

"Girl—"

"I know, I know, I let it get a bit out of control. You sit. I'll find the first aid kit. I'm sure we have one somewhere."

We? He thought she lived alone. So who was we? He was surprised at the stab of disappointment.

Not your business.

"Girl—"

"I'll clear off the sofa. Here. It's okay. Most of it is clean. I think." She stared down at a sweater she picked up in confusion. "Is this even mine?"

"Caley," he said sharply as the door behind him opened.

"Holy shit," Archer exclaimed. Then he no doubt caught himself. "Nice house you have here."

"Sorry…sorry…" she said worriedly.

He narrowed his gaze at her. She was diving from mess to mess without actually making much of an impact.

Nervous. She's nervous.

"Caley, come here," he commanded.

"Uh, Isaac, I'm sure we can get the place tidied up," Archer told him.

He gave his brother a look. "I don't care about the mess."

Archer raised an eyebrow.

"Much," he added. He wasn't that bad about mess and cleanliness. Was he? He grimaced. All right he might have a tiny OCD issue. But that wasn't what he was mainly concerned about.

"Please sit down. I promise, this place will look spotless soon. Well, maybe not spotless. I'm not sure where the broom is. Oh, yes, I do. I'm using it to keep the dryer door shut."

He blinked. She what? Okay, none of that mattered right now. He needed to get her calmed down.

"Caley," he said in a low, commanding voice putting plenty of Dom into his tone. "Come here."

"Isaac," Archer warned.

Archer was a Dom. He liked to tie his partners up in the bedroom. He enjoyed going to his club. But he wasn't interested in anything beyond that. Doc was different. He'd always wanted a relationship where he was firmly in charge all the time. He'd wanted a submissive who was also his baby girl. Who he could restrain and fuck in the bedroom and cuddle and indulge the rest of the time.

Archer was warning him against using that tone with a woman they didn't know. Who wasn't a submissive.

Maybe.

Her eyes had dropped as soon as he used that tone. But then, she was distracted by her worry over the state of the cabin. And by the two hulking strangers standing in it.

For a moment, he thought he might be wrong, and she was going to ignore him. Or tell him off. Instead, she started towards him.

"Put the stuff down on the sofa, girl. We'll get it in a moment."

That was last on his to-do list. First was getting her settled, dry and warm. Second was getting in some wood for the fireplace since the basket next to it was empty. Third was seeing to his head. Fourth was sleep. He didn't even care about food at this point.

She put the stuff down on the arm of the sofa, where it all slid off onto the floor. He winced but didn't say anything. And she didn't seem to notice as she walked towards him.

"What is it?"

He pointed at the bench seat next to the door. "Sit."

She frowned but sat. He went to crouch down, biting back a wince as his head protested the movement.

"Here, let me," Archer said quietly. "You need to go take a look at that head. Think she's right. It could use some stitches."

He'd get to that in a moment. But he did let Archer crouch down in front of her.

"What are you doing?" she asked.

Archer reached for one boot, sliding it off.

"You were traipsing mud through the house," Doc explained gruffly.

"Oh. Right. Shoot. I was so focused on tidying up I didn't even notice." She sighed. "You guys think I'm a total slob, right?"

Well, not a total one. Archer set her boots to one side of the door. Then he stood. Isaac held a hand out to her, helping her stand. Shoot. Her hand was freezing.

"We need to stoke the fire up," he commented to Archer as he undid the zipper on his jacket, slipping it off her. He barely noticed that his own sweater was soaked through.

A woman's care always came first.

"Where do you keep your firewood, Caley?" Archer asked. "I'll bring some in while Isaac helps you get those clothes off."

"I don't think so! Nobody is taking my clothes off but me!"

5

She couldn't believe she'd just said that.

Such a dork.

Then there was the way she'd grabbed hold of her shirt, as though she'd expected him to start ripping it off her.

Yep. Total. Dork.

"Easy, girl. He didn't mean it like that. But you need to get out of your wet clothes," Doc told her in a calm voice. She noticed he kept his hands out at his sides. "I ain't gonna touch you so don't look at me like that. But I do want you to strip off and take a nice hot shower and don't come out 'til you're warmer, got it?"

"He meant to frame that as a request rather than a command," Archer said, trying to smooth over his brother's hard edges. She wondered how often he did that. And why he thought he had to. She saw Isaac's jaw tense at his brother's words. And wondered how much that annoyed him.

A lot, she'd bet.

She got why Archer did it. It was likely not everyone could take Isaac's rather gruff personality. Archer didn't need worry that he might offend her. If he did, she'd tell him.

Their relationship was interesting and there seemed to be some undercurrent of anger between them. But right now, she didn't have time to figure it out.

"No. I didn't. 'Cause a request means she can say no. And I'm worried about how cold she feels."

Archer frowned then reached out to lightly grasp hold of her hand. "Yeah, she's freezing."

"I'm fine. I'll quickly clean up, get some wood and find the first-aid kit. Oh, and show you where you are going to be staying. I only have one spare bed. I—"

Doc reached out and grabbed hold of her hand as she flung it through the air, gesturing nervously. "Caley, get undressed. Get showered. Then you might as well put on your PJs. It's nearly bedtime."

She blinked at him then looked over at the clock. "It's only nine."

"Yeah, and after you've had a shower, it will be close to ten. Which should be your bedtime. Now go." He turned her around.

In what universe was ten p.m. a bedtime? Sheesh. Most of the time, she stayed up until one or two in the morning, especially when on a deadline. She liked to keep going when she was on a roll.

To her surprise, she found herself in her bathroom before she'd even thought about it. Huh. She guessed she might as well shower and get changed. It was a little weird, though. Having two strangers in the cabin.

She made sure her bedroom door was locked. Not that she thought they would walk in...but still...

"This was an idiotic idea, Caley. Should have just driven them into town," she muttered to herself. She sighed and shook her head as she turned on her shower. She shivered in the cool bathroom air. She really needed to get the heater in here fixed. She put her fingers to her temples and rubbed.

The number of things that needed fixing or were falling apart around here stressed her out if she thought about it too much. So in usual Caley-style, she tried not to. Which meant everything fell into more disarray.

It wasn't that she didn't have the money to get it all fixed, it was more that she didn't know where to begin. It all felt too much.

Tackle a bit at a time, Caley Jane. Small bites.

She knew that was exactly what Dave would tell her. It was his fault, though. He'd taken care of all the day-to-day stuff so she didn't have to. And now that he was gone...she was lost. Alone. Afraid. She stepped into the shower.

"I'm doing all right. Everything will be okay. I have it all under control."

If only she had someone to help her. If she'd just had one person to call when it all got too much it might help. But there was no one. She was all alone.

"Could you be a bit more diplomatic," Archer snapped as soon as Caley disappeared.

"Not really." His brother walked over to the sofa where the stuff Caley had been collecting lay in a pile on the floor, he bent over then swayed slightly.

"Oh for God's sake. Will you sit down before you fall over? Exactly how hard did you hit your head?"

"Not that hard. Made of rocks, remember?"

"Yeah. I remember."

Archer had screamed that at him. When he'd refused to let him explain about Evelyn. Fuck.

But to his surprise, Isaac sat on the sofa. He must be feeling a lot worse than he was letting on if he was doing anything Archer said.

"Let me look at it."

Isaac refused to move his hand. "It's fine. Don't need it poked and prodded."

"Fine. Be a stubborn bastard, then. If you don't care, don't see why I should." And he was getting tired of his bullshit. "I'm going to see if I can find some firewood. That fire is about to die out. Do you think she always lives like this?"

Some mess didn't worry him. He wasn't a neat freak like Isaac. But this was a bit more of a disaster than he'd been anticipating.

"Don't know. Guessing so. Someone should be taking care of her. She shouldn't be out here on her own."

"None of our business." Although he couldn't help but agree. "I'll go get that wood."

"I'll come with you."

He whirled around. "No. You won't. Just stay there, you stubborn ass, and rest. You're pale as a ghost and I can tell you're in pain even though you're trying to hide it. Will you just let me look after you for once?"

"You're always doing that."

"What?" Archer raised his hands up.

"Looking out for me. Talking for me. Making excuses for me. I'm a grown man. Don't need you to do that."

Was he doing that? Well, Isaac was his brother, he wanted to have his back. But was it more than that? Was he always making excuses for him? As though the real Isaac wasn't good enough?

"Just trying to keep people from wanting to murder you."

"You're not always with me. I do okay at keeping people from murdering me the rest of the time."

Because he lived on an isolated ranch, surrounded by people, who for some reason, tolerated his cantankerous nature. But he was right...he didn't need Archer.

Sometimes, Archer thought he was the one who needed Isaac. He didn't have a ranch filled with people looking out for him. He had a string of meaningless relationships. Friends who would stab him in the back in a second if they thought they might gain something. And a family who weren't any better. A family that Isaac had separated from a long time ago.

"Sorry. I don't mean to do that. I just...I..."

"You've been doing it all your life. I get it. I was always the fuck-up. But I don't give a shit what people think of me, Archer. That's all you. It's your hang-ups now. If you don't like me the way I am... if you can't accept who I am...then what are we even doing?"

What indeed?

He sucked in a deep breath but before he could say anything, Isaac stood. What he'd been about to say, he wasn't certain. It wasn't like him to be short on words, but Isaac had short-circuited his brain.

"Gonna see if there's another bathroom to take a shower." He moved to the other doors, opening one. "Bedroom." He opened the next one. "Bathroom."

"Do you think we should be going through her stuff?" Archer worried.

Isaac just sent him a look. "I ain't going through her panty drawers. I'm just seeing what's behind these doors."

Archer rolled his eyes and grabbed their bags, setting them in what was obviously the spare bedroom. As he came out, he saw Isaac was still standing in the doorway to the other room.

"Huh," his brother said.

"What is it? Don't tell me she has a torture chamber?"

Her questions when she'd first met him still amused him. The thought of her asking someone else, a stranger who might harm her wiped that amusement away. Why was she living in the middle of nowhere on her own? Isaac stepped inside, letting him move into his place. He looked around the small room. There was a desk with a laptop on it sitting in front of the lone window. Papers were strewn across the desk and then down along the floor.

Seemed it wasn't just the living area that was subjected to whirl-wind Caley.

Then he turned to look at the rest of the room. Surprise hit him. He spotted a huge, oversized bean bag in one corner of the room. Next to the bean bag was a bookshelf, filled with a mixture of adult and children's books. But it was the other corner that really surprised him.

There were train tracks set up and at different places along the track were small buildings and people made of wood. He moved closer. The detail was amazing. Everything looked like it had been created by hand. Unable to resist, he picked up one house and turned it over.

Made for Caley, with love, Daddy.

"Could be her real father made it," Isaac said, looking over his shoulder.

He guessed it wasn't any of their business who made it. And lots of adults had train sets. But there was something about this set. Something special. Made for a little girl with love from her daddy.

"I'm gonna go have a shower. Can you find some firewood?"

"Sure." But this had given him some food for thought. Maybe Isaac would never forgive him for Evelyn. But perhaps he could find someone to replace her in his frosted-up heart. A Little who was in obvious need of someone to take care of her.

6

When Caley stepped back out into the living room, she was surprised to find that the fire was roaring, and the living room was mostly tidied up. Dr. Cranky turned from where he was folding clothes at the table. There were piles of clothes set out. As well as an assortment of other things.

"Hey, you found my flashlight. Awesome." She picked it up. "Been looking for this."

"It was under a jacket. A jacket that you should have worn when you came to get us."

"Do you always scold people you don't know?"

"Only when they do foolish things."

She sighed and pulled the old, plaid robe around her. It had been Dave's, so it hung off her. But like so many things of his, she'd been unable to get rid of it. Having it close made her feel less alone. If she kept his stuff here, then she could pretend that one day he would walk through that door and everything would be all right.

"Thanks for tidying up. You didn't have to."

He just gave her a look with those piercing blue eyes of his. "Nearly tripped on a pair of shoes and grazed the other side of my head."

She blushed, even though she was certain he was exaggerating. She looked up at his forehead which had a bandage on it. "How is it? Are you sure it doesn't need stitches? Are you having blurry vision? Dizziness? Nausea?"

"You a doctor in another life?"

"Ahh, no." She looked away. Right. He was the doctor, not her. "Where's Archer?"

"Having a shower. You look warmer. Feel better?"

"Uh-huh. You found the bathroom then. You've had a shower," she said belatedly, noting his change of clothes.

"Yep."

Right, so he probably thought she was acting like a completely brainless twit. Of course he'd found the bathroom. He'd had a shower.

"Sorry, I'm not used to being around people much."

She nervously twisted at the long sleeves of her robe as he continued to fold her clothes. He picked up a bra and she let out a squeak, snatching it out of his hands. "Maybe I should do that."

"I'm a doctor." He snatched it back.

"So what?"

"I've seen bras. I've seen boobs. You haven't got anything I haven't seen or touched before."

Was he talking about as a doctor? Or a lover? What would he be like in bed? *Intense.* She shivered a bit at the thought.

Stop, Caley.

"Do you guys have anyone you needed to call?"

"No, we're good."

"Really? No, Mrs. Cranky at home?"

She nearly groaned. *Really, Caley? Why did you go and ask that?*

Now he was going to think she was interested in him.

Aren't you? Don't you think he's somewhat cute?

Okay, more than somewhat cute. And she had to admit that the idea he might have someone at home waiting for him filled her with disappointment. It wasn't like she was looking for someone... it had just been so long since she'd been around another man for more than five minutes.

Is that why you're attracted to Archer too?

"Mrs. Cranky?" he drawled.

Oh. Shit. In her anxiety over asking him about a possible significant other she'd failed to realize she'd called him by his nickname.

"Umm, can I rewind the last few minutes?"

"Nope. Mrs. Cranky? Meaning I'm Mr. Cranky."

"No," she replied.

He raised an eyebrow.

"You're Dr. Cranky."

"Seems like an apt nickname to me," a deep voice spoke from close behind her. Too close. How had Archer managed to sneak up on her?

She turned slowly to look at him.

Please don't let him be half-naked.

Please do let him be half-naked.

Oh hell. She was so messed up. When she turned, though, he was dressed in a pair of navy, button-up pajamas.

"Nice pjs, bro," Doc said.

"There's nothing wrong with wearing pajamas," Archer said stiffly. "Just because you prefer the caveman approach, some of us like to be more civilized."

"All you need are the grandpa slippers and a pipe."

Her head went back and forth between them. It was very clear they were siblings. Now that she had a chance to look at them closely, side-by-side, she could see more similarities.

Archer was taller but Isaac was broader, more muscular. Not

that Archer was lacking in that area. Archer's chestnut-colored hair was neatly trimmed, his face cleanly shaven. While his brother's hair was lighter and longer and he sported a short beard.

Archer raised an eyebrow. "I forgot to pack them, my bad. Caley, I brought in some wood for the night. However, there wasn't much out in the barn. Do you have another pile?"

"Oh yes, I have some more coming in a few weeks."

Did she? She couldn't remember now. She needed to write that down.

"Have you seen a notepad around here?" she asked Doc who continued to fold clothes. Including her bras. Oh well, he was right. Wasn't like he hadn't touched them before. And the things that they supported. And hers weren't all that impressive. Come to think of it, though, she could probably use some new bras. She couldn't remember the last time she'd bought one. The one he held currently was looking a little worn.

"Would one of those do?" Isaac nodded over at the pile of notebooks he'd placed on the other end of the long, wooden table.

"Oh, yes, thanks." She grabbed one, looking around again. He pointed at a truly enormous pile of pens.

"Huh, all of these were hidden under clothes?" she asked, picking up one of her favorite pens and writing herself a note.

"No," Doc said. "Some were in the sofa."

She winced, thinking about what else could be under the sofa cushions. "You didn't need to go searching under the cushions."

"Didn't I? Also found around fifteen dollars in change."

"Really? Score."

"I put it all in a coffee mug for you. I haven't looked under the sofa yet, so there may be more to add to it."

"Oh, you don't have to do that. You've done more than enough." She was embarrassed that he'd had to tidy her house.

"Actually, I do," he muttered bizarrely.

"Isaac is a bit of a neat freak," Archer explained.

She stared down at her to-do list.

Check on firewood supply.

She tapped her pen against her chin as she thought about what else she needed to do.

Get truck serviced.

Pleased with herself for remembering that, she put the pad on the edge of the table and turned away.

Archer dove for the pad as it slipped off the edge of the table.

"Whoops. Sorry." She blushed.

Archer set the pad down. Isaac picked it up and looked at it. Then he grabbed the pen as Archer moved to the kitchen and started opening cupboards. Oh drat. She was the worst host. She was vaguely aware of Doc adding things to her list but ignored him and headed towards Archer.

"Can I make you something? Are you hungry? Would you like coffee? Tea?"

"Tea would be lovely. But I can make it." He opened another cupboard and frowned. "Where is all your food?"

"I have food." She moved towards a pantry off to the side which had a large freezer. She pulled up the lid and grabbed a frozen microwaveable meal. "See? I have heaps. What do you feel like? Mac n'cheese? Hmm, you seem more of a shepherd's pie man. Or maybe a roast? Pretty sure I have a roast in here."

"That is what you eat?"

"Sure. I mean I buy some fresh stuff when I go into town."

"And you drive there in that truck with no seatbelt?"

"Uh-huh. It's okay, I drive slow. I used to attach a bungee cord as a makeshift seatbelt but it just got annoying." She drew out a frozen meal. "Score, I have beef or chicken."

"Isaac!" Archer called out.

"He doesn't like to be called that."

"I am not calling him Doc."

She shrugged. No skin off her nose.

"What is it? I'm busy," Doc snapped. She thought it suited him.

"Caley wants to know if we want roast chicken or beef." Archer pointed at the packets of food she held. "She lives on frozen meals apparently.

Doc frowned. "You what?"

"There's nothing wrong with frozen meals," she defended. "They still have all the necessary nutrients."

Right? She actually had no idea. They were convenient and quick, which were her two main criteria.

"They're okay sometimes," Doc answered. "At least we won't get salmonella from them."

"Did he just insult my cooking?" she asked Archer.

"He has a phobia about eating stuff other people cook. Think it's got something to do with his OCD."

"I don't have fucking OCD," Doc muttered. "I just like things to be put away. In their place. And I don't appreciate getting food poisoning. It's not that weird."

Sure. Uh-huh. Not weird at all.

"See, microwave meals are fine," she told Archer.

"You shouldn't be living on microwave meals alone," Doc continued. "You need fresh vegetables, fruit, protein."

It was Archer's turn to give her a look of triumph. Rats.

"It's not like I can just pop out to the grocery store," she mumbled. She shoved the meals back into the freezer. "If you don't want to eat them, that's fine. Help yourselves to whatever you like. There's extra bedding in the closet in the spare bedroom, if someone wants to take the couch. Excuse me, I've got work to do."

She walked into her office, knowing she wasn't exactly being hospitable. But it wasn't like they were invited guests. And she needed a little bit of space right then.

～

"THAT WENT WELL," Isaac stated the obvious.

Archer glared at him. He opened the freezer and pulled out the two frozen roast meals, then searched through and grabbed a third one.

"I didn't mean to insult her."

Isaac stared at the door she'd disappeared into thoughtfully. "Don't know that she was insulted so much as overwhelmed."

Amazingly insightful for his brother. Archer shot him a look as he popped one meal into the microwave.

"What?" Isaac snapped. "You're not the only one who can read people."

"You've never seemed that interested in understanding other people."

Isaac shrugged.

Archer frowned at the microwave, which didn't appear to be plugged in. He followed the cord down. He switched it to a different socket.

Huh.

"Why isn't this thing working?" It might only be a frozen meal, but he was starving. And tired. And it seemed he was going to have to sleep on a couch tonight since there was no way he was sharing a bed with Dr. Cranky.

And he couldn't let his injured brother take the sofa.

"What's the matter? Can't work a simple microwave?"

Archer resisted the urge to hit him. Just. He waved his hand. "Let's see if you do better."

Isaac sighed then a few minutes later, stepped back. "Must be broken."

"Seems there's a few things around here that are. Did you notice the poor water pressure in the shower?"

"And the weak patch in the bathroom floor," Isaac added with a nod. "Got to be a leak somewhere, I'm guessing."

"If it doesn't get fixed, it's going to get so bad she could fall through the floor."

The fact she lived here on her own, with appliances that didn't work and a truck that should have been crushed a long time ago didn't sit right with him.

"Not sure there's a load of firewood coming," Isaac told him. "And she said she uses her broom to keep her dryer door shut."

Archer frowned worriedly. "Think she can't afford to get that stuff fixed?"

"My best guess. Wonder what she does for work. Can't be that many options out here." He looked over at the door.

"I'm not exactly good at fixing stuff but we could see what we can do while we're here," he suggested.

Isaac just grunted. "We'll be leaving in the morning and my head is aching. Doubt there's much we can do."

Isaac regretted the words as soon as he'd said them.

It was obvious she needed some help. Someone to take care of her. That was his big weakness. Being wanted, needed, important. He'd never been wanted growing up. He was the second son. Unnecessary to his parents since they had Archer. Golden child Archer who never did any wrong.

Fuck.

He had to get over this shit. It wasn't Archer's fault that their parents loved him and loathed Isaac.

It also wasn't his fault that Evelyn had preferred Archer to him. He got it. He did. He was an asshole. He could be weird. He could be hard and cold.

Although he'd tried with Evelyn. He'd shown her his Daddy side. He'd thought she wanted all of him. The sternness and the cuddles.

But no, she'd wanted Archer with his nice clothes, his impeccable manners and his penthouse.

He'd blamed his brother for a long time. But really, the person who was most to blame was Evelyn. And him, for being fool enough to take a chance.

He had no intentions of being a fool again.

So he needed to not care about Caley. About the fact she lived in an isolated cabin, that winter approached and she didn't have a good supply of food, a decent truck or enough firewood.

Nope, he wasn't going to care.

He moved to the bedroom to grab his phone.

He wondered if there were any firewood suppliers who could deliver in the next week.

7

C aley stared at the blank page on her laptop screen. That rarely ever happened. She might not know what to say to actual people, but the characters in her head always spoke to her. She never had blank pages. Sure, they might take her on journeys she didn't realize they were going on, but they always spoke to her. Where were they?

She groaned. This is what she got for stopping in the middle of a scene. No, this is what she got for answering her phone.

One of the few punishment spankings she'd received had been when she left the house without her phone. Dave had been a pretty indulgent Daddy. Most of her punishments included time-out and chores, both of which she detested. More than once she'd have thought she'd prefer a good paddling.

Not that she'd earned many punishments. She'd usually done everything he'd asked. She'd been young when they'd gotten together, and she'd looked to him a lot for guidance. She wondered what he'd think of her now. What he'd say if he knew she'd brought home two strange men?

She sighed. Let's face it, the real reason she couldn't concentrate was due to the two men on the other side of the door. She hadn't really been upset about the comments regarding her food choices. Hell, if she hadn't taken umbrage over Dr. Cranky's grumbling about her lack of a jacket, her truck or the fact that he'd tidied up her house, then she wasn't going to be that annoyed over remarks about her cooking.

But she'd needed a break.

And now that she was in here...she kind of wished she was out there.

Plus, her tummy was grumbling.

She glanced around, her eyes settling on her train set. Maybe a bit of play would settle her. But what if they walked in and saw her?

Not worth the risk. Even though a lot of adults had train sets, it wasn't just the train she enjoyed playing with. No, she didn't want them discovering her secret.

She knew all too well how cruel people could be when faced with something different, something they didn't understand.

Stretching, she slumped back in her chair. She had a small headache that she knew was due to lack of sleep and food. She tilted her neck from one side to the other. God, what she would give for a massage. She rubbed her hands, which almost constantly ached. Probably she should rest them more. Or learn how to use dictation. Except she'd tried that before and it had annoyed her so much, she'd actually thrown her one and only tantrum.

Thankfully, no one had been around to see it.

She needed to stop thinking about Dave. It was just making her sad and she couldn't function if she was sad. After his death, she'd gone into a deep depression. If it hadn't been for Murray and his partner, Geoff...

That was part of the reason she'd gone to help these guys. Because she owed Murray and Geoff so much.

A knock on the door made her frown.

She stood and moved to the door, opening it. "What do you want?"

That's a little rude, Caley.

From the way Archer narrowed his eyes, a slight chill filling them, he agreed.

Yikes. She'd sensed some Dom vibes from Isaac, although she wasn't certain if that was just his personality, but until now Archer had been nothing but polite and warm.

But those eyes were filled with disapproval.

She took a breath, let it out slowly. "Sorry, I'm not used to visitors. I seem to have forgotten my manners."

He raised an eyebrow. "That's an affliction that appears to be going around." He looked over at his brother. "I'm sorry to bother you while you're working. I know it's an imposition to have us here."

Now she just felt awful. She really wasn't good at this.

"No, I'm sorry. Really. Can I help you with something?"

"I was trying to heat us up some dinner, but the microwave doesn't seem to work."

"Oh, yeah. There's a trick to it." She glanced over at Isaac as she slipped past Archer, moving towards the kitchen. He was sitting, frowning down at his cell.

"Should you be on your phone?" she asked turning towards him. "Doesn't that hurt your head? I can't imagine it's a good idea for someone with a brain injury."

Isaac sighed and looked up at her. "No brain injury. Just a scratch."

"He's fine," Archer told her, lightly touching her shoulder. "I, on the other hand, am starving. Microwave?"

"Oh. Right. Sorry. I get distracted easily." She moved towards the microwave again.

"What is this trick?" Archer asked.

"You just do this." She thumped the top of the microwave twice with her fist. Then she did the same on the right side. Then she grabbed it and pushed it back and forth a few times. Which wasn't easy, considering it was a huge, clunky thing.

It lit up and she gave Archer a big smile. "See?"

He looked at her then the microwave. He appeared a bit pale. "Are you okay?"

"I...ah..."

"He's fine," Doc called out. "He just isn't used to using kitchen appliances. I'm surprised he knows what a microwave even is."

Archer turned to scowl at Doc. "Just because I don't cook often doesn't mean I can't. And I know what a damn microwave is."

She got a feeling that if she left them to it, they could snipe at each other all night long. She cleared her throat and opened the microwave door, saw the roast beef meal sitting there and then closed the door and set the microwave for five minutes.

"There you go."

"You have to do that every time you use the microwave?" Archer asked.

"Oh, not every time. Just most of the time."

Archer ran his hand over his face, looking tired and worried. She wasn't sure what he was so concerned about. Unless it was his dinner.

"Don't worry, it still works perfectly fine. Although sometimes I do find the middle of my dinners are frozen while the outside is piping hot but then I just eat around the frozen bit and I..." she trailed off as she noticed him pinch the top of his nose. "Have you got a headache?"

"Yes. I do." He stretched. "Think I'm a bit stiff and sore from the accident."

"I'll go get you some painkillers." She moved into the bathroom. When she returned, Archer had his phone in his hand, looking at something online. They seemed to be rather attached to their phones. Doc had barely looked up from his.

She shrugged and opened the bottle of painkillers, tapping a couple out and putting them on the table next to Archer's elbow then she grabbed him a glass of water.

"Thanks, love," he muttered.

She blinked, taken aback by the endearment. But then, lots of people called others sweetheart or honey or love. The microwave beeped and she moved over to it, pulling out the hot meal. She hissed as it burned the tips of her fingers.

"What are you doing? Careful!" Doc grabbed her hand and inspected her fingers.

"Is she all right? Did she burn herself?" Archer demanded and she looked over to see him standing, watching her with concern.

"Just a little red," Doc replied. But he still tugged her over to the sink and turned on the cold water, pushing her fingers underneath.

"They're fine," she told him, drawing her fingers out of the freezing deluge. "I do that all the time. It's not nearly as bad as the last time I burnt myself. I wasn't watching properly when I was pouring the hot water out of a pot and it landed on my foot and I got a giant blister. Now, that hurt. This is nothing."

Doc scowled and pushed her fingers back under the water. "Keep them there."

"But I have to get your meal into the microwave."

Doc muttered something under his breath and held her hand there himself as Archer placed another meal in the microwave.

Finally, he turned the tap off and inspected her finger. "Are you gonna kiss it and make it feel all better?"

She'd intended for it to sound sarcastic. Instead, it came out with a hint of longing. Doc eyed her but thankfully, he didn't say anything. He simply pointed to the table. "Sit."

"Surely, he's not always this bossy," she said to Archer.

"I could tell you that he's not," Archer replied as he set the cooked meal on a plate then put it in front of her. "But I don't like to lie."

Doc continued to mutter under his breath as he returned with an oversized first-aid kit that she knew for sure wasn't hers.

"That's the biggest first-aid kit I've ever seen."

"He likes to be prepared for everything," Archer told her as Doc drew out a cream for her burns.

By the time Doc finished with her finger, it had a huge white bandage around it that was going to make it damn hard to eat or type.

"Umm, do you really think this is necessary?"

"Yes," Doc replied. He stood and grabbing the first-aid kit, walked back into the spare bedroom.

Archer put another meal on the table. He grinned as he saw her fingers. She narrowed her gaze up at him. "It's not funny. How am I supposed to eat? Or type? This is my dominant hand."

She'd likely make a complete mess if she ate her food with a fork held in her left hand. She reached for the bandage, determined to pull it off.

"Don't even think about it," Doc told her, coming back and sitting next to her.

"I can't use a fork with my left hand. My food will go everywhere."

"I'll feed you then." He slid her plate towards himself then forked some up. Instead of pushing the fork towards her, he lightly blew on it. "Too hot. You'll burn your mouth."

Okay, she should probably be weirded out by that. But it was something Dave would have done. And it sent a pang of longing through her. She stood.

"I have to work."

"Sit down."

"I'm on a deadline."

"Sit. Down." His voice grew lower.

She glanced over at Archer, thinking he might be the voice of reason. But he was setting the last meal down on the table. He gave her a concerned look but didn't say anything to rein his brother back in.

Damn it.

"I'm not hungry."

Please don't let her tummy grumble and make a liar of her.

"Caley," Doc rumbled.

Jesus. Again with her name. Why did it sound so sexy when he said it? How was that fair? Her knees went weak and she found herself slumping into her seat. "Fine," she muttered ungraciously. "But I'll feed myself."

"But—"

"Isaac," Archer said warningly.

Finally, he was speaking up. She shot him a look. He gave her a calm look back. "Eat," he demanded.

Great, she was surrounded by two bossy males. She didn't have to do what they said. And the only reason she sat and ate the food was because she didn't want to waste food.

That's what she told herself, anyway.

8

Was she ever going to sleep?

Doc looked over at the door to Caley's office. She'd retreated in there soon after dinner. At least she'd eaten. But she needed sleep as well. He looked at his phone to check the time. Nearly one in the morning. He'd convinced Archer to take the bedroom, claiming he didn't sleep well anyway.

But that was a lie. He'd just wanted the couch so he could keep an eye on her. Well, as much as you could watch someone when they were on the other side of a door.

She should be sleeping. Surely, she didn't need to work this late at night? What work did she do? He scowled and forced himself to stay awake. He was growing soft in his old age.

There wasn't even anything he could use to distract himself. There was no television and the internet reception was patchy at best. Although he had managed to find a local firewood supplier. He'd give them a call in the morning, arrange for a delivery after they'd left. It was just a thank you for giving them a place to stay.

Same as the microwave he was certain Archer had ordered earlier.

Suddenly, the door to her office opened. He forced himself to remain relaxed. He didn't want to give her a fright. The fire let out a soft glow, but there wasn't enough to light up the room so unless she got up close, she shouldn't notice he was awake.

He heard her shuffle. A yawn. Had she fallen asleep in there?

That wasn't good. She should be sleeping in her bed where she would get some real rest.

There was a thump then a low cry of pain. He sat up immediately, spotting her hopping around, holding her foot.

"Caley? You okay?" He jumped up and walked over to her.

"Ouchy. Sorry. I banged my foot on something. Ouch. Crap. Damn."

"Here, let me help." He looked down with a wince, noting that she had banged into the wooden base of the armchair.

He picked her up and carried her over to the sofa. She stiffened in his arms.

"W-what are you doing?"

"Carrying you."

"Yes...but..."

He set her down on the sofa then perched on the coffee table. Grasping her foot, he brought it onto his lap and inspected her toes.

"Wiggle them for me."

She moved them back and forth. "They're okay." She winced as he pressed on them.

He grunted. "You should have turned a light on. You could have really hurt yourself."

"I didn't want to wake you up."

"Wasn't asleep."

"You weren't?"

"Nope."

"Oh, is the sofa uncomfortable? It's probably too short, isn't it? I could sleep out here. You can have my bed. I'll change the sheets." She tried to stand, and he placed his hands on her shoulders to keep her sitting.

"Stay there. You're not changing the sheets."

"Oh, I suppose you could just sleep on top of the bed."

"Girl, I am not taking your bed. You are not sleeping on the couch."

"I don't mind," she told him. "Sometimes I sleep out here because it's warmer."

He clenched his jaw. He didn't like that. Not at all.

Not your business. She is not your responsibility.

But the idea that she was so cold that she needed to sleep on the couch really annoyed him.

"You are not sleeping on the couch. If you need more blankets; you can take mine." Seemed he also needed to order her a heater for her bedroom. He stood and reached out a hand to help her up. She slipped her hand into his and he noticed how chilled it was. He also saw that she'd removed the bandage he'd put on there earlier.

If she was his, she'd be in big trouble.

"You're freezing," he muttered, reaching down to grab the blanket he'd had sitting at the end of the sofa but hadn't been using, seeing as he was lying right next to the fire. He wrapped it around her. "Sit back down until you warm up. Why didn't you open the door to your office to let some heat through? Although you should have been in bed hours ago. What work involves staying up so late at night?" He couldn't stop the scolding note. It was part of who he was, taking care of those around them. Even if he didn't always show his caring in the most thoughtful way.

"I'm a writer. And once I get going, I don't like to be interrupted. If I lose my flow of words, it can take me a while to settle back into a rhythm. I usually don't stop until the words do or my body tells me I need a rest."

"So you do listen to your body?"

She gave him a small smile. "Eventually. I once gave myself a... ahh, actually, you don't need to know that."

He stopped himself from insisting that she tell him. Not his sub. Not his responsibility.

"Think you need to listen to your body a bit earlier, girl. Before you turn into a human popsicle. It's not good to work so late at night. Your body needs rest."

"I had to finish what I was doing."

"Uh-huh. What do you write?"

"Romance."

"Guess you believe in happy-ever-afters then, huh?"

"Don't you?" she asked curiously.

"Nope. I don't think there's any such thing. Nothing lasts forever."

"I guess not." She sounded sad and he immediately felt bad.

"For me, anyway," he told her. "I'm sure for you it might happen."

"I'm not looking for, uh, anything." She attempted to stand again. "I'm tired now, I'm going to bed."

Way to make things awkward.

"Wait. I, ahh, I didn't mean to sound dismissive."

She looked at him. "Some people react oddly when I tell them I'm a romance writer. As though they think romance is a dirty word. Or that I can't be very good, or I'd write something important like sonnets or something."

His lips quirked. Shit. He was starting to wonder if he had a tic or something. "Sonnets? Do people still write sonnets?"

She shrugged. "I dunno. But I like to read romance. I like to write romance. There's nothing wrong with that, right?"

"No, girl," he told her in a soft voice. "There's nothing wrong with that at all."

Her shoulders relaxed and she gave him a tentative smile. "I should go to bed. You need some sleep. Is your head all right? Would you like some more painkillers?"

She really was sweet.

"I'm fine, girl," he said gruffly. "Get yourself to bed. Sleep in tomorrow. I don't want your ass out of that room before ten a.m."

"Seriously. How has no one murdered you already?"

"It's a mystery for the ages."

As she walked into her bedroom, she was aware she was smiling.

Immediately she frowned. She felt light. Almost bubbly. Could be the fact that she hadn't had much sleep in the last week. Or the week before that. Or that she was simply lonely and enjoying having people around. Although the fact that she'd hidden herself in her office most of the night probably negated that.

Or maybe it was that the two men in her house were complete hunks and for the first time since Dave died her body felt alive. She was interested. Aroused.

She nearly gasped at that realization.

She shouldn't feel like that, right?

It felt like a betrayal. Dave had been everything to her. She'd loved him with all of herself. Had planned on spending the rest of her life with him.

Dave's gone.

Confused, upset, she moved to her bed and picked up her stuffed bumblebee, Bumbly. She'd always loved bumblebees, but this toy was special because she'd picked it out with Dave. She also grabbed her snuggly, which was actually just a shirt cut up. Dave's shirt. When Dave was alive, she'd had a soft, fluffy pink blankie. After he'd died, she'd started sleeping in his shirts. But they hadn't exactly been comfortable. So she'd taken to sleeping with one of his shirts next to her, cuddling it. In the end, she cut one up so the buttons didn't end up under her face as she slept, leaving little indents in her skin.

She rearranged the giant sleep pillow. It was long and curled at the top so she slept surrounded by it on both sides. She knew it was something that pregnant women usually used to help support their bellies. But she liked the feeling of being enveloped by it. Like she was in a giant hug.

The kind Dave used to give her.

She climbed into bed and drew up her covers. Her sheets were white flannel with little dachshunds on them. And her duvet cover matched. She pulled Bumbly close. Dave had taken her to a shop in Bozeman to get him, one of the few times they'd been into the city.

As soon as she'd seen him, she'd known he was the stuffy for her. Bumbly was the cutest bumblebee ever, in her opinion. But even better, was what he represented.

A time in her life when she was completely and utterly loved. Safe. Cherished.

Tears slid down her face. Guilt filled her. She shouldn't be reacting to Isaac or Archer. It wasn't right. She wasn't ready.

She couldn't say goodbye. Not yet.

9

A strange feeling filled her as she stared down the tree lying across the road.

She couldn't figure out if it was worry or relief.

She didn't think the wind had been that strong last night. Usually powerful winds freaked her out. But this tree looked old and rotted. It probably hadn't taken much to push it over. And this was further down the mountain where the wind could really rip through.

What was she going to do with the two Docs now?

She'd gotten up early, surprised when she'd been able to sneak past Doc. He didn't seem like the type to miss much. But he'd been snoring softly, his feet hanging off the end of the sofa. She should have pushed harder for him to take her bed. He was probably going to wake up all stiff and sore.

Not that she probably would have been able to convince him. He was more stubborn than an old goat.

She'd wanted to check the road, see if it was possible for her to drop them off at Murray's this morning. The earlier the better for her peace of mind.

Uh-huh, like you really want them to leave.

That was the problem, wasn't it? She didn't want them to leave and she felt guilty about it.

Dave wouldn't want you to feel this way. Dave wouldn't want you to be alone. At least, she didn't think he would.

She'd already checked the creek. Completely flooded. That's when she'd decided to check the road into town and had come across the downed tree.

It seemed that Archer and Doc weren't going anywhere for at least another day. She started turning her truck around. She'd best get back to the cabin before they got up.

Why was she worried about that? They weren't the boss of her, she could do whatever she wanted. Just because Doc told her not to get out of bed until ten didn't mean she had to obey him.

You're a big girl.

Kind of.

Still, she felt nervous as she turned up her driveway, the truck bouncing along potholes that really needed fixing.

She'd have to add that to the list. Maybe she could get a hire-a-hubby. Did those still exist? Get everything done in one swoop.

You could hire an assistant. Urgh, but she'd need someone who was kink friendly. She'd just lucked out when she'd found Daisy to edit her books. Not only was she an amazing editor, she was also a Little. With her own Daddy.

Maybe you should visit her one day.

Sometimes she worried they weren't really friends. After all, she paid Daisy to edit her books. She kind of had to be nice to her, right? If they really met, Daisy might find out that Caley wasn't all that interesting or fun. That she was kind of absentminded and likely a terrible friend.

Yeah, best they don't meet then Caley could at least keep up the idea of having a friend out there, rather than knowing she was all alone.

She pulled up outside the cabin, turning off the truck. The door to her cabin opened and two clearly furious men stepped out.

Uh-oh.

She'd expected that Doc might be a bit annoyed that she'd snuck out past him. He seemed the type who liked to control everything and everyone around him.

She'd seen glimpses of fire in him. Hot to touch, dangerous when he burned. Archer was cooler. Calmer. But there was something under that carefully presented surface.

And both of them were glaring down at her from the porch, hands on hips, their stances so similar she'd almost think it was choreographed if she didn't know them. It was obvious there was tension between them

Despite whatever seemed to be going on between them, it seemed they had united together about one thing.

Her.

She wasn't sure that bode well for her.

When she didn't leave the truck, they obviously grew impatient because one of them started down the steps towards her.

What surprised her was that it wasn't Doc but rather Archer who came towards her. He opened the door to her truck.

"Um, good morning."

He raised his eyebrows. "Is it?"

"You didn't sleep well?" she asked.

"I slept fine. It was when I got up that the problems arose."

"Oh, sorry. Couldn't you find any breakfast?"

His eyebrows lowered. "That's not the problem and you know it, love. What did you think you were doing, sneaking off like that?"

"I wasn't sneaking off," she huffed. "This is my house and my truck and I'm not obliged to tell anyone where I go or what I'm doing."

A shutter came over his face and he stepped back. That heat faded. And at once she felt empty. A little sad. She'd expected him to bite back.

She hadn't expected him to retreat.

"Of course not. I apologize for worrying about you."

She winced at those words. Seemed that maybe she should be the one apologizing. She opened her mouth to tell him that she was sorry, that she wasn't used to having anyone else around, when she saw Doc stomping his way towards him.

"I thought it would be better if I came to get you. He hasn't woken in the best of moods." There was a thread of friendliness in Archer's voice. But she got a feeling her comments had put them back firmly into the polite acquaintance category.

"You mean he sometimes wakes in a good mood?"

"Better than this. Be ready for some scolding."

She braced herself as Doc approached. "What's taking so long? Did she tell you where she's been?"

"She has not. She pointed out that she doesn't owe us anything. We are, after all, strangers who have imposed on her."

She winced at the cold properness in Archer's voice. Yeah. She'd made a wrong move there. Damn it.

"Look, I'm sorry. I should have left a note. I'm not used to anyone being around. I just went to check on the creek."

"You drove your crappy truck out alone after a storm, with what looks like another bad front coming in and you didn't think you should let someone know? You didn't even have your phone with you! What if something happened? What if you'd had an accident? Hurt yourself?"

She blinked as Doc raged at her. Scolding, indeed. To her shock and embarrassment, tears started to well in her eyes.

"Isaac! She doesn't owe us any explanations." Archer turned on his brother with a scowl.

"We didn't know where she was! She was supposed to stay in

her bed and sleep in. She barely got any sleep, then she snuck out, drove off in this heap of junk without a phone. What am I supposed to do? Ask her to kindly leave us a note next time?"

"That's better than yelling at her!"

"I didn't yell. I never raised my voice. And she deserves more than a scolding. She needs a damn good spanking. Should have tied her up, then I'd know she was where I put her."

A sob escaped and they both turned to look at her shocked.

"She's crying," Doc said in a horrified voice.

"No wonder! You're not her Dom. You're her houseguest. You're scaring her."

He wasn't scaring her. He was reminding her of what she'd lost. What she missed.

Having someone who gave a shit about her.

"Love, don't cry. I'll keep the big, mean grouch away from you. Come inside, I have coffee on," Archer coaxed. All the winter in his voice had thawed.

"It...it's not that." She wiped at her eyes. But she did take Archer's hand as he held it out to her. She climbed down from her truck and let Archer lead her inside, his hand firmly wrapped around hers. She'd always loved holding Dave's hand. It had made her feel safe. It also brought out her Little side.

She took a deep breath, pushing that part of herself back. That was the last thing she needed right now. She could just imagine their reactions.

Actually, maybe she couldn't imagine it. What had Archer said to Isaac?

You're not her Dom.

"You're freezing, Caley," Archer commented. He rubbed his thumb over the back of her hand, sending a curious tingling through her body. Shoot. What was that?

She hadn't been attracted to anyone since Dave died. And now, she'd reacted to both Doc and Archer. Mind you, it wasn't like she'd really been around any other men in the last two years. Was it just because she was lonely?

Well, the fact that they're super hot doesn't hurt.

"She forgot her jacket. Again."

Actually, she hadn't forgotten it this time, she just hadn't wanted to take the time to grab it and risk waking Doc up.

They stepped inside and the scent of coffee filled the cabin. "Ooh, coffee."

"I made some, hope you don't mind," Archer said.

"Of course not. You can help yourself to anything. Sorry, I know I've been a terrible hostess."

Archer let go of her hand and she immediately felt the loss. But it wasn't like she could chase after him, clinging to his hand like a toddler in need of reassurance.

House guests. Nothing more.

Doc was behind her, she could feel his presence, but he was silent. She gave him a quick glance over her shoulder. He was frowning down at her. "Didn't mean to make you cry."

"You said I needed a spanking. You don't think that would make me cry?"

"Well, it sure wasn't going to be one for pleasure. So yeah, it would. Doesn't mean I like making you cry. Like it less when I don't know the reason."

"How about because you were being a jerk?" Archer snapped from the kitchen where he was pouring out coffee into three mugs. He also poured a glass of water and handed it to her. "Drink that first."

"It wasn't—"

"You're telling me that you were okay with waking up and finding her gone?" Doc interrupted her. "That you weren't worried when we found her phone was sitting on the kitchen table? That you weren't concerned when she didn't come back for an hour?"

"Course I was worried. But that doesn't mean you've got the right to go all Dom on her."

She looked up at Doc. "You're a dominant?"

He turned from scowling at Archer to her. He blinked, almost as though he'd forgotten she was there. That was flattering as hell.

"Yeah. And you're a sub."

"You can't just come out with it like that, Isaac!"

"Why not? Am I supposed to beat around the bush? Make innuendos to see if she picks up on them? Go slowly, slowly."

"Do you really think she knows what she is?" Archer asked.

"Yep, I do. Which means things will go worse for her considering I told her not to show her face out of her bedroom before ten."

She narrowed her gaze at Doc. If she let him, she knew he'd run roughshod over her. She might be a bit awkward and rusty when it came to socializing, but she wasn't a pushover.

"You're not my Dom. You can't give me rules. And you can't punish me when I break them."

"I owe you ten, brother," Archer commented.

"Ten?" she asked.

"Archie didn't think that you knew what you are." Doc gave her a firm look. "And I might not be your Dom, but that doesn't mean that I'm going to let you run around endangering yourself. What the hell are you even doing here on your own? You should have someone watching over you, making certain that you're safe and healthy."

She used to have that.

"Do you take an interest in all strangers' lives?"

"No. Can't remember the last time I really took an interest in someone else's life who wasn't under my care."

"Under your care?"

"I'm a doctor on a ranch. Everyone there is under my medical care."

Oh right. The way he'd said it, it had sounded like he had a harem of submissives, following his every bidding.

And that hadn't been jealousy she'd felt at the thought. Really, it hadn't.

"But then I found myself in the middle of a storm, staying in a cabin with a sub who is clearly not taking care of herself properly."

"I'm not a child. I can take care of myself just fine."

Doc made a noise of disagreement. Urgh, he was such a jerk. She wanted to...wanted to... strangle him! Kick him!

Kiss him.

Shoot. Where had that thought come from? What was wrong with her? There were so many emotions running through her. Anger. Arousal.

She couldn't remember the last time she'd felt so alive. And she wasn't sure she liked it.

"I have work to do." She turned towards her office. She needed to get away from them for a while. She needed to breathe.

"I don't think so," Doc stated, moving in front of her.

"Out of my way."

"Nope."

"Issy," Archer warned.

"Issy?" she asked Doc, who grimaced.

"Childhood nickname and don't try to distract me. You're not going to work. You worked well into the night. You're going to sit your butt down and explain to me what you were thinking by sneaking off like that. Then you're going to eat whatever I make us for breakfast and drink your coffee."

"And if I don't?"

"Then I'm gonna have to get strict with you."

"You. Have. No. Right." She scowled at Doc.

"Why'd you get upset before?" Archer asked suddenly. He was leaning back against the kitchen counter, studying her intently.

"What do you mean?" She walked towards the table and picked up her coffee. She grabbed her creamer from the fridge, dumping in a generous amount. Seemed she was going to need a pick-me-up to deal with these guys.

"When you got upset out in the truck, I thought it was because Issy was being his usual overbearing self. But you're not intimidated by him at all, are you?"

Doc made a scoffing noise.

"I find him intimidating," she defended.

"Uh-uh, love, no lying," Archer said in a low voice. "My dominant side might be less obvious than my brother's but that doesn't mean I will stand for being lied to. And I think Issy might be right, you need a keeper. How long have you known you were a sub? Have you ever had a full-time Dom? Why'd you get upset earlier?"

Her gaze drifted away from his. The sternness in his voice sent a shiver up her spine.

"It wasn't because you were upset at Issy being so pushy, was it? Was it because you missed that? That you want someone to take charge? That it was nice to have someone care where you were and what you were doing and hold you accountable for misbehaving."

"Goddamn it, how did I forget you're a therapist?"

"This has nothing to do with me being a therapist and everything to do with me being a man and a Dom."

She glanced at Doc then back at Archer. "You're a Dom too?"

"Yep."

She crossed her arms over her chest and stepped away, frowning at them both.

"I'm just doing a favor for Murray, that's all. You have no business trying to tell me what to do or scolding me if I don't do what either of you say. In case you've forgotten we met yesterday. You're both being overbearing and rude. If you'll excuse me, I have deadlines to meet."

She turned and stormed into her office. And she wasn't sad that no one followed her. Really, she wasn't.

"THINK we might have mishandled that one." Isaac looked over at the closed office door with a frown.

Archer took a sip of coffee. He felt a strange sense of satisfaction when he noticed she'd taken the coffee he'd made for her with her. When was the last time he'd done something as simple as make coffee for someone? Everywhere he went, there was someone looking after him.

Even when he went to the club, he was served by a sub. And even though he always gave back, he was nothing if not generous with orgasms, they were never his to take care of beyond a bit of aftercare.

Was Isaac right? Did things come too easily to him? Had he become the kind of guy who just sat back and waited for stuff? For life to happen? When was the last time he'd wanted something that he'd had to actually work for?

"Not so sure."

Isaac raised his eyebrows. "Really? Usually you're the one telling me to stop being an asshole."

"You're always an asshole," he muttered. "But I think you're right in this instance."

"About her being a sub? We already knew that."

"No, in your approach. She wasn't annoyed or scared or upset by you scolding her. I think those tears were relief or sadness. I think that Caley has had a Dom before. For whatever reason, she now doesn't, and she misses it."

"And how the hell do you figure all that?"

"Something in her face. And because she didn't once tell you to fuck off."

"Huh." Isaac looked thoughtful. "Most people do within the first hour of meeting me."

"Exactly. She hasn't told us to leave. She told you that you didn't have the right to top her and she's right, neither of us do."

Isaac frowned. "You could be reading her wrong."

"Could be," Archer said. "But there's something about her. Something sad. And lost." It called to him.

It shouldn't. He was supposed to be setting her up with his brother. Not stealing her for himself. She was completely unsuited for him. Look at where she lived. Isaac's cabin at Sanctuary Ranch wouldn't scare her off. And shockingly, Isaac himself didn't seem to faze her all that much.

She was much better suited to his brother. She needed more than he could offer her.

The door to the office opened and she stood there, looking disgruntled. But again, he got a hint of sadness.

"Forgot to tell you, the creek is still flooded and there's a tree blocking the road in the other direction. You'll be staying here for a while yet."

She shut the door again.

Perfect.

10

Doc paced back and forth along the living room.

"Will you sit down?" Archer asked him impatiently. He was fiddling with something on his phone. The wind was picking up outside. It sounded even worse than it had last night.

"I can't sit down." He wasn't very good at sitting. He liked to keep moving. It kept his mind from thinking too much.

"She hasn't had breakfast. Or lunch." He'd knocked on her door at both mealtimes. Both times, she'd claimed she wasn't hungry.

He'd wanted to march in there and drag her out to the dining table, sit her down and feed her himself. But Archer had warned against being too forceful.

Damn it. He was probably right. If she was his...different story. Her ass would already be red, and her belly would be full. She'd also be having a nap right now after her late night.

Not that he'd have allowed that either.

Shit. Was Archer, right? Was he being an ass? Had he been too overbearing with her earlier? He'd been worried when she'd gotten all teary.

Upsetting little subbies wasn't his thing. He might be brisk and gruff, but he wasn't mean.

At least, he didn't think he was. At one time, he'd been easier going. He'd had more bend in him. More softness. He still tried to find a bit of softness for the Littles on the ranch, but he knew they all dreaded a visit from him.

He ran a hand over his face. Christ. When had he become such a grouch? He couldn't even blame it entirely on Evelyn and her betrayal. It had started earlier than that. But now...now he wondered if he wasn't becoming bitter.

Archer glanced over at the door to her office. "You said she's a writer. Perhaps she's just in the zone and has lost track of time."

"She's going to get sick. She barely slept last night." He sat on the armchair, staring into the fire. "Is she hiding because I make her uncomfortable?" Why had he gone all Dom on her? There was just something about her that stirred him. "Should I apologize?"

Archer's sharp eyes met his. "Do you know how to apologize? Aren't you afraid you'll go up in flames?"

"I'm serious here."

Archer ran his hand over his face, looking tired. "Sorry. I didn't mean to make light of it. Should you apologize? You're right, she's been in there too long without food. Even if she is in the zone with her writing, it's not healthy. Why don't you see if you can coax her out?"

"Coax her out? With what? My charming personality?"

Archer shot him a look. "You've been a Daddy Dom for years, Issy. You know how to talk to an unsure sub."

"Been a long time since I had a Little."

"You're interested in her, though." Archer nodded to the door.

Interested in her? Was he?

Come on, would you really act this way towards a stranger if you didn't find yourself intrigued by her? Attracted to her?

He shook his head. "Doesn't matter if I am. I doubt I'm her type. I'm sure she'd prefer you. Maybe you should talk to her."

Lord knew, Archer was better at dealing with people.

"Why would she prefer me?"

Doc sent him a look.

Archer ran his hand over his face. "Issy, is this about Evelyn? I never wanted—"

"It doesn't matter," Doc interrupted him, not wanting to get into that.

Archer sighed. "Issy, it's clear to me she's interested in you."

Was she? Maybe. But then he thought he'd seen something in Archer's gaze when he looked at her. "Do you like her?"

"Of course I like her. I—"

"No, are you attracted to her?"

Archer appeared startled. "She's beautiful, but she's not my type. She definitely needs more than I could be comfortable giving."

Doc frowned slightly "She may not be a Little."

He couldn't really believe he was considering this. He barely knew her. He'd met her yesterday and he was talking about feeling something for her.

Him. The guy who had hidden himself away in the middle of nowhere, so he barely had to deal with people.

Even though he had a deep need to take care of others. Something that even playing doctor to everyone living on the ranch wasn't fulfilling.

Maybe that was it. He wasn't exactly happy. He'd thought he could at least be content with his life. But maybe he was ready for more. Maybe he'd just needed to figure out this shit with Evelyn and Archer to move on.

Or maybe he'd needed to be tempted by a slightly odd, somewhat messy, curvy blonde who very much needed some guidance in her life.

Hmm. Or a combination of both.

"She might not be interested in me."

"I've seen the way she looks at you. Don't think that's an issue. There is something going on with her, though. Most women wouldn't live like this. Not without a good reason."

He wasn't wrong about that. But that just meant he would need to work at getting her to open up.

First though, was getting her to talk to him.

THE KNOCK on the door brought her out of her scene with a frown.

She turned to the door, trying to pull herself away from Adelaide and Ren's story. This one was a doozy, but she couldn't help but feel like she was missing an element.

She just wasn't sure what the element was. When it finally appeared, she figured she was gonna get a hell of a shock. Some stories were like that. She had them all plotted out. Knew where it was going then *boom*. Suddenly the heroine had a serial killer stepbrother who always considered her to belong to him and didn't want to share.

Ooh. Now that sounded interesting. She wrote that in her notebook. She just hoped she remembered which notebook she'd put it in when she came to find it again. She really did need to organize her desk. She sighed. Hell, she needed to organize her life.

The idea of a personal assistant floated across her brain again. Only how would she ever find a personal assistant when she lived out here?

Another knock and she turned to the door. It could only be one of two people and she was betting on Archer. Doc hadn't knocked the last two times he'd barged in to demand she come eat.

She grimaced. She knew she was being rude. And a wimp. Sure, she'd gotten into the flow with this story, but when she'd come in here, she'd been hiding from the two of them.

Total wuss.

"Yes?" she called out, stretching out her back.

To her surprise, it was Doc that walked in. He shut the door behind him. Uh-oh, that didn't seem like a good sign.

"Why'd you shut the door?"

"I wanted some privacy."

"For what?" She eyed him suspiciously. "If you've come to tell me you really are a serial killer and a cannibal, could you wait until I've finished this book? I've got a lot of people waiting on me to get it out and I'm sure your instincts to torture and kill can wait a few days."

"Girl, I am not here to torture and kill you." He gave her that look. The one she got from people when they thought she was crazy. She'd seen that look enough in her life. She'd moved here to get away from it.

"Was there something you wanted?"

"Let me see your fingers. I haven't checked the burn."

"It's fine." But she held out her fingers. His touch sent waves of heat through her, shocking her. He must have been satisfied because he let it go without a word.

Then he moved his gaze to her face. "I'm not real good at reading people. Apparently, I have the worst bedside manner, but even I can tell I've done something to piss you off in the forty-five seconds since I entered the room. Now, I'd like to say that's a new record, but I don't like to lie."

She took a deep breath, let it out slowly. This was her house. She didn't have to put up with people looking down on her.

"I know I'm weird. I know my brain doesn't always work the way other people's do. I have an overactive imagination."

"Guess that comes in handy for your job."

"Yes, except I tend to go to the worst possible scenario in my head. Which can freak me the hell out. Especially when I'm here on my own."

The house creaked as the wind picked up outside.

"Storm's coming in," Doc commented, walking closer and perching on her desk.

Okay, that was a bit too close. But she didn't move back. She forced herself to look up at him. "I moved here to get away from people looking at me like I'm weird or wrong."

Understanding filled his face. "And that's what you think I just did? That I think you're weird?"

"Don't you?"

He snorted. "I have a phobia about eating other people's cooking. And I have a slight issue with germs and cleanliness. There is nothing normal about me. I can also be extremely blunt, which is why I'm just gonna come out with this. Have you ever heard of age play?"

She felt her lips go a bit numb. Was he... "You're a Daddy Dom?"

"Yep. You've had a Dom before? A relationship with one?"

"My...my husband was my Daddy."

He studied her, his eyes surprisingly kind and gentle. That wasn't something she was used to from Doc.

But then, you hardly know him, do you? And you just told him what is essentially your biggest secret.

"I...I need to finish this book. I have things to do. I'm sorry if I'm being rude but I—"

"Whoa, okay, stop," he told her in a commanding voice, taking hold of her hands which had been flying through the air. "Calm down. Just breathe. In. Out. Nice and slow. That's it. Settle down, girl."

"I'm...not...a...girl."

Okay, that probably wasn't the thing she needed to focus on right now.

"Is that so? Seems you are to me."

"I'm thirty-one years old."

"When you're adulting. When you're Little how old are you?"

There went her ability to breathe properly again. Shit. What had she done? What was she thinking? What if he told people? She'd need to move again. She couldn't move. She had nowhere to go.

"Caley! Caley, listen to me. I need you to settle down now. Just breathe. Little girl, listen to me."

The deep command caught her attention.

"Look at me."

Fuck. No way could she resist that voice. It had been so long since anyone had topped her. She hadn't been certain how she would react. Maybe she wouldn't have liked it from anyone else. Perhaps she might have been able to resist. But something about Isaac spoke to her. Lord knows why, since he seemed to be an asshole. But it did. He intrigued her.

He and Archer both.

Ménages don't happen in real life, Caley Jane. And you don't want one daddy, let alone two.

And she didn't think Archer was a Daddy Dom, anyway. She stared into Isaac's piercing blue eyes. He was a gorgeous man. His skin tanned. His hair dark-blonde. That trimmed beard giving him a sexy look she liked.

"Good girl. Need you to calm down and tell me what's wrong."

She shook her head.

His face tightened. A storm brewed in his eyes.

"Caley, tell me what is wrong. What just happened? Why did you panic?"

She shook her head again.

"We can sit here all day, baby doll. I ain't got nothing to do. Ain't got no place to go. Got nothing to focus on but you. We're just going to sit here until you tell me what's wrong."

Crap. He'd do it too. He was just that stubborn.

"I told you."

He frowned. "Told me what?"

"That I...that I..."

"That you're a Little? Baby, why has that got you so panicked? I told you I'm a Daddy Dom."

Yeah. That's right. He had. She was making an idiot of herself.

"Sorry...sorry..."

He rubbed his thumbs over the backs of her hands. "You wanna tell me why you reacted the way you did?"

"No."

He lowered his voice. "Girl, tell me why you just reacted the way you did."

She wrinkled her nose at the clear command. Then she sighed. "I've just had people react badly before when they found out. I wasn't really thinking clearly. I mean, you obviously weren't going to tell me that I'm a freak and unnatural."

"People said that to you?" Anger filled his face.

She nodded hesitantly. "I didn't really think you'd say that to me," she said quickly, hoping that he wasn't offended by her reaction. "I mean, it sounds like you had something similar happen with your parents."

"Yeah, but I can fucking take it. You're just a tiny thing. Your Dom should have protected you from that."

She snatched her hands back from his, coldness filling her. She could take insults he flung her way. Maybe. Probably not. But it wasn't her that he was insulting. It was Dave.

And she'd never stand for that.

"He did protect me. But it's hard to protect one person against a whole town."

His eyes widened. Shit. She hadn't actually meant to say that.

"A whole town?"

"I don't want to talk about that. I don't want to talk about anything right now. But you didn't know Dave. You don't know how he took care of me. But he did. He was the best man, Dom, Daddy I could ever have hoped for. And nobody will ever take his place. I think you should leave me alone now."

He stared at her for a long moment. She expected him to fight back. She grew tense. She wasn't going to let anyone hurt Dave's memory.

To her surprise he nodded and stood. That was it? He was giving up?

No, not giving up. He's giving you what you asked for.

Yeah, except he hadn't done that up until now. Why now... when maybe there was a part of her that didn't want him to. That wanted him to insist that she come out and eat, that she spend some time with him and his brother.

That lonely, broken, sad part of her that just wanted to feel some warmth. Like someone actually cared about her.

Instead, he was walking away. And a part of her broke just a little more.

He opened the door then turned back. "Where is he? What happened?"

"He died," she whispered.

"And now you live here? All alone?"

She pushed her chin up. "It's what I prefer."

Liar. Liar.

His eyes narrowed. She felt certain he was going to call her out on her bullshit, but a loud yell interrupted them. Followed by pain-filled cursing.

She stood up. "Was that Archer?" Had she heard Archer yell? Or swear?

Doc turned and raced towards the door at the side of the kitchen, which led to the closed-in porch. Why would Archer be out there?

Oh shit! The washing machine!

She raced after Doc, coming to a stop as she saw that Archer was lying sprawled on the floor, groaning. Tangled in his feet was the broom. How had that gotten there?

"Are you okay? What happened?"

"Your washing machine tried to kill me, that's what happened," Archer replied, scowling at the machine in question.

"The washing machine tried to kill you?" Doc asked skeptically. "And just how did it do that?"

"You tried to plug it in," she guessed. "Shoot. I'm so sorry. If I knew you were going to do some laundry, I would have told you. Sometimes it gives an electric shock."

"What?" Doc snapped. "Your washing machine gives off electric shocks?" He turned on her, his hands on his hips. "Do you know how dangerous that is? You could injure yourself!"

"Yes, which is why I always put on my rubber boots first."

Doc started grumbling under his breath while glaring at her as though she'd mortally offended him.

She ignored him, crouching down next to Archer. "Are you all right?"

"Nice someone remembers that I'm the injured party." He glared up at his brother. Uh-oh, they weren't going to start fighting again, were they?

"You're six foot two and weigh two hundred pounds. She's a foot shorter and half your weight."

"Wow. That's the nicest thing you've ever said to me."

"What?" Doc gave her a confused look.

She was five foot four and more like a hundred and thirty pounds. But she'd take it.

Then he frowned. "Imagine what the hell that electric shock could do to her if it put you on your ass."

"It wasn't that which put me on my ass," Archer replied.

"Huh?" Doc asked. "Then what are you doing on the ground?"

"Oh, that's because of the broom that was being used to prop the dryer door shut. The electric shock made me stumble, then I managed to get my feet caught up with the broom and that's when I fell to the floor."

"I'm so sorry, Archer," she told him. "Are you injured anywhere?"

"No, I think I'm okay," he grumbled unhappily. "I've never been taken down by a washing machine and a dryer."

"To be fair, I think it was a washing machine and a broom," she said.

And there was that look again. Like she was a crazy person.

"Don't look at her like that," Doc snarled.

"Like what?" Archer gave his brother a shocked look.

"Like you think she's weird. She's sensitive about it. And I won't have you hurting her feelings."

She felt a little sorry for Archer as his mouth dropped open then shut again then opened once more. He looked like he desperately wanted to say something, he just couldn't work out what.

"I didn't give her a look like she's weird. It's just...every appliance here is a menace."

"I'm so sorry," she said again. "I know I should replace them. I don't do well with change. And I'm used to it and I don't usually have anyone else here..."

"Archer," Doc rumbled.

Archer ran his hand over his face. "No, I'm sorry. You've been kind enough to open up your house to us and I just insulted you. Forgive me?"

"Of course." She stood and held out a hand to him. "Here, let me help you up."

He gave her an incredulous look then turned to his brother. "You're gonna have to do something about that."

"I will," Doc sighed.

"About what?"

"Hey, I'm not anywhere as big as you," Archer said, reaching up for the hand his brother held down to him.

"It's muscle, baby. All muscle," Doc said to her, with a surprising wink. "And I'm big all over."

Archer groaned and she gave him a concerned look. "That was bad, Issy. Real bad."

"You've always been jealous. Poor Archie, he's just never measured up."

She finally got what they were talking about and she could feel her cheeks turning red. At the same time, a smile curved up her lips.

She wasn't sure why Doc was flirting with her all of a sudden. Not after she'd told him to leave her alone.

And he'd agreed.

Why had she done that again? They wouldn't be here forever. Another night or two. A one-night stand wasn't the type of thing she'd ever done. Hell, she'd only slept with Dave. A short fling wasn't denigrating Dave's memory, right?

Doc didn't live here. She never had to see him again. It was kind of perfect. Especially since they weren't alone. Not that she thought he'd try anything weird. But if he did, Archer was here.

Yeah, maybe she'd been too hasty.

11

"Here's some painkillers. Are you sure you're, all right?"

The more Caley fussed over him, the better Archer felt. He didn't know why. He'd had women fuss over him most of his life. But then, she wasn't doing it because she wanted something from him. So why was she doing it? Because of his brother?

He caught them both giving the other one longing looks when they thought the other wasn't looking. He wasn't sure what he'd interrupted with his ungraceful accident, but he had a feeling things hadn't been going well.

Despite Isaac's terrible attempts at flirting.

Jealous of him. Ha! Archer wasn't jealous of that ass's dick. Or anything he could do in the bedroom.

Christ, listen to yourself, man. Next thing you know, you'll be flopping it out and challenging him.

Seemed he would now have to add a washer-dryer to the list of things he was going to need to get for her. Along with a new microwave.

Except that was probably something Isaac would want to do.

He knew that his brother was working on getting firewood for her. But if he was going to be her Dom, then it was his job to make certain she was taken care of.

Not Archer's.

Ouch that hurt. Damn it. Why did he have to like her as well? He barely knew her. Although living together like this, it was difficult not to learn more about someone.

Archer definitely had a certain type he went for. Generally tall, willowy brunettes, maybe the occasional redhead. Someone with a high-powered job. Someone who didn't worry if he missed returning a phone call or had to cancel a date due to work. Someone who liked to submit in the bedroom, where he could make them feel good. But the next morning, they would know the score. They'd leave without a fuss. Because all he was interested in was something casual.

Was that really all he wanted? Casual hook-ups that never meant anything? Women who he never let himself get attached to?

What was wrong with him?

That would never be Caley. She wasn't casual. She wouldn't fall into some box. And she was in desperate need of someone to watch out for her. Over her. She needed more than he was comfortable giving. She required someone like Isaac. Who had to be needed. Who had to be in charge. Who was happy making the decisions.

Being the boss.

Archer could give commands all night long but when the sun came up, he only wanted to be responsible for himself.

Right?

At least that's what he'd always thought.

Damned if he knew what he wanted now. Or why he was so attracted to her.

It could never go anywhere. His brother wanted her. And he would never come between his brother and a woman again.

Maybe she could be between the two of you?

Holy crap. Where had that thought come from? His cock stirred at the idea of sharing her. Of playing with her breasts while his brother licked her pussy.

Shit. Not going to happen. He'd been part of a ménage once before. Years ago, just after college. It hadn't worked out. It wouldn't work now, either. He wanted something different than Caley and Issy.

And besides, he was certain that Issy would never share.

"I'm so sorry, Archer. If I knew you wanted the washer, I would have told you about its quirks."

Quirks? That wasn't a quirk. It was a fucking hazard.

"I'm fine, love. Stop stressing. No harm done. Why don't you sit down? Have a rest."

She gave him a look like he was crazy. But she seemed stressed. Frazzled. He didn't like it. She should be relaxed. Happy. If she was his, he could keep her in the lap of luxury. She wouldn't have to work. Wouldn't have to stress. She wouldn't be surrounded by appliances that were either on their last legs or dangerous. She wouldn't be isolated and alone, she wouldn't worry about where her next paycheck was coming from.

But she's not yours.

And Isaac could do that for her.

"I...I..." She ran her hand through her blonde hair, sending tendrils off at different angles. It was caught back in a bun, which he hated. It should be flowing free. He should be able to run his fingers through it at any time, twist it around his hand so he could draw her head back to kiss her.

Stop, asshole.

Not yours.

"I'll go do that laundry for you. Is it in the washer?" She headed towards the enclosed porch where the ancient washer and dryer were.

"Stop," he barked, surprised at himself.

She whirled, her eyes wide, clearly as shocked he was.

"You're not going near that washing machine. Where did Isaac go?"

"I'm here." Isaac walked out of the porch. He looked at them both. "What's wrong?"

"Caley was going to go do the laundry."

Isaac narrowed his gaze. "You're not going near that machine."

She threw her hands into the air, clearly exasperated. "What am I meant to do when I need to wash clothes?"

"Far as I can see you generally just chuck them on the floor," Isaac replied.

She glared at him, her hands on her hips as she tapped her foot.

"Isaac," he groaned.

"What?"

"I wash my clothes. I'm not a complete slob. It's the putting them away part I have trouble with."

"You're not using that washer," he growled.

Isaac sent him a surprised look. He was obviously channeling his grouchier brother today.

"The washing machine is perfectly safe. I'm going to be using it once you guys are gone. What difference does it make if I use it now?"

"I had a look at it," Isaac told her. "But I don't know enough to tell what's wrong. We need to order you a new one."

She chewed her lip, looking worried. Christ, she probably didn't have the money for a new one. His brother was an idiot sometimes, he should have just ordered one without telling her. Like Archer had done with the microwave.

"I'm sure I don't need a new one."

"You're getting a new one," Isaac decreed.

She sighed. "I guess it is a bit of a hazard. But it will take a while to get a new one up here. And you need your clothes washed."

Isaac sighed. "Tell me what to do and I'll do it."

She gave him a skeptical look.

"Just go with it, love. He's stubborn. He's not going to budge."

She gave him a pointed look. "Yeah, well, I can see he's not the only stubborn one."

He shrugged. What could he say? When it came to her, it seemed he was stubborn. Stubborn and protective.

So long as he didn't get possessive. Because she wasn't going to belong to him.

"Excuse me, I've got work to do."

Isaac watched as Caley fled back into her office.

"Do you think she works so much because she's short on money?" Archer asked.

His brother looked around the cabin. "Yeah, I've had that thought myself."

It was obvious she didn't have much. Everything in the cabin was old or broken. She didn't have an adequate supply of firewood. She worked long hours.

He guessed she didn't sell a lot of books.

Isaac sat, leaning his elbows on his thighs. "I messed up."

"What did you do?"

He sighed. "I insulted her previous Dom."

"Ahh, I'm guessing that didn't go down well with her?"

"No. He was also her daddy."

"So where is he now?"

"He died."

"Aww, Christ. Poor darling." And she'd been left here on her own. Struggling to pick up the pieces. It was obvious she wasn't used to asking for or accepting help.

"Yeah, it sounded like they had some trouble in the town

where she lived, people found out she was a Little and were cruel to her. So he brought her here."

The cabin was cozy, but it wasn't really safe for a woman alone to be living here. There was a lot of work that needed doing. Archer didn't know much about construction work, but there were patches where the floor was soft and when he'd had a chance to look outside earlier, he'd thought the roof looked like it needed replacing.

No, not a place he'd ever allow a woman under his protection to live.

"What are you going to do?"

Isaac sighed. "Maybe she's not ready for someone else. It's not like pushing for this to go anywhere is a smart move. She lives hours away from me."

"Three hours, Issy. That's not insurmountable."

Isaac narrowed his gaze at him. "Maybe I'm not ready."

"Wait...let me go check if pigs are flying right now." He pretended to stand.

"Oh, shut up, you smart ass," his brother muttered.

"She's exactly your type, Issy."

His brother raised an eyebrow. "She's nothing like Evelyn."

"No, thank God," Archer muttered.

"She was more your type."

Now Archer's temper stirred. "So my type is a back-stabbing bitch? That's kind of you, brother." He sighed. "Seriously, Issy, she's perfect for you. She's sweet and submissive, but she'd got some bite to her, so she won't let you get away with Issy-shit."

"Issy-shit?"

"Yeah, like being a grumpy, moody bastard." Another clap of thunder sounded in the distance before Issy could reply.

"Shit. The weather's packing in again." Isaac stood and walked to the door. "I'll get some more wood in."

"She hasn't got much," Archer worried.

"I've got a supply coming as soon as the road clears."

More thunder. Much closer this time. The wind started to rip through the trees as Isaac disappeared out the front door.

Archer moved over to the kitchen; he was going to make a fresh pot of coffee. He wondered if Caley had a generator. If she did, it probably didn't work properly.

It was growing dark. He looked over at the time. He'd make dinner as well. He heated up some canned soup on the stove and Isaac worked on bringing in some firewood. By the time he was pouring soup into bowls, it was fully dark, and the thunder was growing closer.

The wind slammed against the house.

"Here we go," Isaac muttered.

Suddenly, the office door slammed open. Caley stood there, eyes wide, staring at them. Her entire body shook. Small trembles that had Archer tensing.

Isaac got to her first, drawing her in against his body. "What is it, baby? What's wrong?"

"T-thunder," she stuttered out.

"You don't like thunder?"

"N-no. Or the w-wind."

She buried her face into his chest as the wind howled. Isaac picked her up in his arms, carrying her over towards the sofa. He sat with her on his lap.

"Easy, baby doll, easy," Isaac crooned to her. "You're safe. You're safe."

Tiny whimpers came from her. She curled her arms around his brother's neck and a stab of jealousy hit him.

Archer took a deep breath, then let it out slowly. He walked closer and noticed that on the bottom of her fluffy, yellow socks were the words:

If you can read this bring me candy.

She really wasn't his type. No woman he'd dated would be

caught dead in those socks. And all he could think about was how adorable she was.

"Baby doll, calm down." Isaac looked up at him worriedly.

Archer sat beside them. He heard Caley's teeth chattering and frowned slightly. This seemed a rather extreme reaction to thunder and some wind. Surely, she'd been through a number of storms, living here.

And how many had she suffered through alone since her husband died?

"Caley, is there something we can get for you? Something to make you feel safer?" he asked calmly. His hands itched to reach out and rub her back, much as Isaac was doing right now.

"I. . .I. . ."

"It's all right, baby doll," Isaac told her. "Nobody is going to judge you here. Remember, I'm a Daddy Dom and Archer is a Dom as well."

She had her hand twisted in Isaac's shirt as she raised her face to give him a hesitant look.

Poor darling. He got that a lot of people didn't understand their lifestyle, especially when it came to age play. But it hurt that she'd had to experience people's ignorance and cruelty.

He gave her a reassuring smile. "Should I go have a look in your room?"

She looked from Isaac to him, as though searching for any hint of disgust or condemnation. What she found obviously reassured her because her shoulders relaxed. Then another clap of thunder hit, and she buried her face into Isaac's neck.

"Easy, baby doll. Let Archer get you what you need. What is it? A stuffy?"

"My bumblebee and my snuggly. In my bed."

Archer stood immediately, moving to her bedroom before she could change her mind. He stepped in and wasn't surprised to find there was stuff strewn everywhere. Did the woman ever put clothes in her drawers or closet?

He walked over to the bed, which was a mess of sheets. He'd make it for her later. Right now, she needed comforting. He looked over her bed. Seemed she had a thing for dachshunds. There was a huge body pillow on one side of the bed. Did she sleep with that surrounding her? For comfort? He lifted the bedcovers and found a bit of material that appeared to have been cut from a man's shirt and a bumblebee

He picked them both up, along with a fluffy blanket that lay along the bottom of her bed. She seemed to like fluffy things. He carried them back to the living room, where Isaac still held her on his lap, talking to her in a quiet, reassuring voice.

Archer crouched in front of them and held out her toy and snuggly. She reached out and took them, holding them close.

"What do you say to Archer?" Isaac asked her quietly.

Archer shot him a sharp look. His voice was quiet but held a definite firmness. Now might not be the time to go all Daddy Dom on her. But she didn't take offense; instead she shocked him by turning to him, her thumb already in her mouth as she rubbed her snuggly against her nose.

"Thank you, Archie." Her voice had a childlike note and he had to grin at her use of his nickname. He didn't mind. She could pretty much call him whatever she liked, and he'd take it.

Right. And you don't have feelings for her?

"Thumb out of your mouth when you speak, please," Isaac told her.

Archer shot him another look. Isaac just gave him a calm stare in reply. All right, so his brother knew what he was doing. Archer was used to play at the club, to negotiated scenes, where limits and safe words were carefully discussed first.

But this wasn't a scene. This was a baby girl who needed

comfort. She needed to feel safe and secure and that's what Isaac was giving her.

She removed her thumb. "Thank you, Archie."

"You're welcome, poppet." He didn't know where that nickname came from. Instead of examining his need to pull her onto his lap, he pressed the blanket around her. "How about I make hot chocolate? I saw some in the pantry earlier."

"I think hot chocolate is just what Doc ordered," Isaac said with a grin. "See what I did there?"

Archer groaned. But Caley just buried into his chest. She hugged her toy tight, sucking on her thumb.

"Is it good for her to be sucking her thumb?" he asked worriedly.

Isaac shrugged. "Likely not in the long-run but it's all right for now. Baby doll, do you have a sippy cup for the hot chocolate?"

He didn't think she would answer, her face was pressed firmly against Isaac's neck. She didn't seem to have any problem with touching his brother.

"Caley?" Isaac made his voice firmer.

She nodded. "Above the fridge in a box."

Archer gave Isaac a nod. He grabbed the Swiss Miss he'd seen earlier and decided he might as well make them all drinks. Another clap of thunder had Caley crying out and he turned to check on her, even though he knew Isaac had her.

Poor love. He wondered if something had happened to make her so fearful of thunder? Or was it just that she didn't like loud noises?

He reached up above the fridge and found a box sitting on top. It was dusty, as though it hadn't been pulled out in a long time. Opening it up, he stared down at the contents.

There was a large, white sippy cup with a soft, yellow lid and a handle on one side and a bumblebee on the front. There was also a baby's bottle with an extra-large nipple in the box.

Underneath the bottle was a bib. He pulled it out to study it. More bumblebees on the front. It was soft and tied at the back. It was also oversized, perfect for an adult baby girl. Under the bib was a child's plate. It had separate compartments so different foods didn't touch one another. There was also cutlery with more bumble bees on them.

Seemed to be a theme going on.

He put everything away except the sippy cup, but he left the box on the table to show Isaac later. Then he poured out the hot chocolate, making certain to add plenty of cream to hers. He set the mugs down on the coffee table before handing over the sippy cup.

"Hope it's not too hot."

Isaac took it, sipping from it first. "It's perfect, thanks, man."

More wind slammed against the house. He winced. Damn, it was really going for it out there. Far worse than the storm when they'd arrived. The wind hadn't been nearly this fierce. How many more trees were they going to find down tomorrow?

Shit. He was going to have to reschedule his patients because he had a feeling he wasn't getting home by Tuesday. Seemed his four-day weekend had become much longer.

Isaac helped Caley take a few sips of hot chocolate. It seemed she was calming down. Her trembling had eased, and she was no longer making those little whimpering noises.

Thank God.

How was she going to react tomorrow when she realized they'd seen her when she was so vulnerable?

Upset. Maybe angry.

Another crash of thunder and the lights flickered out. Caley let out another loud cry.

"Shh, baby doll. You're okay. I have you."

"Shit. Power's gone out entirely," Archer said. He reached for his phone which had been sitting on the coffee table.

"I found some flashlights earlier, only one had batteries," Isaac told him calmly. "I left it by the door, can you grab it?"

Archer stood and using his phone, he found the flashlight, turning it on. Isaac had grumbled earlier about her lack of preparedness. He added batteries to the ever-growing list of things she needed.

"Baby doll, do you have a generator?" Isaac asked.

"Y-yes, it's in the shed. It h-hasn't come on."

"Should I go check it?" Archer asked.

"No!" she cried out.

He blinked at her in surprise.

"You can't go out there. Don't!"

Isaac shifted her around on his lap. "She's right, man. You can't go out there."

"We're going to go without power instead?"

"Nah, I'll go look at it. I have some experience with generators, at least. You won't know what you're looking at. You come sit with her."

"No! No!" she cried out again, clinging to Isaac. "You both have to stay here."

More thunder. She wrapped herself around Isaac, who gave Archer a surprised look.

"Caley, I'm just going to check the generator and see if I can get it going. We only have one flashlight between three of us, plus the lights on our phones which will soon go dead. If I can get the generator going, at least we'll have power."

"No! It's not safe. Don't go!"

"I'll be fine, baby doll. Come on, let Archer hold you for a bit."

"No! No!"

"Caley, calm down." Isaac put a firm note in his voice.

Archer frowned. Caley wasn't the hysterical type. Yet she seemed terrified of Isaac leaving her.

"I should go," Archer said.

"No one should go! Stay here where it's safe."

"Shit. She's getting herself all worked up." Isaac stood with her wrapped around him. "Caley, listen to me. I'll be fine. I'll be back soon. Sit with Archer."

"Isaac," he said again, but the other man just drew himself out of Caley's hold. She let go, standing there, her arms wrapped around herself.

"Sorry, I'll have to take the flashlight."

Archer handed it over then turned back to Caley, who was shaking and wide-eyed. But her gaze wasn't on him or Isaac, she was staring at the wall, lost in her thoughts.

He kept the flashlight on his phone on so he could see her.

"Caley, love, come back and sit down," he said in a low, soothing voice as Isaac pulled on his jacket and boots and left.

At the bang of the door shutting, she let out another cry and he couldn't stand it anymore. He reached out and placed his hand on her arm. When she didn't turn away from him, he drew her close. She buried her face in his chest and he ran his hand up and down her back.

Knowing he was playing with fire; he kissed the top of her head. Fuck. She smelled good. And she felt perfect in his arms.

He had to stop this. Get some space from her. However, right now, she was a woman in need of care. And he wasn't going to turn her away simply because he was reacting to her in a way that he shouldn't. So he held her as the rain pelted down on the roof and the wind punched through the trees.

Thunder boomed, making the cabin rock. And she screamed. "Daddy!"

Shit.

She fought out of his hold and caught by surprise, he let her go. She raced towards the door. "Daddy!"

Fuck! He ran after her, grabbing her around the waist and lifting her up into the air.

"No! No! Daddy! He's hurt!"

"Caley! Caley! Stop!"

She clawed at his arms and he winced, knowing she'd likely drawn blood. Shit. He carried her back to the sofa and sat with her on his lap. She continued to fight his hold, fierce and vicious as a hellcat.

He wrapped his arms around her, holding her tight. "Caley, calm down."

"Let me go! I have to help him!"

"Caley, I don't know where you've gone right now, but your Daddy isn't out there. He's..." Fuck, not like he could blurt out that he was dead. "Issy left to check the generator."

"He'll get hurt," she cried.

"Issy? He'll be fine, poppet."

"No, no, no, you have to let me help him. I left him last time. I didn't help him." She started to sob. Big sobs that wracked her body, making her shake.

Christ. She was killing him. He couldn't stand it. He tucked her in against him, rocking her and crooning in a soft voice.

"Poppet, Issy isn't hurt. Nobody is hurt."

"He is. He is."

"He isn't. I promise you. And if he is, I'll help him. I'm here. You're not on your own."

"You have to let me go out there."

"I let you go out there and Issy will have my head." Last thing he needed was to return to work with a black eye. That would be an interesting conversation starter to have with his patients.

"But he's hurt."

"Caley, love, he's not hurt. I promise you. He'll be back any second."

"I have to help. I have to help. I can't lose him again. I can't."

Again? Did this have something to do with her Dom's death?

He didn't know and now wasn't the time for questions. He got the feeling she wouldn't calm down until she saw Isaac herself.

"Baby, hush, you'll make yourself ill. Where's your stuffy?" Maybe that would help. The lights flickered on. Thank God, Isaac must have gotten the generator on. He saw her bumblebee lying on the floor. He reached for it, making the mistake of loosening his hold on her. She pushed off his lap and raced for the door. Right as it opened, and Isaac stepped in.

She flung herself at him with a cry.

DOC STARED down at the woman shaking and crying in his arms with shock.

"Caley, damn it, I'm all wet."

He glanced up to find his brother watching her worriedly, her bumblebee held in his hand.

"Caley, calm down, baby. What is it?"

"She's been like this since you left," Archer explained coming towards him. "She kept saying that you were going to get hurt. But she seemed to confuse you with her husband."

He frowned. What was going on? "Caley, I need to get my jacket off. I'm dripping water everywhere." Not to mention getting her all wet as well.

"Caley, here, wrap up before you get a chill." Archer wrapped the blanket around her shoulders, and she stepped back, looking up at his brother in confusion.

"Archer?"

"Yeah, love, come with me back in front of the fire. You're going to get a chill. Come on, now. That's a good girl." His brother spoke in a low, cajoling voice. One he'd never heard him use before. Doc shrugged off his jacket and boots. Then pulled down his saturated jeans.

"I'm going to find a change of pants. Does she need new clothes?"

"Think I spied some pajamas in her bedroom under the pillow," Archer told him. He already had her sitting on the sofa with her sippy cup of hot chocolate in her hands.

Doc moved quickly. He pulled on some sweatpants and grabbed her pajamas from her room. He winced at the mess inside. He'd deal with that later.

When he returned, Archer was talking softly to Caley, who appeared to be in some sort of daze. His brother reached out and brushed some hair out of her face.

"Jesus, man, what happened to your arm?" Isaac asked as he grew closer. There were red scratches down both of his forearms.

"Nothing," Archer said quickly, shooting him a warning look.

What the fuck? Then he looked down into Caley's pale, shocked face.

"I did that?" she whispered. "Oh Archer, I'm so sorry."

His brother's quick reflexes saved the hot chocolate from tipping out of her hand. He set it on the coffee table.

"What's wrong with me? Why did I do that?"

She pressed her hands against her face. He was alarmed by the way she shook. These trembles were far more violent than the other ones.

"Caley, Caley, it's okay," Archer told her, gently pulling her hands from her face. "It's obvious that storms frighten you. You weren't yourself when you did this. You were desperate to get to Isaac."

"She wanted to go out in that to find me?" he asked, shocked. He'd thought she'd done it because she'd been afraid of the storm.

"Yeah. She fought me when I wouldn't let her go out in that."

Isaac sat beside her. "Caley, I'm fine. Nothing was going to happen to me."

"You don't know that. Anything could have happened, and I

would have just been sitting here, doing nothing." The last word was said on a loud cry.

"Caley, how did your husband die?" Archer asked.

Fuck. He was an idiot. Of course there was more to this. He tensed as he waited for her answer. Tears dripped down her pale cheeks. She swiped at them.

"There was a storm. Worse than this one. I've never liked thunder. Was always scared of it as a child. I'd always race to find my mom but if it was at night and my dad was home, he'd send me away. Tell me to stop being a coward."

"Ahh, baby," he crooned to her, drawing her under his arm.

She wiped at her cheeks again and Archer stood, moving into the bedroom he'd been using. When he returned, he held a handkerchief in his hand.

It surprised him, when instead of handing it to her, Archer wiped her cheeks and nose himself.

Archer was acting like a Daddy, which surprised him. Archer moved back onto the coffee table. Doc stared down at Caley worriedly. There was an empty spot inside him, and he hadn't realized until now what a gaping hole it was. Caley could fill that hole. She could be everything he desired.

If he could convince her of that.

Funny, he'd always been against taking on another sub. But maybe he just hadn't found the right one.

"There was a storm, worse than this one. Dave went into town for supplies. The storm hit far sooner than either of us expected. I was writing. I often lose track of time when I'm writing. But before he left, he'd made certain that my cell phone was sitting beside me, charged and turned on. After a few hours, I realized that the storm was getting worse. And that he wasn't home.

"He wouldn't have left if he'd known the storm was so close. He knew I didn't like them. I tried to call him. But there was no answer. I figured it was just the storm. I kept calling. But there was no reply." She ran her hand over her face. "I didn't know what to do. The storm was getting worse. I finally called the sheriff. He said he'd send someone as soon as he could. But they were all busy. And he'd only been missing a few hours."

He rubbed her back as she shuddered.

"I couldn't wait any longer. He'd taken my SUV. So I got in the truck and went looking for him."

"Christ, baby," he muttered.

"I knew I'd be in trouble for leaving the house during a storm. But I just knew something was wrong. I had to find him. But I never expected to find him..." she trailed off with a sob.

He drew her close, kissing the top of her head.

"He must have run off the road. His SUV was upside down. I...I managed to get hold of the sheriff. I don't remember much. I tried to pull him out, but I couldn't. When someone from the sheriff's department arrived, they had to drag me away from him. I was taken to the hospital. Apparently, I was hysterical, and they had to sedate me...they tried to tell me that he died straight away. That there was nothing I could have done even if I had gone looking for him. But I don't believe them...I sat there while he was dying...I...I..."

"Oh, love. No, you didn't know. You couldn't have known," Archer told her.

"Baby girl, he wouldn't want you thinking like this. It wasn't your fault. You aren't to blame."

She sobbed against him, wetting his shirt and he just held her, letting her cry it out.

"What if he was in pain? What if he was waiting for me to help him?"

"Caley. Caley, look at me," Archer told her firmly. He reached out and grasped hold of her chin, raising her face. "Focus on me now. Can you feel my hand on your skin?"

She nodded her head.

"Good girl. Concentrate on your breathing. In. Out. Can you feel Issy has a tight hold on you? Feel how strong he is? How he isn't going to let you go?"

"Yes."

"That's right. He's here. I'm here. Just breathe deep. Hold. Let it out slowly. That's it, love. Relax. We're here."

"I should have gone with him, Archer."

"If you had then you might have died as well."

Doc flinched. Jesus. *Way to just lay it out there, bro.*

Archer just sent him a look. Then he turned his calm gaze back to Caley. "Do you think that's what Dave would have wanted?"

"N-no."

"I didn't know Dave but it's obvious how much you loved him." Archer lowered his hand to hers.

"I did. I do. He was the best Dom, the best D-daddy."

"Then I do know he wouldn't want you to blame yourself for this. You feel guilty for surviving when he's gone. Those feelings are valid. The *what ifs* get to us all. But, love, you let it, and the guilt will eat you alive. And I bet that's not what Dave would have wanted for you. He wouldn't have wanted you to spend your life thinking about what you could have done differently. Would he?"

"I guess not."

"If he was here right now, what do you think he would say?" Archer asked.

"Dude, get your hand off my wife," she said in a gruff voice.

Doc had to grin at that. Would he ever measure up to Dave? Lord knew, he wasn't perfect. He had his shortcomings. More than a few, really. Could he really compete with a dead man? One who Caley still mourned.

"Dave's death was a terrible thing," Archer continued. "It's all right to miss him. To feel sad. But it's not okay to spend your time obsessing over *what ifs*. To not live the rest of your life because you're punishing yourself for being alive when he isn't."

She shuddered. "It's just so hard to let go. I don't want to say goodbye."

"Goodbye doesn't mean you have to forget him, love. But you should spend more time thinking about good memories rather than focusing on the bad ones."

She nodded slowly. "I know. I know he wouldn't want me to keep reliving it over and over. And I was doing better, but tonight... I just lost it. I'm so sorry."

"It's all right. No harm done." Archer smiled at her reassuringly.

She leaned her head against his arm, obviously exhausted. A faint boom of thunder sounded in the distance and she shuddered again.

"She's exhausted and probably cold. You should get her changed and into bed," Archer told him quietly. "She needs some rest."

Doc nodded. He stood and reached down, pulling her into his arms. "Thanks for looking after her, man."

"Anytime."

ARCHER WATCHED the bedroom door close and felt a sharp stab of longing. He examined the feeling, wondering if he was jealous.

There was a bit of that. But most of what he felt was longing. To be in that room with them. Helping to take care of Caley.

Fuck.

It was going to be a long night.

12

Doc carried her into her bedroom.

She was exhausted, emotionally spent. She couldn't believe she'd acted the way she had with Archer earlier. But she'd been lost in the past. She'd confused Doc with Dave. And she couldn't go through that again.

Was love worth the risk of losing someone?

She just didn't know. A few days ago, she'd have said no. But she was so lonely. Was spending her life on her own any better?

God, she was so confused.

"Baby doll, I can hear you thinking from here," Isaac told her. "Put your mind to rest for a while."

"How?" she asked. "I feel like it's whirling around and around, and I can't stop it."

"I can help you, if you can give me a bit of trust."

She thought about that. Could she? She shouldn't. She should be more careful. But who was she kidding? She was here alone with him and his brother. They could do anything to her, and she had no help for miles.

Yet she wasn't afraid of them hurting her. All her fear had been about Doc getting hurt.

"I think I can," she whispered.

"Then just let go for tonight. Let it all go. Stop thinking. All you have to do, right now, is what I tell you to do."

"I…" Christ, could she?

"You'll have a safeword. You can stop it at any time. But this is only about taking care of you. It's not about sex. It's not about me. It's all about you. Okay? There's no play, nothing sexual. I just…I have a deep need to take care of you, baby doll. It's about who I am. My need to care for those around me. I can see you're struggling. I want to ease that."

"So you'd do this for anyone?"

He snorted. "Ahh, no. I haven't taken care of anyone like this in a long, long time. Last time I tried; it all went horribly wrong. You're special, Caley. You're not like anyone else."

The tension in her eased. It was what she needed to hear. She didn't want to just be a person in a long list who he took care of.

She was special.

"Okay," she whispered.

"Okay." He set her down next to the bed.

"What do I need to do?"

"Just listen to me. Do you want to go Little?"

She shook her head. It might be easier in some ways, but she wasn't ready for that. She'd shown him her Little side briefly. That was all she could manage right now.

"No? That's okay. Whatever you're comfortable with. Although, for the record, I think your Little is adorable, and I would love to spend more time with her."

She could tell he meant every word. More tension eased. Jesus, he was potent. Archer was like Scotch. Smooth with a burn. But Isaac, he was a craft beer. Unique, with a bite.

"Okay, baby girl. For tonight, I'm just Doc or Sir. Whatever you would like. What's your safeword?"

"Banana."

"Banana?"

"I hate bananas."

His eyes twinkled. "That so?"

"Uh-huh. They smell bad, they taste bad. The texture." She shuddered. "Ick."

"Are you a fussy eater, baby doll?"

She flushed. "Maybe a bit."

He raised his eyebrows. "You can't survive on frozen meals and snacks."

Well, why not?

"Come on, let's get you out of those clothes and into your pajamas."

She glanced down at what he held in his hands. They were old, faded flannel pajamas with pictures of wiener dogs on them.

"Got a fondness for dachshunds?"

"Yes. I think they're so cute."

Maybe she should get a dog. Although she should probably get something big that would also serve as protection.

"Arms up, baby."

"Umm." She was not ready for him to see her naked.

He studied her then nodded. "I'll go brush my teeth in the other bathroom. You get ready. I expect to find you in bed in ten minutes, understand?"

"Yes, Doc."

He lightly brushed his lips against her forehead. "Good girl."

He looked at her bed. "I'll make that when I get back. What's this?" He pointed at her body pillow.

"I, umm, I sleep with it. I find it hard to sleep. This helps. It makes me feel secure."

He nodded. "You need your sleep."

She quickly got changed after he left, throwing her clothes in the hamper. Well, she threw them at the hamper, only her pants landed in it.

She'd get the rest in the morning. She yawned and stumbled her way into the bathroom to get ready. She really was exhausted. It had been an eventful day and evening. What time was it?

As she climbed into bed, glancing down at her clock. Holy hell, it was nearly midnight. And she'd gotten up early this morning. No wonder she was exhausted. She left the lamp on a soft glow. She hated sleeping in the dark.

It hadn't worried her when Dave slept beside her. But sleeping on her own was scary.

Being on her own was scary.

She knew she'd relied on Dave for a lot, but she hadn't realized just how much until he was gone. And so was her sense of place in the world. Her safety net.

Her door opened without a knock. Doc walked in, dressed in just a pair of low-slung sweats.

Holy hell.

That was a sight. He didn't head towards her, but he moved to the other side of the bed.

"What are you doing?"

"Getting into bed."

"Oh."

Wait a minute.

She sat up. "You can't sleep in here!"

"Why not?" He climbed into bed.

"Because this is my bed. I'm in it," she added inanely.

Like he can't see that, Caley.

"I know, that's why I'm sleeping in here. Can't say as I've ever slept in sheets with dogs on them before. Do you need the lamp on to sleep?"

"Umm, yes. But...but you can't sleep in here with me!"

"Caley, come here." He lay on his back, looking up at her. What did he mean, come here?

"I am here."

"No, I mean lie down next to me. You can still sleep with the body pillow, but just let me hold you for a moment."

She shook her head. She couldn't do that, could she? That sounded far too intimate.

You just agreed to let him take over.

Yes, but she hadn't thought he would actually want to sleep with her. She'd only slept with one man.

"Girl, ain't nothing happening here but some cuddling and some sleep. You can't handle that much then I'll sleep on the floor. I won't lie, I'm getting on in years so that's gonna be a bit hard on my body. But I'm not leaving you tonight. You need someone here. Someone to make sure you don't get scared during the storm or stay awake all night. Because you desperately need sleep, don't you?"

For some reason, tears welled. Because he actually seemed to truly care about whether she slept or not? Because he was willing to sleep on the damn floor just to ensure that she was all right?

Maybe all of the above?

"I don't sleep much anymore."

"I've noticed," he said dryly.

She smiled. "I often wake up and can't get back to sleep. What if I wake you?"

"If you wake up then I want you to wake me," he said firmly.

She wouldn't be doing that. No need for both of them to be awake.

She rubbed her head.

"Girl, what did you agree to just fifteen minutes ago?"

What had she agreed to? Lunacy, that's what she'd agreed to.

"To letting you take control."

"That's right. And what are you doing right now?"

"Trying to control the situation."

"Called topping from the bottom."

"I didn't realize we were doing a scene."

"We're not, baby doll. I don't really scene. I'm this way all the time."

"You mean you're wanting a 24/7 sub? A slave?"

"Not a slave, no. I don't require that level of obedience. But I do need to have the ultimate say. If I had a sub, she'd also be my Little. When she was Little, I'd pick her clothes, I'd get her dressed, I'd decide what we did that day. But I'd always put her first. Her needs, her safety. She would be my responsibility and I take that seriously."

"But she wouldn't always be Little?"

"No, but even when she wasn't, I'd still be the boss. She'd have more freedom to wear what she wanted. To do what she wanted. But if she left the house, I'd want to know where she was going, how she was getting there, when she'd be coming back. If she was going to be later than expected, I'd need a call to tell me that. I'd require her to be careful with her safety even when I wasn't around to watch over her. There would be no speeding, no texting while driving. No walking around at night alone. And if I couldn't trust her to take care of herself then I'd need to be with her."

Wow.

It was more than what Dave had required of her.

And yet, didn't you always wish for more? Want him to take things a step further?

"What if she disobeyed you? What if she stayed out late and didn't call you?"

"First, it would be completely disrespectful, since I would be worrying. I would never do that to her. Second, it would put her at risk since I wouldn't know where she was and if something went wrong, I couldn't be there to help her. So she'd earn herself a harsh punishment."

"Like what?" she whispered.

"Likely the belt or a paddle."

"Oh."

"Oh?" He raised an eyebrow in amusement. "You ever been spanked with a paddle or belt?"

"No, Dave only ever used his hand on me. He didn't spank me very often. I was a good girl."

"I'm sure you were. But I also think you have a tendency to overlook self-care. That would end up in you going over my knee. What about when you were Little? Did he spank you when you misbehaved?"

"Sometimes. Mostly I got time-out."

"Hmm, I usually use time-out before a spanking. To help get a Little into the right frame of mind. Now, you have a choice, girl. You can either say your safeword or you can do what I asked and lie down."

"Asked?"

"All right, commanded."

She took a deep breath and thought about it for a moment. She had agreed to let him take control. In fact, she'd wanted it. She desperately needed sleep. Her head ached. Her heart hurt. She just wanted some blessed oblivion for a while.

Not being in charge will give you that. If you're not in control, you don't have to worry or stress.

Before she talked herself out of it, she lay down. He immediately pulled her against him, resting her face on his chest.

"Comfy?" he asked, wrapping a big arm around her.

Comfy? Hell, no, she wasn't comfy. She was pressed up against one of the hottest men she'd ever seen in her life. His skin was warm and smooth beneath her cheek. She could hear his heart beating. He had a light smattering of chest hair. It was sexy as hell.

"Easy, girl," he said in that rough voice of his. "Ain't nothing going to happen. I'm just going to hold you. All I'm doing tonight is taking care of you. I ain't gonna touch you, no matter how much you beg me. So don't go doing that, cause it's just sad."

She snorted out a laugh. Okay, the last thing she'd expected to be doing tonight, was lying curled up against Isaac Miller, with a smile on her lips.

He was so fucking crazy.

"I just want you to sleep, girl. Just empty your mind and sleep. Ain't nothing or no one that can hurt you while you're in my arms. So you just listen to the wind, to the rain and know that you're safe from it all. Safe in my arms."

She took in a shuddering breath, then let it out slowly.

He ran his hand slowly up and down her back. "Deep breath in. Slowly out. Here, put your feet between my legs. Jesus, they're freezing. The rest of you warm enough?"

Her eyes were drifting shut. Warm? She didn't think she'd been so warm. Normally, she had to layer up for bed. Just her pajamas weren't enough. She needed a sweater and socks, sometimes Dave's robe.

No, don't think about Dave right now. If she did, she might not be able to sleep.

And she desperately wanted to sleep.

In his arms.

She woke up cozy and warm. With a yawn, she stretched, groaning at the pull in her back. She might need to look at a new chair. She was falling apart.

Her arm slammed against something solid. Something that was definitely not Bumbly. It was then she realized that she wasn't pressed up against her body pillow.

But rather an actual body.

She threw herself back with a gasp and slid right off the edge of the bed, landing on her ass.

Ouch.

"Oh, shit, baby doll." A sleepy-eyed, hair-tousled, bearded face looked over the edge of the mattress down at her. "What happened? Are you all right? Are you hurt?"

Just her ass. And her pride.

She closed her eyes, lying on her back. She was an idiot. Total dork.

Had she seriously just fallen out of bed?

Her eyes flew open as she was picked up in the air and placed down on the bed. She gaped up at a concerned-looking Doc as he started running his hands over her body.

"Where does it hurt? Your bottom? Your back?"

Oh God.

She had to face facts. She wasn't that good at looking after herself. She definitely wasn't good at taking care of her stuff. Or keeping on top of anything except work, which she'd thrown herself into in order to try to stop thinking about Dave.

But this...oh, she'd missed this. Even if he was over-the-top protective, Doc actually cared.

It wasn't something she'd ever thought she would have again.

"I'm fine," she told him, trying to sit up.

He held her down. "Stay there until I check your bottom. Let's roll you over."

And then she was lying on her front as he raised the back of her pajama top. He lightly pressed down on her back. She let out a groan.

He stopped. "Sore?"

"Not from the fall. It was already sore."

"It was? Why didn't you tell me?"

She rolled slightly over to look up at him. "I sit at a desk for long hours. It's bound to get sore. And my hands and shoulders. Just part of the job."

He frowned. "You need to take more breaks. Stretch. You need an ergonomic desk and chair. And you should tell your Dom when you're hurting so he can help you."

She sucked in a breath. "My Dom?"

He gave a nod without a hint of hesitation. "Your Dom. I'd be your Daddy too, but I don't think you're ready for that yet."

"Ahh, no. I'm not entirely sure I'm ready for anything yet."

"You let me take control last night. You trusted me enough for that. To sleep in your bed. Are you attracted to me?"

She nearly snorted. "Ahh, yeah, there's no issues on that front."

He grinned. Actually grinned. Had she seen him smile yet? Sometimes his eyes twinkled. Briefly. But actually smile? No.

And it was a thing of beauty. Her heart raced. Her clit actually throbbed. Without being touched.

Good Lord, a woman could live and breathe for a smile like that. Sacrifice everything to see that every day.

So why are you hesitating? Give that man everything he wants.

Because she'd given a man all of herself once. And when he was taken from her. . .she'd fallen into a dark place. She knew she couldn't go back to that place. Wasn't sure she'd find a way out again. Even though she knew logically that just because Dave died didn't mean that anything would happen to Doc, it still made her hesitate. Made her wonder if she was strong enough.

"Good to know," he crooned. "Because I think you're gorgeous, girl. Smart, caring, a little odd at times—"

"Hey," she protested. But she did it with a grin. Because let's face it, she could be totally odd sometimes.

He rubbed her lower back. "I know it was hard on you, losing Dave. I'm not a replacement for him. I wouldn't want to be. But I do feel a pull towards you, Caley. And I think you feel the same. So how about you give me a shot? I'll stay here awhile and we'll explore things. As much as you feel comfortable with. I don't need to see your Little yet. I understand how much trust that takes. But I am a dominant guy. I can't hold that back."

"Yeah, kind of seen that already."

"I can help you," he told her seriously. He rubbed her back as he spoke, and she lay on her front. "I can help you get a bit more balance in your life. You work too much. You don't eat or rest enough."

"I need to work," she warned.

"I get it. I wouldn't stand in your way. But can you honestly tell me you need to work as much as you do? You might actually get more done in a shorter amount of time if you weren't running on caffeine, no sleep and zero calories."

She smiled. "There's calories in the creamer."

He snorted when she groaned as he reached her shoulders. "Not good ones. What do you say, girl?"

She sighed. "You'll leave eventually."

"Can't guarantee forever. You might be begging for me to leave. I've got it on good authority that I'm not easy to live with."

She didn't know. If he gave massages like this, she could forgive a lot.

"But we can face that hurdle when we get to it. Sometimes, you've just got to have a bit of faith that things will work out the way they should."

"Didn't take you for a believer in fate."

"I'm not. But I'm not the sort of person that stands back and lets life come at me. If I want something, I go for it. Sometimes it doesn't always work out. But I've worked hard for everything I've gotten. Makes me appreciate it all the more. Let me Top you. Nothing heavy. A few rules. Bit of punishment if you disobey. Doesn't have to be anything sexual. Doesn't have to be any age play."

She thought it over as he continued to rub her back. She

should likely say no. Save herself heartache. But then would she always regret it? Always wonder? When was she ever likely to get an offer like this? And from someone like Isaac? Gorgeous. Dominant.

If she said yes and then couldn't do it, she could always safe-word out.

And she had Archer as back-up. Not that she didn't trust Doc but there was something about having Archer here that made her feel safe.

But he's not part of this. You need to remember that.

"All right," she said quietly, before she could talk herself out of it. "But I can't...I don't know that it will go anywhere. I have so much baggage where Dave is concerned. I'm not sure I can ever give you anything more."

"You can try. That's all I ask. Let's just try. If either of us don't want more, then it doesn't go further."

"All right. Do I have to call you Sir, though? I've never been much into that."

"No, you can call me Doc."

"I rather like Issy."

He groaned. "Of course you do. Now, let's have a look at this bottom. Make sure you didn't hurt yourself."

"I didn't. It's fine," she said hastily as he reached for her pajama bottoms.

He raised an eyebrow. "My main priority, as your Dom, will always be health and safety. And I don't compromise on those things. I also don't do things by half-measures. So if I need access to your body to ensure your health or safety, I expect to be given that, understood?"

Oh. Holy. Hell.

"Yes, Doc."

"Good girl. Use your safeword if you need to. I'll stop what I'm doing. We talk. We discuss. Then we decide how to move forward."

"All right."

He lowered her pajama bottoms then her panties. She went stiff. Could feel herself blushing as he studied her ass.

"Easy, baby doll. You ain't got nothing to be embarrassed about because this ass is perfection. Also, I suspect it won't be the last time I see it. I fully expect this bottom will be feeling the palm of my hand sometime in the near future."

"You'll spank me?"

"Yep. Unless it's a hard limit."

"Oh, umm, no. It's not. I've always had a bit of an obsession with being spanked."

"Yeah? If you have any desires, wants, needs, you can tell me. I won't ever make fun of you or be shocked."

She didn't know why she'd held back so much with Dave. Maybe she'd been worried it wasn't something he wanted.

"Your bottom doesn't seem to be bruised." He ran a finger down between her cheeks. "Tell me your hard limits."

"Can I pull my pants up?"

"No, I like you just where you are. Remember, you can always use your safeword, but unless anal play is a hard limit, I want to explore a bit."

Explore her bottom? Holy hell.

"Caley? Is anal play a hard limit?"

"No."

"Ever had someone take you here?"

"No."

"Been plugged?"

"No."

"Hmm. Lots of fun times ahead for you then."

Yeah. She got that feeling.

He pressed her ass cheeks apart to massage her back hole lightly. Oh God, it felt so good. She should protest. She wasn't sure they were at this stage. But then he ran two fingers over her hole, and she shivered with delight.

"Yeah, my baby doll likes that," he murmured.

"Is it weird to do this when we haven't kissed?"

A bark of laughter erupted out of him.

Ooh. That was nice.

"You know what, baby? Didn't think of it but it is definitely weird. Then again, neither of us are particularly normal, right?"

"No, we're not," she said quietly. How often had she wished she could be normal?

"Hey. Normal is overrated."

Was it? If she was normal, she'd still have her family. Then again, if her family loved her shouldn't they accept her the way she was?

"Yeah. You're right."

"That's my good girl."

To her disappointment he pulled his finger away. "Shit. Hard to concentrate." He drew her panties up but continued to rub her bottom. "Hard limits?"

"Anything hard impact, like a whip or cane."

"Paddles? Belt?"

"They're fine."

Was this really happening? Was she living an alternate reality? Sometimes she daydreamed, caught up in the stories of her mind and made things up that seemed so real. Was that happening, right now?

"Anything else I need to know?"

"I wouldn't like to be humiliated."

"I'd never want to do that to you, baby doll. Not my kink. I like having a Little. A baby girl who looks to her Daddy for protection and safety and care."

What if she couldn't ever give him that?

"But that takes a lot of trust. And we don't need to have that right now. It's enough you're giving me your trust to let me take control in some areas. I want you to communicate with me, Caley. I want to know if you're scared, angry, unsure, horny."

She snorted at the last one. She had a feeling she'd always be aroused around him.

"Don't hold back out of fear, all right? Honesty and communication are important."

"I understand. I do tend to go into my head when I need to think something out. I like to mull over things."

"That's fine. But you have to tell me you need time and then when you are finished mulling, you've got to tell me what you're thinking. And you can't take too long doing that mulling or I'm going to interfere."

Hmm, yes, patience wasn't his strong suit.

"Anything you need from me?"

"I..." Oh hell, could she ask for orgasms?

"Baby doll?"

"I guess...maybe I...don't sleep well."

"I'm going to help with that. Think maybe I should get some rails for the side of the bed, don't want you falling out again and hurting yourself."

"That's the first time I've fallen out of bed."

"Hmm, you forgot I was in bed with you, huh?"

Maybe. "I know I work too much...it was a coping mechanism after Dave died. I have trouble pulling back."

"I fully intend to help with that too. Most of your rules will be around health and safety and they will be strictly enforced. Somehow I think you need that."

It was almost like he could read her mind.

"Now for my limits and needs," he told her. "I'm a deeply

dominant guy. I've already told you honesty and communication. Lies are something I cannot tolerate."

"I understand."

"I can be a bit blunt and gruff. I can be overwhelming. You need to tell me if I'm too much because I don't always see the line. Sometimes I blast right over it."

"O-okay."

"I enjoy bondage. You okay with being restrained?"

"Y-yes."

"Spreader bars? Ropes?"

"I've never tried them. But I'm willing."

"Good girl. That's not something I'd do with your Little by the way. You ever gift me with her, and she'll be pampered and cherished. Adored. But she'll also have her rules to follow. Daddy wants his Little safe, secure and under his watch. Always."

Oh Lord. Maybe it should have sounded scary or smothering. But it didn't. None of it did.

"If you were mine. Fully mine, sometimes I'd tie you up and play with you. I'd hold you on my lap with your legs spread and play with your clit, your nipples, bringing you to pleasure over and over. But when I'm Daddy, then I'd have my Little girl bundled up in my lap. In a onesie with a bottom flap or wrapped up tight in a blanket, swaddled if she needed more from me. You can be as needy as you want with me, Caley. I want it all. I crave it.

"Neither my sub nor my baby girl would be allowed to go anywhere without my knowledge. Not to control you but because of safety. If you were ill, I'd take complete charge. If you wake at night, then you need to wake me up. You'll be required to get enough sleep and to eat well, to take care of yourself. Exercise is also part of that."

She groaned. She hated exercise.

"My Daddy side is less strict, but I think you need strong boundaries, but also some gentleness."

She thought so too. But she knew he'd meant it when he said she had to show him where the line was and pull him back when he stepped over it.

Otherwise he would consume her.

Archer would help with that. Archer had a good read on people. He'd see when she was pushed too far without her having to say a word. Archer would know when to push her out of her head.

But Archer isn't a part of this.

"You've tensed up, let's see what we can do about that."

He slapped his hand down on her bottom.

Holy shit. That stung!

But then he rubbed the abused cheek and she let out a small whimper of pleasure.

"Okay, girl?" he asked in a gruff voice.

"Ahh, yeah," she said on a sigh.

"Good. That means I get to do this." He lay her on her back then leaned in to kiss her.

And it was stunningly, shockingly amazing. The kiss was no quick peck on her lips. This kiss ravaged her.

"I'm gonna go wash up. You're gonna do the same. I'll make you some breakfast then you can do some work before lunch."

Oh hell, work.

She let out a cry as she saw the time. Holy shit. She should already be several thousand words deep by now. She jumped out of bed. He followed more slowly.

"Girl, come here."

"I can't! I'm late. I don't even have time to eat."

"You're gonna eat," he told her in a deep voice. "And you have time to come here. Two minutes won't make any difference."

She took a deep breath to calm herself. Of course it wouldn't. She walked to him.

He tilted her face up with one hand. "I'm going to take care of you, Caley. I'll show you that you can trust me. With all parts of yourself. That's a promise."

Then after laying that on her, he walked out.

Sheesh.

13

She stood, stretching. Her right hand was aching, and she knew she should take a break. She'd written a lot despite her late start.

The weather outside had calmed down a lot during the night. It was still pelting with rain, but at least the wind had stopped. Still, there were branches everywhere.

Clean-up. Yay.

Not exactly her strong suit.

A knock on her door had her turning. Doc pushed his head in.

"Ahh, good, you've stopped. Didn't want to interrupt you in the middle of a scene. Lunch is nearly ready. Time to wrap it up now."

"I think I should eat it in here. I have some more to write."

"You'll take a break and eat it out here."

Bossy bastard. But the thought was an affectionate one.

When she walked out, she saw him stirring something on the stovetop.

"Yum, what's that smell?"

"Found some ground beef in your freezer so I made meatballs. They're not as good as my grandma's but they're better than another night of frozen meals. They're for dinner, though. Grilled cheese for lunch."

Her tummy took that moment to rumble.

"Ahh, Caley, what is your poison? I thought we could have aperitifs later on, before dinner." Archer walked in from the back porch, carrying some bottles of spirits.

Isaac snorted. "Aperitif."

Archer just rolled his eyes. "I found these earlier and you have some juice and soda. Thought I would experiment. Do you like cocktails?"

"Oh, I'm not much of a drinker but one would be nice before dinner."

"How are your hands?" Doc asked her.

"Sore." She looked down at her swollen hands. He stepped forward and gently took her hands in his.

"They don't look good, Caley. They're swollen. You need to start looking into dictation before they get really bad."

She sighed. "I hate using dictation. It takes so long to train it to my voice. And then it's so slow to edit."

"Seems to me it would be worth the time considering the state of your hands. You need to start doing some form of exercise as well."

"What my brother meant to say is that exercise would help you from getting too sore sitting at a desk all day."

"That's what I said, isn't it?" Doc glowered at his brother.

"Ahh, I suppose I should," she said quickly. "It's just not that easy out here. I could go for a walk but I'm kind of scared of wildlife."

"You live in a cabin in the woods and you're scared of walking outside?" Doc gave her a funny look.

She knew it sounded ridiculous.

"There's yoga and Pilates," Archer offered. "You can do free classes online I expect."

That actually wasn't a bad idea. The microwave beeped and Isaac pulled out a heat pack.

"Hands up," he ordered.

She raised them up and he placed the heat pack on the table. "Put your hands on there. Not too hot?" he asked when she'd done as ordered.

"No, it's good. Thank you."

He doubled it over, so it also lay on top of her poor hands. Ahh, that was bliss.

"Keep them there for at least ten minutes," he ordered. "Do you need a painkiller?"

"No. I don't think so."

He gave a short nod and returned to the pot.

"Archer, did you get hold of the rental company?" she asked.

"Yes, once Mal gets up here to tow it down, they'll take it from there. They'll also deliver another rental when I need it."

"That's good," she said, even as she felt a stab of sadness at the idea of them leaving.

Archer held up a bottle of vermouth. "I might not be much of a cook, but I mix a mean martini. Think I'll make up a batch later."

Doc shook his head. "How are we brothers? What is wrong with beer?"

"Nothing. If it's a good craft beer."

"Brother," Doc started.

She knew if she let them get started, they'd never stop.

"I didn't even realize I had any alcohol."

"Yeah. Found some out in a box in the woodshed."

"That's weird. You did?" A tendril of worry unfurled in her gut. "Why would there be alcohol out there?"

"I don't know, love," Archer said. "You didn't know it was there?"

"No. Dave didn't drink much once we moved out here. He,

uhh, he lost his job after he was arrested for driving under the influence."

"He did?" Isaac asked.

Archer shot him a look that she barely caught.

"Yeah, I didn't think he'd been drinking that much. It was when I still lived at home. He wanted to go out for dinner and a drink. We went to this place in the next town. I asked him if he needed me to drive, but I hadn't had my license long and I wasn't used to driving in the dark. I didn't think he'd drunk that much, or I would have insisted we take a taxi."

"Wait, are you saying that he was driving after drinking and he had you in the car?" Doc demanded. The look on his face clearly said he thought Dave was an idiot and she pressed her lips together. This wasn't fair to Dave. He wasn't here to defend himself. And she shouldn't be bringing up old stuff.

"Isaac, easy," Archer warned.

"Are you saying that it was okay for him to drive with something so precious in the car without a care for her safety? Bad enough he risked all the other people on the road and himself, but to risk the person he was most responsible for?"

"It wasn't like that," she said.

"What? You weren't his then?"

"No, I was, it just...he was under a lot of pressure. I noticed he was drinking a bit more, but he said it was a rough patch. Soon after that, he lost his job and we moved here. I just didn't think he was drinking anymore. Was he hiding it out there from me?"

"Sounds like it."

"Isaac!" Archer snapped.

"What?" Doc looked genuinely confused.

"Love, you can't know what reason that booze was out there. Maybe he put it out there and forgot about it. If you didn't see signs of him drinking, then likely he wasn't. But whether he was or wasn't, it doesn't matter now."

Tears blurred her eyes and she glanced down at her lap.

"Hey."

She glanced over at Archer who was crouching next to her. "Don't think about it. It will just mess with your mind. So what if he was drinking? What is knowing that going to achieve now? All it's going to do is hurt you. And it doesn't change anything. Not how much he loved you. Not your memories of him. All right?"

She gave him a tremulous smile. He had this way of making everything seem better. Of calming her. "Yeah, thanks, Archer. It just hurts, the idea of him hiding something from me. Makes you question everything, you know?"

"Yeah, we know something about that," Doc said to her, coming to sit at the table. "I'm sorry, Caley. I didn't mean to sound so judgmental. Just the idea of you in a car with a person who is intoxicated," his face turned grim, his jaw clenching, "makes me furious."

"I should have insisted on driving. It was really my fault."

"No, love, it was not," Archer said firmly. "That is something Issy and I will agree on. That was not your fault. He had a duty of responsibility to you as your Dom and as your man."

"It was on him to protect you," Doc added.

She sniffled. "I always thought Dave was protective, but you two are a different breed all together."

Archer mock-frowned. "Not sure I like being lumped in with this guy." He pointed at Issy.

"Right back atcha, brother."

Archer stood. "Love, shall I put the booze away? I can if it upsets you."

"No, I'd like a drink later. Unless, do you think that's wrong?"

"No. Not wrong at all." Archer's hand rested briefly on her shoulder. Warmth filled her at his touch. "I'll get you some water."

"Thank you." She smiled up at him, feeling exhausted.

He placed a glass of water down beside her.

"Keep those hands in there for another few minutes," Doc bossed.

Archer winked at her. "He's so shy and retiring. I don't know how we'll ever get him to speak up and say what he wants."

She bit back her grin as Doc shot his brother a look. Doc put down plates of grilled cheese. She picked up one half of a sandwich and took a big bite.

"Oh man, that's so good."

Both men were grinning at her.

"What? Is there something on my chin?"

"Yeah, baby doll. Just a little." Doc got up and grabbed some paper towels and then sat and wiped her chin.

"Sorry." She blushed, dropping her gaze down. She should probably try to eat with more manners.

"Have you talked about Dave much, love?" Archer asked gently after a few more minutes of eating.

"Not exactly a lot of people to talk to around here," she muttered. "After he died, Murray and Geoff would come to check on me, but I didn't much feel like talking to them."

"How long ago did Dave die?" Archer asked.

"Over two years ago now."

"And you've lived here on your own ever since?" Doc asked.

"Yes."

"You've said a few things about your family and the town you lived in, you don't keep in contact with them?" Archer asked.

"Ahh, no. I haven't spoken to my family since we left Spencerville."

"Where's that?" Doc asked.

"Small town in Kansas."

"Is that where you met Dave?" Archer asked her.

"I was working at the local motel in reception. Dave used to stay when he was travelling. He was a salesman. He was always super polite. A gentleman. So kind and sweet.

"It took months before he even asked me on a date. I thought he was shy. But apparently, he'd been worried about our age difference. I was only twenty when we met. He was forty. He was my guide into BDSM. It took several dates for him to tell me what he was. I didn't really want to hear it. My mother was always submissive to my father. She never stood up to him. We always did what he wanted. Had what he liked to eat for dinner. Or went on vacation where he wanted to go. It was like she didn't have a mind of her own. I didn't want that. But he explained that being a submissive didn't mean I was a doormat. That I ultimately had all the power. Eventually, I decided to give it a chance. For the first time in my life, it was like I felt right. I felt at peace. I could shut off my mind and just be."

"Felt good, huh?" Doc asked.

"Felt better than good. I hadn't realized how busy my mind was. I'm always thinking. Always imagining things. Sometimes, the stories in my head feel so real it's like I've actually lived them. Dave was the one who encouraged me to write them all down. I'd never even thought of trying to write. He was everything to me. Unfortunately, the rest of the town found out about our relationship. Someone took photos of us in the motel room. They circulated through the town. The sheriff even paid Dave a visit and told him to get out of town before he was arrested for sexual assault."

"Oh, baby doll," Doc crooned, rocking her.

"Some of the photos were of me in Little mode, playing with a doll he'd bought me. There was another photo of him spanking me. That was one of the few times he ever spanked me and it was tarnished. People were awful. They called me all sorts of names. My parents told me to leave town. I've never felt so less in my life, you know what I mean?"

"Yeah," Doc said quietly. "I do, baby girl."

"What are you talking about?" Archer asked. "When did you feel like that?"

"When our parents disowned me."

Archer blinked. "Disowned you? But they told me that you left. That you wanted nothing to do with them."

"Yeah, well, they lied," Doc said bitterly.

"Why would they disown you?" Archer asked.

"Mother caught me watching some BDSM porn. Stuff with age play in it. She called in Father. Both of them told me I was sick. Depraved. After a lot of yelling and insults, they told me my choice was to be reformed or leave. I told them to fuck off and I left."

"What the hell? Why did you never tell me?" Archer demanded.

Doc shrugged. "I dunno. Guess I was embarrassed."

"Jesus Christ, Issy. I know they can be uptight, but I didn't realize... I could have stood up for you. For God's sake, I'm a Dom as well. What are they going to do, disown both of us?" Archer followed with his own plate and they were soon facing off against one another in the kitchen.

Doc snorted. "They'd never disown you. You could tell them you'd committed armed robbery and stolen the pope's hat and they'd ask you if you needed their help covering it up."

"That's not true."

"Come on, Archer."

"Well, maybe I would have walked away from them, ever think of that?" Archer asked.

Oh, this was not going to go well.

"Ahh, guys, maybe we should all talk about this some other time—"

"Walked away from them? Why?"

"For you, you idiot!"

"Guys, I really think we should just—"

"You can't walk away from it all for me," Isaac yelled. "They need you."

"And I need you! What don't you understand about that, Issy!

Soon as I get home, I'm telling them I want nothing to do with them until they apologize to you."

"Not happening," Doc told him.

"It is!"

"You guys need to calm down," she interjected, standing.

"Like hell!"

"It's happening!" Archer insisted.

"I'm not letting you do it."

"Why? Because you like being the black sheep in the family? Or because you can't be happy!"

"I've tried to be happy before, remember? It didn't fucking work."

"Guys!" she yelled.

They ignored her, glaring at each other. So she did the only thing she could think of. She picked up the glass of water Archer had given her and threw it at them.

Of course, she'd meant to just throw the water. She was horrified as the glass slipped from her hand and smashed against the counter behind them.

Her hands came to her mouth. "Oh God, I'm so sorry. Stay still. I'll get the broom. Don't move, you might stand on glass and hurt yourselves."

Both men gaped at her.

"Did she just throw a glass at us, brother?" Archer asked.

"I do believe she did, brother," Doc replied, crossing his arms over his thick chest and giving her a foreboding look.

Oh great. They were united by their irritation with her.

"I didn't mean to."

"You didn't mean to?" Archer asked. "The glass just spontaneously erupted out of your hand? Strange."

"Very odd," Doc agreed.

She huffed out a breath. "I was trying to throw water on you and the glass accidentally went with it." Guilt filled her again. They could have been hurt. "I really am sorry."

"So you meant to throw the water," Doc said.

"You were arguing. You weren't listening." And she had a feeling she should be running.

"Come here, little girl." Doc crooked a finger at her. She shook her head and stepped back.

No way was she gonna do that.

"Here. Now." He pointed at the floor then looked down at it with a grimace. "Actually. Stay where you are. I'm coming to you."

"I'll take care of the glass," Archer said.

Was that a flash of regret in Archer's eyes? Of longing? Pondering that distracted her long enough from Doc and she failed to notice that he was standing right in front of her.

"Oh shit." She turned to run but he picked her up, swinging her over his shoulder.

"No! Put me down!" She wiggled on his shoulder, trying to free herself.

A sharp slap landed on her butt. "Stay still."

"Nooo!"

"Brother, can you handle this?" Issy asked.

"Yep," Archer replied. "Can you handle her?"

"Oh, with pleasure."

Another smack landed on her bottom and she gave an outraged squeal. Then Doc turned and stomped towards her bedroom.

Shit. Shit. She raised her head to look back at Archer, hoping to plead with him to help her.

The look of complete longing on his face made her gasp. It was quickly gone. He turned away and hurried out of the kitchen. But that look. It made her heart hurt.

Did he. . .could he possibly want her too? Or was she imagining it?

Of course you're imagining it.

Doc carried her into her bedroom and locked the door. Then he set her down on her feet. He placed his hands on her hips, giving her a stern look.

"Want to explain yourself?" he asked. A drip of water made its way down his forehead and along his nose before falling onto the floor.

"Umm, not really."

"Not. Really?"

She studied him, trying to gauge how upset he truly was. His shirt had splotches of water on one sleeve, but most of it seemed to have gone on his face.

Whoops.

He whipped off his T-shirt and wiped it over his face and hair.

Her mouth went dry at the sight of all the muscles.

Oh wow. Yum.

Lord help her if she ever saw him fully naked. She might be rendered completely mute.

"Much as I enjoy the way you're staring at me, girl, it's not going to distract me."

That wasn't the reason she'd been staring at him, but it was a good idea.

"Are you sure you couldn't be distracted?" She sent him a hopeful smile and attempted to flutter her eyelashes.

"You got something in your eye?" He gave her a concerned look.

She sighed. "My seduction technique needs work."

His eyes widened. "You were trying to seduce me?"

Eek. She hadn't thought that through. Had she been trying to seduce him? Not exactly.

"I. . .I. . ."

"Easy, girl. Just breathe," he told her gruffly. "I know you're not ready for that. You're just gonna have to wait to have all of this."

He ran his hand through the air, indicating his body. He gave an exaggerated huff of air. "Know that's hard for you, resisting me. But if I have to tie you up to get you to keep your hands to yourself, I will."

She rolled her eyes, her tension easing just as she knew he'd intended. Although his gaze had grown all hot as he'd mentioned tying her up.

"You're dying to tie me up, aren't you?"

"Then at least I know you'd stay where I put you."

"Dear Lord," she muttered. How much more of a caveman could he be?

"Would also stop you from throwing glasses at my head."

"I didn't throw a glass at your head!"

Although right now she was tempted...very tempted.

"Throwing things at other people is very naughty behavior. Throwing things at your Dom. Big, big trouble."

"I was trying to get the two of you to stop fighting."

His face softened slightly. "Were we upsetting you, baby?"

"I don't like it when you fight."

He reached out and cupped the side of her face. "Then we'll have to make sure we don't fight in front of you again."

She noticed he didn't promise not to fight with Archer. She bit her lip. "I wish you guys could work things out."

"Hey, there's a lot of stuff between Archer and I that we need to work out. We've got to do that our way. What isn't acceptable is doing it in front of you. That won't happen anymore, okay?"

She wasn't sure it was entirely what she wanted. She didn't want him to think she couldn't handle the arguing. It just wasn't something she was used to.

"I'm sure we'll still snap and snarl at each other. But you're right. We need to talk this shit out." He grimaced. "Christ, can't believe I just said that."

"Poor Doc, allergic to talking."

"Poor Caley, about to get her bottom spanked."

Her mouth dropped open. Her hands came around to protect her bottom. "What? Why? I didn't do anything!"

"Didn't do anything? Did I imagine the water on my face?"

"I was just trying to get your attention! To stop you guys!"

"Would it be acceptable if I threw water in your face?" He took a step closer to her.

"Well, no, but. . ."

"You could have hit one of us with that glass. . .would that be acceptable?"

"It was an accident."

"I understand that, which is why I'll go easy on you. But you still intended to throw the water, didn't you? And what if you'd then stepped on the glass and cut yourself?"

"I was going to put shoes on to clean it up."

"Or you could have not thrown anything in the first place."

"You admitted that you shouldn't have been arguing, does that mean you're getting a spankin' as well?"

"Unfortunately for you, girl, there's only one of us that gets spanked when they mess up. And it ain't me. Pants and panties off. Turn around, hands on the bed."

Her eyes widened. She gaped at him.

He studied her for a moment. The hard look on his face faded into understanding. "If you're not ready for this step, I get it. We can stick with a scolding and corner time."

Scolding and corner time versus a spanking? She knew which she'd rather.

She licked her lips nervously.

"You have a safeword," he reminded her. "You can use that anytime."

"I know," she whispered. "Dave would never have spanked me for this."

He flinched. "I'm not Dave, sweetheart. I wish I could bring him back for you. But I can't. I also can't replace him. I'm sorry for pushing too far too fast. I'll—" He turned away and she realized he'd misunderstood her.

"No, wait, you don't understand." She reached for his arm.

He turned back. "I can only be me, Caley."

"And I want you. I do."

"There's nothing easygoing about me. I'm gruff. I don't have much of a filter. You break the rules, and I won't just give you a slap on the wrist. You'll be over my knee, with my handprint on your ass. I can be soft and indulgent, but I can also be strict and hard. And I'm too set in my ways to change."

"I don't want you to change, Issy, that's not what I meant. I just...I barely know you and yet I care for you so much. When Dave and I first met, I needed that softness. I needed gentle. I still do. But I think part of me always wished for some more firmness. And that makes me feel guilty, for thinking that way."

"Oh, baby. You shouldn't feel guilty."

"I know."

"Every relationship is different. Doesn't make one better than the other. Or somebody better than someone else."

HE HATED that she felt so conflicted over this.

But he understood and he wouldn't push. If she needed him to back off, take things slower, he would. Last thing he wanted was for her to feel railroaded. And he knew he tended to do that. He was the one that always went full speed ahead while Archer took a slower, more thought-out approach.

"It's up to you. Tell me you need more time and we'll settle this with a hundred lines and ten minutes in the corner. Or pull your pants and panties down and turn around."

He wasn't sure what way she was going to go. He kept himself back, forcing himself to be patient. It didn't come easy to him. But for her, he'd try.

He fully expected her to ask him for more time. So he kind of froze in shock as she started pushing down her pants. She sat on the bed and drew off her fluffy socks and pants. Then she stood again. She looked up at him. He made certain to keep his face neutral. He didn't want her to do this because he wanted it. But because she needed it.

"You're sure?" he asked as he reached for her pink, cotton underwear.

So cute.

He was certain Archer would insist on buying her silky, sexy underwear and he could see her in those too.

Fuck. Where had that thought come from? What was wrong with him?

"No," she said. "But I want to try. I want to do this."

"For you? Don't do it for me."

She looked at him steadily. "For both of us."

He gave her a nod and she slipped her panties down. She was completely bare. Open to his gaze.

Giving him a look of trepidation, she turned around, revealing her gorgeous ass. It was rounded and plump. White. It was going to show up every smack of his hand perfectly.

He heard her take a breath then she bent over.

His cock pressed against his jeans uncomfortably and he had to reach down and adjust himself.

"Good girl," he told her in a low, rough voice. He actually had to clear his throat. Jesus, she had him so tangled up. "Spread your legs."

She pushed her thighs apart.

"Lean down further, rest your forearms on the bed, bottom nice and high in the air."

That put not just her ass on display but the pretty folds of her pussy as well. Perfect. He wanted to test whether his guess was right, and she was going to find some pleasure in her punishment. Not that she'd be allowed to come. While he wasn't that upset with her, he thought this was a good opportunity to test whether she was ready for this part of him. The disciplinarian. This was a small introduction. Better to do this now than wait until a bigger transgression when he might have to be harsher with her.

He moved up behind her, grabbing her cheeks with both hands and rubbing them. He felt her jump then settle as she realized he wasn't starting in on her punishment immediately.

"You are so fucking sexy, girl. This ass. Those legs. That plump, pink, pretty little pussy. I'm going to need a cold shower after seeing all of this."

"I could help you with that problem."

As nice as that offer was, he wasn't taking them there yet.

Slow and steady would win him the subbie. And the Little. Who he couldn't wait to meet again.

This was all about building her trust in him. About her figuring him out. About her knowing that he would never allow her to be harmed again. Never let anyone treat her like less than the fucking princess she was.

He moved so he was standing side on. He rubbed one ass cheek briefly before giving her a sharp slap.

"Just so you know that last smack wasn't anything to do with your punishment."

Slap! Slap!

Her ass was already turning a nice shade of pink. Delicious.

Smack! Smack!

She groaned.

"You were very naughty throwing water at us."

Slap! Slap!

By now both of her ass cheeks were red. Her breathing had

quickened. He paused for a moment, giving her a chance to breathe and for him to assess her.

He gave her lower back a small rub. "You're doing well, girl. Proud of you."

Smack! Smack!

He moved his hand lower, focusing on where her cheeks and thighs met.

"Ow! Ouch! Shit!"

"No swearing," he commanded. "That's two more."

"Nooo!" she cried out. He took her in, noting the tense way she held herself but also the glistening dew on her lower lips.

Yep. Turned on.

"I'm going to give you the rest all at once." He smacked his hand over and over on her ass until it was red, and he knew it had to be burning. Soft sobs filled the room and he stopped. He quickly sat on the bed and drew her onto his lap, holding her tight and rocking her.

"You're okay. You're all right, little one. You did so well. Good girl. My good girl."

Daddy's good girl. The words burned in him.

He wanted that so badly. But for now, it was enough for her to submit to him. To his rules. To his discipline.

But he wanted to show her his softer side too. That he could be a good Daddy to her Little. That he wasn't always stern and brisk.

She sobbed into his chest, her breath sending electric flashes of arousal washing through him. He kissed the top of her head.

"I'm sorry I threw the water at you and Archer."

He kissed her forehead then her two cheeks before pressing his lips against hers. He slid his tongue along her lips, pressing it between them. Wrapping his hand in her hair, he drew her head back to ravish her mouth.

When he pulled away, he stared down into her glazed, hazel

eyes, at her plump, swollen lips with a sense of utter satisfaction. And an almost overwhelming need to take more.

"All is forgiven." He continued to hold her, reveling in the feeling of her heat and softness in his arms. "I didn't go too hard on you?"

"No. I felt bad when that glass slipped from my hand. If it had hit you or Archer," she shuddered. "I'd never have forgiven myself. While I didn't want a spanking, I guess in the end, it made me feel better."

"Good girl for telling me that. I know it's not easy to admit to what you need. Now, what I need is to go have a cold shower. Want to join me?"

He grinned down at her as she laughed. "Ahh, I'll pass. Although it could be good on my hot ass."

"Can't have that. Don't want my good work going to waste." He winked to let her know he was joking. He stood her up and helped her put her pants and panties back on. Much to her chagrin and his delight. He'd crouched down to help her get them over her feet, which had put his face at the perfect height to get a good look at that pussy.

Her scent tempted him, teased him until he felt his mouth actually water with the need to taste her.

He wondered what she tasted like. Sweet? Tart? Creamy?

Cold shower here he came.

14

Caley walked tentatively out into the living room. Her cheeks were bright red. She hadn't given much thought to how much noise she was making when Doc spanked her. But now she wondered just how much of that Archer had heard.

He was sitting at the table and glanced up from his phone as she walked in.

He looked her up and down and she tensed.

"You're still in one piece then, wasn't sure from all that screaming," he teased.

Her face burned even brighter. "Oh God. Couldn't you do the polite thing and not mention it?"

A grin filled his face, although she noted that it didn't really reach his eyes. It made her want to cuddle him until his smile was more genuine...

She wasn't usually like this. There was just something special about Doc and Archer. Soon, though, they'd both be gone soon, and she'd be on her own.

I don't want to be on my own anymore.

She sat and closed her eyes at the thought. She should take all the memories she could with Doc. Why was she even holding back?

"Hey, I didn't mean to upset you," Archer told her quietly.

She opened her eyes and noticed him giving her a worried look. "I won't say anything again, love. I'm sorry, I didn't mean to tease you."

"No. No, it's okay." She grinned. "I guess I was making enough noise to wake the dead."

He snorted and stood. "I made coffee. Want some?"

She'd noticed Archer was rarely without a coffee in hand or was in the process of making one. Seemed he might have a bit of an addiction.

"Yes. Thanks."

What would she do when they left? No Archer making coffee and watching her with gentle eyes. No Doc to challenge her and make her laugh.

He handed her favorite mug over. Her fingers brushed against his and a small shiver ran through her. Shit. What was that? She dropped her head to hide her reaction and took a sip of coffee. Made perfectly.

As usual.

Where Doc liked to bluster through, Archer was more careful. Watchful. Anyone who belonged to him, wouldn't get away with much. They'd be closely guarded. But she knew they'd also be ridiculously happy. Because once Archer set his mind to something, she was pretty sure not much would dissuade him.

He was a man who got what he wanted.

"I'm sorry about before, Archer." She forced herself to look up at him.

"We shouldn't have been arguing in front of you. We'll try not to do that again."

It was almost exactly what Doc had said to her. She wondered if either of them knew how similar they thought.

Archer frowned. "He did give you aftercare, didn't he?"

Okay, her face had to be beet red by this stage. "Yes."

"Good. Thought I was gonna have to kick his ass for you." He grinned at her. Then he walked over to the sofa and grabbed a cushion.

Walking back, he nodded to her. "Stand up, love."

He placed the cushion on her seat and she gently sat back down.

"Got sick of watching you shift around like you had ants in your pants."

"Umm...oh...thank you." She buried her face in her cup of coffee. "I didn't mean to throw the glass, but if it had hit you..."

"It's all right, love. All is forgiven now. Where is he now?"

"Um...having a cold shower."

Archer grinned again. This time it actually did reach his eyes. "Poor bastard."

"Hey!" she protested, but she couldn't help but grin as well. It was nice to feel attractive. To know that Issy was so affected by her that he had to cool himself down.

Yeah, it had been a while since she'd felt like that.

"Are you missing a lot of work?" she asked worriedly, nodding at his phone. "You could use my laptop if you needed to."

"You mean it's not attached to you?" he teased. "I wouldn't have to use a crowbar to pry it from your hands?"

She snorted. "Hell, I didn't mean the one I'm using now. I've got about four. Or maybe five."

His eyes widened. "What do you need with those many laptops?"

"Ahh, well, I have a problem with throwing them out. When I upgrade, I usually just store the old one. Some of them still work okay. I hate change, but I know I have to replace my laptops when they start acting up or running too slow. So I compromise and keep all the old ones."

"Well, thank you for the kind offer, love. But I'm all right at the moment. I have been known to do Skype sessions; however I wouldn't trust the internet not to cut out on me."

She nodded. "Yeah. Reception isn't always that reliable and especially in this sort of weather."

"Hopefully, I'll be headed back to Dallas soon. I've had Susan, my personal assistant, move all of my appointments until later in the week."

A pang filled her at the thought of him leaving.

"Hey, you okay?" He reached out and tilted up her chin.

She gave him a small smile. "Yeah. Guess I'll just miss you."

"I'll miss you too."

She cleared her throat to disperse the pleasure those words brought.

"If you need me, I'm only a phone call away," he told her. "No matter what you need to talk about. Dave. Your parents. How annoying Issy is being."

She giggled at that.

"Any more of that coffee?" a deep voice asked from behind her.

She turned to find Doc standing there, staring down at them. He was wearing a new shirt and the same jeans. His feet were bare. She didn't know how he stayed so warm when he hardly wore anything.

Not that she was complaining.

He folded his arms across his chest as Archer made him coffee. "A cushion?"

Oops.

"I got it for her," Archer told him.

Doc raised an eyebrow. "Part of a punishment is having to sit on a hot, sore ass."

"She apologized. And there was no harm done."

Doc sighed. "You're lucky he's such a softie, girl."

Yeah. She was.

"I've got some work to do. Can I trust the two of you not to be at each other's throats for a while?" She gave them both a pointed look as she stood.

ARCHER WATCHED his brother pull Caley down onto his lap. His face was stern but there was a twinkle in his eyes that he hadn't seen in years. He whispered something in her ear, making her go red and glance over at Archer.

Then he lifted her off his lap and turned her towards the office, giving her a slap on the ass. "I'll come get you when it's five."

"Five?"

Doc gave her a pointed look. "You're finishing at five."

"I have deadlines."

"You've also got dark smudges under your eyes and you look a bit pale for my liking. What do you think, Archer?"

Oh no.

He should tell his brother to keep him out of this. It wasn't his business. But he did care about Caley. More than he should. Definitely more than he wanted to.

He was attracted to her. When he'd heard her crying out earlier, he'd had to fight the urge to join them. To insist on having his share of her ass. To give her a cuddle afterwards and hold her while she recovered.

Aftercare was pretty much his favorite fucking thing in the world.

It killed him that he wasn't included.

But there was no way he was going to get between his brother and his sub. Never again. Even though he'd never wanted Evelyn, never encouraged her, if he wanted any hope of a relationship with his brother then he had to keep away from Caley.

However, he couldn't hold back his opinion.

"You do look tired, love. An earlier night wouldn't hurt. How much would you really get done if you're tired?"

For a moment she looked like she might fight him. But then her shoulders slumped, and she nodded.

Archer cleared his throat then gave Caley a small smile. "I'll have your drink ready for when you finish."

"Oh, right. Yeah. I guess I can get enough work done by then."

"That would be wonderful. Tell me, Caley, do you play poker?"

"Um, no, I've never tried."

"Well, we could try to teach you, couldn't we, Issy?"

"Strip poker?" Heat entered Issy's face as he stared over at Caley who blushed.

Strip poker? Was his brother trying to torture him?

"Or maybe we could play for small change," he suggested.

Isaac turned her with a soft push on her back. "Work, baby."

When she shut the door to the office, Isaac turned to him. "We shouldn't have been fighting in front of her."

"Agreed."

"It upset her. She's not good with any sort of confrontation."

"I know. She has a deep need to take care of people. To make sure that they're happy. You'll have to watch that she doesn't give too much. Like she does with her work."

Isaac opened his mouth then closed it again, looking thoughtful. "You're good with her."

"What do you mean?" He took a sip of his coffee.

"You got her to agree to finishing work early. She was going to argue with me."

"Well, sometimes you tend to command rather than cajole."

"You're a Dom too."

"Ahh, but according to you I'm far too easy and indulgent. And I'm only dominant in the bedroom."

Isaac snorted. "Yeah, I'm starting to wonder about that. About whether you're just sneakier. Your dominance is there, it's just quieter."

"That's amazingly insightful, little brother." And not necessarily a welcome insight.

Isaac ran his hand over his face tiredly. "We need to talk about shit rather than continuing to argue."

Well, okay. That was an unexpected breakthrough.

"Agreed."

Isaac let out a breath. "Did you know that our parents were disappointed that I wasn't a girl?"

Archer frowned. "What?"

"I overheard them talking about it one night. They were discussing whether to try again, but the doctors said that Mother shouldn't have another baby. That it wasn't safe. Then they discussed whether to adopt but Father said that he would rather have a boy of his blood than a girl who did not share his DNA. Like we were fucking interchangeable."

Jesus Christ. What the fuck?

"When was this?"

"I was eight."

"I'm so sorry. That was a fucking shitty thing for you to overhear as a kid." Or as an adult.

"Yeah. They never wanted me. It was probably a relief to them, to find some reason to push me out of the family. I'm not ever going to have a relationship with them again."

"I get it. They can't treat you like that. It was just wrong. And hell, if you're perverted, so am I."

"Now, Archie, we both know I'm more perverted than you."

"It's not a fucking competition."

His brother just grinned. Idiot.

"We are not holding a 'who's more perverted' competition."

"Aww, because you know I'll win," Isaac joked.

Archer was glad he found something funny. Because he was feeling decidedly unamused. "Right, so Mom and Dad are assholes. That's agreed. But about Evelyn…"

Isaac sighed. "She was a mistake. I was blinded by her. I thought she was everything I'd ever wanted, and she played me." Isaac looked away then back at him. "I felt like a fool."

"Issy." He leaned forward, his heart hurting for his brother.

Isaac waved him off. "Don't. Really. I don't want your sympathy. I don't deserve it. I acted like a kid who'd had their favorite toy taken from them. I know it was all her. I always did. Just didn't want to admit that I'd been played like a fool. I treated you badly, man and I'm sorry for it."

"I didn't know she was interested in me. She wasn't even my type."

Isaac sent him a look of disbelief. "Not your type?"

"I'm not a Daddy Dom."

"Yeah, well, I don't think Evelyn was even a Little."

"What do you mean?" Archer frowned.

"Think she was playing at it to reel me in. She used me to get to you."

"Seems like a pretty elaborate plan just to get to me. Pretending to be a Little. Getting involved with you. Why didn't she just come straight to me?"

"I don't know. Maybe she just saw her opportunity and ran with it. Perhaps she was just using me then met you and realized I was her stepping stone."

"I don't know how she ever thought that I would choose her over you."

Isaac looked at him. "What do you mean?"

Archer frowned. "I mean, I don't know why she thought I would open my arms to her when she'd fucked you over. Like I would want anything to do with someone that hurt you. Didn't you know that?"

He could tell from the look on his brother's face that he hadn't known that.

"Issy, you didn't know that? You don't know that I'd take your side over anyone else's? You're my brother. I'm always here for you. I never wanted Evelyn. I didn't do anything to encourage her. I let her into the apartment because she said you were coming to get her soon. When I found her naked in my bed...I felt ill. I tried to get her up and out. I fucking told her I wanted nothing to do with her. That's what you walked in on, me trying to get rid of that skank."

Isaac leaned forward, resting his elbows on his legs. "I should have stayed to listen to you. Should have answered one of your calls, instead I ran away to lick my wounds."

"All the way to a ranch in the middle of nowhere Montana." Archer winked at him to let him know he was teasing.

"It's my home now."

"I know. I'm glad you found your place."

Isaac nodded then stood. "Good. So can we damn well stop talking this shit out? You know I don't do good with feelings and emotions and shit. Rather hit something than sit down and discuss it."

Archer just rolled his eyes.

"You'd think Caley would at least have some beer around here. Something to make me feel more manly."

"We could go try to wrestle a bear or chop down a tree or something if it would make you feel better."

"Maybe another day." He eyed the door to the office as though thinking about going to find his woman.

"Don't even think about it. She's working." Archer stood and stretched. He knew what his brother's problem was. He wasn't used to not having much to do. Archer felt the same.

"You could let me punch on you a while. That would get rid of this excess energy." Isaac shook out his hands.

"Think Caley might object to us fighting in her house."

"Then we'll go outside."

Archer raised an eyebrow. "Wrestling in the mud? Sounds more like that would be Caley's fantasy than yours."

He nearly winced as he said that. He hadn't meant that he was part of Caley's fantasy but Isaac just grinned.

"We'd be doing her a favor. Give her some inspiration for her books. With the added bonus of getting her all worked up." Isaac wriggled his eyebrows.

Archer grinned. Although he didn't object to giving Caley inspiration. "She let you read anything yet?"

"No. I keep asking but she says no. I'll wear her down."

Archer knew Isaac wouldn't stop until she gave him what he wanted.

15

Caley groaned as she laid down her hand. "I'm crap at this."

Archer grinned. He was much freer with his smiles than Doc was. "You're getting better, love. We've been playing for a while."

"And you have a crap poker face," Doc told her bluntly.

"Issy," Archer scolded.

"What? She does! Lucky we're not playing strip poker. Well, lucky for her. Not for us." Doc wiggled his eyebrows up and down.

Archer gave his brother a look but didn't say anything. Things seemed a lot better between them tonight.

Doc had gotten her at five on the dot. It had taken her a bit to finish off her scene, which he'd grumbled in the background about, but Archer had managed to keep him off her back. He'd pestered her for a while about reading what she'd written. But she didn't want him reading it. Not yet. She'd written ten thousand words today. And in eight hours, rather than her usual eleven or twelve.

Maybe there was something to getting more rest and having

regular breaks. She wasn't ready to admit that to Doc though, his head was already big enough.

Doc had corralled her into doing some stretches while Archer mixed them up some drinks. Which Doc had continued to rib him about. But there had been a lighter note to his teasing. That darker note, the tension between them had eased. Maybe that fight earlier had been the breakthrough they'd needed.

She wished it could have happened without her getting her butt spanked. Sitting on it all afternoon hadn't been possible. She'd ended up stacking her laptop up on a whole bunch of books and standing.

Which had been surprisingly comfortable, and she might try doing that each day for a while.

After the stretches, which she'd moaned about but had felt quite good on her poor body, she'd sipped the cocktail that Archer mixed. Then they'd eaten meatballs, which she'd only spilled on her clothes three times. Archer and Doc managed to eat them without spilling a drop.

She'd told them it was unnatural.

Then came the poker. Thankfully not strip poker.

She lay back on the sofa with a groan. "I suck."

"You don't suck," Archer told her. "You're new at this."

"I just don't have the brain for it. My brain is wired for words. Not card games. I even suck at Go Fish."

"Hey." Doc reached over and tugged her up into a seated position. He grasped hold of her chin. "I know you're joking around, but you need to stop speaking about yourself like that, understand?"

"Like what?"

"Saying that you suck." His face was serious as he stared down at her. Why would he object to that?

"Why? It's the truth. I do suck at cards."

"It is not the truth and say it one more time and see where you end up." Doc gave her a stern look before rising and walking into her bedroom. Where was he going?

She looked over at Archer. "I don't really get it."

"Part of being a good Dom, hell, part of being a man, is taking care of those we take responsibility for," Archer explained. "When you gifted him your submission, it became a promise between you and him. And not just one of pleasure and pain. But one of well-being. You give him your submission, Issy gives you his protection and care. That includes mental and physical. Putting yourself down, means you're speaking badly of someone Isaac holds dear. You."

She could feel herself going bright red. "But we...this is...we don't know where this is going."

"But you have agreed to be his sub while we're here?"

"Yes," she whispered. She didn't know why she was so embarrassed by this conversation. It wasn't like Archer hadn't heard her being spanked earlier.

"Then he's going to treat you as such. Something precious. I'm not criticizing, and you don't have to answer, but did Dave have any training as a Dom?"

"Ahh, he'd done some playing before. But he'd never had any formal training."

"You ever go to any clubs?"

She shook her head. "After everything that happened back home, I could never have gone anywhere public. We left Spencerville, found this place and bought it. After everything, it was such a relief not to be so scared. Not to be judged constantly. Sure, it's lonely sometimes. But I always have my stories."

Issy came back and crouched down in front of her. He placed his hands on her thighs. "Ever thought about moving from here?"

She shook her head. "No. Move? I can't move. Where would I go? I can't leave here. This is where Dave..."

She swallowed, cutting herself off. Talking so much about Dave to Issy probably wasn't the thing to do, right?

"It's okay, you can talk about him."

"Seems like you haven't had anyone else to talk to," Archer added. "It's good to get it out. You don't want to bottle everything up. Believe me, we know how badly that works."

"Me. He means me. I bottle shit up, stew on it and let it eat away at me," Doc told her dryly.

"The two of you seem better," she ventured tentatively.

"Yeah, we had a talk," Archer told her.

Doc stood, reaching out a hand. "Come on, your bath is ready."

"My bath?" He'd run her a bath? She reached up and he took hold of her wrist rather than her sore hand, just another sign of how careful he was with her. It was something she could too easily get used to.

Which wasn't a good idea considering these guys would be leaving soon.

"Yep. Will help with your sore muscles. Then I'll give you a rubdown before bed."

"You sure I can't wash your back?" Isaac asked.

"No. Thank you for running me a bath. But I got this."

He noted the way she couldn't quite look at him, instead, she kept her gaze on the floor, her cheeks red.

He reached out, tilted her face up and kissed her gently. "You have nothing to be embarrassed or ashamed about. I'll let you take this bath on your own. Just this once."

She sighed. "Anyone ever tell you that you're a pushy bastard?"

"Language," he scolded. But his eyes twinkled. "And yes, all the time. Enjoy. I'll go whip Archer's ass at another game of poker. When you're finished, stick your head out the bedroom door and holler. Then get on the bed, face down, naked. I'll give you a backrub."

"Okay," she whispered.

"Okay, Doc or okay, Issy," he said in a deep voice.

"Issy?" she teased. "I thought you didn't like that nickname."

"It's growing on me."

She glanced up, met his gaze and her eyes skittered away. How the hell had Dave been so lucky to find a natural sub like her? And then to discover her Little side.

Yeah, he was a lucky bastard.

And now, so was he. He gave her a last kiss then strode out of the bathroom, through the bedroom and back into the living area where Archer was pouring himself another of those godawful cocktails he'd made.

"Pour me another," he said.

"Thought you said they taste like cough syrup."

"They do. But I need a drink." And Caley didn't have any beer.

"She kick you out while she took a bath?" Archer guessed.

"Yes." He frowned as he sat. He could have demanded that she let him stay, let him help her. But that would go against the purpose of having her take a bath in the first place. To relax and unwind.

"Surprised you didn't just tell her you were staying."

"Thought about it. But she's kind of shy about her body." That wasn't the only thing she was shy about. "She's reluctant to show me her Little."

Archer sat across from him. "It's only been a few days, man. You have to realize you're already moving fast. Give her time."

He tapped his fingers against the arm of his chair. He didn't want to waste time. If there was one thing he was not, it was patient.

"She's happy to have me touch her."

"Which just tells you how much she does trust you. And how vulnerable she feels letting her Little out."

"Have you ever just known that something was right? That someone was meant for you?"

"No," Archer replied quietly. "Because I'm thinking if I had, then I wouldn't let that person go." A strange look crossed his face. "You feel that about her, though?"

"Yeah. Guess I'm wondering if she feels the same."

"Because she's holding back."

He gave a nod. He wasn't used to talking about his emotions and shit. But if there was one person he could talk to, it was Archer.

"I've missed this." He practically spat the words out. They made him kind of uncomfortable. Like he was admitting a weakness. And he guessed in a way it was.

"Me too," Archer replied.

"Didn't miss Evelyn, you know. Maybe for the first week I told myself I did. Told myself it was all about her, the reason I was so upset. But the truth is, I never really missed her. She wasn't as important to me as I'd thought. It wasn't her I was upset about losing."

Archer leaned forward. "I was always there, Issy. You only had to call me."

"Couldn't. Stubborn. Too much damn pride."

"Yeah, well, I guess we're both at fault for not speaking up about things in the past. And things are good now. I'm here for you now."

"Yeah. Ditto." Verbose, he was not. "So how do you reckon I get her to trust me more?"

Archer looked thoughtful. "With what she's told you about her past, I'm frankly shocked she trusts you as much as she does."

He frowned, not liking that. "Those narrow-minded assholes."

She should have been treated like the treasure she was. Not ridiculed and hurt.

"A lot of people don't understand the lifestyle. They think that just because it's different and it doesn't fall into their conception of normal, that it must be wrong."

"Ass fuckers."

"Well, some people don't understand that either."

"So you really think it's just time she needs?"

"Wouldn't hurt you to let her see your vulnerable side."

He groaned.

"Don't go making that noise," Archer told him. "You've made breakthroughs in talking to me."

"Breakthroughs, gag."

"Must you always act like a child when I try to speak to you about your feelings?"

"Hmm, let me think about that...yep. Pretty much."

"And how are you going to help her with her issues around trust and being vulnerable if you don't get hold of your own?"

"Aww Christ." He had a point. And he knew it. Bastard. "Fine."

"You both have a lot in common. You were both hurt and rejected by people who were supposed to love you unconditionally."

Yeah, except for him it had been just two people. And he was a big guy.

She'd only had Dave. And Isaac wasn't convinced he'd been good enough for her. Driving under the influence with her in the car? He'd kick the other guy's ass just for that.

"You think talking about that with her will really help?"

"I do. And I think it will also help you."

"You always did like talking. Even as a kid, you wouldn't shut up."

"Not all of us prefer to pretend that we are emotionally shutoff."

He wasn't pretending.

Well, mostly.

"It will help her understand that you've experienced what she has. And it will help her see that you're willing to open up to her. Trust her with your issues. So she can trust you with hers."

"Right. That's all."

"That's all."

"You make it sound fucking easy."

"I know it's not, Issy. I do. But I know that Caley is special. It's only been a few days, but I can see that. She lost part of herself when Dave died. She's smothered her needs, her desires since then. Work has become her everything. She needs to know that it's okay to be that vulnerable with someone else. To allow herself to open up to someone else."

"What if she decides she can't? She defends him, even when he's in the wrong."

"We didn't know him. We can't determine what sort of man he was. Caley loved him, though. And he's not here to defend himself. My advice, don't say anything to disparage him. It will only hurt her. And there's no point to it."

He took a deep breath, let it out slowly knowing that his brother was completely right.

The door to the bedroom opened. "Umm, Issy? I'm done."

Archer grinned as the door shut. "See that nickname is taking off."

Doc shot his brother a look. "You're an asshole." He reached out to squeeze his brother's shoulder. "But thank you. Your advice is actually okay."

"Don't strain yourself with the praise there, brother."

Doc flung the middle finger behind his back as he walked towards the bedroom door. But he was grinning as he did it.

16

"Rise and shine, it's exercise time."

She cracked open an eye. Stared up at Issy. Why was he smiling? That didn't bode well for her.

More and more she was thinking of him as Issy. Doc was strict and grouchy. A disciplinarian. Issy was sweeter. She liked both sides of him. She promptly shut her eyes again.

"Caley, time to wake up."

"Don't wanna. Is it the weekend?" Not that she didn't get up and work in the weekends anyway. So it didn't matter if it was or wasn't. But she'd had such a good sleep and she wanted more.

"No, it's Monday, baby doll. Far as I can see you never take a day off. We're gonna fix that."

They were? Hmm, she wasn't so sure about that. She had a routine. Her routine did not involve being woken up by a sexy, drop-dead gorgeous guy.

Huh. Maybe that was where she was going wrong. Because it seemed her day should start with that.

"Caley, wake up. Or I'm going to find an incentive for getting you up."

"Incentive? I might like an incentive." Her clit tingled as all sorts of thoughts flooded her mind.

"Girl, tell you right now I fucking love the look on your face. However, we don't have time for that and exercise."

"Isn't that considered exercise?"

"Come on, get up." He rolled her onto her front and landed several hard smacks on her ass. She didn't feel much through the bed covers, but still, the intent was there.

She got onto her hands and knees and nearly screamed as she saw the time. Shit! How was it so late? How had she slept in so long?

"Oh God, you should have woken me up an hour ago. I don't have time to exercise." Or shower. Or have breakfast.

"Exercise. Then you can shower while I make breakfast. Then work."

"I can't."

"Did you get enough work done yesterday?"

"Well, yes, more than enough," she replied honestly.

"And that was working less hours than usual?"

"Ah, yep."

"Is your body sore? Hands aching? Back sore?"

"Not as bad as usual."

"Exercise is good for your body and mind. Gets the blood flowing. It will help with the aches and pain. And help you concentrate. I don't want your body giving out on you in a few years because you didn't take a bit of time now to look after yourself. I know what I'm talking about. Trust me, I'm a doctor."

She sighed. "You know just because you're a doctor, it doesn't mean you know everything."

"It doesn't? You sure about that?" He grinned.

Yep, she was in trouble.

～

"Come here a minute." Issy patted the sofa. It was late afternoon and Caley had just finished work. Archer had given some bullshit excuse about chopping some kindling in order to give them space.

She sat next to him and he placed the heat pack on her lap. She put her hands down and he wrapped it around them. He really needed to get her onto doing more dictation.

Small steps.

He'd already started restricting her work hours. He knew it was a risky move. It could backfire on him. But so far, she'd reacted well. She was already looking better just from a couple of days of only eight hours behind her computer as well as better sleep.

So far, his bedtime routine for her seemed to be helping her sleep issues. But he was aware that he still had a way to go to get her health to optimum. She was still a bit pale. And there might be times she had to work longer hours. He wasn't trying to interfere with her work. It was important to her and he got it. He also thought she had to be struggling financially so it was no wonder she was so work-focused.

Once Dave died, she'd thrown herself into work to keep herself busy, from thinking about his death. But he was going to give her other things to focus on. And if she needed money, then he was going to need to work out a way to help support her financially as well.

But those thoughts were for another day. Right now, he was going to open up to her.

Fuck. This was hard.

"Everything okay?" She'd grown tense beside him, and he realized he'd gone too long without talking.

"Everything is fine, baby doll. How many words did you write?"

"Nine thousand today. I'm actually ahead of schedule."

"Guess that exercise got the blood pumping, huh?"

She narrowed her gaze. "Perhaps."

Seemed that was all she was going to allow. They'd see. What she didn't realize was that exercise routine had just become a regular thing in her life.

"When am I going to get to read one of your books?"

She blushed bright red. She did this every time. Why would she be so embarrassed about something she obviously loved?

Was it because she didn't think they were very good?

"Uhh, never."

"Never?" That didn't sit well with him. "Why can't I read them?"

"Be-because...I don't know. I don't feel comfortable with you reading them."

Okay. That cut deep.

She must have seen something in his face because she slid one hand free of the heat pack and reached for him.

"Keep your hand in there," he ordered.

She slipped her hand back into the folds of the heat pack. "Issy, you don't understand. It's not you. It's...I don't let anyone I know read them."

"What? Seriously? Even Dave?"

"No one."

"But..." He didn't get it. "How could he stand not having read them?" Doc was curious as hell. Even more so now that she was being so secretive.

"I don't know...I guess...what if he didn't like them? Or what I wrote about? Or some of the characters...they have a lot of me in them and some are nothing like me. I just write what I feel. What if you read them and think that what I'm writing is about you? And it makes things awkward between us? What if you think they're crap?"

"First of all, I won't think they're crap. I can guarantee that."

"You don't know that."

"Do people buy your books?"

"Yes."

"Do they like them?"

She nodded. "Oh yes, I get a lot of messages from people who enjoy them. Of course, there are people who don't like them either."

"All right, if I don't like them then I won't tell you."

"No, I don't want you to lie to me. I just...I don't know. It feels like letting you read them would be like standing up in front of an auditorium full of people naked."

"What if I looked up your name?"

"I write under a pseudonym."

"Huh. All right, I won't push." For now. "But just know that I'm dying to read them." He cleared his throat. Time to open up. "I'm not the best at talking about stuff that has affected me."

"I get that," she said quietly.

"You know a bit about my parents. Archer didn't know the full truth of what happened. Not until I told him the other day, after our argument. We sat down and talked it out."

"Oh, so that's why you guys had some tension between you."

"It was one reason. Most of it was my fault. I never told him what happened, and he believed my parents' version. I was in medical school, but I'd come home for the holidays. I tried not to do that, especially if Archer wasn't going to be around as a buffer. I was always the second fiddle to him. Not that he wanted it that way.

"Anyway, Archer wasn't able to get home. All flights into Chicago had been grounded due to snow. I'd just made it home. Lucky me. My parents weren't happy. You could tell they wished it was the other way around and it was Archer who had made it home, not me."

She reached out and squeezed his hand. This time, he didn't

tell her to put her hand back. He started to gently massage it. She let out a low noise of pleasure.

"You give the best massages," she muttered.

"Why thank you, baby doll. I promise my hands have multiple talents."

She stared at him for a moment before letting out a bark of laughter. "That was terrible."

"Huh, it was some of my best work."

She gave him a soft smile. "It wasn't even close to your best work. Tell me the rest."

He sighed. "So you know my mother caught me watching BDSM porn. I had just started to explore my sexuality. I was exploring what I liked. At the time, I wasn't sure what exactly that was. I just knew I liked the feeling of being in control in the bedroom. Mother had a fit. She told my father what she'd seen. They went through my room. Found some magazines. And some stuff on age play that I'd been looking up on my computer. I wasn't sure I was even into that. That I wanted to be a Daddy Dom. I was just curious. I told you how they reacted. They thought I was depraved. That I needed to be reformed and when I wouldn't agree, they kicked me out. It was Christmas time. I had no way of getting back to college. My granddad died the year before; besides Archer, he was the one I was closest to."

"Those assholes."

"I was walking down the road when a neighbor stopped and asked me what was wrong. I just point blank told him. He took me into his house. I spent two nights there before flights resumed and I could get back to college. I was there a week before college admin called me in and told me that my parents were refusing to pay my tuition. I had three months left then had to make my own way."

"Oh, Issy, that's terrible. I'm so sorry."

"I know it doesn't measure up to what happened to you—"

"What are you talking about? They kicked you out at Christmas. Cut you off. There is nothing that isn't bad about that. And you never told Archer?"

"Well...I just figured Archer would take their side. They were always close to him. So, I ignored his calls until he came to talk to me in person. By that time, he was angry. Our parents told him that I'd stormed out after arguing over something and had refused to come back."

"So they straight-out lied to him."

"Yep."

"And he believed them?"

"In fairness to him, I did have a habit of going off like a hothead when I was younger. And I didn't tell him what actually happened."

"Oh, Issy."

"I know. I was young and hurt."

"You've never spoken to them again?"

"No. Archer has tried to act as mediator. But I've no interest in making up with people who could treat me like that."

She swung her arms around his neck, and he pulled her onto his lap. "I'm so sorry that happened to you, Issy."

"I'm more sorry it happened to you. People can be small-minded. Although, in my parents' case, I think they were always looking for some reason to reject me."

"And they don't know that Archer is a Dom?"

"No, but even if they did, they'd probably ignore it. No way they'd cut themselves off from the golden child."

"Are you angry with him about that?"

"With Archer? For being the favorite?"

She nodded.

"I was. Then. I'm not now. I know he didn't ask for it. Doesn't even want it. I know in the end that I got the better deal because I no longer have to be around them and their poison. No, I'm not angry with him anymore.

"I can see how that created a rift between the two of you."

"It wasn't just that. There was also Evelyn."

"Evelyn?" she asked cautiously.

He sighed and rubbed a hand over his face. "After the Navy, I took a job as an ER doctor in Dallas where Archer lives. Figured I'd try to mend fences. Things were okay between us. Probably would have been better if I'd told him the truth of everything. He was pissy at me for leaving him to deal with our parents, who have never been easy."

"So who was Evelyn?"

"My girlfriend."

"Oh." Her eyes were wide, and she seemed to be holding back. No doubt she had a hundred questions.

"Just let me get this out, all right? It's not easy to admit what a fool I was."

She frowned at that. "If I'm not allowed to say that I suck, then I don't think you're allowed to call yourself a fool."

"Except with me, it's the truth."

"What happened, Issy?"

He couldn't deny, he liked when she called him by that ridiculous name.

"I thought she was the one. Fell for her hard. Didn't notice that Archer was more her type than me. Archer lived in an upscale penthouse while I had a run-down two-bed I was supposed to find time to renovate. Archer had a successful practice, whereas I worked long hours as an ER doctor. Archer had all the manners. I was blunt and socially awkward."

She scowled. "I'm not going to like this woman, am I?"

"Good news is, baby doll, you're so different from her it's not funny. Makes me wonder what I saw in her in the first place. Guess I was lonely and she played me well."

"She used you to get to Archer?"

"Got it in one, girl. She used me to get to big brother. Only Archer didn't want her. I went to his place one night, dropping something off. I can't even remember what. Found her in his bed, naked. With him standing over her."

"Oh my God."

"I didn't want to hear his explanations. I just jumped to the conclusion that they'd been having an affair. I stormed out. In the space of a week, I'd quit my job, put my shack on the market and taken a job at JSI."

"JSI?"

"Jensen Security International. Kent Jensen hires mostly ex-military. I'm their resident doctor."

"Why does that sound familiar?"

"Don't know. They're a big firm. Best in the world."

She shook her head, uncertain where she would have heard about JSI before. "So what happened after that?"

"After that? Well, I've barely spoken to my brother in three years. Over the years he's tried to explain what happened. I wasn't willing to listen. Until now."

She sucked in a breath. "All this time you've been angry at him?"

"I was angry. Then I was hurt. Then I became kind of bitter. And then he convinced me to come on a weekend away with him and I said yes, because I miss him, and I got sick of him moaning at me. Turned out to be the best thing I ever did."

"How did she get in his bed?"

"She talked her way into his apartment, then while he was in the bathroom, she stripped off and climbed into his bed. When I got there, he was trying to get rid of her but I just saw my naked girlfriend in his bed."

"What a bitch."

"Total bitch."

"I feel so sad for you and Archer, all those years wasted."

"I know. My fault."

She shook her head. "I get why it was hard for you to trust. I feel the same. It's hard when you've been rejected by people meant to love you."

"Yeah, seems we both have something in common." He kissed her forehead. "I wanted you to know that I know what it feels like to be rejected because of your desires and needs. And that I'd never do that to someone else. Especially not someone I was meant to protect and care for. You're safe with me, baby doll. Your Little is safe with me, when you're ready to show her. I just thought it might be easier, if I told you my secrets for you to trust me." He sat her on the sofa. "Now, I better go get Archer before he takes off a finger."

"It's dark out. He's not really chopping kindling, is he?"

"I doubt it. I don't know if he even knows how to wield an axe properly but he's probably freezing his ass off."

17

She slipped quietly from the bed. She'd stopped using her body pillow with Doc in the bed. She didn't need it. She'd been awake for around half an hour. Since he'd been in her bed, this was the first time she'd woken and been unable to fall asleep again.

He rolled over and she froze. She knew he'd said to wake him, but she couldn't do that to him. He needed his sleep. They shouldn't both be sleep deprived.

With a yawn, she moved out of the bedroom, wishing she'd been able to find her slippers. Luckily, there was a blanket on the sofa. She picked it up and carried it into her office.

She drew it around her as she started up her laptop.

She blinked at the screen blurrily. She needed to get her brain moving. She started doing some spell-checking, which didn't really require her brain to work.

"What do you think you are doing?"

She screamed as she jumped out of her seat and turned. Doc stood in the doorway, glaring at her.

"You scared me!"

"You scared me when I woke up and found you gone."

"Sorry, I woke up and couldn't get back to sleep. I didn't mean to wake you."

"Well, you should have," he told her grouchily. "That's what I told you to do." He came forward. "Is your work saved?"

"What? Oh yes?"

He put the lid of the laptop down gently then reached for her, pulling her up into his arms.

"What are you doing? I was working!"

"No, you're not. You're going back to bed. You need sleep."

"I won't be able to go back to sleep."

He yawned as he carried her through the living room. "We need to work on that. But what you should never do is sneak out of bed without waking me."

He deposited her on the bed then moved in next to her. He tilted up her chin. "I have an idea of how to get you back to sleep, if you're willing."

"What is it?" she asked, feeling slightly breathless.

Leaning in, he kissed her. "I'm going to make you come. Hard."

She gulped. "You think that would work?"

"Only one way to find out. If you say yes."

"Yes," she murmured. God, she was so ready for this. Having him in her bed each night, waking up to him each morning, seeing him without his shirt on, wanting to strip off his boxers until he was completely naked.

Yeah, she wanted this.

He sat up and then drew her nightgown off, folding it and placing it at the end of the bed. Always tidy. Only the lamp was on, lending a soft glow to the room.

"Close your eyes."

She complied and he leaned in to kiss her. Then his mouth moved along her cheek to her ear. "All I want from you is to lie there and enjoy. Understand me?"

"Yes," she replied.

"Yes, Doc."

"Yes, Doc," she repeated.

"That's my good girl." He kissed his way down her neck, then cupped her breast, wrapping his mouth around her nipple. A small gasp escaped her.

"You don't have to be quiet," he told her. "And you don't have to ask permission to come."

Thank God for that.

He moved to her other breast, lapping at it. She ran her fingers through his hair, her hips thrusting. It had been so long since someone had touched her like this. She hadn't realized how much she needed it. Missed it.

He ran his tongue along her tummy.

"Issy!" she cried out.

"That's right, baby. Say my name." He drew off her panties then pressed her legs apart. He parted the lips of her pussy and took a long, slow lick.

Whimpers escaped her.

He circled her clit, flicking at it. She knew it wouldn't take much. She was so close already. He pressed a finger into her passage.

"Fuck, you're tight. Come, baby. Come hard for me."

He firmly lapped at her clit. She could feel it. Taste it. She was so damn close.

"Come now," he commanded.

Pleasure engulfed her like a flame. She cried out as she fell over the edge. But it wasn't a straight drop. It peaked then fell. Peaked then fell. The orgasm was extreme, it took her over completely. So it took her awhile to realize that she was now lying on Doc's chest as he lay on his back on the bed, his hand rubbing her back.

"You always come so hard?

She blushed. "Umm, is it polite to ask a woman about how hard she comes?"

He threw back his head and laughed. Oh yeah. She could definitely get used to that.

"Girl, there is nothing polite about sex. It's dirty. It's messy. It's fucking satisfying. But it should not be polite. And while I'm not always the best at communication you can damn sure bet your ass, I will ask you all sorts of probing questions when it comes to sex. Can't do my job as your Dom properly if I don't know exactly what you need, now can I?"

Well, when he put it like that...

"That was the strongest orgasm I'd ever had." She immediately felt a surge of guilt. Was that betraying Dave?

"Do you have any toys?"

"No," she whispered, blushing hotly.

"A romance writer without a vibrator. Say it isn't so."

"Mine broke and I didn't get around to replacing it."

"Now that is a damn shame. Tell me, are you the sort of writer that has to act out everything before you can describe it, or do you have a very active imagination?"

"Umm, some things I've tried."

"Yeah? What haven't you tried?"

"Ahh...well..." Christ, she could see exactly where this conversation was going. What could she give him?

"Figging."

"You've written about it?"

She nodded.

"Well, we'll need to see if we can give you a real-life experience."

Yep, she'd guessed correctly about where he'd been going with that. And she felt pretty safe, considering she knew there was no ginger in her house.

Dodged a bullet there, Caley.

"Umm, Issy?"

"Yeah, girl?"

"Can I...shall I..."

"Spit it out." It wasn't said in a mean way. Just his usual, blunt Doc way.

"Touch you?" she squeaked.

"You can touch me as often as you like. But if we're talking about my cock here, and I damn sure hope we are, then I'm going to make you wait for that."

She pouted.

"Don't pout now, girl. It's cute as hell but it's not going to be used to manipulate me."

Well, damn.

"Now, it's time for sleep," he told her. "You wake up again, then you make sure to wake me. Oh, and you're getting your butt spanked for this in the morning."

She yawned sleepily, not even concerned about her impending spanking.

Then he started to massage her scalp. Oh. That was nice. She yawned, finding herself relaxing.

He gently rolled her onto her front and rubbed her shoulders. Even better. He found all of her knots, massaging until she was a pile of goo. And then he rolled her back, tucking her into his chest.

Almost immediately, she drifted off to sleep.

"Do you think she knows it's her turn?" She heard Archer ask.

"That's her thinking face. She's probably plotting the destruction of one of her characters."

"Hmm, as long as she's not plotting against us," Archer replied.

"Entirely possible, bro. You're kind of annoying."

"Me? What about you? You're the one who made her get up

this morning and exercise. Then you set about organizing her wardrobe. Women don't like it when you touch their underwear," Archer advised.

"Oh, she likes it when I touch her underwear just fine," Issy said slyly.

That brought her right into the here and now. "Issy!" she scolded, feeling her cheeks grow red. She thought back to the spectacular orgasm he'd given her when she couldn't sleep last night. She shifted around on her seat, pressing her thighs together.

She stared at the two of them. They were in the midst of another poker game. They were both sinfully gorgeous. It was kind of unfair how beautiful they were. She felt inadequate. She ran her fingers through her hair, feeling it tangle. Did she even brush it today?

"Okay, I'd really like to know what you're thinking now?" Doc drawled, placing his cards face down on the table.

Her mind raced as a possibility just occurred to her in her story. "I just got an idea. I have to go write it down. Is there a notepad somewhere?"

"Ahh, I believe I put about three in the Caley-basket today," Archer told her as he stood and strode towards a basket near the front door. Where had that come from? And why was it there? And how long had it been there?

"You didn't notice it, did you?" Doc sighed.

"Umm, no. How long has it been there? What's it for?"

"You owe me ten dollars, brother," Archer crowed as he picked the basket up and hauled it over to where Caley and Doc still sat at the dining table.

"I thought she would have noticed it when she went outside."

"That was your mistake," Archer told him. "She rarely goes outside. And she doesn't tend to notice things unless she trips over them."

"Guys," she said with exasperation. "*She* is sitting right here."

Archer, at least, had the grace to look slightly sheepish. Doc just kept frowning. "Knew I should have put it in the middle of the room."

"And risk her tripping over it and injuring herself? Like you'd do that."

Archer was right. Doc had been almost fanatic in keeping the cabin clutter free. Or Caley-clutter free since these two were ultra-tidy. At first, she thought it was his OCD at work, until she'd tripped over a chair which had been left pulled out of the table. From the way he'd reacted, you'd have thought she'd chopped her foot off.

It had been over-the-top, but definitely sweet.

Archer set the basket down next to her. She looked down, shuffling through for a notebook and a pen. There was a whole lot of stuff in here. More notebooks. A scarf. A sweater. Even a pair of bumblebee slippers.

"I wondered where these went," she said, pulling them out and putting them on her feet. Then she looked over at Archer and Doc.

But they didn't give her a funny look. Archer just winked at her. They weren't exactly sexy or sophisticated. She bet none of the women Archer had slept with would have been caught dead in these slippers.

She ducked her head, opening her notebook to hide her thoughts. Then her mind turned to the basket again. "Why is a whole lot of my stuff in this basket?"

"It's everything you leave around the cabin during the day," Archer told her, picking his cards back up.

It was? She looked down at the basket. She'd left all that lying around just today? Yikes.

"Although I found the slippers in the spare bedroom," Isaac added. "Don't know when or how they got there."

"I'm so sorry. You guys don't have to pick up after me."

"Oh, I'm working on a plan to help you pick up after yourself." Isaac winked at her.

Uh-oh. She wasn't sure about the sound of that.

She started writing down her ideas in her notebook to hide her thoughts about his plan. She drowned out their voices as she wrote everything out. There, that was perfect. It filled in her plot hole. She sat back with a smile. She wondered if she should go write it out now.

She glanced over at her office door.

"You're finished for the day, girl," Doc told her.

"But it would be better to get this written down now."

He eyed her for a moment. "How long?"

"An hour? Maybe two?"

He glanced over at the clock. "You can work until eleven. But that means you sleep in tomorrow. No getting out of bed before ten."

Drat. She wanted to argue, but at the same time she knew how stubborn he was.

"All right. Deal."

"Come give me a kiss before you get to work."

She glanced over at Archer, feeling herself blush, which was ridiculous.

She walked around the table and leaned down to kiss his cheek. But oh no, he wasn't going to let her get away with that. He drew her onto his lap, leaning her back slightly so he could ravage her.

When he drew away, he winked down at her. "Consider that inspiration."

She groaned at his smug look. Inspiration? More like distraction now that her clit was throbbing, and her lips were swollen.

As she walked into her office, she couldn't help but wonder

what Archer kissed like. Would he be firm and demanding? Or soft and gentle?

Urgh, Caley, you have got to stop this.

"CALEY? WHAT ARE YOU DOING?"

The shock of hearing Archer's voice made her wobble on the stool. She let out a gasp as she realized she was about to fall. Two big hands wrapped around her waist, steadying her, then lifting her to the floor.

Her breath caught, her heart racing as she felt his chest pressed against her back. Goosebumps covered her skin and gulped nervously. Then suddenly, he stepped back away from her. Her legs shook slightly.

Archer cleared his throat. "Caley? What were you doing?"

She turned then leaned back against the counter behind her, trying to give them both some space. There was no denying how gorgeous he was. How potent.

"I, umm, I thought you were working," she said brightly. He'd commandeered one of her old laptops and had been working in the spare bedroom. Issy was outside, doing some work on her gutters now that the weather had calmed.

"I was. Then I came out to get some coffee and saw a naughty sub standing on a wobbly stool. Why didn't you come get me if you wanted something from a high cupboard? Is that how you always access things that are up high?"

"I don't usually store much up there."

He raised an eyebrow. He was so debonair. So put-together.

Unlike you.

"So what were you after?"

"Umm, well, see..."

"Okay, now I'm really curious." He moved closer and she stepped back hastily, almost stumbling.

He stilled, frowned. "Caley?"

"Oh. Sorry." *Calm down. You're acting like a dork.* She glanced up at the cupboard. "You really don't need to see what's up there."

"I definitely need to see what's up there."

He reached up and pulled out a box. He placed it on the table. His eyes almost bugged out of his face as he looked inside.

She found herself blushing as he drew out bags of cookies, boxes of chocolates and candy. Then more candy.

"It's my, umm, stash," she confessed. "I put it up there so it's not so easy to get to then I won't eat it all at once."

He gave her a firm look. "I should hope not. This is enough sugar to last you a year."

Well, maybe a month or two.

"And just what were you after?"

"Oh, ahh, maybe some cookies." She pointed to a bag of chocolate chip cookies. Her favorite.

He turned and grabbed a small plate. "Milk?"

She'd been planning on taking the bag back to her office. But it would be nice to share some with him. "Oh, yes. I'll grab the milk."

"You'll sit. I'll get everything."

So bossy.

So like his brother.

She sat and watched him move around her kitchen. He poured them both a glass of milk and she frowned as he placed just four cookies on the plate.

"Umm, where are yours?"

He snorted. "Love, if you think you're getting more than two cookies, you can think again."

She pouted as he sat across from her. He wiggled a finger at her. "Uh-uh, you can put that away. It doesn't work on me."

It didn't? Well, that sucked.

She grabbed a cookie, dunking it in her milk then sucking on it. She noticed him staring at her and she blushed.

Way to be unsophisticated, Caley.

But he just grinned at her and picked up his own cookie, dunking it.

"You dunk your cookie too?"

His eyes widened. "Doesn't everyone?"

She smiled and sunk her cookie into the milk again.

"Next time you need something up high, you come get me, understand?" he told her with a firm look. "If you'd fallen and hurt yourself, Issy would have had my hide."

She rolled her eyes at the exaggeration, but nodded.

"You're good for him, you know," he told her, surprising her. "He's more relaxed. Happier. I haven't seen him smile this much in years."

"Really?" she asked.

"Really. How are you feeling with him? I know it must be an adjustment for you, having us here when you were used to being alone."

She bit at her lip. "It is. Dave was...he was nervous of something bad happening again like in Spencerville and so was I. So we've never really gotten to know the people in town. And I only got closer to Murray and Geoff after his death. I thought I was good with being so isolated but now...now I realize I was lonely."

"People aren't really meant to be on their own."

"I'm nervous, though. I know that Issy wants me to show him my, uhh, my Little..."

"And you're scared of being vulnerable? Of being hurt?"

"Yes." He could read her so well. "I want to open up. To show that side of myself. But I just can't seem to take that next step."

"It's understandable that you're having trouble after losing Dave and after what you went through."

The door banged open and Issy stomped in. Archer let go of

her hand and she moved it back, missing the warmth of his touch. But she stood with a smile, wrapping herself around Issy as he came close. He held her against him and she sighed happily.

"Everything okay? What's going on? Hey, are those cookies?"

"Everything is fine. And yes, they are," Archer answered with a wry grin.

"Awesome."

18

"I just spoke to Mal." Archer walked outside through the mud to where Doc was chopping up wood. He stopped and wiped at his forehead with his arm. They'd been here at Caley's cabin for six nights now.

"Who?"

"The guy at the local garage. He said that there's a crew currently working on the downed tree and he ought to be able to get through to get my rental vehicle by tomorrow. He can give me a ride back down the mountain. The rental company already has another vehicle waiting for me. I figure I can drive to Bozeman and get a flight back to Dallas."

Fuck.

That meant Archer would be leaving. Should he be leaving too? He couldn't stay here forever.

But he also wasn't ready to leave her.

"I'm not ready to go."

"I don't blame you. If I had Caley in my bed, I wouldn't be willing to go either." There was a hint of longing in Archer's voice. Was his brother lonely? Used to be that Archer had a gorgeous woman on his arm almost every weekend. He wasn't a player, exactly. He always made it clear to the women that he had no intention of getting into a relationship with them. Still, he'd never lacked for companionship.

Maybe seeing him with Caley had shown Archer that he wanted something more meaningful. A sense of sadness filled him. Now that he'd patched things up with his brother, he was reluctant to say goodbye.

"I don't know where to move from here," he admitted. "She still hasn't shown me her Little." And he needed that part of her. It was who he was. He knew himself; he wouldn't be happy if she permanently kept that part of herself back.

And neither would she.

Archer studied him for a moment. "You spoke to her about Evelyn? About our parents?"

"Yeah, couple of days ago." Still nothing. He'd noticed her pulling into herself more than usual. Could be the book she was working on, but he had a feeling she was thinking about everything he'd told her.

"I don't think Caley is the impulsive type. Well, other than letting us stay here with her. But that was kind of out of her hands unless she was willing to leave us out in the cold."

Doc nodded. "I know. She likes to mull things over."

"But sometimes thinking too much can be detrimental," Archer added, reading his mind. Why had he gone so long being angry at his brother? "But I think you've made more headway than you realize."

"How do you mean?"

"You've been topping her almost since we got here. She now has a nighttime routine, a bedtime, rules to follow. She has to eat regularly, exercise."

"You're right," he said slowly.

"She's worried about getting hurt, but she wants to take that next step. So maybe you should give her Little a bit of a subtle nudge."

Yeah, except how did he do that?

His mind whirred, thinking. "Do you think the rental car company would bring the car up here?"

"If I pay them enough, they will. Why?"

"Just thinking I could take over the rental. Don't like to be up here with her crap truck as our only transport option. If you can get a morning flight out of Bozeman, I'll drive in, drop you off and do some shopping."

Archer frowned. "Shopping? You hate shopping...ahh...I see. You're not going subtle at all, are you?"

"Brother, you hurt me. Subtle is my middle name."

Archer just shook his head.

IT WAS hard to say goodbye.

Far harder than she'd expected. She didn't want him to go. She'd gotten used to him being here.

At least Doc was staying. But for how long? He wouldn't be patient with her forever. She just didn't know why her Little was still afraid to come out. After everything Doc had told her about himself, after giving him her submission in bed, after allowing him to boss her around when it came to her work, her eating, her sleep.

You'd think it would be a no-brainer to let her Little out.

But it just wasn't happening. And it kind of worried her. What if it never happened? What if he grew impatient with her and gave up? What if he left?

He'll have to leave at some stage, Caley. What are you going to do then? He has a life. A job. Putting your head in the sand over all of that doesn't make it go away.

He only lives a few hours away.

What? And you think he'd be happy visiting? That he'd want to do long-distance?

Groan. She really should have thought all this through before she agreed to anything. And now...now she was in so deep she couldn't end things. It would break her. He would have to do it.

Which he would likely do soon with the way she was holding back on him.

And now Archer was leaving. Her partner in teasing Issy out of his grumpy moods. She liked having someone to gang up on him with her. Although she got the feeling that in anything serious, he'd be on Issy's side.

She didn't want him to go. But that was incredibly selfish of her.

"Hey, Caley, don't look so glum," Archer sat down on the sofa beside her. He reached over and gave her hand a small squeeze. "I know being left with this guy is a daunting prospect, but if his bossiness gets out of control, you can call or FaceTime me. I'll help you corral him, okay?"

She gave him a small smile. It was early in the morning and they were headed to Bozeman. Archer to catch a flight. Issy to do some shopping. For what, she wasn't sure. Although she guessed some of it was for groceries.

Issy had wanted her to say her goodbyes last night rather than getting up so early, but there was no way that was happening. She'd just start work once they left and be able to finish early.

For the first time since Dave died, she had something else to do other than work. She used it as a crutch. A way to protect herself. A distraction. But she was now ahead of schedule, so it wasn't like she had an excuse not to take some time off.

"I could come with you guys," she offered again.

Archer shook his head. "You've nearly finished your book. And airport goodbyes suck."

The rental people had brought the car up the mountain last night. She hated to think what Archer had paid them to get them to do that.

"We best go," Issy said. He held out a travel mug to Archer. "Here's the first of your twenty daily coffees."

"I don't drink that much," Archer said, standing to take the mug. "But thanks."

"Caley, there's a fresh pot of coffee there. Enough to last you through the day. Don't drink any more than that. I've put a big bottle of water by your desk. I expect that to be all gone by the time I get back. And there's a sandwich in the fridge for your lunch. Stop and eat it. Understood? I'll text you a few times during the day, I expect a text back within thirty minutes or I'll start calling."

"Sir, yes, Sir."

Archer grinned while Issy rolled his eyes. "Such trouble." He drew her close and gave her a kiss then a sharp smack on the butt that had her yelping. "Behave yourself or your ass is toast when I get home. I'll be waiting in the car."

He walked out, surprising her by giving them some privacy. She looked at Archer for a moment. He studied her.

"Well..." he said.

She threw herself at him, wrapping her arms around his waist. She knew she should probably have held back. But she couldn't.

"I'll miss you," she whispered, squeezing him so tight he could probably scarcely breathe.

Don't go. Stay.

She didn't say the words, of course. They weren't fair. He had a life of his own. He couldn't stay here just because she wasn't ready to say goodbye.

"Miss you too, poppet," he said quietly. "Remember, our friendship is not dependent on your relationship with my brother. You can call me anytime, for anything. Understood?"

"Yes." She had to bite off the Sir. He wasn't as overtly dominant as Issy. Definitely more understated. Much like the man himself. But it was still there. And while in the beginning she'd thought him less dominant than his brother, she'd come to realize he just kept that side of himself tightly under rein.

She wondered what would happen if Archer ever lost some of that epic control. If he let himself actually fall for someone.

She had a feeling he might blow Isaac's overprotectiveness out of the water.

She leaned back to look up at him. He bent down and pressed a kiss to one cheek then the other.

"Good luck with my brother, poppet. Remember, under all that gruffness, he's a really good guy. He'll take care of you. If you let him. It's okay to rely on other people. Sure, sometimes you get hurt. Sometimes they leave. But that's life. Time to start living again, Caley."

Time to start living again, Caley.

Goddamn, Archer. Did he know what he was doing to her with those words? She still held a lot of guilt about Dave. About feeling like she was betraying him by being with Issy. That was likely another reason her Little was still locked away.

She trusted Issy. Knew he wouldn't betray or harm her. She rubbed her pounding head; she should stop and take something for her headache. Last thing she needed was to get a migraine. But she only had ten more pages to edit before she could send this off to her editor.

So she persevered, ignoring the call of her bladder and the rumbling of her tummy. If she got this done, maybe she could have a rest before he got home. She sighed, rubbed the back of her neck and dove back into her story.

19

Doc pulled up outside the cabin. It had been a long day and he was glad to get back to Caley's place. He opened the back of the rental vehicle and drew out his bags of shopping. Going shopping always put him in a foul mood and he was trying not to give in to that.

Saying goodbye to Archer at the airport had been harder than he'd thought.

Stupid, not like he couldn't go visit his brother whenever he wanted. He hadn't been back to Dallas since he'd basically run off two years ago. But things were different now. It almost felt wrong not to have his brother with him.

He shook his head at the idea.

It took a couple of trips to unload the truck. He knew that Caley would still be busy working, but he didn't want to interrupt her until he was done. He didn't want her to insist on helping him. It was far too cold for her to be traipsing in and out of the cabin.

Mind you, the inside of the cabin wasn't that much warmer since she'd let the fire go out. He shook his head. Part of him, the

Daddy side, didn't actually want her touching the fireplace. But he knew that wasn't possible

He quickly started the fire then put the groceries away before putting his other purchases in the spare bedroom.

Archer's room.

Don't be ridiculous, man. He glanced at the clock with a frown. The coffee pot was empty, and the sandwich was missing from the fridge. So at least she'd eaten today. And gotten up and moved around.

He knocked on her door. He heard her let out a cry and pushed his way through the door, looking around frantically.

"What is it? What's wrong?"

She gaped up at him, her hand on her chest. "Oh my God. You gave me a fright."

"I gave you a fright? I heard you yell out and thought something was wrong. You've taken years off my life."

"I wasn't expecting you back so early."

"Early, girl? It's nearly five."

He frowned as he took her in. Her hair had mostly fallen from the bun she'd put it in this morning. Even though she was bundled up, but she still looked cold. And pale. There was a tightness around her eyes as though she was in pain. She reached up and rubbed at the back of her neck.

Sore muscles? Or a headache as well?

He caught sight of the bottle of water next to her desk. Mostly full. Okay, that wasn't good. A plate sat on the desk with a half-eaten sandwich. So not only had she not finished her lunch, but she'd eaten it while still working.

Oh, she was in so much trouble.

"You didn't hear me pull up or empty out the truck?" he grumbled.

"Umm, no," she said hesitantly as though sensing his upset but not entirely certain about the cause.

He folded his arms over his chest. "Finished your book?"

"Oh yes. I did. Sent it away to my editor. And I started plotting out a new one. And I got some social media stuff done. I'm actually well ahead of schedule."

"That's good because I think you need a day off. Doc's orders."

She smiled. "Well, I guess I have to obey then."

"Hmm, seems to me you had some other orders to obey and you didn't."

"What do you mean?"

He pointed at the nearly-full bottle of water. She glanced down, wincing as she did. "Did I not tell you that you were to drink all of that?"

"Whoops."

"Noticed all the coffee is gone. Which means you're mostly running on caffeine right now since you barely ate any of your lunch. Which can happen when you don't stop to eat."

Another guilty look. "I'm in trouble, aren't I?"

"Oh yes. Now tell me why you keep wincing. What hurts?"

"My head. Could be from sitting so much today."

"Could also be from not enough water and food. You ever get migraines?"

"Yes. Sometimes."

He grunted, not happy with that reply. "Right, any punishment is going to have to wait until you're feeling better. Come on, let's get you some water and painkillers."

"Umm, first, I really need to go to the toilet." Her cheeks blushed as she stood, pressing her legs together.

Damn. His Daddy side rose, wanting to take her to the toilet himself. But he gave her a nod. She rushed off and he grabbed the water and found some painkillers and crackers, taking them into the bedroom. Probably the best thing right now for her was some sleep. He heard the toilet flush. Then the sound of retching hit him.

Shit!

He rushed into the bathroom, to find her bent over the toilet. He quickly knelt beside her, grabbing her hair to keep it off her face as she threw up. Soon nothing was left to come up and it was just dry heaves.

She groaned, slumping back against him.

"Caley? Talk to me." Worry filled him as he took her pulse. It was racing. She felt chilled. Ill? Or a migraine?

"Headache is worse than I thought. Sorry. Need dark. Quiet."

"Okay, hush. Stop talking. Let me take care of things for you."

He picked her up and carried her into the bedroom, laying her on the bed. "Be back in a second. Stay there."

SHE WASN'T PLANNING on going anywhere. For quite a while.

She sighed with relief as he closed the curtains.

"Need black-out ones," he muttered. Then there was silence. She wondered if he'd left, but she couldn't open her eyes to check.

God, the taste in her mouth was awful. She wondered if she could make it to the bathroom to brush her teeth.

She needed to move slowly. She sat up. Her head thumped, pounded.

"What are you doing?" a whisper-yell made her whimper.

"Bad taste. Mouth."

"I'll get you some mouthwash and a bowl to spit it out. Lie back. I'm warming up your heat pack. Drink this."

She lay back without opening her eyes. He'd half-propped her up against some pillows and he held a glass to her lips. She drank some water then the glass was removed.

"Here's some mouthwash, swirl it around. I'll place a bowl under your mouth. That's it. Now spit."

She groaned quietly as it dripped down her chin. "So gross."

"This is nowhere near the grossest thing I've seen; I promise you," he told her in a low, quiet voice, wiping her face once more. "I'm going to go get the heat pack and make you a bottle. Is there anything else you need?"

A bottle?

Maybe she should ask about that, but she couldn't find the energy to care. He was being so kind and caring. She wanted more.

She wanted it all. All of him. Was this what his Daddy side was like? She'd seen his stern side. And she had seen his caring side. But she thought this was something else.

"Bra. Off."

"Yeah. Thought that might be the case. Let me see if we can get you comfier. Sit up a bit and I'll undo it." He very carefully and gently took off her top layers. She shivered slightly, whimpering.

"I know, baby. I know. Here, let's get this torture device off and get you into your favorite nightie." As soon as her bra was off, he put her nightie over her head. She kept her eyes closed. He laid her down and slid her pants off.

"I've put Bumbly in beside you and your snuggly is next to your face." Then the covers were slid out from under her and she was tucked in tight, with the covers under her chin. When he returned a few minutes later, she was nearly asleep.

"Got your heat pack. Gonna put it under your neck."

She whimpered as he raised her. "I know, baby doll. I know. I've got you."

Oh, that heat felt so nice against her tight muscles. "Here's a bottle. Might help settle your stomach."

Something rubbery was pressed against her lips. Was it an actual bottle? With a nipple? Was it her old one?

"Open up. Open up for Da—uh, for me."

Tears filled her eyes, falling down her cheeks.

"Baby doll, don't cry. Shh. Shh, now." He gently wiped her tears from her cheeks. "I can see I'm gonna have to keep an even closer eye on you. Can't have you getting into this state again.

Here's the bottle. Good girl. It's just like a chocolate milkshake, but it's got lots of good things in it like protein and vitamins. I bought it today for you. There you go."

He fell silent and let her drink. She fell asleep with the nipple in her mouth and the knowledge that he really did want this. To be her Daddy. To take care of her.

SHE FELT LIKE GARBAGE.

Pure and utter rubbish. Her head had stopped thumping at least. And she had only thrown up the once.

Go her.

Hmm, just maybe she'd pushed herself a bit hard yesterday. And well, most of the days since Dave died. It wouldn't hurt her to take a day off now and then. Although she thought she'd been better since Issy appeared in her life and forced her to take regular breaks and eat and sleep.

You know...all those things she neglected to do when left to her own devices.

The door to the bedroom opened and the man in question entered. She couldn't believe the way he'd looked after her last night. Dave had been a bit squeamish when it came to vomit. Actually, most bodily fluids. Her vomiting would likely have set him off.

Maybe it was because Issy was a doctor.

Or maybe it was just him. Issy.

"Hey, baby doll." He walked forward. "Hoped you'd sleep a bit longer. How you feeling?"

"Like I've been run over by a truck." Her throat was scratchy, sore. Issy picked up a bottle of water from her bedside table. She tried to sit and groaned. She was not only sore, but her muscles were like jelly.

"Here." He sat next to her, then helped her half recline against his chest. He held the bottle up to her mouth. She tried to untangle her hands from the sheets, but they were trapped under the covers.

"Let me," he told her. "Just relax. You're in no state to do anything today."

She gulped a few drinks of water. Then he set the bottle aside and moved her, so she was back to lying down. He rested a hand on either side of her body.

"You didn't look after yourself yesterday."

"I know," she said guiltily.

"I trusted you to follow my orders."

"I know."

"I'm not happy that you disobeyed me and that you pushed yourself so hard that you ended up with a severe migraine."

It actually wasn't as bad as some she'd had, but she figured now wasn't the time to tell him that.

He sat up then grasped hold of her wrist, taking her pulse. "It's better. It was racing yesterday. Too much stress and caffeine. Did you have plans for today?"

The look on his face told her there was only one answer to that.

"I thought I might take the day off."

He grunted. "You'll likely be taking more than just one day off. You've pushed yourself too hard for too long, baby doll. You're reaching breaking point and I don't like it."

She didn't much like it herself.

"I know," she whispered. "I've been trying to lose myself in work since Dave died. But it's not healthy. That's not the first migraine I've had, not even the worst one. I've gone more than twenty-four hours without sleep because I was working so much then collapsed into bed for days. I never had trouble with sleeping before. And I never worked more than fifty hours a week. And some weeks a lot less. I only developed these migraines after he died."

"All right. So, that was easier than I thought. I had a whole speech prepared."

She had to grin at that.

He narrowed his gaze. "Can still give it to you, girl."

She wiped the grin off her face. "I think I've got the gist of it, Issy."

"Do you? Because from now on, there will be no more working yourself into a state. You knew what I expected from you while I was gone, and you didn't follow the rules. When you're feeling better, you're going to be punished for that."

She bit her lip. Drat.

"The answer to that is 'yes, Issy'."

"Yes, Issy."

"Bought a few gifts for you while I was in town."

"Do I no longer gets them 'cause I was naughty?"

His eyes widened and she realized how childish her voice had sounded. She waited for the worry, the panic. None came.

He blinked then his shoulders relaxed. "No, baby, you still get your presents. But some of them you might not like."

How could she not like a present?

"One of them is a rewards and punishment chart. I'm going to set it up while you're resting today. I'll explain how it works later."

A rewards and punishment chart? Yeah, she didn't like the sound of that.

"I'm not sure I feel like eating anything yet." While her head felt a lot better, she still felt a bit queasy.

"Did you like the drink last night? It's a protein shake with added vitamins. Thought it might be good for you to start drinking it regularly."

"I did. Thank you." That was so thoughtful. "Will it be in the same bottle? Like last night? Is it my old bottle?"

It had been in the same box as her sippy cup.

He'd been walking towards the door, but he turned at that question and looked down at her. "I bought you a new one, actually. That old one hadn't been used in a while. Would you like that again?"

She took a deep breath. This was still hard, but she wanted to try. She wanted to reclaim that part of herself. "I'd like it in my bottle, please, Daddy."

He cleared his throat, and something filled his face. If she had to guess she'd say it was a mix of pleasure and relief.

"Sure thing, baby doll. Daddy will go get that ready. You stay in bed and wait for me to come back."

"Umm, Daddy?"

"Yes?"

"I gots to go," she whispered.

"Silly Daddy," he quickly said. His facial expression didn't show any hint of disgust or embarrassment. Seemed she was the only one who found talking about bodily functions embarrassing.

He walked over to the bed and pulled down the covers. "It's a bit chilly in here. I'm going to keep the door open to let the heat from the fire in." He picked her up, cradling her against his chest as he carried her into the bathroom.

"Daddy, I can walk."

"Not today, you don't. Today, you're getting the full baby girl treatment. You haven't been well and you're going to let Doctor Daddy take care of you."

"Doctor Daddy?" She giggled.

He winked as he set her feet on the floor. Brr, the tiles in here were cold. He frowned at her feet. "You need some socks on." He reached under her nightie and whipped down her panties before she even knew what he was planning to do. Then he pressed her back, so she sat on the toilet.

"Here, you go potty and I'll go grab some warm socks. Do not move until I get back here to help you. I need to give you a check-up too. Can't believe I haven't done that already."

A check-up? Oh no. She was very glad he hadn't done that already.

She quickly peed. She'd just tidied herself up when he returned. Her panties were still around her ankles. He helped her stand then drew them back up.

"Daddy! I can do that myself."

"'Course you can. But why should you when Daddy is here to take care of you?"

Jesus. How did he do that? How did he just suddenly find the perfect thing to say? He lowered the lid on the toilet and sat her back down before pulling on a pair of bright pink, fluffy socks. They had eyes and a nose round the toes. They were super warm and soft, and she fell instantly in love.

"These aren't my socks."

"They're one of the presents I bought you," he explained before he helped her stand then turned her to the counter. He ran the water and squirted some soap on his hands before he started to wash her hands. He ran his hands over hers, scrubbing every inch.

She didn't know what it was. They were just her hands. It shouldn't feel special. But it did. After drying them, he picked her back up.

"You really don't have to keep carrying me, Daddy."

"I don't want you getting dizzy and falling over. Besides, I've waited a long time to carry you."

See? Bam! He just kept hitting her with these moments of sweetness.

When he walked with her into the bedroom, she saw that he'd laid a blanket out on the bed. He laid her down on her back on it.

"Is this a new blanket?"

"Yep. I know how much you like soft things. I also know how

cold you get." He wrapped one side of the blanket over her, then the other. Her arms were trapped but she wasn't held in tight. She knew she would be able to escape if she really needed to. Then he sat, leaning against the headboard with her on his lap. He reached over and grabbed a bottle from the nightstand. She hadn't even noticed it sitting there.

She blushed a little. It was different seeing it in broad daylight than in the safety of darkness. But she'd told him this was what she wanted. She rested back against one arm and he reached up with the bottle, pressing the nipple to her mouth.

"That's it, baby doll. You drink it down. Hopefully it will help rehydrate you as well. Then you can rest in bed while I make you something to eat.

Hmm. She had a feeling she'd be getting a lot of rest today. Well, it wasn't like she was up to doing much. And if he really wanted to carry her around and take care of her...

Who was she to argue?

Doc picked up his phone as it rang.

"Hello, brother, long time no see."

"Issy, how are things going?" Archer asked. There was an odd note to his voice. Doc walked over to the bedroom door and glanced in to find Caley was fast asleep. She'd protested having to take a nap when she hadn't been up for long, but she'd been asleep almost as soon as her head hit the pillow.

After she woke up, he'd feed her some lunch then give her a check-up before he gave her the rest of her presents. He should have been taking better care of her before now. The guilt ate at him as he shut the door.

"Things are okay here. You all right?" Doc asked.

"Ahh, yeah, just came back to a full workload. You know how it is."

Actually, to be honest, his workload was fairly light. Sure, the JSI guys got themselves hurt on a regular basis and living on a ranch meant there was often an injured cowboy around, but it was nothing like his work schedule when he'd been an ER doctor while in Dallas.

Which gave him plenty of time to dedicate to Caley. Once he convinced her to move home with him, that is. But he was determined that when he returned, she'd be by his side. Thankfully, Kent had given him the go-ahead to take some time off.

"How's your girl?"

His girl. Yeah. He liked the sound of that. And if something felt like it was missing, he pushed that thought aside. What could possibly be missing?

"She's better."

"Better? Was she not well? Is she all right? Do you need my help?"

Doc frowned. "Whoa, man, calm down."

"Sorry."

"I'm a doctor, remember? If she's not well, I've got it."

"Yeah. She's just...she means a lot to me too. Not like that. She's your girl. But I got close to her while I was staying there."

They had gotten close. And when she'd talked about Archer earlier, he'd seen a hint of sadness in her face, which he hadn't liked. His girl shouldn't be sad. He wanted her to have everything she desired.

"Issy? You gonna tell me what's going on with Caley?"

"Oh, uh, sorry. Yeah. She's fine. She just pushed herself too hard. Got home last night and she'd barely eaten anything or drunk any water. Ended up getting a severe migraine. She vomited."

"Shit. Poor darling."

"She's doing a lot better today; I've just put her down for a nap."

"Yeah? She might need a check-up."

"Read my mind, brother."

"You're gonna work on getting her to take better care of herself."

"Even better, I am going to take better care of her myself," he said.

"What about when you have to leave?" Archer asked.

"Then she'll be coming with me."

There was a beat of silence. He expected Archer to start lecturing him about how he couldn't force her to go with him, which he had no intention of doing, he just wasn't going to take no for an answer.

Those were two totally different things.

In his eyes, anyway.

"Just remember that she's still emotionally fragile, Issy. You have to tread carefully when it comes to the loss of her husband. And changes in her life. Just go easy. Promise me?"

"I'll try."

"Right. Which is a bit like you trying to be subtle," Archer muttered.

Yeah. Pretty much.

"I will try to be mindful of Dave and his memory, all right?" He didn't intend to bad-mouth the guy.

"Okay, when she feels better will you get Caley to call me? Sounds silly, but I kind of miss being with you guys."

"Hey, that doesn't sound silly at all. We're great to be around. Barrels of fun."

"Caley, maybe. You on the other hand, yeah, not so much."

Too bad they weren't FaceTiming. Giving someone the bird just wasn't as satisfying when they couldn't see it.

ARCHER HUNG up the call and had to fight against the urge to throw his phone at the wall.

You self-sacrificing idiot.

He heaved in breath after breath, trying to calm himself. He had never felt so out-of-control in his life. Every part of his life was carefully thought out. From what his career would be, to where he lived, to what he wore and who he associated with.

Who he dated.

Caley was a curve ball. The total opposite of who he thought he should want. She wouldn't fit into his life smoothly. She wouldn't make things easier.

Is that really what you want? Someone who is easy? Or do you want someone you love? Someone who makes you feel alive?

His world had been gray, now it held color.

Issy loved her. He needed her. He'd be good for her.

You could be good for her too. You could stop her from sinking into her head. You could get her to talk. You could stop them both from hiding away.

He could round them out.

But she was Issy's not his.

He wanted his brother to be happy. He wanted Caley to be happy.

He just wished it wasn't his happiness he had to sacrifice.

20

She lay on the bed, feeling a bit nervous.

"How long since your last check-up, baby doll?" Issy asked her. He walked into the bedroom, carrying a black bag. She hadn't even realized he had that with him. It must have been in the spare bedroom.

"Umm, I guess, maybe since before I left home. So over five years ago?"

He froze then stared down at her with a frown. "You haven't been to the doctor since then?"

"No. I hardly ever get sick. Just the migraines. And sometimes I get a little light-headed, but I think that's a low blood sugar thing."

He grumbled something under his breath.

She was shocked that she'd fallen asleep earlier. She'd felt sure she would lie there, counting sheep. But no, she'd slipped off almost as soon as she'd laid her head down. Then when she'd woken up, Issy had actually let her sit at the dining table to eat before he'd brought her in here for her check-up.

Something she was sooo looking forward to. Not.

"Do you need the potty, baby doll?" he asked as he grabbed a stethoscope out and started breathing on the round, silver end. Obviously warming it up. That was so sweet.

"Ahh, no. I'm all right."

"Do you have a set of scales?"

"Umm, yes, not sure if they work. They're in the bathroom cupboard."

He went and retrieved the scales and then placed them on the wooden floor.

"Okay, they work all right. Let's get all your clothes off."

"I have to take my clothes off?" she asked in a high-pitched voice.

"Gonna be hard to give you a proper check-up with your clothes on, baby doll."

Yes, but, naked? Well, he'd already seen her naked so she guessed she shouldn't be shy.

"Let's get you on the scales quickly then underneath the blanket to keep you nice and warm." He helped her strip off, leaving her panties and T-shirt.

"Let you keep that until you're nice and warm under the blanket.

She climbed on the scales. Not really watching the number. It had been a while since she'd weighed herself.

"Huh," she said when she saw the number.

"Huh?

"I haven't weighed myself since before Dave died. I used to do it once a week, religiously. I've lost quite a bit of weight."

"How much is quite a bit?"

"Umm, thirty pounds."

"Yeah, thirty pounds is a lot to lose. Back on the bed, let's get you under the blanket."

He placed the blanket over her, making her whip off her T-shirt first before covering her up from chin to toes. She wasn't actually that cold, but she was grateful to be covered. It was strange being nearly naked when he was dressed, even if his gaze hadn't lingered on her boobs at all.

That had been a little disconcerting.

The first part of the examination was pretty typical. He took her pulse. Then her blood pressure, telling her it was on the low side. Then he'd felt her glands, looked in her mouth and ears.

"Right, baby doll, how often do you examine your breasts?"

"Umm..." Had she ever done that?

"Caley," he said in a scolding voice. He lowered the blanket down, exposing her breasts. Her nipples were hard peaks. "You're not too cold? We can move this into the living room if you are."

She should go with the excuse. But it was toasty warm in here. Her nipples were just traitorous little hussies who seemed to be at Issy's beck and call.

"I'm okay," she croaked out.

Was it possible for her to be any more embarrassed? Really?

He's given you several orgasms, Caley.

It seemed to be his cure for her waking up at night. He'd make her come before massaging her neck or head until she fell back asleep.

"You have beautiful breasts, baby doll," he murmured to her. She opened her eyes and looked up at him.

"They're small."

"They're perfect." There was no mistaking the sincerity in his voice. And Issy didn't lie. He wasn't even one to say something in order to spare someone's feelings. If he said it. He meant it.

She almost thought that might be what she liked most about him. There was no subterfuge.

"Let's see if we can warm them up a bit." He shocked her by leaning over and taking one nipple in his mouth while his hand cupped her other breast, the palm brushing against her tight bud.

She groaned, pressing her body up, trying to get closer to him. He suckled on her nipple for long moments then drew back and blew over it. She shivered at the feeling that travelled through her body.

He moved to her other nipple, engulfing it in his mouth.

Okay, maybe his honesty wasn't the thing she liked most about him. Maybe it was his mouth.

The man was multi-talented. He drew back, staring down at her with warm eyes. "Such a beautiful girl. My girl."

His girl.

And then there was this soft, caring side which she wasn't sure many people got to see.

There was a lot to like about this man. He might have his flaws, but he wore them loud and proud. He didn't hide them away, like a dirty secret.

Like Dave did with his drinking.

Don't think about that. Like Archer said, he wasn't here to defend himself and all it was doing was causing her pain.

"Caley? You okay?" Issy stared down at her with concern in his eyes.

"Yes. I'm all right."

He studied her for a moment but didn't question her like Archer might have. Guilt flooded her. She shouldn't be thinking of Archer right now.

God, she missed him though. It was okay to miss him, wasn't it? He was her friend.

"Reach up and put your hand behind your head. That's it."

He was surprisingly efficient as he examined her breasts and she relaxed slightly.

"Good, everything feels good. I'll make sure to do that each month."

A pang hit her as he spoke of the future. She took in a shuddering breath as he lowered the blanket further, revealing her stomach.

"All right, baby doll?"

"Yeah."

"Tell me if there's any pain or anything. We'll need to get some bloodwork done. But I don't have the equipment with me for that. I'm guessing it's been a while since you've seen a gynecologist."

"Umm, I've never seen one."

He placed his hands on either side of her, leaning down, a hint of anger in his eyes. "Never?"

"No," she replied, wondering why he was so angry.

He looked away; his jaw clenched. "All right. We'll add that to the to-do list."

"I'm not sure I want to see one." She bit her lip, worrying it.

"I can take care of that for you if you want."

Okay, so what was worse? Having him examine her or a complete stranger?

"I'll make an appointment with a gynecologist," she squeaked.

His lips twitched. "Don't trust me?"

"No...it's not that. It's just..." she glanced away, feeling silly. *He's a doctor, Caley.*

"When you want me down there, you'd rather it was for pleasure?"

She gaped at him then rolled her eyes at his smirk. "Something like that," she muttered.

"It's okay, baby doll. I'm teasing. I get it." He leaned in and kissed her lightly. "But just so you know, some medical role play can be fun. Especially since I'm a doctor and have access to all the good medical equipment."

Medical role play? Her body stirred at the thought. She hadn't written a book about that yet, but imagine if she had some real-life experience to add in. Except, would he be happy about that? It wasn't like she'd mention his name, but maybe he'd feel like he was being used.

"Okay, you're off in your head again and I want you here."

"Sorry," she croaked.

He pulled the blanket up. "I'm going to go get a few more of your presents before I take your temperature. See if I can keep you focused and your mind off work."

She felt bad that she'd kind of blanked out on him. But why didn't he just take her temperature first? It didn't take that long to stick something in her ear or mouth.

When he returned, he held one of her plates. Did he have a snack for her? Was that her gift?

Then he put the plate down on the bedside table and she leaned up on one elbow to look at what was on it. Her mouth dropped open in shock at the sight of two dildos, one was small and black with a wide end. Anal plug. The other was pink and long and had a power button at the end. There was also a tube of lube. He then pulled a glass thermometer from his first-aid kit and placed it on the plate. It looked thicker than any thermometer she'd ever seen.

"Umm, Issy…" she said with worry in her voice.

He glanced down at the plate then at her. "I washed them all, don't worry."

Not what she was worrying about. But now that he mentioned it…yay for cleanliness. Not that she'd expect anything else from him.

"That wasn't exactly what I was worried about. Are you planning on using all of those?"

Amusement filled his face. "Why yes, baby doll. I am. I'm going to get you to roll over onto your tummy then I'm going to position the vibrator against your clit and turn it on. Then I'm going to take your temperature. After I've done that, I'm going to put this tiny plug in your bottom."

Tiny?

"That doesn't look so tiny to me."

"It's tiny in comparison to my cock and that's what we're working you up to taking."

Holy crap.

She hadn't thought about all the prep work. Even though she should have. She'd written about anal sex. It was just different when faced with it...when faced with what exactly was going in your butt.

"Can't you take my temperature with one of those thermometers that goes in your ear?"

"I could," he said cheerily. "But I'm not going to."

She gaped at him. He didn't have to smile while he said that.

"You seem awfully happy about sticking things up my butt."

"Your bottom is a thing of beauty," he told her. "And yes, it makes me extremely happy to stick things up it. Roll onto your tummy, I'll grab some pillows to put under your hips."

She groaned as he lifted the blanket. But she rolled over obediently. She had to admit, as embarrassing as it was, that she was a teensy bit curious about what the plug would feel like.

All in the name of research, of course.

Caley, you are so full of it.

He pushed some pillows under her hips, raising her up then settled the blanket over her upper half.

"Just relax, baby doll." He rubbed her lower back. "Remember that you have your safeword. If at any time you get scared or something hurts, then you can use it."

She took a deep breath in, trying to relax her tense muscles.

"Good girl. That's it."

She heard a buzz and looked over to find he'd picked up the vibrator. A blush filled her cheeks and she hid her face in the pillow. When she'd woken up this morning she'd had absolutely no idea that this was what she was getting herself into.

"Spread your legs. That's it. Let's just slide this under you. Is that in a good spot for you?"

A good spot? Her eyes had practically rolled back in her head. It felt like fucking heaven.

Her breath came in quick pants. A sharp smack landed on her bottom. "Caley, words."

Oh. Crap. Right. Really? She had to speak? That seemed unfair.

"Yes, it's good."

"Yes, Daddy or yes, Issy."

"Yes, Daddy."

"Good girl." He rubbed the spot he'd just smacked. "Come as often as you like and make as much noise as you desire. I want to hear you come."

Oh hell. Oh crap.

Her bottom cheeks were parted and a dab of cool lube was applied to her back hole before a wet finger slid inside her. The nerve endings in her ass seemed to dance into life. It was unexpected. And it sent her crashing over the edge. Her pussy clenching down, shivers racing through her body.

"Well, now, that was quick."

Too quick? Oh no, how embarrassing.

"Shh, I can hear you thinking. There's no rule about how long it has to take you to come," he told her as he removed his finger then something firm and cool was pushed into her bottom. The thermometer.

"Just relax. Good girl. I'm going to push the thermometer inside you and then I'll leave it there while I clean my hands." The cool, thick thermometer filled her ass. "There you are, keep that in there." She felt the bed shift as he stood. "Damn, that's a pretty sight. I'll be back in a minute."

He walked into the attached bathroom while she lay there, her bottom bare, legs spread. A vibrator buzzing against her sensitive clit and a thermometer in her bottom.

Maybe she should have been embarrassed by that. But she was too turned-on to worry too much about how she looked.

She wanted to come again. Her folds were slick with her need.

Her passage clenched, wanting something to penetrate her. Take her.

Daddy returned and sat next to her on the bed. "Good girl. Oh, look how tense you are. You need to come again, don't you?"

"Y-yes," she cried out.

He slid the thermometer out of her bottom. "Temperature is good. I'm going to put the plug in now, baby doll. Just take a deep breath. That's it."

She felt her cheeks part and something firm was pressed against her hole.

"Now out."

She breathed out as he slid the plug into her bottom hole. It stung a bit and she had to focus on not tensing up. But as soon as it was in and she clenched around it, she could feel her need growing higher.

"Good girl, now roll onto your back. I'm going to help you come again. You've been such a good girl you deserve a treat."

He helped her roll onto her back. The vibrator slid down onto the mattress and she had to concentrate on not letting the plug slip out. That would be embarrassing. He moved so he was lying on his stomach between her open legs. Reaching out, he parted her lower lips and took a long lick of her juices.

"Damn that's delicious, baby doll."

A vibration hit her entrance and she realized then that he'd picked up the vibrator. He pressed it slowly into her pussy until she was filled in both holes.

Fuck. Fuck. She needed to come so badly.

"Look how wet you are. All slick and in need. I'm going to plug you every day. Work on stretching this asshole until you're ready to take me there."

She groaned at the thought.

"Every night, when you finish work, I'm going to have you pull your pants and panties down then bend over and part your bottom cheeks. Then I'll push the plug nice and deep into your asshole. You're going to wear that plug while you sit at the table and eat your dinner. Then while we snuggle on the couch."

Oh Shit. Shit!

She wasn't going to last much longer. As though he realized how his words were affecting her, he stopped talking and started flicking at her clit with his tongue. She lost the ability to breathe as she was thrust over the edge, her orgasm rushing through her with the force of a bull let free from a pen.

She shuddered as he withdrew the vibrator and pulled the pillows out from under her. He then wrapped the blanket around her and walked into the bathroom with the vibrator and thermometer, probably to clean them. The man had a thing about cleanliness.

When he returned, he sat next to her, leaning against the headboard. Then he reached over for the bottle of water. "Sit up a bit, baby doll. Drink some water."

She half-reclined against him, not even bothering to reach for the bottle. She knew the drill by now. After drinking some water, she snuggled in against him. He ran his hand up and down her arm.

"Are you sure I can't do the same for you?" She didn't look up at him, too embarrassed by her offer. She wasn't exactly sophisticated.

He wasn't going to let her get away with that, though. He reached down and tilted up her chin, so she was staring up into his firm, blue eyes. "When I think you're ready for more, then you can have your mouth and hands on me as often as you like. Well, when I'm not inside you. And you'll need to brace yourself because I am going to be taking you every chance I get."

"That sounds nice."

Umm. Whoops she hadn't meant to say that out loud.

But how would he know when she was ready when she didn't know? And how long would he wait?

"Don't you have to go back to work soon?"

She knew he'd talked to his boss about some extra time off, but there had to be a time limit on that.

He snorted. "Kent was so happy I was taking time off; I think he nearly wet himself."

"Issy!"

He grinned. It was a slightly evil grin. "Think they all believe I'll be less crotchety if I have a vacation. Idiots."

She rolled her eyes at him. "So he's really okay with you having time off?"

"Baby doll, even if he wasn't, I'd still be here. But I promise you, if I let him have your number, he'd probably call you up to thank you. Do not worry. I'm here until you realize you can't live without me."

That might have already happened.

SHE STARED at the whiteboard as she sat up in bed. The plug shifted in her ass, sending a wave of arousal through her.

Uhh, so yeah, who'd have thought she'd have enjoyed having a piece of plastic up her ass so much?

After she'd recovered from her orgasm, Issy had gone and retrieved some more of her gifts. One of which she was looking at right now.

The whiteboard was about the size of a ledger-sized piece of paper. Across the top was written, Caley's Rules.

Then numbered down the board, were a list of rules.

1. No lying

2. No putting herself in danger i.e. no speeding, texting while driving, meeting with strangers alone
3. No disrespecting herself or her Daddy
4. Bedtime is 10 p.m. unless she is in Little mode when it is 9 p.m.
5. No working more than fifty hours a week or more than ten hours in a single day
6. No skipping meals
7. Must drink eight glasses of water a day and have no more than four cups of coffee a day
8. Must tell Daddy before she leaves the property, and let him know where she is going and if she will be late when returning
9. If Daddy texts or calls her, she must reply or call back within thirty minutes
10. Must listen to Daddy
11. Must attempt to pick up after herself

"Are you sure you didn't miss anything?" she asked, gulping at the list. Sheesh.

"Well, I ran out of room for anything more. But if we need to, we can buy a bigger whiteboard."

Was he insane?

"Thought it best to write it all down, then you can't claim you forgot a rule. Not that that is an acceptable excuse for not following the rules, anyway."

Lord help her. She studied the rules again. Was it bad that the one she figured she was going to find hardest was the last one?

"I don't even notice that I'm dropping things, how am I going to pick things up?"

"Don't worry, baby doll. I don't expect you to suddenly change overnight. That's why we have the Caley-basket. At the end of the day, you're going to go around with your basket and pick up all the stuff you've left behind. Hmm, and we'll start with a count of ten. If you've left less than ten items out, you get a smiley face on the reward side of your chart. If you leave more than ten, then it's a frown on the punishment side."

Yeah, that was another 'gift'. The rewards and punishment chart was really just another whiteboard with a line down the middle. She earned smiley faces and frowny faces and at the end of each week, they got added up.

She glanced at the two jars he'd placed on the dresser. They were filled with cut-up pieces of paper. One jar had a sticker on the front that said Rewards, the other had a sticker that said Punishments.

Apparently, all those bits of paper had either punishments or rewards on them for her to choose from depending on whether she had more frowns or smiley faces at the end of the week.

She really wasn't sure how she felt about that.

"You should know that for each time you break a rule, you do get an immediate punishment. So, say I caught you texting while driving, I'd likely pull you over my knee and paddle your bottom thoroughly. Then you'd also get a frown on your chart."

She gulped. So she got a punishment when she originally broke the rule then another one from her jar if she got more frowns than smiley faces at the end of the week.

Oh. Crap.

"You're still owed a punishment for yesterday. I didn't give that to you immediately because you weren't well. That is likely the only time that I will delay a punishment." He grabbed a whiteboard marker and started marking frowns on the whiteboard. She got frowny faces yesterday for not eating, not drinking and not obeying Daddy.

Oh. She was in so much trouble.

～

WHILE ISSY WAS COOKING DINNER, she grabbed up her phone and opened her contacts. She missed him. She just wanted to talk to him.

She called him before she could second-guess herself. If he didn't want to talk to her or was busy, he didn't have to answer.

"Hello, love."

"Hi," she whispered shyly then cleared her throat. "Is this a good time? I can call back later. Are you still at work?"

"No, love. I just got home."

"I just wanted to call and make sure you got home okay." It was lame, she knew. Basically, she just wanted to hear his voice.

"I did. Thank you." Those warm tones soothed something antsy inside her. "I spoke to Issy earlier. He said you had a migraine last night? Are you all right now?"

"Oh yes. Too much caffeine not enough water. I'm still in bed. I've been here all day."

"Poor baby, is Issy taking good care of you?"

She blushed remembering that orgasm. "Yes."

A low chuckle came over the phone that made her blush. It was like he could read her mind.

"He's got this reward and punishment chart for me though." She explained it to him, pouting as she did.

"Aww, you know how to avoid the punishment jar, though, don't you?"

She huffed out a sigh. "Yes." She didn't want logic, she wanted sympathy. "Still think it's mean."

Another laugh. She smiled. She liked that she could make him smile. There was something in his voice. Something sad or maybe it was tiredness.

"You sure you're all right?" she asked him. He was always there for her. Talking her through things. Helping her see things in a different light. She hadn't realized until he was gone, how much she'd come to rely on his calming influence. His advice. His help.

With Issy, she could be vulnerable and know he would take care of her. She could let go. With Archer, she could tell him anything. He'd never hurt her. In fact, he'd done the opposite, he'd help heal the wounds on her soul.

They both had.

"I'm fine, love. Just missing you guys. I think I even miss that rundown shack of yours. I definitely don't miss the microwave or washing machine."

She was giggling as Issy stepped into the bedroom, his eyebrows raised in question.

"I've got to go. I think dinner is ready. Take care, Archer."

"You make Issy take care of you," he replied.

21

Now that was a damn pretty sight.

His girl with her nose in the corner, her panties down around her ankles, which were spread wide. She was wearing a nightie since she'd only just gotten up and he'd had her hold it up to her waist so as not to cover her bottom.

He had to reach down and adjust himself.

It had been two days since her migraine. He'd made her spend all of yesterday in bed, which she'd done with hardly any complaint. That, more than anything else, had told him how exhausted she was.

Today, he knew he'd have trouble getting her to rest and stay off her laptop. Which is why he planned on having her spend the day in Little space. With a bit of help from him.

It wasn't just for her benefit. He wanted to spend time with her Little. Craved it. Happiness flooded him. Unlike anything he'd felt before. If only he didn't keep feeling like something was missing. He guessed it was because she hadn't committed to moving in with him. But he knew he had to give her time.

"Come here, baby doll."

She dropped the nightie and reached down for her panties.

"Uh-uh, I didn't say you could get dressed again."

She turned; her eyes wide.

"Keep the nightie up around your waist. But lose the panties. I don't want you tripping over them. Pick them up and bring them here."

She slipped her panties off, holding onto them as she raised her nightie once more, revealing her pretty pussy. Damn. His cock throbbed. He wished he could lay her down and feast on her.

But that was for later. Right now, she was owed some punishment.

As she drew closer, her eyes widened as she saw the item sitting on the sofa next to him. "Uh, what is that?"

"That is Caley's naughty girl paddle. Isn't it pretty?" It was a teak color and was long with a rounded end. "It's hand-crafted and even has an ergonomic handle. So I won't hurt myself if I have to paddle you for a long time."

"You won't hurt yourself? That's what the person who made that paddle was worried about?"

He grinned. "Well, he wasn't worried about how much it was going to hurt the person receiving the spanking, that's for sure."

"Oh dear Lord."

He finally took pity on her. "Don't worry, baby doll. I'm mostly going to use my hand. I'm just going to give you a few with the paddle at the end so you know what it feels like. Because next time you disobey me regarding your health, you'll be getting your butt paddled until you can't sit for days. Either that, or I'll be taking my belt off."

He saw her gulp. Didn't hurt for her to be a bit worried, not if it made her think twice about not taking care of herself when he wasn't around.

Not that he planned on going far.

He patted his lap. "Over you go."

She drew closer, giving that paddle a look filled with trepidation. But she slowly placed herself over his lap. He drew her in close, placing one hand on the small of her back while he rubbed her bare bottom cheeks with the other.

She was tense to begin with, but as he kept rubbing, the tension started to slowly ease from her muscles.

"Can you keep your hands out in front of you or do you need me to hold them?"

"I can keep them there. I think."

"Good girl. Let me know if that changes. What's your safeword?"

"Bananas."

With that, he smacked his hand down on her bottom. He heard her take a surprised gasp of air in. But he didn't give her time to recover. His hand landed again and again. He didn't pause to scold her this time or to rub. That last spanking hadn't been a truly serious one. After all, he'd known she hadn't deliberately thrown that glass. And she hadn't been in danger.

This was entirely different.

Gradually, she started to shift around on his lap. Her feet tapped against the cushions of the sofa.

"Daddy! Daddy, stop!" she cried out.

"I'm sorry, baby doll. But this spanking has to be far harder than your last one." He moved his hand lower, to the top of her thighs and started spanking her there. She started wiggling, trying to escape and he held onto her tighter, gripping her around the waist as he made certain to redden all of her ass.

Gradually, she stopped fighting and lay there, just sobbing.

Poor baby.

He felt terrible that there was more to come. But not so bad that he wouldn't follow through and give her everything she needed. This is what she required. She'd been floundering without a dominant figure in her life. Someone to give her boundaries. If she'd been left on this path, she'd have worked herself into an early grave.

Not on his watch.

"Baby doll, do you know why this spanking is so much harder than your last one?"

She was silent for a moment. "I g-got sick."

"And you got sick because...?"

"I didn't t-take care of m-myself."

"That's right. This is a far more serious transgression and I need you to know how serious I am about your health. It is not something I will ever take lightly. Not because I'm a doctor but because I ..."

Love you.

Nope. Not the way to blurt it out. But now that he'd thought the words they felt right. He was ready to shout them from the rooftops. However, he knew they were likely to scare her off. Most people would see it as too soon. But he wasn't most people.

"Care about you."

"I care about you too," she whispered.

He rubbed her lower back. "Keep your hands where they are, baby doll. Once we get this part over with, I'm going to hold you for a long time. Then I thought you might enjoy some Little time, what do you say?"

There was a beat of silence and he thought she was going to reject his suggestion. Then she nodded and sniffled. "Yes, please, Daddy. I-I'd like that."

"That's my girl. It's a count of six. Two smacks for each rule you broke." Before he finished speaking, he'd smacked the paddle down on her ass. She tensed then let out a loud cry.

Another smack of the paddle. Another cry. By number three, she was trying to roll herself off his lap. He held her steady and applied the last ones quickly, not making her wait.

After the last one landed, he rolled her over, holding her tight against him, careful not to let her full weight rest on her bottom.

Shit. He would always do what was best for her. And putting her over his knee for a well-deserved hand-spanking or one for fun, he had no issue with. But those smacks with the paddle had almost killed him.

Still, if she ever put herself in real danger, he wouldn't hesitate to redden her ass with his belt or the paddle. Because she meant that much to him.

She meant everything.

"What do you think, Daddy?" Caley bit her lower lip as she held up the collage picture she'd made. She'd been cutting out bits of paper and gluing them onto a giant white piece of paper. Then she'd put more glue on top and sprinkled glitter all over it.

"What was that?" Issy walked out of the bedroom with a basket filled with what she assumed was dirty laundry. Mostly hers. Guilt filled her. She should be helping.

But before she could open her mouth and say something, he paused, his mouth dropping open slightly as he stared down at her. She looked around, at the glitter on the floor and her clothes and all over the coffee table where she'd been working.

And then there was the mess of paper, with small bits lying everywhere from what had been cut off.

Oh. Whoops. For someone with his OCD issues this was probably torture for him.

"Sorry, Daddy. I'll clean it all up."

He closed his eyes and his mouth moved. She was fairly certain he was counting. Then he opened his eyes again. She gave him a guilty look.

"It's okay, baby doll."

It was? It didn't look like he actually thought that.

"But you will clean all this mess up," he said sternly.

She nodded. Uh-huh. She totally would. It was okay if some got swept under the rug and sofa, right? What he didn't know wouldn't hurt him.

He gave her a skeptical look. "What did you make, baby doll?"

"Oh, it's a picture for you!"

"That's gorgeous," he said in a much less strained voice.

"Are you gonna hang it on the 'frigerator?"

He blinked then looked over at the fridge where all her magnets were now lined up in neat rows.

Seriously. They were lined up. He'd organized her fridge magnets.

"Never mind," she said sadly, dropping her face to stare at the floor. "I know it's not that good."

"Hey now," he said sternly, stepping forward to grasp hold of her chin. He raised her face. "That is a gorgeous creation and I would love to put it on the fridge."

"You would? You don't think it's too messy?"

He shook his head. "I'm sorry, baby doll. I know I have a few, um, quirks, but I also know I need to find a line between tidy and psycho."

She had to grin at that.

"And if it makes my girl sad then I am definitely not striking the right balance. You have my permission to point out what an uptight ass I'm being."

Her eyes widened. "I get to call you an uptight ass?"

"Ahh, no. That's not very polite. But you can tell me that I need to ease up." He had set the laundry basket down when he walked over to her. He took the picture from her hand then walked to the fridge and put it up. She got up and followed him. "There. How does that look?"

"Great, Daddy." She bounced excitedly on the tips of her toes. "Does you want me to do the laundry?"

"Certainly not," he replied. "Littles do not use the washing machine. And my girl definitely does not use *that* washing machine."

"I've used it lots before, Daddy."

"Well, no more. You're getting a new washing machine."

She frowned. A new one? But she was used to this one.

"I donts need a new one."

"This one is dangerous, and you do need a new one. Now, stay here while I go do the washing. Then I'll help you clean up."

"I thought I'd make a picture for Archie. Unless you think he wouldn't want one." She bit her lip. Was it all right that she wanted to make one for his brother? Or was it weird? Would he think it was weird? It was just...she missed Archer so much.

"I think he'd love one, baby girl. We can mail it when we next go into Bozeman."

"We're going into Bozeman?"

"Yes, we'll need to go get some groceries next week and you need to visit a gynecologist."

Oh. Freaking awesome. Most Littles might get to go to the movies or an arcade.

She got the gynecologist.

He must have seen something on her face because he grinned. "Don't worry, baby doll. If you're a good girl, Daddy will take you to do something fun as well."

"Like what?" she asked suspiciously. "Get a flu shot? Have some blood taken?"

"Hmm, both good suggestions, I'll add them to the list."

She groaned. She needed to learn to stop while she was ahead.

22

———————

Doc looked over at Caley's clay creation. He'd gotten her some the other day to play with, thinking that it might be good for her hands. He was trying to coax her into figuring out how to use the dictation software that she owned but had never used.

He'd spent today stacking the load of firewood that had finally arrived while Caley worked. She hadn't been terribly impressed that he'd ordered and paid for the firewood without her knowledge. When she'd told him she was going to pay him back, well, he hadn't been too happy about that.

When she'd stomped her foot, the beginning of a tantrum, and called him a couple of not-nice names, he'd ended the argument with a hand spanking then sent her to spend fifteen minutes in timeout.

Afterwards, her mood had been a lot better. Although she still wasn't happy about the wood. She wasn't going to be impressed when all of Archer's gifts arrived, which should be any day now. But she could call Archer and have a chat with him.

He frowned, thinking about his brother. He'd been surprisingly hard to get hold of lately. In fact, he'd only spoken to him twice since he'd left nearly a week ago.

Of course, in the last two years you've only spoken to him a handful of times.

But that was before...when he'd been holding onto a foolish, misplaced anger.

He and Caley had settled into a bit of a routine. He brought her coffee in bed in the morning, they got up and did some light stretches and exercise. Then after breakfast, she worked while he did some things to tidy up the property. After dinner, they spent time together, with her in Little space. This was his favorite time of the day; when they were together, and both of them were relaxed.

"That looks great, baby doll. It's time for your bath soon. This is your five-minute warning."

He'd learned about the need to give her warnings rather than just spring things on her. She did not do well with change.

"Couldn't we skip the bath tonight, Daddy? I want to do some more playing."

"Nope. We could not. A bath is important for your bedtime routine." He'd managed to instill a routine, hoping it would help with her sleep. He'd give her a bath then comb and braid her hair before putting her to bed with a bottle of warmed up chocolate protein shake.

"And you haven't picked up your stuff yet, either," he reminded her sternly.

She groaned. He just gave her a look. She got up with a huff and grabbed the empty basket then started walking around, picking things up. He'd put her rules board and her reward/pun-ishment chart up on the wall. Where she could see them every day. The punishment and reward jars were kept on the mantel of the fireplace. So far, she had slightly more smiley faces than frowns, but he wasn't betting on that lasting.

"Remember to go through the bedroom and your office," he

called out. He followed her into her office to make sure she got everything. His gaze went to the train set and he walked over, sitting down to study it.

"Dave carved it all for me," she said quietly, kneeling beside him. She picked up one of the small people. "This one is me."

He carefully took the piece from her, looking it over. "He was really talented."

"He would carve wooden toys and sell them over the internet. He had a lady who made the outfits for the people. But he always worked on pieces for me." She ran her hand over one of the houses.

"He forgot a bit on your doll, though."

She frowned, glancing over. "What? Where?"

"The red bottom." He turned it around and lifted the material of the dress.

She rolled her eyes. "Not everyone has an obsession with my bottom the way you do, Daddy."

"Just as well. If anyone else tried to touch your bottom, they'd lose their hand. Right, show me your basket."

He pulled everything out, one by one. "Twelve."

She bit her lip. "Are you sure?"

"Count it out for yourself."

She slowly and carefully counted everything. He put each item back in the basket as she counted it. Her shoulders slumped. "Twelve."

"Go mark a frowny face on your chart."

"At this rate, I'm gonna have more frowns than smiley faces." Yesterday she'd earned a number of frowns for that tantrum she'd thrown.

Doc turned and walked into the living area with the basket of stuff. He paused as he heard his phone ring. He picked it up and frowned as he saw Kent's name.

. . .

CALEY SIGHED LONG AND LOUD. She dragged her feet as she made her way to her chart. She heard Issy answer his phone. She didn't pay much attention as she put another frowny face on her chart. This was not going to end well for her, she could tell.

She turned as she heard Issy swear. His face was twisted in a scowl.

"Fuck. Can't someone else go to him?" he snapped.

He sat and rubbed at his temple. She moved behind him and leaned over the sofa to rub his shoulders.

"Yeah. Yeah, sure. No, I think it will be quicker and easier for me to drive than fly. Yeah. Got it."

She paused then straightened. What was going on?

Issy grunted then ended the call without a goodbye.

"You're leaving, aren't you?" she whispered, her stomach trying up in a knot.

He stood and turned towards her. "Baby doll, I don't want to. If there was any way that I didn't have to, I wouldn't."

"What's happened?" she asked, suddenly worried. "It's not Archer, is it?"

"No. No, Archer is fine. It's work. One of our guys has been shot."

"Oh God. A friend? Is he in the hospital? You need to go home to help him?"

"Wouldn't exactly call him a friend. More like a thorn in my side, bane of my existence, pain in the fu...flipping butt," he said hastily. "Zander isn't exactly friends with anyone. And he doesn't follow any rules. He also won't let anyone but me fix him up. So he's currently holed up in one of his hidey-holes in Colorado, and is waiting for me to come doctor him because Lord forbid, he be normal and go to a hospital."

"He's been injured and he's refusing to go to a hospital?"

Issy sighed and moved into the bedroom, pulling out his duffel bag. He grabbed a few pairs of underwear, jeans and shirts, putting them neatly into his bag. Even in a rush, he took care.

"Yeah, Zander isn't normal. He's paranoid. He trusts very few people. Unfortunately, I am one of those people. That's what happens when you save a guy's life. Suddenly, they think they can call you up every time they get shot!"

He moved into the bathroom to gather up his toiletries and she followed him. "Wait, this has happened more than once?"

"Uh-huh. Zander gets hurt a lot. As well as being paranoid and anti-social, he also pisses people off on a regular basis. If he keeps doing this, I might shoot him. And it won't be a flesh wound."

"How long will you be gone?"

He zipped up his bag. Then turned to her. "I'm not sure, baby doll. It depends how bad the wound is. Maybe a couple of days."

She bit at her lip. "Should I...should I come with you?" Some panic filled her at the thought of it. She hadn't been away from this cabin for more than a few hours. Just enough to go get supplies. But she also couldn't imagine being here without Issy.

You would be fine if Archer was here.

But he wasn't.

Issy cupped her face between his hands. "I wish I could take you with me. Believe me, I would. But Zander won't let me on his property if you're with me."

"Oh. All right."

"What I do want you to do, is to follow all the rules. I expect an honest accounting on your chart. Understand?"

"Okay. I guess I can do that."

"No working long hours. You need to eat and drink. You have my cell number. Go grab your phone and I will put Kent's in as well. That's my boss. If, for some reason, you can't get through to me then you can call Kent."

She very much doubted that she'd need to call his boss, but she let him put his number in her phone.

"I'll try to call but don't worry if you don't hear from me until tomorrow night, all right? And, baby girl, I expect you to take care of yourself or there will be trouble when I get back."

She rolled her eyes and he spun her around, popping her sharply on the bottom. Then he turned her back and drew her into his chest, holding her close. "Be good. I'll miss you."

She wrapped her arms around his waist. She didn't want him to leave. What if he left and decided that she wasn't worth returning to? What if...

"Hush, Caley," he murmured. "Whatever you're thinking, just stop. I'm coming back. I'm not leaving you. The only way I'm leaving here permanently, is with you by my side." He took a step back, giving her a firm look. "I am never leaving you. You. Are. Mine. I want you to come home with me, live with me, be mine. I've got to go."

Caley watched him drive off, until his rental vehicle disappeared around the corner in the driveway.

Feeling bereft and lost, she stepped inside the cabin and locked the door.

I am never leaving you.

Thing is, he couldn't guarantee that. And losing him...

It might just break her permanently.

WHY HAD HE LEFT HER?

Archer drummed his fingers against the desk in his office. He had one more patient due in about an hour. He should be spending this time more productively. He stood and moved to the wide windows, looking out at the Dallas skyline.

Why hadn't he stayed and fought for her?

Because the person who you would have fought for her was your brother. The person you've been trying to mend fences with for years. The person who deserves her love, needs it.

I need it too.

He pushed his hand into his immaculately pressed pants. Pursuing Caley would have been a disaster. He knew that. Plus, there was no guarantee that Caley would pick him.

On the surface, Isaac was the one who suited her. Isaac would happily live the hermit life in a cabin in the woods. He'd chop wood and fix things and fuss over her. And she'd be free to be herself. She could write, she could let her Little side have free rein.

He couldn't give her any of that. He lived in the city. He had a career that he loved, mostly, he had people he cared about, sort of, he had a life here. He wasn't about to give that up...

Not even for Caley?

This was ridiculous. There was nothing he could offer. And if he'd have tried to fight for her, he'd have lost his brother.

What if you could have both?

It was something that he kept going back to. It wasn't just a relationship with Caley he desired. He loved his brother. When they'd managed to move past their issues, they'd worked well together.

You could love her together. Dominate her together. Take care of her together.

He groaned. It was madness. Okay, so he'd done it before, but only for a few months.

And not with Issy and Caley.

There was another problem as well, though. He wasn't a Daddy Dom.

But couldn't you be? The idea doesn't freak you out. Just because you never have been doesn't mean that you couldn't be. For her.

Or at the very least he could dominate her in the bedroom. Even he could see she desperately needed rules and for someone to enforce those rules. He would very happily spank that delicious ass if she was naughty.

He sighed. He had to stop thinking of her.

Maybe he should head to the club tonight. Get out of his own head. Find a brat to spank.

And pretend she was a certain sweet, absent-minded blonde-haired poppet.

Damn it. He needed to know she was all right. He walked back to his desk and grabbed his cell. If he called her, though, he might interrupt her work.

Instead, he brought up his brother's name. The call went immediately to voicemail. That wasn't unusual, Isaac wasn't generally one for socializing. He often went days without returning a call.

His phone buzzed in his hand and he was surprised to see her name on the screen.

"Caley? Is everything all right?"

"Archer, umm, hi."

"Hi, love."

"I was calling because I received a new microwave and a washing machine/dryer combo."

"Oh good, they arrived."

"Archer, you shouldn't have bought that for me. It's too much."

"It's not too much. It's entirely necessary. Did they set them up for you?"

"Umm, they set the washer up."

"Let Issy set up the microwave, it's too heavy for you to be carrying."

"Oh, Issy isn't here right now."

"He's not? Where is he?" he demanded.

The door to his office opened and his assistant walked in with a cup of coffee for him, but he ignored her.

"Has he gone into Bozeman for the day?" he asked when she didn't answer.

"Uhh, no, he left."

"He left?" he yelled.

He was aware of his assistant staring at him, wide-eyed. He gave her a wave to let her know everything was fine. Then he tuned her out.

"Love, what do you mean, he's left?" he asked, forcing himself to speak calmly.

"I, uhh, Archer, you yelled." She sounded completely shocked.

"Sorry, Caley, did I scare you?" He turned and saw his assistant still gaping at him. He gave her a small frown and she quickly turned and left.

"Umm, I just...I've never heard you yell."

Why did he leave her? What the hell was he thinking? Had they had a fight? Why hadn't he called Archer? He'd have...

Swooped in to save her.

Hero complex, much?

"He, umm, he got called into work."

"Called into work? Someone on the ranch is ill?"

"Sort of," she hedged.

"Caley," he growled, not impressed at her half-answers.

"I'm not sure how much to say."

"All of it," he told her firmly. Damn it, why hadn't Isaac called him?

"But Da—I mean Issy might get angry with me." There was a lost note in her voice.

Poor baby.

"He won't get angry with you," he said soothingly. "If he gets angry at anyone, it will be me."

"But I don't want the two of you to argue again. I don't like it when you argue."

"You won't know, because we aren't going to argue in front of you again. Tell me, Caley."

His voice was pure Dom now.

"He had to go to Colorado to help one of the guys who he works with. He got shot!"

Colorado? But the ranch was in Montana. And why would he have to go to help this guy? "Why didn't he go to the hospital?"

"Apparently he doesn't trust them. He doesn't trust anyone to help him except Issy. That's why he had to go."

"And he just left you alone?" What was he thinking?

"I've lived by myself for years, Archer. A few days is fine. He's coming back." There was a note of uncertainty in her voice.

Damn it, Isaac! Didn't he realize how vulnerable she was right now? If he left her too long, she could well convince herself that he wasn't going to return. That he didn't care about her as much as she did him. She could well decide that she was betraying her love for Dave by falling for Isaac.

He could lose her.

"Of course he's coming back, love. Did he not tell you that?" If he hadn't reassured her of that before he left...

"Archer, he wants me to move in with him. Before he left, he said he wanted me to move back to his home. With him. That he wouldn't be leaving again without me with him. I...I..."

Holy shit. He could feel her panic from here. What was Issy thinking, laying that on her right before he left?

Jesus Christ.

"Poppet, breathe. Just breathe. It's all right. He doesn't expect that right away. That was just Issy's way of telling you how serious he is about you. How much you mean to him."

"What if I want that too?"

"What?" Whoops. He hadn't actually meant to say that.

"What if I want to be with him. He's only been gone half a day and already I miss him like crazy. I feel so lost. First you left, now him. I don't know if I can be here on my own anymore. But it's too soon, right? And what about Dave? How am I meant to leave here? Leave Dave? Leave it all? Archer, I..."

He heard her sniffle.

"Poppet, listen to me. It's all right to have doubts. It's okay to feel conflicted."

"Is it? I feel like I'm being torn apart. To choose one option seems to disrespect how much I loved Dave. But to choose the other option, to not have Issy in my life, I'm not sure I can do that, Archer."

"Because you love him." He felt so happy for his brother. Yet at the same time, it was like his heart was breaking.

"I love him," she said the words on an amazed breath. "It's too early to feel that."

"Nobody says there has to be a certain timeframe in which you fall in love."

"Everyone says that. Everyone has an opinion."

And she had experienced firsthand how much people's opinions could hurt.

"Well, fuck them," he said.

She drew in a breath. "Archer, you swore. First you yelled, then you swore. Are you sure you're all right?"

He ran his hand over his face. "I'm fine, poppet. I miss you."

"I miss you too," she said quietly. "I'm scared, Archer. It's not just letting go of Dave. It's leaving here. It's my safe place. It's scary out there. I'm such a coward."

"You are not a coward," he said fiercely. "And I do not want to hear you call yourself that again, understand me?"

"O-okay."

"You have every right to be scared after what you've been through. It's understandable that you would be worried about leaving your home. It's what is familiar to you. But, baby, you have to know that Isaac is not going to let anything happen to you."

"He can't be there to always protect me."

"Not always, no. But it isn't often that he leaves the ranch. And everyone on the ranch will be there to watch out for you."

"But what if...what if they don't like me or who I am?"

He was struck silent for a moment. "Has Issy not explained about Sanctuary?"

"Explained what? How most of the people who work for JSI live there?"

"That's it?"

"Uhh, yes."

"He left a bit out. Love, the majority of the men who live there are Daddy Doms. It's a place where women are cherished and protected. If anyone ever made you feel bad about who you are, they'd be kicked off the ranch. And that's probably after they got an ass kicking."

"That's...that's...really?"

"Really, baby. I can't believe Issy didn't tell you all this."

"I guess we've had other things going on."

His brother was an idiot.

"I'm just scared. I've forgotten how to be around other people."

"Then take it slowly. There's no right way of doing this, Caley. You do what feels right for you. But I can guarantee that anyone who meets you will love you."

Like he did. Fuck. He loved her.

She let out a shuddering breath. "You always know what to say to help me."

"Hey, it's my job," he joked. He winced. Fuck. He shouldn't have said that. He heard her breath hitch.

"Not that I think of you as a patient or anything. I didn't mean it was a job to talk to you. I love talking to you, I just..." Shit. He hadn't stumbled over his words like this since he was a teenager.

"It's okay," she said quietly. "I know what you mean. I like talking to you too."

He let out a deep breath, trying to calm himself. "You can come to me about anything. I'm here for you. Issy is coming back. He would never leave you."

"Sometimes people don't have a choice."

"No, they don't," he said with sympathy. "But you have to decide whether taking a risk is worth it. You can spend your life protecting yourself from all harm and hurt but never truly living. Or you can love, you can live, and you can risk loss. Caley, do you need me to come to you? I can."

Only with a hell of a lot of reshuffling and probably a pissed-off assistant and patients. But he'd do it. For her.

"No, Archer, that's all right. I know you have a lot to do there. And this conversation has helped more than you can know. A very wise man once told me that it was time to start living again. I think I should take his advice."

"He does sound wise. And handsome, very handsome."

CALEY WAS GIGGLING as she ended the call with Archer, placing the phone on the kitchen table as she looked over at the brand new microwave he'd bought her. It probably cost more than the rest of her appliances put together.

He was right, though. Lifting it herself wasn't a smart idea. She grabbed her heat pack and put it in her old microwave. Her hands were aching a bit today and Issy wouldn't be happy if she didn't take care of them.

She closed her eyes and took a deep breath, bringing up Issy's face. She missed him. She loved him. She wanted to be with him.

It was time to say goodbye.

There was only one way she could think to do that properly. Grabbing her jacket, she put it on. Then she put on her boots and stood.

She ignored the beeping of the microwave. She'd reheat her heat pack when she got back. This was more important.

CALEY LOOKED out across the small stream where she'd scattered Dave's ashes. This was one of his favorite places to go. He claimed he thought better when he was here. So it had only been natural for this to be his final resting place.

She thought she'd probably keep this property. Maybe it could be their holiday cottage or something. She took a deep breath, letting it out slowly. Archer was right, she'd always carry a piece of Dave with her. But if she didn't take this chance with Issy, she'd always regret it.

"I love you, Dave. I always will. And I will never forget you. You were everything to me. My hero. My love. My Daddy. I hope you understand and that you approve of where my life is going now. I think you would. Not sure you'd like Isaac. But he takes care of me. He wouldn't let anything hurt me. I think he loves me. I love him." She crouched and pulled off her glove, running her fingers in the freezing cold water.

"Goodbye, my love."

Turning, she started back down the dirt road, feeling lighter than she had in a long time. It was time for the next chapter.

It wasn't until she was halfway back home that she smelled it. Smoke? Holy shit. Where was that coming from? She started moving faster. It was now growing dark. She'd forgotten her cell phone, not that she'd get much reception up here.

There was a gap in the trees, and she let out a loud cry as she saw the flames ahead of her.

Her cabin? Oh God. She raced forward, barely noticing the branches slapping at her, scratching her face. She tripped over a root of a tree, wrenching her ankle. But her fear and the adrenaline meant she didn't even feel the pain. She stumbled on.

Bumbly! Her laptop! Her train set!

She reached for the front door, screaming in pain as the heat seared her skin. She got the door open, though, coughing as smoke assailed her. The back of the house was engulfed in flames.

Oh God. Oh God.

She attempted to make her way to her office, but the smoke was just too thick. The heat was so intense. She changed direction, moving to her bedroom. She screamed as the cabin creaked then the roof at the back collapsed.

Moving on instinct, she stumbled into her bedroom. She quickly grabbed Bumbly and her snuggly, disorientated, the smoke thick and insidious, she moved to the window, opening it, crying out as her hands protested.

She practically dived out the window then rolled away, right as the roof completely caved in. Taking just about everything she owned and cherished with it.

23

Caley coughed. Her lungs burned. There was a beeping noise that appeared to be in time with the throbbing in her head.

Something was over her mouth. She reached up, trying to bat it away, shocked to realize her hands wouldn't work.

What was going on?

"Easy, Miss Ryan, you're in the hospital. You have an oxygen mask over your face since you inhaled quite a bit of smoke. Your hands are bandaged up as well. Just relax. That's it."

She blinked, looking up into an older woman's lined face. She appeared brisk, slightly tense but her eyes were kind.

"Hello, Miss Ryan. I'm Jenny, your nurse for this shift. You're in the hospital in Bozeman."

Bozeman? She was in Bozeman?

What had happened? She'd inhaled smoke?

Her cabin. Her cabin had caught on fire. Everything was gone. She whimpered, trying to speak.

"It might be hard to speak for a bit. You should just relax and concentrate on breathing. You're safe in the hospital. You were airlifted here after someone called about the fire and the authorities arrived and found you. We're trying to find a next of kin for you."

She shook her head, worried they might call her parents.

"Easy. You can't dislodge the oxygen mask. Everything is fine. Why don't you go back to sleep?"

She got the feeling the nurse gave her something to help her sleep, because all at once a wave of drowsiness overcame her and she was out.

THE NEXT TIME she woke up, the throbbing in her head was slightly less. And she no longer seemed to have an oxygen mask on. Instead she could feel prongs in her nose belonging to oxygen tubes. She guessed that was progress.

She glanced around. She needed a drink of water desperately. She saw one sitting on the bedside table and reached for it, shocked to see the white bandages on her hands.

What had the nurse said? Had she burned her hands? She recalled opening the front door to her cabin and the heat searing her hands. Tears dripped down her cheeks.

Everything was gone.

At least you're alive. No one was hurt.

The door opened and someone in dark pants and a light green dress shirt walked in. He was carrying a tablet in his hand. A nurse entered behind him.

"Ahh, Miss Ryan, you're awake. Excellent. How are you feeling?"

She blinked at him.

"This is Doctor Reynolds," the nurse explained kindly. "I'm Emily."

She nodded. "My...my cabin?"

The doctor frowned. "I'm sorry. We don't have information about that. I'm sure someone will be in touch about your home. We're just here to assess your physical condition."

The doctor was brisk. Not unkind. But her tender emotions couldn't handle much right now. Tears slid down her cheeks.

"Oh, honey, it's all right. Are you in pain? Is it your hands?" Emily asked, moving closer. She looked to be in her sixties and spoke to her soothingly.

She shook her head. "No pain. Just my throat."

"Smoke inhalation. We need to keep you in a few days to monitor you. Your hands have second-degree burns. I'm afraid they could take a while to heal. You're going to need help when released. Have you got someone who can take care of you?" the doctor asked.

"I...I...my phone was in the cabin."

"Poor thing," Emily sympathized. "We can call someone for you. Husband? Parents?"

She shook her head. "I can't remember his phone number. My boyfriend." She stopped to cough. "Maybe you could call his brother for me."

Archer would be able to get hold of Issy. And maybe Archer would come himself.

"Of course."

"Good. Good," the doctor said. "You're on pain relief for your hands. We'll keep an eye on your oxygen levels. You were lucky, Miss Ryan. Too much smoke inhalation can kill."

Lucky. Yeah, that's how she felt.

EMILY FROWNED.

Her stomach dropped. They'd had to google Archer's name to

find where he worked and call him since she didn't know his private number by heart.

"Is he busy? Not there?"

"His assistant said he couldn't take our call at the moment, but that she would leave him a note. I'm sure he'll call back, dear."

Of course he would. It was Archer.

"Could you also look up the number for Kent Jensen. Or JSI?" she asked. If they couldn't get through to Archer, she'd have to call Issy's boss.

"Right. I have a number here for JSI. Want me to call and ask for Kent Jensen?"

Emily hadn't queried why they weren't calling her family. Maybe she thought she had none. Which was actually pretty accurate.

"Yes, please," she said after a moment. She felt bad about taking up the nurse's time. But she was lost and alone.

Everything was gone.

Emily dialed the number and asked for Kent. "Yes. It's for Caley Ryan." She rattled off a number and hung up. "He's in a meeting."

Disappointment flooded her. But she couldn't expect instant results. What would Issy do when he called and couldn't get hold of her? He'd get mad then worried. She felt so terrible. What was she going to do? Her laptop was gone, although at least everything was saved to the cloud. But everything she had of Dave was gone. All her stuff.

She let out a small sob.

"There, there, honey. Everything will be all right."

She nodded, trying to give Emily a small smile. But she wasn't sure she believed that. Not at all.

∼

THE DOOR to her room opened. She glanced over, wondering if the policeman who'd just visited was back with more questions. She'd explained what had happened, then suffered through a scolding about entering a burning building, before he'd given her a sympathetic smile and left.

She seemed to be getting a lot of those smiles lately.

But it was Emily returning and she had a phone pressed to her ear. She smiled at Caley.

"Here she is. I'll have to hold the phone up to her ear as her hands are bandaged. No, she'll be all right as long as she takes care. Right."

Emily pulled the phone away from her ear.

"Is it Archer?" she asked eagerly.

"No, honey, it's Mr. Jensen. Very intense and demanding young man he is too." Her smile told Caley that she wasn't upset by his manner.

She held the phone up to Caley's ear. "Hello?"

"Hello, Caley?" a masculine voice said warmly. "This is Kent Jensen. How are you?"

"I've been better."

"I heard, sweetheart. Are you in any pain? Are they looking after you all right?"

"Yes, everyone here has been nice. I think I'm on the good painkillers." It was a bit strange to be speaking to a stranger about this, but he seemed nice.

"Good. Sweetheart, I've tried to call Doc and Zander, but their comms are down at the moment. Not sure if Doc told you but Zander is kind of paranoid. We're going to keep trying, but it might be easier for me to send someone to get Doc and I'll come to you. How does that sound?"

"That's not necessary."

"Actually, it is." His voice was firmer this time. "Doc is going to lose his mind when he finds out you're injured and in the hospital. Someone needs to be there to take care of you until he can."

She coughed. He didn't say anything, waiting for her to finish. "I...I really want Doc."

"I know, sweetheart. I'll do my best to get him there as quickly as I can."

"Can you...do you know Archer?"

"Doc's brother? Sure, I know him. Do you want me to call him?"

"My phone is gone. I can't remember his number. We left a message with his assistant, but he hasn't called back yet."

Because he's too busy. You shouldn't bother him.

"I think we have his personal number on file."

"Oh, you know, actually, maybe don't bother—"

"Caley, I'm going to interrupt you. Sorry, sweetheart. But I need to tell you that it's not a bother. And that we need someone with you asap. Considering I'm far closer than Archer, I'm still coming even if he does as well. All right?"

She let out a small sob. "All right."

"And I'm going to send someone to find Doc. I need to send someone expendable in case Zander decides to kill them."

"W-what?"

"Oh, don't worry about that," Kent replied cheerfully. "I'll be there in a few hours. Just rest."

24

"I have blueberry or banana."

Kent Jensen was not a guy who took no for an answer. Nor was he a guy who was afraid of going after what he wanted. That was clear.

He was tall and broad. Handsome. Although not as handsome as Doc or Archer. He'd arrived last night, just before visiting hours were over, but he'd managed to charm the new nurse into letting him stay longer.

He'd booked a hotel room close by and when he'd left, he'd promised to be back early with some breakfast.

He was a man of his word too.

"I'm really not hungry."

"I thought a muffin would be nice and soft on your throat. Now, I'm kind of partial to blueberry myself, but don't let that sway you in your choice."

It also seemed that Kent Jensen had a problem with listening.

He placed both muffins on the tray that rested next to the bed. It contained her untouched breakfast. He lifted the lid and wrinkled his nose at the food underneath. "Don't blame you for not touching that stuff, sweetheart. My Abby would turn up her nose at it too. Now, Abby is fond of blueberry as well."

"Abby is your wife?"

"Ahh, well, I haven't asked her yet. But I plan to." He grinned, warmth filling his face as he talked about his girlfriend. "She wanted to come as well, but I thought that might be too overwhelming for you. Doc said you've been living by yourself for a while."

"Umm, yes." Archer said that most of the men who lived at Sanctuary were Daddy Doms. Did that mean Kent was?

Sympathy filled his face. "I know you must be overwhelmed, sweetheart. I've sent someone to get Doc. Archer should be here soon. When I spoke to him yesterday, he was catching the first flight he could get on. He sounded pretty upset. When he gets here, I'm going to go out and check what's going on with your cabin, all right?"

"You don't have to—"

He gave her a stern look and she pressed her lips together. They were dry and chapped. She wished she had lip balm. She wished she could ask Kent to see if he could find Bumbly and her snuggly. She remembered rescuing them from the fire. But she wasn't sure where they had gone, and she'd been too embarrassed to ask anyone.

"Now, which muffin are you going to eat?" He glanced down at her hands. "Did someone offer to help you eat?"

"Oh yes. But I'm really not hungry." Eating was the last thing she felt like doing.

"The nurses told me you haven't eaten since you were admitted. If you want to get out of here, sweetheart, you need to build up some strength."

"I can't."

He sighed. "All right, but Doc is going to be seriously mad when he gets here and finds out that you haven't been eating. I just want you to know that I'm going to absolutely throw you under the bus."

She gaped at him then she saw the humor in his eyes. "You wouldn't."

"You kidding? I so would. I'm petrified of Doc's temper."

"That makes two of us," someone said from the doorway.

"Archer," she said on a hiccupping sob. She gasped in a breath that started of a coughing fit.

Hell of a welcome.

SHIT. Fuck.

Terror had been his constant companion since he'd received that call from Kent Jensen late yesterday afternoon.

Caley was injured. A fire. In the hospital.

Alone.

She looked so lost and ill. Her face was pale. There were dark smudges under her eyes. She seemed small and helpless.

And he didn't like it. In fact, he fucking hated it.

"Caley, love." He dove forward, helping her sit up so he could lightly pat her back. He glanced over as Kent handed him a glass of water. When she stopped coughing, he eased her back and held the glass up to her lips.

"Easy, poppet. Small sips. That's it."

She sat back and put the glass back. Kent gave him a curious look. But he didn't have time to decipher that. He ran his gaze over Caley, noting her oxygen levels and heartbeat on the monitors.

"How are you feeling, love?"

"I'm all right," she said.

Uh-huh, sure she was.

He ran his fingers through her hair. "Don't lie to me."

She stared up at him then her shoulders slumped. "I've been better."

"Has the doctor been in yet today?"

She shook her head.

"All right, I'll have a chat with him about your care. Your hands got burned in the fire? Are you in pain?"

"No, I'm on some good painkillers, I think."

He bet. Poor darling. "Were you in the house at the time? What happened?" He'd been frantic since receiving the call from Kent. He'd basically just headed to the airport with the clothes on his back, arranging a ticket on his way. He'd arrived too late last night to visit. He'd wanted to be here earlier, but Susan had called with some questions about shifting patients around.

"I don't know. I left to go speak to Dave. To where I scattered his ashes further up the mountain, at this spot he used to like."

He nodded.

"When I started back down, I could smell the smoke then as I grew closer, I could see that the cabin was on fire."

"So you weren't near it? How did you burn your hands?" This didn't make sense.

She glanced at him quickly then away. "Umm."

"Caley," he said warningly. He knew a guilty look when he saw one.

She flicked her gaze up to him then over to Kent. "I'd rather not tell you."

Oh no. That was not going to happen.

"Caley, you're going to tell me. Right. Now."

"Will this come under patient-doctor confidentiality?" she asked, sounding desperate.

He stood there, arms crossed over his chest, his best Dom look on his face. "You're not my patient, poppet. So if you're asking me whether I'm going to keep this secret from Issy the answer is no. And you should know that even if I did agree to that, Issy would get it out of you anyway."

"Issy?" Kent said with some amusement. "I'll remember that. Also, I wouldn't agree to keep that a secret."

"Thank you for coming," Archer told him, reaching across to shake the other man's hand. "I appreciate it."

Kent nodded. "I've got someone tracking down Doc and Zander. Unfortunately, they seem to have moved location."

Archer frowned. "Moved? Without telling you where they were going?"

"Well, it was likely Doc didn't know where they were going."

"Doesn't Zander work for you?"

Kent looked somewhat exasperated. "Zander does what he wants when he wants and somehow, I still pay him." He shook his head. "But he's the best at what he does so I give him a lot of leeway. But I am worried about Doc."

"You think something has happened to him?" Caley asked, looking worried.

Archer sent Kent a look. He better not upset her.

Kent gazed at him rather coolly. "Doc will be fine physically, sweetheart. But he's going to be in an extremely foul mood. Especially as it seems Zander either has his phone and has turned it off, or he's got a jammer that is suppressing any signals. He'll be doubly mad when he finds out what you've been through."

There was something on Kent's face. A warning. Archer felt himself flushing. He knew Kent was wondering why Archer was so protective of Caley. But she was his brother's girl. He was allowed to be. Right?

"Tell me what happened, Caley." Archer turned back to her.

"Okay," she whispered. "When I got down to the cabin, I saw that the back was all on fire. I thought that maybe I could go through the front and get..." she looked over at Kent, "Bumbly."

She spoke so quietly, that he could barely hear her.

"Fuck. Please don't tell me you went back into a burning cabin to get a stuffed toy."

"I...I..."

"Jesus, Caley, what were you thinking? You could have killed yourself! Over a damn stuffed toy! Shit! Of all the—"

"Archer!" Kent said sharply, interrupting him.

He glared over at the other man who nodded at Caley. Who was staring up at him with wide eyes, tears dripping down her face.

"Oh, poppet, I'm sorry." He hadn't meant to upset her. It's just... he could have lost her! She could have died.

She could have died and he wouldn't have told her how he felt about her.

No, you can't lay that on her now. She's vulnerable. Hurting.

"Dave gave me Bumbly," she said. "I know it was stupid. I thought maybe I could get my laptop, but my office is at the back of the cabin. So I...I...grabbed Bumbly and my snuggly and I went out the bedroom window. I burned my hands on the front door. I didn't realize it would be so hot. I'm sorry, I know it was stupid."

Her gaze dropped to her lap and her shoulders shook.

"Way to go," Kent whispered, glaring at him. He reached up to pat her shoulder.

"I got this," Archer told him with a scowl. He sat on the bed, facing Caley. "Look at me. Look at me." He raised her face up with his hand on her chin. "I'm sorry."

Her face was filled with misery. "What for?"

"For getting angry at you. I shouldn't have done that."

"It was stupid to go back in for a toy and a snuggly. It's just that Dave gave them to me and now I don't have anything of his. My train set..." She sobbed.

Oh God, he was such an asshole. Remorse filled him. He was supposed to be better than this. He didn't lose his temper. He was always rational. Calm.

Except when it came to those he cared about most. Isaac. Caley.

"I get it, poppet. It's something I never, ever want you to do again but I know why you did it. And I'm sorry I got so mad."

"You never get mad."

"I do. When someone I care about a lot is in danger or risks themselves or I'm worried about them. But I shouldn't have spoken to you like that. Forgive me?"

She gave him a small smile. "Of course."

He leaned forward and gave her a kiss on the forehead. "Thank you, love. You're far more forgiving than I would have been." He drew back. "I'm guessing your cell phone was in the cabin and that's why you didn't call me straight away?"

She nodded. "I didn't know your number by heart or Issy's. So the nurse called your offices and your assistant took a message and said she'd get you to call back. Then we called JSI and Kent called back."

"I was in a meeting." Kent shot him a look. "What's your excuse for not calling back?"

He felt frozen. Cold. "I never got the message." It could have been a mistake on his assistant's behalf. But he would most definitely be questioning her.

"Thank you for coming," Caley said. "I'm sorry to pull you away from your work. I know you must be busy. I wouldn't have called you but I..."

Her voice cracked and so did his heart.

"Love, what did I tell you about calling me?"

Those hazel eyes stared up at him. "That I can do it for anything."

"And I will always come if you need me. Always. Don't worry about my work. That's my concern. Not yours. Your only worry should be getting better, understand?"

"But what am I going to do? I have nothing, Archer."

He wiped away her tears. "That's not true. You have Issy. You have me. And we're not going anywhere, understand? You're not alone, Caley."

He pressed another kiss to her forehead. His attention was pulled from her as Kent stood. Shit. He'd forgotten the other man was even there.

"Could I speak to you for a moment, Archer?" Jensen asked. It was broached as a question, but he heard the command in it.

"Sure. Be back in a minute, love."

"Caley, I'm going to head up to your cabin. You say you rescued Bumbly and a snuggly? Have you got them? Did anyone give them to you?" Kent asked her.

Caley's face went bright red.

"It's all right, love. Kent is a Daddy Dom. He has a Little of his own."

"I don't know where they are," she told Kent.

"Would you like me to find them for you?" Kent asked gently.

"I...I...yes please."

"I'll see if I can find out whether anyone knows how your cabin caught on fire and where they went. All right?"

She nodded then Archer followed him into the corridor. Jensen turned on him, his gaze assessing.

"She's Doc's girl, yes?"

He stiffened. "Yes, she is. But I care about her."

Jensen studied him for a moment. "Oh, I think you more than care for her."

Archer scowled.

"You love her, don't you?"

"That's none of your business."

Kent grunted. "Does Doc know?"

"No," he told him. "And I'd appreciate it if you didn't tell him."

Kent nodded. "Are you gonna tell him?"

His shoulders slumped. "I don't know. It will make every-thing...complicated."

Kent snorted. "That it will. You know, when you walked in the door her whole face lit up. Haven't seen her with Doc, but I assume she does the same with him?"

"She does. They're good for each other. I'm not here to get between them."

"That's good. Doubt Doc would allow that anyway. Didn't think he'd ever find someone who could, uhh, appreciate his uniqueness."

Archer had to grin at that. "Caley's special."

Kent patted his shoulder. "You're prepared to take care of her, give her what she needs until Doc can be tracked down?"

"I can take care of Caley."

Kent nodded. "She's fragile at the moment. She needs some careful handling."

"I'm a psychiatrist, I think I can handle it."

"Yeah, I don't really think the doctor part is in charge right now. You're acting on emotion."

"Look, I know I shouldn't have gotten mad just now, but she walked into a damned burning building."

"I get it. And when she's feeling better, I'm sure Doc will tan her hide. But right now, that's not what she needs."

"I know. I've got this."

"She hasn't been eating. Doubt she's sleeping much. She's lost everything and Doc isn't around. I'm just trying to look out for her."

"I appreciate that," Archer forced a patient note into his voice. "But you don't know her. I do. Don't worry, I'll take care of her until my brother returns."

"And then what?"

He frowned. "What?"

Kent folded his arms across his chest. "I got some friends who share a girl. Works well for them. Means one of them can always be around to take care of her. Watch over her. Could work well for someone who has experienced loss like Caley has."

"Are you suggesting I should share Caley with Doc?"

Kent shrugged. "You saying you haven't considered it?"

"Yeah, I have. I thought walking away was the best thing. For both of them. But..."

"But you can't stop thinking about her. Wanting her. You should tell them." Kent frowned. "Well, I wouldn't tell Caley right now. She doesn't need to feel torn between you both. But if you told Doc and he was open to the idea..."

He shook his head. He couldn't see it happening. "You don't know about our history. There was a woman...it doesn't matter."

"And so you're prepared to just walk away from her?"

"Shouldn't you be looking out for Doc's best interests?"

"I figure you're already doing that. Maybe it's not Doc's interests or yours that I'm thinking of. Maybe it's hers. She kept asking about you. And when she did manage to get some sleep, it wasn't just Doc she called for." Kent turned and walked away.

Fuck.

25

She could hear the whispers. The giggles. She knew something was wrong. Someone spat at her as she walked past a group of people. Spittle hit her cheek. She reached up and wiped it off.

Shock filled her. This was the town she'd grown up in. She knew everyone here.

"You disgust me! You're filthy!" someone screamed.

She turned, looking in shock at her third-grade teacher. Mrs. Peach was always so nice to everyone. But her face was twisted. Filled with anger. Hate.

Suddenly, Caley knew it wasn't safe for her here. Not at all. She turned and ran. She knew it was cowardly, but if she stuck around then they might all turn on her. Her breath pounded in and out of her lungs as she raced. She heard a thump of footsteps behind her. Someone yelled but she couldn't understand what they were saying.

Oh God! They were chasing her! What happened when they caught her?

Suddenly a car pulled up around the corner in front of her. The passenger door opened.

"Get in!" Dave yelled.

She dove in and he took off before she had a chance to shut the door or put on her seatbelt.

"Turn around. Put your belt on and close the door." *His voice was sharp. He'd never snapped at her before. But with the situation they were in, she couldn't blame him for being snappy.*

"Those bastards." *He glanced around as he drove. She wondered where he was taking them.*

She was trembling. Her stomach clenching tight. She was a mess. She let out a sob.

"What's going on? What happened back there?" *Tears slid down her face.*

"Someone took photos of us in the motel," *he told her.* "They must have a hole in the wall or something. I don't fucking know."

Dave never swore. He was always so calm. Then he slammed his fist into the steering wheel. "I got called into headquarters this morning. They fucking fired me."

"B-because of the photos?"

What would he do? Would he leave and find a job somewhere else? What would she do?

"They said it was because of the DUI the other night, but I'm sure that was only an excuse."

She rubbed her hand over her face. "What will you do?"

"I have to leave. I can't stay here. The sheriff warned me I'll be arrested if I stay."

What? That was insane. How could the sheriff threaten to arrest him? They hadn't done anything wrong. "Caley, I want you to come with me."

Come with him? Leave her home? But was it much of a home? Her parents barely knew she was alive and now it seemed the whole town was out for her blood. She was just spat on and chased.

"I-I don't know." *She hadn't known Dave that long. Could she go away with him?*

"I'm leaving, Caley. You have two hours to decide." *He stopped* outside her parents' house. "I care about you, Caley. What we're doing isn't wrong, but I know that no one here will accept it. If we leave, we'll have to go somewhere more isolated."

She nodded, shaking. He was right.

"Come with me, Caley. I'll take care of you. I have some money saved. You can finally write those books in your head. It will be fun."

It sounded frightening and freeing at the same time. "I'll call you." She climbed out and slowly entered the house. At first, she thought no one else was there. Then she saw movement from the living room. Her mom stood up and turned.

"Mom? I—"

"How dare you!" her mother screeched as she rushed towards her. She swung her arm, slapping her palm against Caley's cheek.

Pain exploded in her face. She stood there in shock, her cheek stinging. Tears filled her eyes. Her mother had never hit her. She'd never even spanked her. In fact, most of the time she barely noticed Caley was alive.

"George! She's here!"

Her father thundered down the stairs. Trembles shook her entire body. What was happening?

"You sick little bitch!" Her father yelled. "How dare you shame this family! I was going to run for mayor and now you've ruined everything. My reputation. My business."

"W-what?" Running for mayor? His business? What was he talking about?

"We're ruined," her mother wailed. "We'll be lucky if anyone talks to us again. I had to turn off my phone because of all the calls about you."

"I never want to see you again. Not in this house. Not this town. Now leave!" Her father's face was mottled. Her mother looked ill. Her father came towards her, his arm raised.

And Caley knew there was only one choice.

She fled.

"Caley!"

Into a burning building. Fire everywhere. Heat. Smoke.

"Love, wake up."

She couldn't breathe.

Issy! Archie! Help!

"Poppet, wake up now!"

She came awake, startled to see Archer leaning over her. Her body was trembling, her lungs burning for air, fear a stench in the air. And there he stood, his face filled with concern.

She lunged at him.

"Hey, hey, easy, love. You're all right. I'm here. Shh. It was just a nightmare. You're safe. I have you. You're safe."

She was always safe with him. With both him and Issy. Issy was like the ocean. He could be turbulent and rocky but with hidden depths. Archer was a calm, still lake. Always there. Steady. Rock solid.

God, she'd missed him.

"Easy, love. You're safe. I'm here." He rubbed his hand up and down her back in long, soothing strokes.

"Sorry. Sorry," she told him.

"Don't be sorry," he replied. "Was your nightmare about the fire?"

"It started off with...with me being run out of Spencerville then it ended with the fire."

He leaned back, sitting on the bed facing her. She wanted to pull him back, to snuggle in where it was safe.

"Are you all right? Did you hurt your hands? Do you need me to get the nurse?"

"No, I'm all right."

He frowned. "No offence, poppet, but you don't look all right to me. Why don't you tell me about the nightmare? Sometimes it helps. It gives our fears less power when we talk about them."

Spoken like a therapist. But maybe he was right. She cleared her throat then told him about the dream.

"And you left that same day?" he asked once she'd told him it all. He was right, she did feel better.

"Yes. Once we moved into the cabin, we didn't often leave. Just when we needed to get supplies and things. It was always just the two of us. And now...the cabin is gone."

"Oh, poppet. I'm sorry for the way your parents and the rest of that town treated you. You know that it isn't a reflection on you but them."

"I-I guess."

He cupped her face between his warm hands. Safety. Security. A feeling of peace came over her.

"I know," he said firmly. "You, Caley Jane Ryan are beautiful inside and out. Your parents should have been proud of the amazing person you are. Instead, they only cared about themselves. They didn't deserve you. Just because people don't understand something doesn't give them the right to judge or hurt others. Not everyone is like that. Not everyone will hurt you."

She took in a shuddering breath. "You're right."

He grinned. "Course I am. I'm always right."

She rolled her eyes. "You sound like Issy."

Something came over his face. Worry pinched at her. "Archer?"

"Hmm?"

"Are you all right? Is it work? Do you need to get back?"

Please don't go.

"What? No. No, poppet. I'm not going anywhere. Not until Issy gets here. I was just talking to him while you were napping. He's on his way."

"Really?" He'd called and she'd missed it?

"He won't be here until tomorrow, apparently he wasn't actually in Colorado. Zander moved them."

Thank God. She'd missed him so much.

"I should have been more careful. Those appliances weren't safe. I kept using them, knowing that. One of them probably started the fire. Destroyed everything."

"Oh, baby. You can't know what started it."

He drew her gently against him. Safety surrounded her. His scent engulfed her. Warmth filled her. Being held by Archer felt so right.

And that was why she forced herself to move back.

"Everything I had of Dave is gone. The train set, the village, the little people. His clothes. All of it, gone." She didn't care about her stuff; it could be replaced. But that train set...she let out a sob.

"But Dave isn't gone, love. He lives in you."

She knew that was true. But she still wished she had more. She still mourned what she'd lost.

"It's okay to feel sad, love. I know it must feel like losing him again. I know this won't bring back what you lost, but did you have insurance?"

"I don't know." She bit her lip, feeling like an idiot. "Dave handled that stuff."

"That's okay. Whatever you need, Issy and I will replace for you. You don't need to worry about money."

She frowned in confusion. "I don't need you guys to buy stuff for me."

"Love, I'm not letting your pride get in your way. You need to replace the things you lost. You need clothes at the very least."

"No, I mean, I have money of my own."

"You might need that money. Let us do this for you. Save your money for a rainy day."

"What the hell would I buy with over a million dollars on a rainy day?"

Archer blinked. "What? I thought you were broke?"

Huh? "Why would you think that?"

"Umm, maybe because you were using appliances that should have been thrown out years ago. Because parts of the cabin were falling down. You had barely any firewood!"

"Oh yeah. Those things."

"Caley," he said warningly.

"You know I'm not always good at practical things. I get side-tracked and forgetful and I find change hard."

He sighed and shook his head. Then he started to laugh. He laughed until tears ran down his cheeks. She loved the sound of his laughter even if she had no idea why he was laughing.

"What's so funny?"

"Sorry, love, just thinking about Issy's reaction once he finds out."

"He won't be mad, will he? I didn't mean to keep it from him." She bit her lip worriedly.

He reached out and freed her tortured lip. She froze, her breath trapped in her lungs as a jolt of heat rushed through her.

She slammed back at the same time as he moved away, looking torn and conflicted.

"Sorry." He cleared his throat. "Issy won't be mad, love. It would be hard for him to be mad at you about anything."

"I know that honesty is important to him."

"It's always important, but maybe more so in a relationship like yours. But this will be fine, so don't worry about it. Now, that wasn't a very long nap. The nurses said you didn't sleep much last night. Every time they checked in on you, the T.V. was on."

If she could read, she would but she couldn't hold anything with her hands, so T.V. it was.

"Is there anything I can do to help you sleep?" he asked with concern.

Issy always gives me an orgasm. She blushed at the thought of saying that to Archer.

His eyebrows rose. "Hmm, I'd like to know that thought."

She shook her head. Nope. He might be able to get most things out of her, but not that.

There was a knock on her door and Kent walked in. She gave him a small smile.

"Hey, Caley. You're looking...not much better than you were this morning." Kent gave her a concerned look. Then he turned to Archer. They seemed to have some sort of silent communication and Archer gave him a nod.

What was that about?

"I've spoken to Doc. He's speeding his way here as we speak, so I'm going to head back to Sanctuary. But I did bring you a few gifts."

He set his bags on her bed and reached into one, pulling out Bumbly.

"Oh!" She cried out, reaching for the toy. He handed it to her, and she unselfconsciously hugged it.

"He was a bit muddy and worse for wear, so I cleaned him up for you. Along with this." He handed her over her snuggly.

Tears filled her eyes, dripping down her cheeks.

"Hey, poppet," Archer told her worriedly. "Don't cry."

He drew closer and she leaned into his chest, letting him hold her. His hand ran through her hair. "Shh, everything will be all right, Caley. I promise. Everything is going to be fine."

"Thinking maybe you might sleep a bit better, now? I know Abby would be lost without Bun-bun," Kent told her.

He spoke so freely about Abby and her Little side. As if it was nothing unusual. And there was always a clear note of affection in his voice. It was obvious he cared about her very much.

"And I also got a few things to tempt you to eat." He drew out a small box filled with donuts. Two cupcakes, also in individual boxes. As well as an assortment of deli sandwiches. Then he pulled out a chocolate milk and a strawberry milk.

"At least there's one healthy thing in there," Archer grumbled, looking over the assortment.

"The sandwiches are for you, man." Kent winked at her.

"Are you trying to put her into a sugar coma?"

"Just trying to tempt her to eat. I made sure everything was soft for her throat."

Archer turned to her, giving her a concerned glance. "What would you like to start with, love?"

She really wasn't hungry. More than that, she wasn't really comfortable with one of them helping her eat.

"Oh, and I got straws for the milk. Metal ones. Environmentally friendly."

That surprised a smile out of her. "Chocolate milk."

"Okay." Archer reached for the chocolate milk, opening it and putting the straw in. Then he held the straw up to her mouth. She took a long sip, letting out a small sigh of pleasure as it soothed her throat.

Yummy.

Some dribbled down her chin, as she drank too quickly. Mortification filled her. But Archer just calmly reached for the napkin and wiped her face clean.

"All right. What do you want to start with?" He looked down at the food skeptically. "Not sure I would call most of this actual food. Sugar, additives, and fat."

Kent rolled his eyes. "How about a donut, sweetheart? I'm partial to the jam-filled ones."

She looked at the donuts. "I'm all right." But that one with sprinkles and pink icing did look awfully nice.

There was a beat of silence and she glanced up to find Kent staring at Archer.

"How about this one, love?" Archer reached over and tore a piece off the one she'd been looking at. He held it to her lips.

She blushed, feeling shy.

"You don't eat it and I'll have to," Kent patted his tummy. "Then I'll have to go home and explain to Abby why I've got sprinkles and pink icing all over my shirt."

She had to smile at the image of the big, tough man covered in sprinkles and pink icing.

She opened her mouth and Archer popped the piece of donut into it. He fed her a couple more bites while the two men talked as though there was nothing out of the ordinary about one of them having to feed her. When she'd had enough, she lay back tiredly.

"Why don't you rest, love?" Archer asked her. He walked to the sink along one wall and wet a cloth then he came back and gently washed her face.

Ooh, that felt really nice. She hadn't been able to shower. The nurse had offered to help her shower, but she felt a bit weird about that.

Issy would be here soon. He'd help her.

God, she missed him.

She wrapped her arms awkwardly around Bumbly. She felt her snuggly being pressed to her face.

"I'm just going to say goodbye to Kent then I'll be back, okay?"

Anxiety filled her at the idea of being alone but she nodded. "Okay."

ARCHER WALKED out of the room behind his brother's boss. Kent turned to him as he shut the door.

Kent frowned in concern. "She's okay?"

Archer shook his head. "It's going to take her a while to recover."

Kent nodded. "The fire marshal is looking into the fire. But might take a while until they figure it out. You'll call me if you need anything."

It wasn't a question.

"Thank you for everything. I'm sure I'll see you again some-time." When he visited Caley and Issy. God, how was he going to do that?

"Oh, I'm sure of that. You know, I could use someone with your skills working for me."

He raised his eyebrows. "You need a psychiatrist?"

"For everyone on the ranch. Have you ever thought of targeting your services to people in the lifestyle? A lot need some help, yet don't want to go to a vanilla therapist. So to speak."

It had been something he'd toyed with.

"Anyway, give it a thought. The offer is there."

"I can't move to Sanctuary."

"Why?"

"Well...it's in the middle of nowhere. I prefer the city."

Kent rubbed his chin with his finger. "Ahh, that's the excuse you're going with."

"It's not an excuse."

"No? Is that really the reason? Or is it because you can't be around Caley without letting your feelings for her show?"

"Do you blame me? How torturous do you think it would be to see them every day? To always want what I can't have?"

"And I'm telling you maybe you can have it. If you're brave enough to ask."

"It wouldn't work. Even if Issy and Caley agreed to that, I'm not...I can't give her what she needs."

"What? A man that loves and adores her? That would do anything for her?"

"I'm not a Daddy Dom," he hissed.

Kent grinned. "You're not? Huh, that's not what I've seen."

"What are you talking about?" Archer asked, confused.

"You don't have to label it. But I think you could definitely give her what she needs." He patted Archer's back. "Good luck, man. Look after her."

Like he'd do anything else.

HER NIGHTMARE WOKE HIM. Not that he'd really been asleep. Just dozing in an armchair next to her bed. The nurses had tried to get rid of him, but he'd charmed them into letting him stay.

Like he was going to leave her.

She whimpered, her head thrashing back and forth. Shit. Poor darling. No wonder she didn't want to sleep. Every time she drifted off, she had a nightmare.

"Easy, love. You're safe."

She didn't react to his words. In fact, her whimpers grew louder. He got out of the chair and sat next to her, clasping hold of her upper arm.

"Poppet, I'm here. You're safe."

"Issy. Daddy."

Maybe she didn't want him. Maybe she needed Issy. And only Issy.

Self-doubt ate at him.

"Archer!"

His eyes widened at the sound of his name coming from her lips. He leaned in, mindful of her hands.

"I'm here, poppet. You're safe."

Another whimper, quieter though. Working on instinct, he carefully moved her over then lay next to her on the bed, gathering her close. He'd be in trouble if he was caught by one of the nurses. But he'd do whatever it took to help her.

Immediately, he felt the tension in her ease.

"You're safe, baby girl. My gorgeous little poppet. Your smile like sunshine. You've brought color to my cold world, did you know that? Thought I was happy with my life until you tripped your way into it."

"Archer," she said on a breath. He knew she was still sleeping, but it was like she could hear him.

"I made a big mistake, poppet. Walking away without at least trying to fight for you." He sighed. But there was a lot to think about. "I love you, darling girl. All of me loves you. I'll give you whatever you need. How you need it. What I can't do is stay away from you indefinitely. I nearly lost you." She let out a quiet noise. "Hush. You're safe. I'm watching over you."

Another small whimper. He leaned in, his mouth against her ear.

"Daddy's here, poppet." No, that wasn't quite right. He wasn't Daddy. "You're safe. Papa won't let anyone hurt you."

She fully relaxed, slipping into a big sleep. And a feeling of rightness came over him. Maybe he couldn't be exactly what Issy was to her. But he'd have his own part in her life.

If Issy didn't kill him, that is.

DOC RACED INTO THE HOSPITAL, his heart pounding.

She was hurt. There had been a fire.

He hadn't been there.

Guilt was flaying him along with the terror. He hadn't been there, and she'd gotten hurt. Damn Zander anyway. The asshole had a jammer that had prevented him from using his phone.

He should have just left him.

He'd been gone less than four days. He didn't think anything would happen in that time.

He'd been wrong.

He was never leaving her again. She was far too precious to him. He ignored a warning from a nurse to slow down and moved to the room number he'd been given, opening the door.

And he froze at the sight that greeted him.

He knew Archer was with her. It was the only thing that had kept him sane. When he'd talked to Archer, she'd been sleeping, but Archer had given him the lowdown. Her cabin had caught on fire, it and everything in it was completely gone. She'd run into a burning fucking building to grab a damn toy. He'd sworn long and loudly upon hearing that.

Archer had to calm him down, reminding him that she hadn't been thinking rationally. That she'd lost everything.

She was in the hospital with second-degree burns to her hands and suffering from smoke inhalation. If she had someone to take care of her, they would likely release her tomorrow.

Well, he'd see to that. She was coming home with him and she'd be lucky if she wasn't grounded until she was fifty.

Later. That could all come later. Once he'd ensured her health.

But none of that was what made him pause in the doorway. He was struck still as Archer wiped Caley's face gently with a napkin. Then he picked up a sandwich, feeding her.

It was an innocent gesture. There was nothing untoward about any of it. But there was something so intimate in the way they stared at each other.

Doc studied his brother, noticed the soft smile on his face. Then he looked to Caley. She stared up at Archer, happiness radiating from her.

He frowned. Something stirred inside him. Jealousy? Suspicion?

"What's going on here?"

26

She started choking on the sandwich that Archer had just fed her. He ended up leaning her forward and patting her back.

"Spit it out, love. Spit it out!" He held his hand cupped under her mouth.

Eww. Gross.

"Caley, spit. Now."

She spat it out, her nose wrinkling in disgust. Archer didn't look as though it bothered him in the slightest. He just grabbed a napkin and wiped up the mess.

"Issy. Why did you have to yell like that? This is a hospital. She's recovering." Archer turned to glare at his brother.

Issy was here.

She smiled as she turned to look at him. Then she saw something hard on his face. Her smile dropped. Why was he so upset? Was it something she'd done? But how?

Did he not want her anymore?

Panic flooded her. Archer turned to her; his eyes filled with concern. "Don't worry, love. He's not angry at you."

"Don't call her that." Issy stepped forward, his hands curled into fists. "How long?"

"What?" she asked. "How long what?"

"Hush, love," Archer said quietly. "He's not talking to you."

Archer had been her rock since he arrived. He'd cajoled her into eating. Kept her entertained. Cheered her up when she'd fallen apart. She didn't know what she would have done without him. And she didn't understand why Issy was so angry.

"How long have you wanted her?"

She gasped in a breath. "Issy, what are you talking about?"

"Love, I told you to hush." Archer's voice was firmer this time. A hint of steel.

"Don't give her orders. She's not yours."

"I know she's not mine," Archer said in a low voice. "Issy, think before you say anything more."

"Think? Think about what? Are you trying to take her from me? Like Evelyn?"

"That's not fair. You know I had no interest in Evelyn. She fixated on me. And nothing has happened between me and Caley. And before you say another word, you might want to remember that your submissive is injured and in a very vulnerable place right now. You might also remember that you promised we wouldn't argue in front of her."

They both turned to look at her and that was when Issy's blurry image softened.

"Baby doll, don't cry. I'm not upset with you."

"I...I don't u-understand why you're m-mad. Archer's been here, t-taking care of me. I...there's...he's not..." A sob broke free and Issy strode forward. He carefully drew her into his arms, rocking her back and forth.

He spoke to her in a quiet, reassuring voice. "I'm sorry, baby doll. Shh, hush now before you make yourself ill. I'm so sorry I gave you a fright."

She drew back and looked up at him. "I've missed you so much. I'm glad you're here. I love you, Issy."

He drew in a sharp breath but before he could say anything, she continued on. "You don't have to say it back. But I realize now that I can continue to live my life, scared of what might happen, hiding away, keeping myself safe or I can actually be brave, take a risk and find true happiness. Even though I'm scared something will happen and I'll lose you, I know that I would forever regret it if I didn't tell you how I feel. If I didn't take a chance. I'd take a few weeks of happiness with you over a lifetime of loneliness without you."

"Baby doll, fuck, I love you too." He cupped her face between his hands. "I have never been so terrified as I was when I found out that you'd been injured. You are everything. And I plan on having forever with you, but even if I don't, know that every moment I spend with you is the happiest of my life."

He kissed her. It was soft, gentle and exactly what she needed. When he drew back, he wiped the tears off her cheeks. "I should have been there, I'm so sorry I wasn't. That's never going to happen again, because you're going to be grounded until you're fifty."

"Grounded, why?"

"For running back into a burning fucking building and taking thirty years off my life."

"Oh, that."

"Oh, that," he repeated. "But we'll talk about that later. Just suffice to say that I am not letting you out of my sight for a long time. How are you feeling? You look tired and as though you've lost weight."

"I'm all right. Archer has been looking after me." She glanced around, worry filling her. "Where is he? Where did he go?"

"He left soon after I pulled you in for a hug," he told her calmly.

"Issy, I don't understand why you were so angry at him. What did you mean about how he wants me? Archer doesn't feel anything towards me."

Doc wiped his hand over his face. He was tired, hungry, he'd spent the last few days thinking about his girl, wanting to be with her, torn with his need to do his job and be with the woman he loved. So when he'd stormed into the hospital room and seen his brother leaning over his girl, the look on his face one of love and worship...

Well, yeah, he'd lost it.

Fucking idiot.

"Issy? You don't think that I...that Archer and I..."

"Baby doll, of course I don't think that. I wasn't thinking...I've been frantic these past twelve hours, trying to get to you, worried about you. I hate that I wasn't here for you. Taking care of you. I'm angry at myself about that."

"But why? You had to leave. You had to go help Zander and you couldn't have known something would happen."

"I left you in a cabin on your own, with no one around for miles, in a house that was damn well falling down around you." He shook his head, berating himself.

"Issy, you couldn't have known there would be a fire. I've lived there for years on my own."

"Yeah, but you weren't mine then. Christ, I'm not sure how I'm going to let you out of my sight from now on."

"I'm fine. I'll be all right." She licked her lips. "Is that offer to, uhh, to move in with you, is that still, uhh..."

He interrupted her awkward question by putting his hand gently over her mouth. "You're moving into my cabin on Sanctuary Ranch. No buts. No arguments."

He removed his hand as tears welled in her eyes. "That's good.

Since I now seem to be homeless." Her eyes widened. "Not that that is the reason I want to move in with you. I'd already made my mind up that I wanted to come with you to Sanctuary, especially after talking to Archer and—"

"What has my brother got to do with this?"

"Oh, we had a talk, before I left the cabin to say goodbye to Dave, where Dave's ashes are. That's where I was when the cabin went on fire..."

"Wait, baby, calm down. Why don't you start from the beginning, tell me everything?"

He was silent as she went through everything. The new appliances arriving, her talk with Archer, her trip to say goodbye to Dave, the fire, trying to get hold of him and Archer. Then Kent and Archer arriving.

He sighed. Fuck. He owed his brother a big apology. "I need to talk to Archer."

She nodded. "He's been taking good care of me. Coaxing me into eating and sleeping."

His gaze narrowed. "You haven't been doing either of those?"

She shrugged. "Hard to eat with my hands bandaged. Plus, I haven't had much appetite. I lost all my stuff, Issy. Everything I had of Dave's."

"I know, baby doll. I know there were things that are irreplaceable and I'm sorry you lost them. But what's really important is that you're all right."

She sniffled, nodding. He drew her close, rocking her back and forth. "Everything is okay, baby doll. I'm here. I'll take good care of you."

"You owe Archer an apology. All he's done is been here for me. He's a good brother."

Issy nodded. He agreed. He'd been an ass to think Archer would ever make a play for Caley. He trusted his brother.

He'd make it up to him. He just hoped Archer understood.

ISAAC WALKED out of her room fifteen minutes later, telling her he was going to go find something for her to eat. He didn't like how drawn she was.

He was reaching for his phone as soon as the door to her room shut behind him. He found his brother's name and called him.

"I'm in the waiting room on this floor. It's empty," Archer greeted him.

He hung up without a word and headed down to the waiting room. He walked in and looked over at his brother, freezing in shock.

Archer looked...defeated.

He'd never seen him like that. His older brother might be a pain in his ass at times, but he was always a calm in the middle of a storm.

A rock.

"I'm sorry for the way I reacted," Isaac told him. He felt ashamed of his behavior. Archer had been here taking care of his girl and he'd jumped down his throat. All because of his own insecurities.

Archer let out a humorless bark of laughter. "Don't. Don't apologize when it's me that should say sorry to you."

"Why? Look, I'm tired, hungry and stressed. I read something into what I saw that I shouldn't have. I know you didn't want Evelyn's attention and I know —"

"I love her, Issy."

Doc took a step back, feeling like he'd been sucker-punched. He what?

"She doesn't know any of this, so don't blame her. But I can't keep quiet. I love Caley. I think I have since the moment she asked me those ridiculous questions about whether I was a serial killer.

Or at least that was the start of it. I didn't mean to. God, my life would be so much easier if I didn't feel this way."

Issy gaped at him, barely able to breathe. This was not the conversation he'd thought he would have. "You never said anything."

Archer grimaced. "Because I thought I could leave without it hurting. I was fucking wrong. It hurts every fucking day I'm away from her. I didn't think I could give her what she needs. What you can give her. I thought you were better for her."

"And now you don't think that?" Was he going to try to take her?

"No. God, no. Issy, I don't want to take her from you. I don't think I could. She loves you."

"Then what the fuck do you want?" Issy demanded.

Archer ran his hand over his face. "I nearly lost her, Issy. We nearly did. I can't live my life without at least knowing that I tried to...that I did everything possible to..."

"Archer, fucking tell me."

"I want to share her."

Doc stared at him. A million emotions ran through him and he struggled to grab onto one. The one he managed to grasp hold of probably wasn't the best one.

Anger.

"Share her? Share her? She's not some freaking toy you pass around, Archer!"

Archer flinched. "I know that. I would never disrespect her like that."

"You think this is respectful?"

"It is if it's what she needs, Issy. What she desires. What if what she wants is both of us? Are you going to deny her that? Do you really find it so objectionable to share her with me?"

What she wanted?

"Have you talked to her about this?"

"No. Of course not. She's not in a position to hear this. She needs time to heal, to get over the loss of her home."

"Then you're going to leave now. And we're both going to forget you ever said this."

Archer flinched. "Issy—"

"Don't call me that. Leave, Archer. And just don't call me for a while." He turned away.

"I'll leave, but I'm not giving up."

Doc winced. He didn't turn. "She won't go for this unless I'm okay with it. And I'm not okay with it."

He stormed away.

ARCHER STARED at the door for a few beats. That could have gone better. He sighed, and ran his hand over his face. He could have chosen a better time. A better way.

Fuck.

Now, Issy was going to dig his heels in. What if he poisoned Caley against Archer?

No. He wouldn't do that. This might be a shock, but he knew his brother. He tended to react first and think after. He'd think about this. And hopefully, he'd realize this was what was right for all of them.

Archer would give him time, much as it killed him. But while he was doing that, he'd get the ball rolling in other areas.

Because he wasn't giving her up.

He took out his phone and found the number he'd put in there.

"Hello?"

"Hello, Kent? It's Archer Miller. About that job offer..."

27

Caley looked out the windshield at the cute cabin. It was surprisingly pretty. It had a small porch out the front, but she knew from Doc's description that there was a larger one out the back. It was bigger than she'd thought it would be considering she knew it only had two bedrooms. She knew he had a clinic at the main JSI headquarters which was a few minutes' walk away. The drive here had been picturesque. There were cabins dotted through the trees, most down on the flat but some further up the mountain where JSI headquarters were.

So, this was home.

She'd been discharged from the hospital this morning. Thank God. She hadn't thought she could stand another night in there. Issy had seemed just as eager to get home as she was to leave. She'd thought about asking to go up to see the remains of her cabin, but she wasn't ready to face that yet.

He'd bundled her into the car. She was surrounded by pillows to cushion her hands and to allow her to nap. And she'd actually managed to have a small one.

"What do you think?" he asked as he stopped his truck. Kent had arranged for it to be delivered to him.

A pang of sadness filled her as she thought of Archer, she didn't understand why he'd left without saying goodbye. Issy had told her he had to get back to work. Which was likely true, but he couldn't have taken a few minutes to say bye? And since he'd left, Issy had been acting odd. Withdrawn. Quiet.

She hoped he wasn't regretting letting her move in with him. Worry churned in her gut.

"It's really cute."

"You sound so surprised."

She was. He didn't seem the type to care about where he lived. But then again, he was a neat freak, so it was no wonder everything looked spotless. How quickly would she drive him nuts with her messiness?

Self-doubt was really killing her. She could barely do anything for herself with her hands bandaged. Nightmares were tearing up her sleep. And she felt kind of bereft, lost. Maybe it was just because she was missing work.

"Of course not." She gave him a bright smile. He didn't look like he bought any of it.

She wondered what she was going to do about clothes. She could buy some stuff online, but she couldn't use her computer yet. Not that she had one. She sighed sadly.

"Hey, what's wrong? You don't like the cabin?" He reached over and grasped hold of her chin gently turning her face to him. "You don't want to live here?"

"No, the cabin looks lovely. Far nicer than mine."

"You're worried about moving in here? With me?" There was something vulnerable in his voice that she wasn't used to.

"No," she said firmly. "I want to live here, with you. I'm just..." *Just tell him, Caley.* "Do you regret it? Offering me a place to live? If it's too soon, I can find somewhere else, somewhere close by. You don't have to do this just because I have nowhere to live. And I'm injured."

His eyes had grown wider with each sentence. "What the hell? What nonsense are you spouting? I asked you to move in with me before I left, remember? This has nothing to do with the fire. What part of 'I love you and I'm not letting you out of my sight' did not compute with you?"

"It's just...I guess you've seemed a bit quiet since Archer left. And I was worried..."

"That I'd changed my mind?"

She nodded.

"I have not."

I have not? That was it? She gave him an exasperated look.

"Baby doll, you are mine. You're staying mine. End of story."

"But what if I annoy you? I'm not easy to live with. I'm messy and I spend a lot of time in my own head, I don't always notice what's going on around me and I—"

"Baby doll, I know all this. I've lived with you."

"Only for a short time."

"Nobody is perfect. We both have flaws. I'm a neat freak."

"And bossy."

"That too."

"And blunt, anti-social, temperamental—"

"Okay, you need to stop now before you talk yourself out of living with me," he grumbled.

That wasn't going to happen but she nodded.

"I'm sorry I've been quiet and withdrawn. I've had stuff on my mind."

"Archer?" she guessed.

"Yeah, that's some of it."

"Will you tell me what happened?"

He sighed. "Can you give me a while? I'll tell you eventually. I just need to process it all."

She nodded. She could do that.

"All right, let's get you inside and into bed."

"Nooo, I don't want to go to bed. I've spent days in bed." She pouted.

"Because you're injured and recovering. Wait there for me."

He walked around to the passenger side and reaching in, undid her belt, pulling her out into his arms.

"I can walk. It's my hands that are injured."

"Are you forgetting about your ankle?"

"It was just a twist; it's not even swollen anymore."

He just grunted and carried her inside. To her surprise, the door was unlocked. But then she guessed security wasn't much of an issue around here. They walked straight into the cozy living room, where the fireplace was already lit and crackling away. The fireplace had built-ins on either side, half-filled with books. There was a rug on the floor and a sectional in front of the fireplace. Mounted up high was a large T.V. The kitchen was towards the back of the room, making a big, open-plan area. It was warm and inviting. But that wasn't what caught her attention.

Across the beams of the ceiling was a large banner that read,

Welcome Home, Caley

It looked like it had been hand-painted. There were also pictures of flowers, hearts and stars. And a big heaping of glitter scattered on top.

"Looks like the Littles have been busy," Doc commented, walking to the sofa and setting her on it. "You can stay up for a while before you go down for a nap."

"That was so kind of them."

Doc grunted, looking at the floor. "And seems they left a trail of glitter in their wake. Gonna need the vacuum cleaner."

She bit back a smile at his grumbling, knowing it was hot air without any real heat behind it. He walked towards the small, circular table set between the living and kitchen area. It had a series of gift-wrapped items.

"What are those? It's not your birthday, is it?"

"No. These are all for you." He pulled out his phone as it buzzed. "It's Kent. He says everyone wanted to replace some of what you lost in the fire. He forced them to leave all the gifts here because he thought you might be overwhelmed by their presence here when you got home."

That was thoughtful. And kind. From Kent and all the Littles. She didn't even know how many there were or their names, other than Abby.

But she was going to have to learn sometime. And they'd already shown that they were incredibly kind. She'd never had someone do something like this for her. Not even on her birthday. And she didn't even know them.

You're going to need to be brave.

"Tell him they can come over."

He eyed her. "You sure? They're all very kind and caring, sometimes a bit bratty but I don't want you to feel overwhelmed or pressured."

"I don't. I won't." She tried to brush her hand through her hair. "I probably look like a fright though. I haven't had a shower in days. What if I stink? Is there a mirror somewhere?"

He walked over and crouched down beside her. Then he kissed her forehead. "You look beautiful as always. You don't need to do anything. They're going to love you the way you are. Remember, I would never allow anyone to harm you. In any way."

She stared into his firm gaze.

"All right. I'll tell them they can come over and give you their gifts but only for an hour. You need a nap."

She sighed. He could go from sweet to bossy in two seconds flat.

But she kind of liked it.

However, she'd never tell him that.

28

"Oh, you poor thing," Abby said, sitting next to her on the sofa and staring down at her bandaged hands.

She and Kent had arrived soon after Issy texted Kent back. They'd been the first to get there. And Abby was just as sweet as she'd imagined. They were followed quickly by Ellie and her husband, Bear. He was as quiet as his wife was bubbly. Then Zeke had pushed in his girlfriend, Eden who was in a wheelchair. She was also Kent's sister.

Clint and Charlie, Kent's brother and his fiancée, had come with them. Last had been Macca and Gigi, who had the most gorgeous accent.

Now all the men were in the kitchen area talking quietly while all the women had gathered around her.

"I'm all right. It doesn't hurt too much. And they will probably heal up in another week or so."

"But you can't even open your presents," Ellie said, sitting down on her other side. "I'll have to help you."

Eden rolled her eyes. "Like that's a hardship. Ellie loves to open gifts."

"Who doesn't?" Gigi said with a smile.

"Ari says she wishes she could be here, but she and Bain had to go to New York to meet with her record label," Abby told her.

"She's amazing. She hasn't lived here long, but she's so kind and lovely," Ellie told her.

The door opened and she turned her head to see a dark-haired woman bounce in, followed by a big, fierce-looking man.

"Sorry we're late. I was finishing up some editing."

Caley knew that voice. She'd spoken to her several times but never seen her in person.

"Daisy?" she asked.

The woman paused and so did the man behind her, looking her up and down, assessing.

"Yes?" Daisy asked warily. "Do I know you?"

"I'm Caley."

"Yes." She still looked puzzled.

Caley blushed. Idiot. "You know me as CJ?" She made it into a question in case she was wrong.

"CJ?" Daisy squealed. "Oh my God! How did I not know it was you? Why did Doc not tell us!"

"Tell you what?" Issy asked, coming over.

"That she's CJ Bennett!" Daisy said. "I would have come to the hospital if I'd known. Oh, CJ your house. All your stuff. Your laptop!"

Tears started to roll down Daisy's face and a comically horrified look filled the face of the man behind her, who could only be Jed.

"You're CJ Bennett!" Gigi gaped at her. "I love your books so much."

"Wait, you've read her books?" Issy asked. "That's your pen name?"

She nodded, embarrassed.

Daisy moved away from Jed who had been hugging and talking to her quietly. Abby moved over and she sat next to Caley.

"Of course!" Gigi answered. "You mean, you haven't?"

"I haven't been allowed to yet," Issy said dryly. "And she's never told me the name she writes under."

She blushed slightly.

"They're amazing books," Gigi said.

Caley shook her head, looking over to Daisy. "I should have put it all together. I knew when Issy mentioned JSI that I'd heard of it before. I don't think you ever mentioned the name of the ranch you lived on and it just didn't click. I can't believe you live here."

"And now so do you! Imagine what we can get done together."

"Get done?" Issy asked.

"Issy?" Jed asked, his lips twitched.

Issy glared at him. She looked up at him, worried that she'd messed up by calling him that. But he must have caught her thought because his face softened.

"I'm CJ's editor," Daisy explained.

"Caley," she said softly. "Call me Caley."

Daisy sniffled. "Oh, Caley, I'm so sorry about your home."

"It's all right," Caley said, looking out at them all, feeling more at ease than she'd have thought possible considering they were a room full of strangers who knew her deepest secret. "It seems I have a new home."

I WANT TO SHARE HER.

Fuck Archer. Just fuck him. How could he just lay that on him? Share her? Was he fucking kidding? Why would Issy do that?

Except maybe...maybe this wasn't about him. His brother was

miserable. That was easy to see. Issy had the girl. He could keep Archer from her.

Except what did Caley want?

Issy glanced over at Caley to check on her. She looked pale and tired. But there was a smile on her face. And there was a lightness to her that he hadn't seen before. He knew then that this was the right move. For too long, she'd been on her own. She needed people around her that cared. That would look after her if anything ever happened to him. He never wanted her to be on her own again.

"She looks better than she did," Kent commented to him.

Only Daisy, Jed, Clint, Charlie, Kent and Abby were left, the others having gone once the presents were opened. He could tell by the shocked look on Caley's face that she hadn't imagined anyone doing something like this for her. She was now surrounded by a pile of gifts, from soft blankets to bumblebee slippers to fuzzy socks.

He was going to have to figure out how to spoil her.

Better but not great. He knew she was hurt by the way Archer just left. And he couldn't tell her that was his fault. That he'd snapped at his brother and told him to fuck off.

Christ. What had he done?

"Half expected Archer to be here with you."

"Why is that?" he asked, stiffening.

Kent took a sip of the beer he'd helped himself to from his fridge. "Offered him a job."

He spun to gape at his boss. "You did? Why? Why would you need a shrink?"

Kent looked around then nodded to the back porch. "Come talk out here."

Doc glanced over at Caley. Kent turned to his brother. "Clint, watch Caley, will ya?"

"Why? What trouble can she possibly get up to when she's bundled up in a blanket with both her hands bandaged?"

Kent just stared at him.

"Yeah, okay," Clint replied. "Clint's Little-sitting service is here."

Doc rolled his eyes at Clint's grumbling. Truth was, the big guy watched over and protected everyone on this ranch. Whether they wanted his help or not.

Doc walked out with Kent. "Well? Why'd you offer Archer a job?"

"Is that so bad? Are you not getting along with him again?"

He ground his teeth together, looking out at the woods. "He loves Caley."

"Told you, did he?"

Doc swung back to him. "You know?"

"It's pretty damn obvious. I think the only one who doesn't know is Caley."

"So you knew he loved her, and you offered him a job? Have I done something to piss you off?"

"Pretty much daily. And yet I still care about you. Which is why I'm going to tell you this, don't let your pride get in your way of happiness. Yours, your brother's, but most importantly, Caley's."

"What the hell are you saying?"

"Archer loves Caley. You love Caley. You and Archer love each other. So..."

"You think we should share her?" he asked. Had everyone around him taken fucking crazy pills?

"Is that so crazy? I know several ménage couples. Hell, Bain was telling me that Ari's three best friends are looking for a woman to share and there's three of them."

"Yes...but...what..." He tried to speak. To protest. To tell Kent he was way off base.

But what if he wasn't?

"You left something out."

"What's that?" Kent took another sip of beer, looking completely relaxed.

"How Caley feels about Archer."

"So I did." Kent turned towards him. "How do you think she feels about Archer?"

Unease churned in his gut.

"Look, I shouldn't be interfering. This isn't my relationship. It's just...I love you, man. I don't want to see you throw something away that could work. I don't want you to lose your brother just when you've found him again. What if you could have your girl and your brother in your life? A permanent ménage ain't for everyone and I'm not saying it will be easy, but it could also mean that one of you was always watching over your girl, there to see to her needs, giving her twice as much love and affection. Your brother loves her, he'd be there for her no matter what. And for someone who has lost as much as she has, well, she deserves as much love as possible, don't you think?"

29

Hours later, as he helped Caley into the bath, Kent's words were still plaguing him.

The bastard.

After everyone had gone, he'd put Caley down for a nap and tidied everything up. And he'd discovered there was one gift that hadn't been opened. It had been lost under a pile of wrapping paper. But he'd recognized the handwriting on the card.

Knowing he shouldn't, he'd opened it.

Dear Caley,

I know everything probably feels overwhelming and you might feel a bit lost. But remember, Issy makes a good rock. He'll stand in the storm. He'll be your strength. If you ever need me, call. Here's something to help you feel more normal.

Archer

THAT BASTARD.

Doc could only imagine how much pain he had to be in.

Loving her and so far away from her. And he was still backing him up. Doing what was best for everyone else.

But was Archer being away from them what was best for her? Hell, was it even best for him?

Could you share her? If it was what she wanted?

Fuck. Back in the cabin, he'd liked it being the three of them. Liked having Archer to bounce things off.

If Archer had been there when Doc had to leave, the cabin would never have gone on fire.

He groaned. Christ. Was he really considering this?

"Daddy?"

"Yes, baby doll?" he asked.

After her nap, Caley had woken up in pain and a bit grouchy, which was unlike her. So he'd settled her in the living room watching a cartoon with a glass of chocolate milk with a straw and had tried to coax her to eat. He'd ended up having to get strict with her, then had felt terrible as she'd started to sniffle.

He had to tread carefully. Still, he couldn't let her get away with not letting him take care of her. She needed plenty of sleep and good nutrition to get better. And once she started feeling better, he had no doubt she'd get frustrated by her bandages and restriction.

Then he'd have to get firmer with her.

He had wrapped her hands in plastic bags, not wanting her to get the bandages accidentally wet. He ran a cloth over her chest and those pretty breasts with her peach-colored nipples.

Easy, man.

She's not up to that yet.

"Are you okay?" she asked worriedly.

Crap. He'd kind of zoned out on her again.

"Just working through that problem."

"With Archie?"

"Yeah." He washed down her tummy. "Why don't you lie back?"

"My hair will get wet."

"I'll wash it for you." He helped her lie back then he moved to wash her legs.

"I thought we might have heard from him." There was a sad note in her voice and he instantly felt like an asshole. What if Kent was right? What if she needed Archer too? Could he deny her anything that she needed?

Short answer was no.

But he still wanted to think on this for a bit. There wasn't just the logistics of this sort of relationship. There was the fact that Archer lived in a different city. He couldn't imagine his brother living here, with them.

And he couldn't imagine living anywhere else.

He sat her back up and grabbed a cup to wet her hair.

"I was spoiled today."

He turned her face around, so she was looking at him. "If anyone deserves it, baby doll, it's you."

She gave him a small smile. "I didn't think I would ever have this again. A feeling of being home. Of being loved."

He lightly kissed her lips. "Welcome home, Caley. We're gonna make lots of happy memories here."

"I know."

He finished washing her hair then lifted her out of the bath and quickly dried her off. He rubbed the towel through her hair.

He grabbed some clean panties. They were a pale pink with clouds on them. A gift. He felt bad that he hadn't thought to buy her anything before they left Bozeman. Although he had ordered a few things online for her last night while he was trying to sleep in that uncomfortable hospital chair. The nurses had tried to kick him out, but there had been no way he was leaving her.

He took note of the way she was pressing her legs together. She hadn't been to the bathroom much today. The nurse had helped her first thing this morning then he'd helped her while they'd been waiting for everyone to arrive. And that was only because he'd made her go.

Poor baby, he knew it had to be hard to let others help her, but she shouldn't hold it in. It wasn't healthy.

"You need the potty, baby doll?"

"Yes," she whispered. "But I can do it myself."

He eyed her hands which were still thickly bandaged. "Not until those hands heal a bit more."

Her cheeks were flushed.

"Baby doll, you don't have to be embarrassed. It's my privilege to help you. This is what I thrive on, taking care of you. I need it."

She stared at him then sighed. "It's just embarrassing."

"You can't hold it, baby doll. You'll give yourself a UTI." He frowned. "This isn't why you're hardly eating, is it?"

She looked away guiltily.

Right. Enough of that.

"Caley, you cannot refuse to eat because you don't want help to go to the bathroom. I cannot allow that." He kept his tone kind but firm. He grasped hold of her chin raising her face. "Do you need me to take more control?"

"I don't...I don't know. I still feel kind of lost. Even though I can tell I'm going to like it here, I don't know what to do. I can't work. I can't feed myself. I can't dress myself. I can't even go to the toilet on my own."

"Then let Daddy take over. You need time to recover, to work through what happened. I know it will take more than a couple of days. But let me take the reins for these few days. Let me make the decisions. You can spend the entire time in Little space or just some of it. And you always have your safeword. You can use it anytime."

"Yes, okay. It might be easier for me to accept help in Little mode."

He rubbed his thumb over her cheek. "Would it be easier if I put you in diapers?"

She gaped up at him. "No! That wouldn't be easier."

He studied her. "Okay but know that not eating is no longer an option for you. Come on, go potty then I'll get you in your nightie and into bed."

CALEY KNEW she was blushing as he helped her use the toilet. It wasn't easy to accept that level of help. From anyone. Once he had her nightie and panties on, he lifted her up and carried her to bed.

"Right, rules, Little one. Hmm, I'm going to need a new whiteboard, rewards/punishment chart and some jars."

"I don't think that's necessary, Daddy," she said quickly.

"Oh, I think it is. We hadn't even gotten to use your jars. But don't worry, it's all up there." He tapped his forehead. "I'm sure that there's some spare whiteboards at JSI I can use in the meantime."

Awesome.

He set her down next to the bed then pulled the covers back. The bedspread was a plain gray, but the bed itself was soft and lush.

He put some pillows behind her back. And she rested back. "I'll go get you a bottle in a moment."

"You have a bottle here?"

"Kent grabbed me some supplies. He also got that nutrition shake you like. You need it more now than ever." He looked at her hair. "I need to brush out your hair. I think I saw a hairbrush in your pile of presents."

He returned quickly with a wooden hairbrush. The back of it was very flat and shiny. She scooted forward so he could sit behind her and brush the tangles from her hair.

"Now, your rules are all the same as before. Except, since you'll be in Little space and you need extra help, there's no getting dressed by yourself, no going to the toilet on your own and no getting up on your own. Understand? I've ordered a camera monitor to help with nap times and if you sleep in so I'll know when you wake up. I know it's hard to let me help you with more intimate things like going to the bathroom, but if I'm not worried by it you shouldn't be either."

She guessed it made sense. She still knew she wasn't going to like it. There was a small pull on her hair, and she realized he was braiding it.

"And your big-girl rules from before still apply," he told her, slipping out from behind her. "Let me get your bottle."

She snuggled into him as he fed her the bottle, her eyes getting droopy. Her lack of sleep over these past few days was catching up to her. She felt him tuck her in, Bumbly and her snuggly next to her. She was so glad that Kent had found them.

Something rubbery was pressed to her lips and she instinctively opened them, freezing at the feel of what could only be a pacifier was pressed into her mouth. She didn't know how she felt about that, but she was willing to give it a go.

She realized now how much she missed their nighttime routine. She lay down and he massaged her scalp until she drifted off to sleep.

Fire. Heat. Smoke.

She opened her mouth and screamed for help.

But nothing came out. No one could hear her. No one was there.

Issy! Archer!

"Wake up, baby doll. Easy," a rough voice told her as she woke and she realized a firm hand was shaking her. She opened her eyes, staring up into Issy's concerned face. He must have left a light on somewhere because it wasn't fully dark.

"Sorry," she whispered. "Nightmare."

He kissed her forehead. "About the fire?"

She nodded.

"Poor baby. Want to talk about it?"

She shook her head. She'd already talked it to death. She wanted to forget.

"Go back to sleep," she told him, feeling bad that she'd woken him.

His face grew stern. "Is that the way things work?"

"No." She should have known better.

"The rules haven't changed. If you wake up in the night, you're to wake me as well." Heat entered his gaze. "Now, it's my job to help you get back to sleep."

Her breath caught. She nodded, her heart racing for an entirely different reason.

"Can you put your hands above your head? I don't want you to hurt yourself."

She raised her hands above her head, and he pushed back the bed covers before drawing up her nightgown and latching onto her nipple.

Oh fuck. Oh Christ.

She wondered if he'd take her now. If he'd let her touch him, taste him.

And then his mouth moved down her stomach and he was drawing off her panties before he lay between her legs and started toying with her clit. He began to feast.

He ate her. Tortured her. Teased her. Drove her up to the edge then drew back until she was moaning, her heart racing. Finally, he thrust two fingers deep inside her as he flicked at her clit until she fell over the edge into bliss.

Then she couldn't think at all.

30

"Caley do it!"

"Caley, cannot do it," Issy replied calmly, although she could tell he was becoming increasingly unhappy with her.

These past few days had brought them closer than ever. She'd spent most of her time in Little space. And it had been freeing. Sure, there were times when adult Caley came out. Mostly during the middle of the night when she either couldn't sleep or was woken by a nightmare and he would use his fingers or mouth on her.

Issy's care and attention was helping her slowly heal. Physically and mentally.

There was just one snag. She hadn't heard from Archer. She missed him. Missed talking to him.

Oh, and there was one other issue. Her daddy's continued insistence that she be treated like an invalid.

"Caley can do it," she told him, her bottom lip coming out in a pout.

"Caley, sit down and let me feed you."

"Caley feed herself. I is a big girl."

"Your hands are still healing."

They were, but they were a lot better. So much so she only had to wear the lightest of bandages and she could go to the toilet on her own now. That was something to celebrate.

But that was the only allowance he'd made. And she was feeling a burst of independence. She also thought it was probably time to get back to work. Although there was a part of her that was enjoying having a break, she missed working as well.

First, though, she needed a new laptop. Oh God, just the thought of shopping for a new laptop made her feel stressed.

You can do it.

"Caley, I'm going to count to three then you better have your bottom on your chair and be ready for Daddy to feed you lunch."

Not happening.

"One."

She shook her head.

"Two."

Uh-uh.

"Three."

She gave him a stubborn look. He stood and trepidation filled her. Uh-oh. What had she been thinking?

"I'm sorry, Daddy. I sit now!"

"I appreciate the apology but it's not getting you out of your punishment. Come here." He drew out her chair but instead of waiting for her to sit in it, he sat and crooked a finger at her.

Oh dear. She really was in trouble.

She shook her head, her hands moving behind to her bottom as though to protect it.

"Caley, come here. Now. You do not want me to get up and come grab you. I can promise you that."

She was starting to really regret her choices.

"Daddy, can't I have a do-over?"

"No, you cannot. You've needed this for a while now, but I haven't wanted to spank you while you were recovering. However, since you seem to think your hands are healed enough that you can do everything yourself then it seems you're well enough to get punished."

He may not have spanked her but she usually went into time-out at least once a day. Turns out, she wasn't the best patient. He'd created a new chart and two more jars. By now, the frowny faces well out-weighed the smiley faces and she knew she was going to be pulling something out of the punishment jar come Sunday.

"Caley, last warning."

She scampered over to where he sat.

"Don't run!" he barked at her. "You could trip and hurt yourself. Over you go."

He helped her lie over his lap. She was wearing a T-shirt, sweatpants and a pair of fluffy, bright orange socks. A gift from Daisy. Every day one of the Littles who lived on Sanctuary visited her, sometimes they even played with her, helping her with her clay or her coloring since she couldn't really do any of it herself.

He drew down her sweatpants and panties.

"Daddy! Can't we talk about this?"

He started rubbing her bottom. "What would you like to talk about, baby doll?"

"Abouts how I shouldn't get spanked!"

"And why not? Daddy asked you to come to him. He gave you a count. You had your chance to sit like a good girl and eat your lunch. Now you've earned yourself some punishment in order to remember to obey Daddy and because tantrums are never acceptable. It's a count of twenty then ten minutes of corner time."

Noo!

"Place your hands behind your back. I'm going to hold your wrists, so you don't accidentally bang your hands and hurt yourself."

What about the hurt that was going to be applied to her ass! He was always concerned with her harming herself. Even while her butt was being reddened.

She placed her hands in the small of her back and he carefully held her wrists together. Then his hand descended on her butt.

Smack! Smack! Smack!

Holy crap. He certainly wasn't taking it easy on her. That was for sure.

Slap! Slap!

All too soon her ass was burning. Tears welled in her eyes and she sobbed, kicking her feet.

Smack! Smack!

She finally gave up fighting. She knew she wasn't going to get free. His hand laid down smack after smack. Her bottom throbbed. Her skin burned and when he was done, she was sobbing. He turned her over, holding her on his lap for a long moment, rocking her gently and kissing her forehead.

Once she'd stopped crying, though, he set her on her feet in front of him, holding her hips. She was standing there just dressed in a tight T-shirt. She must have kicked her pants and panties off while she was over his knee.

"Over to the corner, baby doll."

She turned and moved to the corner. She was well acquainted with this corner. She sighed, closing her eyes as she spread her legs and pressed her forehead against the corner, poking her bottom out.

"Good girl," he told her quietly.

That praise filled her with warmth. She knew she was acting like a bit of a brat because she was starting to get frustrated. She was ready for her hands to be fully healed.

"Right, come here, baby doll."

She turned, having to remind herself not to run as she moved back to where he sat on the chair. He drew her onto his lap once more. "What do you have to say for yourself?"

"I'm sorry I was naughty and didn't listen to you, Daddy. I know you're only trying to take care of me."

"You're starting to get frustrated; I get it. But your hands still need time to get better."

She nodded. "I've really liked spending these days in Little space, but I also miss working. I think I'm ready to spend some more time as adult me."

"All right. Your hands aren't up to typing, though."

"I know, I'll need to learn dictation. I also need to get a laptop. And a printer." She sighed. "I hate buying new stuff."

"I would never have known," he told her dryly. He gave her a wry smile.

She licked her lips. "I was also thinking that maybe it was time for...I mean, you did say once I was ready that you would let me... that we could have sex," the last two words were said quickly, her voice a high squeak.

"I did, didn't I?" His heated gaze looked over her. "I didn't want to touch you while you were recovering."

"It's only my hands that are injured. There's nothing wrong with the, uhh, rest of me." She groaned. "I'm so bad at sexy talk."

He stared at her. "That was your attempt at sexy talk?"

She hid her face in his shoulder. "Yes."

His chest moved and she knew he was laughing at her. "Don't laugh. I don't know how to talk sexy."

"Well, we'll have to practice, won't we?"

"So we can have sex? Tonight?"

Something moved across his face. "No, not tonight."

Her face fell. He didn't want her? But that couldn't be right. How many times had she felt his erection press up against her in bed?

"Don't look at me like that. It's not that I don't want you. It's because, damn can't believe I'm about to say this. But I think that the first time I take you, Archer should be there as well."

He realized what he'd said at the same time as her mouth dropped open.

"Why would your brother be here while we have sex?"

He cleared his throat. It took a lot to embarrass him, but he could feel his cheeks redden.

"Ahh, well, that could be because I think we should share you."

Her mouth closed then opened then closed again.

You're making a real mess of this, man.

"If that's what you want," he said hastily, wincing as he realized how what he said could be misconstrued. He took a deep breath and let it out slowly. "Caley, I'm going to ask you something and I want you to answer me honestly. Can you do that?"

Her eyes wide, she nodded.

"Do you love my brother?"

"Of course, I do. Archer means a lot to me but that doesn't mean—"

"No, I mean do you *love* my brother? Do you find him sexually attractive? Say you met him under different circumstances, and I wasn't around, would you be in a relationship with Archer?"

"I don't understand. This is all hypothetical. You are here. Archer isn't."

"Just answer, baby. Please."

"I...I..." Tears filled her eyes.

"Fuck, I'm making a mess of this. Listen to me, okay. You and I, we are solid. I am going nowhere. No matter what. Hell, probably not even if you wanted me to leave. Understand?"

"Yes."

Just say it. "Baby doll, Archer loves you. He wants you."

She shook her head, tears slipping down her cheeks. "I'm with you. I love you."

"I know you do, baby doll. I love you too. But what if you could have both of us? Me and Archer? A permanent ménage. A relationship with us both. I know it seems like I've come up with this out of the blue, but I've been thinking of it for a while. Ever since... since the hospital when he told me he loves you and wants to share you. If you don't want it then nobody will force you. But I think that you might love Archer too. Do you?"

SHE GAPED UP AT HIM.

He'd lost his mind. What was he even thinking? A permanent ménage? Was this a trick? To see if he could trust her? If she said the wrong answer would he send her away?

Her breath came in short, sharp pants.

"Caley? Girl? Whoa, calm down."

She felt herself being lifted then set on a soft surface. A fluffy, warm blanket was wrapped around her. A hand pressed lightly against her chest.

"Caley. Everything is all right. You're safe. Breathe nice and slow. That's it. Nice and slow."

Her panic started to subside, and she blinked to clear her vision, confused to find that tears were dripping down her cheeks. She looked around. She was now sitting on the sofa and the ultra-soft blanket that Charlie and Clint had given her as a gift was wrapped around her shoulders and over her lap.

Issy was on his knees in front of her, his eyes filled with worry as he watched her carefully.

"Baby doll, what was that?" he asked carefully. "Why did you panic?"

"I didn't know how to answer!" she wailed.

He frowned. "Just answer with the truth."

She sobbed out a breath. "T-the truth? But what if I say the wrong thing?"

His face cleared as understanding filled it. "The wrong thing? There is no wrong answer. No matter what you tell me I'm not going to be mad. If you say you don't feel anything towards Archer, that's fine. If you say you have feelings for him, then that's fine as well."

"It is?" She looked at him in bewilderment. "But with Evelyn—"

"That was completely different," he told her. "Evelyn isn't you. Evelyn used me to get to Archer. I know that's not the case with you. If I said I didn't want this, that I didn't want to share with Archer, what would you say?"

"I'd never do anything to hurt you, Issy."

"I know, baby. I think I always knew he had feelings for you. I guess I needed time to work it through. I've also spoken to some other people in ménage relationships."

"You've spoken to people about this?" She wasn't sure if she was dreaming right now.

"I wasn't trying to go behind your back. I just needed to get my head on right before talking to you about this. And I needed to know how it could work, if it could work because the stakes are high. You and Archer are so fucking important to me. I didn't want to fuck this up. Well, more than I have."

"What do you mean?"

"When he told me in the hospital how he felt about you. That he wanted to share you, I got angry. I told him to leave and not contact me for a while. But after I had time to think, well, back in the cabin, when it was the three of us, it felt right. He was there to balance things out. He'd be there when I couldn't be. But he's not just a back-up plan. He's the steady influence. He's the one who would kick our butts if we got too far into our own heads."

"He'd make us talk," she said quietly.

"He'd also fucking take your side in far too many things," he grumbled.

"I don't know, I think he'd side with you plenty."

He grinned. "All his life, he's done the right thing. Including walking away from you. But it doesn't feel like the right thing to me. Does it to you?"

"No," she whispered.

"I know it won't be all smooth sailing. But we'll figure out some ground rules. You need him. I need him. You call for him in your sleep, you know."

"Oh God." She did?

"You call for me too. You need both of us and truth is, it might take both of us to look after you."

She huffed out a breath at that. "I'm scared."

"What scares you most?"

"Losing you."

He placed his hands on her hips. "Not happening. Understand me? Never happening. I'm on you like glue. You couldn't pry me off you with a crowbar."

"Well, I'm probably going to need some space now and then," she joked.

"Why?" he said seriously.

She rolled her eyes. "We both have jobs."

"Yep. Good thing is, my job doesn't take me away from the ranch that much. But when it does, if we go ahead with this, Archer would be here to take care of you."

Her gaze narrowed. "You're not suggesting this just so I always have someone watching me, are you?"

"Of course not," he told her. "It's just an added bonus."

She rolled her eyes at him. "But he lives in Dallas, he has a life there. A career. Would he want to move here?"

"Kent offered him a job. I'm sure he'd take him up on it. And if I'm willing to share and you're going to submit to two bossy dominants, I think he could give up his pretentious penthouse and boring career."

"Issy!"

"Baby, he's the one that suggested this. He wants it. I mean, if you'd prefer someone else…"

"Issy!" She whacked his shoulder.

His eyebrows rose. "Did you just hit your Daddy? With an injured hand?"

"No."

He tilted his head to one side. "I think that should be a new rule. No hitting either your Daddy or your Dom. Especially when you're injured."

"Is that what he would be? My Dom?" How would that work? He wasn't a Daddy Dom. Would he be comfortable with that side of her? Would she only be Little when she was with Issy? She didn't like the sound of that. It seemed like she would have to hide who she was again.

"You're still thinking too much. Whatever happens, I'm here and I always will be. Understand?"

She nodded.

"You want to think about it?"

"No," she whispered. If she thought too long, she'd chicken out. Take the safe road. Like usual. Would she be happy not knowing whether it could have worked? *Time to start living, Caley.*

"I'm in. Let's do this."

31

"What if he's not here?" she asked.

The taxi had just dropped them off outside the building where Archer owned the penthouse apartment. She swallowed nervously. She'd never been to Dallas. Never been to Texas. Even though it was night, it was decidedly warmer here. The taxi driver had been friendly, but she hadn't been able to talk much. Her stomach was in knots.

What if Issy was wrong? What if he'd changed his mind?

What if he wanted them to move here with him? She couldn't live in the city. She loved Sanctuary. She'd only been there a week, but she felt so at home in Issy's cabin. And everyone there was so nice. It had taken her a while to adjust to people coming around a lot, Issy had grumbled that his house had turned into Grand Central Station, but he never turned anyone away, especially if it was one of the other Littles.

She never thought she'd find a place where she could be herself. Where she wouldn't be judged for being different.

Sanctuary was that place.

But there was a piece missing. Archer. But what if he didn't want to move?

She still couldn't believe he'd bought her a laptop. Well, actually, she could. These guys were constantly spoiling her. But dictation software had already been loaded on the laptop, and he'd also included some headphones with a mic. All top of the range.

But it had been his note that had made her tear up.

"Baby doll? Caley?"

She turned to look at Issy.

"There you are. You're worrying too much. Everything is going to be fine."

He was always so confident. So certain. She wished she could be more like that. She always seemed to be waiting for the worst to happen.

Issy pressed on the button for the penthouse. No answer. She shifted around. They should have called him. What if he was away? What if he wasn't happy to see them?

"What should we do?"

Issy brought out his wallet and she watched with amazement as he drew out a card which he held to the reader pad next to the door.

The door opened and he picked up both of their bags. She'd learned her lesson about not picking up her own bags at the airport. He'd given her a sharp slap on the ass, right there in public, as she'd reached for her bag. She'd gone bright red, but after a glance around the only people who seemed to have noticed were an older couple. The woman had given her a knowing wink.

She wondered if there were more people around who were into this sort of stuff than she'd realized. She'd always thought she was weird and odd. But maybe not.

He led them through a very nice foyer with shiny tile floors and high ceilings. There were two elevators and Issy pressed a button, the doors to the one on the right opened immediately. He stepped in, swiped the card and pressed a button for the penthouse.

"This card only allows access to the penthouse floor," he told her. "Archer gave it to me years ago."

The elevator doors opened after a smooth trip and she followed Issy into a small foyer with just one door leading off it. He swiped the card again. Then entered a number into a pin pad.

"He never changes his alarm code. He needs to be more careful. Especially now that we have you to take care of."

Except Archer didn't know that. Maybe he didn't want that.

Urgh. She wished she could stop worrying.

The lights turned on automatically and her mouth dropped open as she walked through the door and into a huge open-plan living area. The furniture was all dark. Everything looked clean and shiny. The kitchen white with marble countertops. A huge T.V. was mounted in front of a sectional.

But none of that was what caught her attention. No, she was drawn to the huge floor-to-ceiling windows looking out at the lights of the city below.

"Wow. This is amazing."

Issy grunted. "I prefer mountains, trees and the stars. But it's okay."

It was more than okay. Although she understood what Issy was saying. She forced herself to turn and take in the rest of the penthouse. It was swank and sophisticated. Very Archer.

Very much not her.

"Probably hired someone to decorate the place. It's pretty bland and boring but at least it's tidy."

She nearly rolled her eyes at this statement.

Issy walked to the fridge and opened the door. "Urgh, craft beer. I guess it will do." He drew one out as well as a bottle of orange juice, which he poured into a glass for her.

"Here, baby doll. You haven't drunk much today." He set the glass down on the counter then opened his beer.

She felt weird making herself at home without Archer here. "What if he doesn't want us here? Should we be in here?"

"He's not gonna call the cops on us." He tapped his fingers against the kitchen bench. "I'm gonna put our stuff in the spare room. Drink your juice."

Bossy.

But she drank the juice. And she did feel a bit better. She guessed she had been getting low in blood sugar.

Issy returned with a frown, his phone pressed to his ear. "He's not answering his phone."

"Do you think he's all right? Why would his phone be off?"

"I can think of one reason. I can find out for sure if he's there. But question is, if he is there do you want to go to him?"

"Go where?"

"To the Twisted Thorn, the BDSM club he belongs to."

"A BDSM club?" she repeated. Nerves fluttered in her stomach.

"You don't have to go. But he would have put his phone on silent and left it in his locker if he's there."

What was he doing at this club? Would he be...

"Is he playing with other subs?" Her voice was louder than she'd intended.

Issy looked surprised then he smirked. "Ooh, jealous, baby?"

"No." She blushed. Yes. She watched him closely to judge his reaction. But he didn't seem perturbed by her possible jealousy.

"I very much doubt it."

"Find out," she said.

Issy grinned. "All right. Let me make a call." He grabbed his phone.

Shit. What was she doing? She knew nothing about going to a club. What did she wear? Would she have to participate?

But under the panic was a tendril of excitement. Think of all the research she could do.

"Is Gray there?" She heard Issy ask into the phone. Then he swore. "Shit. Is he? All right, is Hunter there? Yeah, I want to speak to him. Put him on. When isn't he in a bad mood?"

She turned, pulled out of her musings at the note of impatience in Issy's voice. "Yeah, Hunter? It's Isaac Miller. Yeah, I'm in Dallas. I didn't run away with my tail between my legs," Issy growled.

She raised her eyebrows at his angry tone.

"Listen, Hunter. I need a favor." He pinched the top of his nose. "Is Archer at the club tonight? Right. Yes. I know you're not his PA. Christ. We're here to surprise him. Yes, we." He looked over at her and rolled his eyes. "We need access to the Twisted Thorn for the night. Two of us. She's my sub. Her name is Caley. I don't think it's any of your business. Will you give us access? She won't be playing with anyone but me. Fine, we'll sign an agreement at the front desk. Yes, she has a safeword, I'm not a fucking tourist. Shit. All right. Yeah, I owe you one."

Issy ended the call with a sigh.

"Who was that?"

"Hunter Black, one of the owners of the Twisted Thorn, I was hoping to speak to Gray, one of the other owners. He's far more reasonable. Hunter is going to leave passes for us at the front desk. We just have to sign some documents about liability and an NDA as well as fill in some info on your limits and health. Paperwork alone will probably take a damn hour. He's such an ass and now I owe him a favor. God knows what he'll want."

This Hunter didn't sound like someone to mess with.

Issy turned his gaze on her. "Let's see if we have something to dress you in."

∽

Issy hadn't been wrong, the paperwork had taken a while to work through, but he'd helped her. Just as well since her nerves meant she could hardly operate a pen.

Caley felt decidedly underdressed as they entered the club. Or maybe that should be overdressed since most of the people in the club seemed to be wearing next to nothing at all. They walked through the bar area first and it hadn't seemed all that different from ordinary bars.

Once they entered the dungeon, it was another story. There was a bar in here as well. And a few Doms and Dommes stood around it. Most dressed in tight black fetish wear. Issy was dressed in a black shirt and jeans. Many of the men here didn't bother with shirts.

But it was the submissives that made her feel out of place. One submissive walked by, being led by a leash. She wore what seemed to be a simple, tight black dress but there were cut-outs for her breasts to fit through and her nipples were clamped with a chain going from one to the other.

She gulped.

Issy had dressed her in what was actually a nightie. It was a pretty nightie. Made of satin, it had lace at the bottom and along the top. She'd objected when he'd pulled it from her luggage, but he'd insisted. And she hadn't been allowed a bra or panties. The nightie stopped at mid-thigh, so she was going to have to be careful not to bend over.

At least he'd let her wear a long jacket on the ride over in the taxi.

The nightie was white, and her nipples were pressed against the material. She tried to cross her arms over her chest, but Issy gave her a sharp look.

Right. No trying to hide herself.

He'd given her a crash course in the rules. No looking at a Dom or Domme in the eyes. No speaking unless spoken to. And always do what he said.

God. She hoped they found Archer soon. She was terrified. If she had boots on, she'd be shaking in them. But apparently, she wasn't allowed shoes. They'd been left out with her coat.

"Ahh, so this is the little subbie you wanted to bring to the club so badly," a big voice boomed.

She glanced up; her eyes widened as a huge man stomped towards them. This wasn't a guy you'd wish to meet in a dark alley. There was something cold and dangerous around him. He was wearing a tight black T-shirt and blue jeans.

She was aware of people turning and staring at them. Whispering started up. Panic filled her. They were judging her. Finding her wanting. She didn't belong here.

"Easy, baby doll." Issy placed a hand on the small of her back, instantly calming her.

Issy was here. Nothing bad would happen.

"Don't be scared of Hunter. His bark is worse than his bite."

This was Hunter Black? Holy shit.

"I object to that. My bite is just as bad as my bark, isn't it, baby?" He turned and she saw a woman she'd missed while she'd been focused on everyone else in the room.

The dark-haired woman was gorgeous. Petite. She couldn't be with this big beast of a man, could she? But then a miracle happened. Hunter's face softened as he glanced down at the tiny woman. He reached out a hand and she took it, stepping forward.

"Your bark is definitely worse than your bite," she said quietly. "Hello, Sir."

This was addressed to Issy and she started in surprise. She looked up at Issy.

"Call me Doc, Cady," he told her. "It's good to see you, sweetheart. You're looking well."

"I am."

"Of course she is. I take good care of her." Hunter turned his ice-blue gaze to her. "Hello there, little one."

She was surprised at the softer note in his voice.

"Hello, Sir," she said, remembering Issy's coaching.

"You want me to book out one of the rooms for Littles?" Hunter asked.

She jolted. How had he guessed? She looked up at him, then remembered not to meet his gaze.

"It's all right, little one, you can look at me. Not a big stickler for all these rules. I just like to come here and spank Cady's ass, give her a fucking spectacular orgasm then shoot the shit for a while."

"Hunter, you own the place," Issy told him.

"So?"

"You're meant to set a good example."

"I am? Well, hell, that sounds boring. Maybe I should sell up. You looking to invest, Doc?"

Issy rolled his eyes. "No, actually, I'm looking for my brother." He glanced down at her. "And not the Little room for tonight, I think, but maybe a medical room?"

"Closed or open?" he asked weirdly.

"Closed."

"Consider it done. Will Archer be joining you?"

"Hopefully."

"Good, he's been moping around like someone stole his lollipop." Hunter's gaze moved to her. "Hopefully you'll cheer him up, huh, sugar?"

She gulped. "I'll try, Sir."

ARCHER DIDN'T EVEN KNOW why he'd come to the Twisted Thorn tonight. He was having a fucking miserable time. Much like his life these last few weeks. Since he left Montana. Since he left her. He looked out across the dungeon. He didn't feel much like playing. Didn't feel like doing anything. Maybe he should volunteer to be a monitor tonight. Or he could go check on the Littles.

He'd never been interested in taking watch over the Littles before.

"Sir?"

He glanced over as Susan approached him. He managed to suppress another groan. Why had he said yes to his assistant joining the same club he went to?

Because you thought it didn't matter when Gray asked you if it was all right.

But he didn't want to see Susan right now. He'd dressed her down for not passing on Caley's message and she'd tearfully told him it was an oversight and wouldn't happen again. So he'd kept her on. Still, he was annoyed with her. And he didn't feel like seeing her outside of work.

She was dressed in a tight black corset and a black thong.

Yeah, it felt wrong to see his assistant so scantily clad.

Fuck. Was he going to have to find a new club? Or maybe he should just give up on this altogether since he couldn't find much interest in playing.

Susan knelt beside him and placed her hand on his knee. He frowned. What was she doing touching him without permission? He opened his mouth to reprimand her when she spoke up.

"Please, Sir, will you—"

"We interrupting something here?"

His head snapped around at the deep rumble and he gaped up at his brother. What the fuck? What was he doing here? He stood, paying little attention to Susan who still knelt at his feet.

"Isaac? What are you doing here? Is it Caley? Is she all right?"

Surely, he would have called him if something was wrong with her. Why would he come here? Had he left her at home?

Then a vision in white stepped out from behind his brother. She was wearing an almost see-through nightie, it was clear she didn't have a bra on and knowing his brother, she wouldn't have underwear either.

Christ, what was Issy thinking? She was like an angel in a sea of sharks. He could see them circling. Her sweetness and innocence shone brightly. Issy would be fighting them off all night, especially since few people probably knew him. It had been years since he'd been a member.

"What are you doing bringing Caley here? She doesn't belong here!"

Caley flinched and Isaac scowled. "I'm sorry, would you rather we left you here with your friend?"

"What friend?" He glanced down at where Isaac gestured. "Oh. Susan, go back to where the unattached subs are. If you approach or touch a Dom again without permission, you will be publicly punished."

He heard a gasp and realized it had come from Caley. Susan left, her face tight with anger. Caley looked shocked, and uncertain. Which just fueled his belief that she didn't belong here.

"Isaac, explain why you brought her here."

"We're here because we came looking for you, asshole," Isaac bit out at him. He placed his arm around Caley, supporting her. She leaned into him.

They looked perfect together. And once again, he was on the outside.

"Why?"

"Aww, baby, don't make me make them stop," a deep voice pleaded behind him.

He whirled to see Hunter Black standing there. The big Dom was staring down at his wife, Cady, who gave him a firm look back. Archer honestly didn't know how she put up with him.

"I wanna see the drama play out."

Cady sighed and gave him a pointed look.

"Fine. But I'm taking this out on your butt. Gotta have some fun tonight." Hunter was practically pouting as he turned to them.

"Maybe you all want to take this somewhere private. The room you wanted is available now, Doc. Room 3b."

3b. That was a medical playroom.

"You brought her here to play with her? Issy, she's never been to a club before."

"I know that." Issy scowled at him. "Fuck, why am I even here?"

"I have no idea, that's why I'm asking."

"See, baby, they wanna do this in public," Hunter drawled. "They don't care if we watch along with everyone else."

Archer scowled at the meddling man. He couldn't resist sticking his nose into Archer's life. But Isaac nodded.

"Come on, Caley. Even if Archer isn't willing to listen to us, we can at least have a play. I've often fantasized about playing a doctor."

Caley smiled up at Issy then turned her gaze to Archer, looking pensive. "Archer?"

He started at her voice. Then she licked her lips and looked nervous. "Sorry, I'm not supposed to talk to you first, am I? Oh God, you're not going to publicly punish me, are you?"

"Easy, baby doll," Isaac told her. "You're my sub. If anyone punishes you, it will be me."

Archer frowned. "You're not punishing her."

"No, I'm not. But I'm about to take a damn bullwhip to you, if you don't start listening to us."

With that, Issy turned away and led Caley with him. But she looked over her shoulder at him, her eyes filled with a deep sadness.

And he could do nothing else but follow.

32

Despite her curiosity, Caley barely looked around the room that Issy led them into. She did note the table in the middle that resembled one you might find in a doctor's surgery. Only it had a series of straps attached to it at the top, the middle and on the stirrups that rested out from the sides of the bench.

Issy led her over to where there was a desk with a big leather chair. There were two other chairs sitting there and he gently pushed her into one. It wasn't a bad idea for her to sit considering her legs were trembling.

Archer walked in and shut the door behind him. "You requested this room?"

"Yep."

"If you wanted to play out a doctor-patient fantasy, couldn't you have done that at home, in Montana? After all, you have all the equipment since you are an actual doctor."

"For God's sake, Archer, of course we didn't come all the way here to play out a fantasy. We're here for you."

She saw the other man jolt in reaction to Issy's words.

"For me? What's wrong?" Archer's gaze moved over her as though trying to search out an injury.

"Nothing's wrong, other than you being an ass."

She reached up and took Issy's hand, tugging on it. He immediately turned to her.

"Do the rules apply in here?"

He looked confused for a moment then that cleared. "No, baby doll. Not right now. You can speak freely with just me and Archer here."

She forced herself to stand, not wanting to feel at a disadvantage. She swallowed. "Archer, we came here to find you when you weren't at your apartment."

Archer was still frowning. "I still don't understand why."

"It's because...well...we..."

"Spit it out, baby doll," Issy said dryly.

"Do you still want to share me?"

Okay, she hadn't meant to just come out with it.

Archer opened his mouth, but she kept going. "A ménage, a permanent one. A relationship, not just for sex. Issy said you brought it up at the hospital. That you walked away originally because you thought that was better for me and for Issy. But the thing is, I miss you, we miss you. Issy has done some research into ménage relationships. And well, we think we can make it work. If you're still willing...I mean if you still want...me," she finished lamely as he just gaped at her.

She looked to Issy who stared at her in shock as well. Archer he didn't say a word.

"Archer?" What was he thinking? Why wasn't he talking?

"Easy, baby doll. That's his thinking face. Give him a minute."

Archer gave Doc a sharp look. "You're an ass."

"I think we all know this by now."

Archer rubbed his hand over his face. Then he looked to his brother. "I thought you didn't want this."

Issy shrugged. "I changed my mind."

"That simple, huh?"

"No, not that simple," Issy said sharply. "Fucking barely slept in past two weeks. Been going over scenarios. Been talking to people who are in these sorts of relationships. Learnt about the advantages and disadvantages. None of this is simple."

Archer winced. "Sorry."

"But what it comes down to is, am I willing to try? Am I willing to try to give Caley what she needs? You what you need. And me what I need."

"You?" Archer asked.

Issy shrugged. "Won't lie. There were many times I wanted to be selfish. But the thing is, I have to give Caley what she needs. It's built into me. And the fact that it's you, my brother, well, I don't hate that. I miss you. I think that we all have something to add to this relationship. And I think it will be stronger with all of us in it. Besides, I do this and I'll be her favorite."

"Issy!" she protested.

He just grinned.

"And what do you want?" he asked Caley. "You're the most important person in this. How do you feel about me? Do you want me? Or am I second fiddle to Issy? An afterthought? Another cock in the bedroom?"

"Another cock? I barely know what to do with one cock, two kind of terrifies me!"

Issy snorted and she glared at him. "Don't laugh at me!"

"I agree this isn't a laughing matter!" Archer scowled at his brother. "If we do this, I want to fully be part of this relationship. Just as important to you as Isaac."

"So you really want this?" She guessed she still hadn't fully believed he'd want this. "Even though it means sharing me and we live in different states and I'm kind of forgetful and clumsy and I'll likely never be sophisticated and worldly?"

He stepped forward and cupped her face between his hands. Then he kissed her. Ravished her. This kiss was dominant. He took complete control.

And she loved it.

When he drew back, she was panting heavily, her body thrumming with lust and need.

"I love you the way you are. I don't want you to ever change, understand me? I can deal with the logistics, I can work everything out with Issy that needs to be figured out, what I can't change is how you feel about me. So?"

"You love me?" she asked.

"'Course I damn well do. Loved you almost from the moment I met you and I've been fucking miserable without you. What I don't know is how you feel about me?"

Archer stared down at her intently.

"I love you too. I've missed you so much. When you walked away without saying goodbye, I thought I might never see you again." Tears dripped down her cheeks. "I know this idea sounds weird, but if we can make it work then I want to try. I don't want to spend my life with regrets. I feel like for so much of my life, I've hidden from everything, too scared to do anything. Now, I'm going to be brave. I'm going to live. And I want to spend the rest of my life with both of you by my side."

"I'll never walk away again; this I promise you. This is it. Your only chance to get me to leave."

She threw herself into his arms kissing the side of his chin as he held her tight.

"Oh, love, how I've longed to feel you in my arms. To have you here with me." He lifted her off the ground, her feet dangling in the air. He set her down but kept her pressed into his side. He'd grown slightly tense as he stared at Issy.

She looked over at Issy, who appeared relaxed, his arms crossed over his chest as he leaned against the desk.

"You sure you're okay with this?" Archer asked him.

"Jesus, I know you like to talk, but how many times do I have to say it? I wouldn't be here if I wasn't sure."

"You're not jealous at the idea of sharing her?"

"Maybe when the idea first came up. I would be with anyone else. But it feels right to share her with you, brother."

"Sharing's caring," she quipped.

Archer stared down at her with a frown. Grasping hold of her chin, he tilted her face. "There won't be sharing with anyone else, love."

"Definitely not," Issy barked, scowling at her. "Just because I'm sharing you with my brother, doesn't make me any less possessive of you."

"Nor me."

Oh dear. She hadn't thought this part through. "I'm gonna be in double trouble now, aren't I?"

Issy grinned. "Yep. It's the perfect scenario. When I'm not around, Archer can keep an eye on you. Baby doll, with both of us taking care of you, you won't even have the opportunity to get into trouble."

She sighed like she was terribly put out but, on the inside, she was happy dancing. She'd never be alone again. She had the two men she loved and adored.

How had her luck changed so much? Was this fate handing her happiness after so much shit and tragedy in her life?

"What about the fact that you live here and we live at Sanctuary? I know you have your job and that you love living in the city—"

He kissed her then drew back to smile down at her. "I've already handed in my notice for my job. And I am going to sell the penthouse."

"You have?" she asked.

"Yep, Kent offered me a job a while back. I've taken him up on it."

"That bastard never told me you'd accepted the job," Issy grouched.

"I asked him not to."

"So you're moving to Sanctuary? With us?" she asked ecstatically.

"I am."

Another thought occurred to her. She glanced up at Archer. "Are you okay with the, umm, with my Little," she rushed out.

He frowned. "Why wouldn't I be?"

"Because you're not a Daddy Dom."

"Poppet, if you have to go into Little space, then that's what you do. My job is to provide you with what you need."

"What I need right now is to stop talking this to death," Issy complained. "We've only got this room for another hour and I want to play. Besides, our girl here needs some stress relief."

"I hope that's a code word for orgasm."

Archer sighed, shaking his head. "Such a naughty subbie. Did you even tell her the rules?"

"I did." Issy grinned.

"Does she know how to find her position?" Archer asked in a deep, commanding voice. A shiver ran up her spine.

Position?

"Oh, you mean this? I've read about it lots." She got onto her knees, straightened her spine and put her hands palm down on her thighs. Which she kept together.

"Not bad. You've never been to a club, have you?" Archer asked.

"No."

"No, Sir."

Her eyes widened and she glanced over at Issy who seemed to be happy to let Archer take the lead. "This is more his thing, baby doll. I learned early on that I was a Daddy Dom. While I've been to clubs, I prefer a more relaxed approach."

Archer just snorted. "Relaxed is one way to describe it. As you know, Issy likes to do things his own way."

"What can I say? I'm a rebel."

"Issy," Archer said warningly. "Do you want to play this out?"

"Sure do," Issy said, walking over to grab a doctor's coat and slipping it on. "I'll get everything ready."

"Do you see what I had to put up with growing up?"

"You wouldn't have him any other way. Sir," she hastily added on as he raised his eyebrows.

Then he surprised her by crouching, his face softening. He reached out and grasped hold of her chin. "Are you sure you're okay with this, love? With me being part of your relationship?"

"It feels like I was missing a piece and now I'm whole."

His eyes warmed. "Yeah, that's what it feels like for me too. Instead of a piece, it was my whole damn soul."

"Oh, that's nice. I might use that in a book."

He looked down his nose at her. "Is that what you're doing here? Getting research?"

"No! We came here for you," she said quickly, almost tripping over her words.

He grinned. He was teasing her. The jerk.

"I know, love. But if you get some new material that's a bonus, huh?"

She nodded shyly.

"Now, are you okay with having me dominate you? Have you talked to Issy about limits?"

"Umm, yes. We talked about them a while ago and before we came in here tonight. Dave was my daddy, but we never really did anything like this. We never even had a safeword."

"It's always better to err on the side of caution. What's your safeword?"

"Bananas."

"Good. Tonight we're just going to play out a simple medical play scene. Are you all right with us spanking you?"

She cleared her throat.

"She's cleared for paddles, straps, and crop," Issy told him. "Nothing that makes a hard impact or a loud noise."

Archer nodded. "Restraints?"

"Yes, that's fine," she replied.

"Sexual contact?"

Her face blushed bright red. "Yes, I'd like that."

Okay, that was kind of a dorky thing to say.

"We'd all like that," Issy said dryly.

Archer turned to look up at his brother. "What? Like you haven't been taking her every minute you can."

"He hasn't," she said.

Archer swung back. "What?"

"He was waiting for you," she whispered, feeling her cheeks go bright red.

Shock filled Archer's face then he grinned and stood. "Aww, brother I'm touched. You do love me." Archer pressed his hand to his chest, and she giggled.

"Keep going and the only touching you'll be doing is your hand on your own cock," Issy grumbled.

"Don't worry, I'll touch it for you," she offered.

Both men turned to her and she groaned. "I did not mean it to sound like that."

Archer shook his head. "Will I ever be able to get the two of you to stick to protocol?"

"Protocol is boring," Issy told him. "I like our way better."

Archer looked down at her then nodded. "I like our way too. What about her injuries? She's no longer wearing bandages."

"Her hands have healed well," Issy told him. "However, they

are still a little tender. So no wrist restraints or using her hands. Otherwise, she's good to go."

"Good." Archer watched her hungrily. "There's just one thing wrong with this picture. Caley, spread your legs."

ARCHER WATCHED as her cheeks went bright red. She was so gorgeous. Her blonde hair was loose tonight, probably at Issy's insistence since she usually wore it pulled back in a twist. The white negligee was a good choice, although he was surprised Issy dressed her in something so revealing. He didn't think his brother would want her so exposed to other eyes, even if her outfit was pretty tame compared to most.

"I can't," she whispered.

"What do you call me?"

"Sir." She looked to Issy.

He shook his head. "I'll accept the usual. Doc, Issy or Daddy."

She gave him a small smile. Something shared between the two of them. Archer waited for a surge of jealousy; it wasn't there. He knew that didn't mean he might not feel jealous at times. But he would work that out himself. Or with Issy. She wouldn't be brought into it.

They would protect her at all costs.

"I can't, Sir."

"Why not?"

"Because I don't have any panties on." The words were said in a hushed voice, her eyes wide.

He made certain to hide his smile. "As I would expect. If you were wearing panties, it would be a count of ten immediately."

Her mouth dropped open. "Oh. Really?"

"Really, Sir."

"Really, Sir?"

He gave a sharp nod. "Now spread your legs."

She looked to Issy but whatever she saw on his face must have reassured her because she pushed her legs apart. It was clear how comfortable she was with his brother. It didn't matter, he'd get her to that level with him as well. Where she obeyed his commands without hesitation.

He had to remind himself to go carefully. She was still a newbie in so many ways.

She spread her legs and the negligee moved up her thighs, exposing her bare pussy.

Delicious.

"Words are required tonight, Caley," Archer told her. "A nod of your head isn't an acceptable answer, understand? Because one of us may be doing something and miss it."

"I understand, Sir."

Archer looked to Issy "Does her pussy taste as sweet as it looks?"

"Sweeter. That's how we've been helping with her insomnia," Issy told him.

"She's still having trouble sleeping?" He didn't like the sound of that.

"It was getting better, until the fire. We have a bedtime routine. Bath, bottle and massage. Then if she wakes up in the night, she's not allowed to get up without waking me. Normally another orgasm or two will get her nicely off to sleep again. Sometimes another bottle."

Archer nodded, noting the way she gaped at Issy. "You'll have to get used to this, love. We're going to have to discuss your care constantly to make certain we're on the same page."

She swallowed. "Oh, dear Lord."

"For tonight, you may speak whenever you like, as long as you remember to be respectful. I want you to ask questions if you need to. If you need to slow things down, you can say yellow. If you need things to stop, red or bananas. We are going to act out a scene. You ready for that?"

"I'm a patient? Sir?"

"Yes. Issy is the doctor and I am your husband."

Her mouth dropped open slightly and he worried for a moment that she wouldn't react well to that. "Yes, Sir."

"Good girl. If anything hurts, you safeword immediately." He helped her stand then he led her over to the door, pretending to rap on it.

"Here we go, love." He winked at her.

33

Her heart was thundering, a mix of nerves and excitement.

"Yes? Come in," Issy barked out in a grouchy voice.

He turned to look up at them with a frown as they walked into the room. "You're my next patient?"

"Yes, I'm Archer, this is my wife, Caley."

Issy grunted. "My secretary said that you're having problems bringing her to orgasm."

Archer made a funny noise, like he'd been punched in the gut. She couldn't help but giggle. Archer gave her a stern look, but Issy just winked at her when Archer wasn't looking at him

"Yes, that's right," Archer said in a strangled voice. "Are you able to give her a full examination?"

"Oh, I can do that. Get her up on the table. On her back, feet in the stirrups."

"Come here, love." He led her to the bench and lifted her onto it.

"Thanks, snugglebum," she replied.

He froze and stared at her aghast.

"If you're my husband, don't I get to call you by a cute name?"

He groaned as Issy started laughing.

"You don't need a cute name for me."

She pouted. "Well, that's no fun."

He sighed. "Fine, but only in here. No one out there would understand."

"Dunno, think Hunter might be interested," Issy added with a wicked glint in his eyes.

"Mention that nickname out of this room and you won't sit down for a week," Archer warned in a dark voice that told her he meant business.

She nodded frantically, then remembered she had to give verbal answers. "Yes, Sir."

"Lie back. Let's get you settled."

He placed her feet in the stirrups, placing cuffs around her ankles to keep them in place. Then he spread her legs wide, exposing her fully. She blinked up at the ceiling.

Holy shit.

"Normally, we would restrain your hands," Issy said. "Instead you will need to keep them at your sides." Issy stared down at her. "But move them without good reason and that's ten, understand?"

"Yes, Issy."

"Yes, Doc," he told her.

"Yes, Doc."

He fiddled with the monitors, placing a small cuff on her finger. To her surprise the screen lit up with her heartbeat. It actually worked?

Then he grabbed his stethoscope, listening to her heart. "Have you noticed anything different about her body lately?"

"Her breasts are very tender. And her nipples are often hard."

She gasped. They were not! And how would Archer know? Oh wait, this was role play.

Issy moved the stethoscope around her chest, brushing her nipples several times. Deliberately, she was certain.

"Let's expose her breasts and examine them. I have something to test how sensitive she is." He reached into a drawer and drew out a Wartenberg wheel. She only knew because she'd researched them once. She'd never actually had one used on her.

"Now, this won't do." Issy fingered the material. "Your wife needs to be completely naked for this next part."

Wife. Her heart raced at that. She could get used to the idea of being Archer's wife all too easily.

It's just a game, Caley.

Archer helped her sit then he drew off the negligee, throwing it away. Issy cleared his throat. With a roll of his eyes, Archer picked up the negligee and folded it before placing it on a chair. It seemed even in roleplay, Issy liked to have everything just so.

Archer ran his gaze over her, his eyes darkening. She wondered if he liked what he saw. He leaned in, his lips brushing against her ear, sending a rush of pleasure through her body.

"You are gorgeous, love. I don't think I could ever grow tired of looking at your body. I'm dying to touch you, to taste you all over."

Yeah. She could go for that.

Issy held the wheel up for her to look at. "Ever used one of these?"

She shook her head, feeling a pinch of trepidation.

"How do you reply, pumpkin cupcake?" Archer said in a low voice.

Her eyes widened at the nickname and then she grinned. "Sorry, honey bunches, no I haven't, Doc."

"Well, I'm just going to use it lightly on your skin." He ran it down the side of her arm. It wasn't painful, in fact it was rather pleasant.

"How does that feel?"

"Good," she whispered.

He replied with a smile then ran it over the underside of her breast. She gasped as her skin became electrified in its wake.

Oh, holy hell.

"Judging by your wife's reactions, her breasts are very sensitive." Doc ran the wheel across each breast, and she shivered, biting on her lip. Archer reached up and teased her lip free.

"No biting," he warned her then ran his finger over the seam of her lips as Doc moved the wheel between her breasts.

She gasped as he moved over her nipple. Archer pressed his finger into her mouth. "Suck," he commanded.

That shouldn't have been as much of a turn-on as it was. The wheel ran down her stomach. Where was he going? She tensed, but Archer moved his finger out of her mouth and ran the wet digit across her nipple.

Oh, that felt so good. Doc moved the wheel across the top of her mound then lightly along each outer lip of her pussy.

"Her reactions show that she is very sensitive. I'm not sure why you had such a problem getting her to orgasm," Doc told Archer as he put the wheel away and reached into the drawer to grab something else.

Archer's jaw clenched but he said nothing in return.

"I have a special implement that will gauge her arousal levels." Doc pulled out an anal plug. "It has been sterilized and is replaced after every examination."

She thought he probably added that part for her benefit. Still, she gaped at the plug. It was bigger than any she'd had. He attached a cord to the end of the plug then pressed a button on the base. The plug started to buzz. It couldn't actually gauge her arousal, could it?

Archer leaned into her ear. "It's just a bit of play. It's only a vibrating plug."

Oh. Issy grabbed a tube of something out of the same drawer. He squirted lube on to his hand and started coating the plug.

Then he sat on a stool that had wheels on the base and wheeled himself between her legs, so she could only see the top of his head.

Holy hell.

"Please start manipulating her nipples. I'll judge her arousal levels as I insert the plug."

She felt his finger prodding at her asshole and tried to relax the way he'd taught her. Archer chose that moment to brush his fingers gently over her nipples. She gasped. She knew she was already wet. She could feel the slickness on the lips of her pussy.

"Relax, breathe out," Issy told her.

She took a breath and let it out and he pushed his finger deep inside her. "Her pussy is nice and wet," Issy commented. "She obviously has very sensitive nipples. Use more pressure."

As Doc started moving his finger in and out of her ass, Archer plucked at her nipples, applying more pressure. Her heartbeat started racing and the machine beeped.

Issy looked up. "Heartbeat has increased considerably. I do believe your wife would benefit from anal play. Is this something you have experimented with?"

"Not yet. But we will be soon."

Oh, dear Lord help her.

Issy removed his finger. Then the plug started to prod at her bottom hole. "Deep breath in again. Now out."

The plug was pushed slowly into her asshole as Archer played with her nipples. Shit. Having the two of them work together on her body was almost too much. She was overwhelmed by sensation.

The plug was pushed, slowly and firmly into her asshole. It burned slightly. She felt full. And she loved it.

Issy turned the plug.

"Her pussy is saturated. I'm going to clean her up a bit and taste her."

What did he mean....ohh. She groaned as he took a long lick of her pussy. He lapped at her. Cleaning her up? Holy shit, he was just making her wetter. His tongue flicked around her clit and she could feel her orgasm approaching.

Archer must have sensed it because he raised his mouth from her nipples. "No coming without permission."

"Nooo," she cried. How could he be so cruel?

He gave her a stern look. "You come without permission and I will turn you over and redden your ass with my belt."

He wouldn't. She swallowed, unwilling to take that chance. She had to fight to pull herself back from the brink. Issy was too damn good with his tongue. Then she felt a vibration in her ass and realized he'd turned on the plug.

"Oh. Oh. Please!"

"Please what?" Archer asked her, staring down at where his brother had his mouth buried between her legs.

"Please let me come."

"Hmm. What does the doctor think?"

Issy raised his head, his lips glistening with her juices. "I believe it would be good for her to learn to wait."

That asshole.

He stood and wiped at his mouth with the back of his hand, reaching down to turn off the vibrator. "I'm going to wash my hands. Perhaps you could continue to clean her pussy."

Archer looked at her hungrily.

She groaned as he moved between her legs. His mouth immediately zeroed in on her clit, his tongue moving with such light flicks she could barely feel it. She cried out, trying to grab him, wanting to push him closer. Wanting him to stop teasing her.

"Uh-uh, what did we say about moving your hands?" Issy barked.

Oh shit.

"Sorry."

Issy shook his head, although there was a twinkle in his eyes. Archer pulled away from her pussy, causing her to moan out a protest. She needed to come.

"Undo the bindings, I'll hold her legs while you punish her," Issy told him. "What would you like? Paddle? Strap? Crop?"

"Crop," Archer answered. Issy handed him a riding crop from that same drawer. Was that thing like a gateway to Narnia? How much could it hold?

Wait. Crop? Holy hell.

Then Issy raised her legs up, pressing them against her stomach, his arm under her knees. It put her ass completely on display. She had to clench around the anal plug.

"Don't you lose that, love," Archer warned as he ran the base of the crop over her ass lightly.

Then he tapped it against her bottom. Okay, that wasn't as bad as she expected. The next smack of the crop was slightly harder. It stung but nothing like she'd built it up in her head. He lay down smack after smack, increasing the burn until her body was trembling, her ass on fire but she'd experienced harder spankings over Issy's knee.

When he was finished, he dropped onto his seat and started licking her pussy. Issy still held her legs. It was insane. And oh, so hot. She felt her orgasm rush up.

"Please! Please can I come?"

"Come, girl," Doc growled at her. "Come hard."

Archer made a growl of agreement and she immediately fell over the edge, her release rocking her body as she screamed with pleasure.

"Fuck yes."

Doc let go of her legs and Archer moved his mouth from her pussy, putting her feet back into the stirrups.

"Damn, you taste good, love," he told her.

She heard a crinkling noise and glanced over to find that Issy was now naked and rolling a condom over his thick erection. Archer slid out of the way as Issy moved between her legs. He grasped hold of her hips. "Ready for this?"

"Please!" She was dying to feel him take her. He grasped hold of his cock, pressing it slowly into her pussy. She cried out as he filled her. He was slow but relentless, his shaft thick and delicious.

Finally. Finally.

There was movement beside her and she turned her head to find Archer stripping off. She hungrily ate up at the sight of him. He had a slighter build than Issy, but was taller.

And his cock was thick. Gorgeous.

He grasped hold of the shaft, running his hand back and forth.

"Jesus, man, she likes watching you do that. She just clenched down on me so fucking tight." Issy sounded like he was in pain.

"You feel so good, Caley. So fucking good." He leaned over her, brushing his lips against her. She smiled up at him as he stood up and thrust deep once more.

Archer moved closer and she licked her lips as his dick came into her eye line.

"Want a taste, love?"

"Oh, yes please."

"Open up then."

She parted her lips and he slid his dick into her mouth.

"Just relax and breathe, let me drive it. If you need a break, raise your hand."

She didn't know how they did it, but they seemed to work in tandem, one pulling out as the other drove in. Archer moved in softer, shallow thrusts, not wanting to overwhelm her, she guessed. She loved the slightly salty taste of him.

"Fuck, I'm close," Issy groaned.

A hand cupped her breast, a thumb swiped at her nipple. Then a finger was pressed against her clit. She could feel her pleasure rising. She was going to come again.

"Come, girl. Come with me!" Issy yelled. She felt him drive deep then her own orgasm washed though her, flooding her pleasure. Archer pulled out of her mouth and she was barely aware of him putting a condom on. But then Issy left her, Archer taking his place. Issy took care of his condom, chucking it in a trash can before walking over to her. Archer was rubbing her lower tummy in small circles as she came down from her high.

Issy kissed her gently, lightly. "All right, baby doll?"

She smiled. "Yes."

"Good girl. Can you take Archer as well? Or are you sore?"

"I can take him."

"Thank fuck," Archer said. He slid a finger over her sensitive clit, making her shiver. "Issy, kiss her."

As Issy ravaged her mouth, Archer took her, rode her. She didn't think she could possibly come again, but he found a spot inside her that made her scream. And he kept driving his dick over that one spot until she saw stars, her orgasm catching her by surprise. Archer let out a shout as he followed her over.

The three of them lay slumped together, her heart was racing, and she knew Issy and Archer weren't in a much better state.

"I should punish you for coming without permission," Archer told her. "But I don't think I have the energy."

"Later," Issy told him. "After all, we have the rest of our lives."

Yeah. She liked the sound of that.

34

She was completely over this damn dictation.

There was nothing wrong with her hands anymore, anyway. She glanced over at the door. She had commandeered Archer's home office. They'd been here two days now. Even though, Archer had already handed in his resignation, he couldn't just leave. He had patients in his care. Some of them he was going to continue with via Skype, others he needed to get settled with new therapists.

Rather than return to Sanctuary, they'd decided to wait here with him.

Caley had decided it was time to make an effort to get back to work. She missed writing and she was getting way behind in her schedule. They'd brought her new laptop with her, which she'd thanked Archer for profusely, so she'd taken over his home office to get some words down.

It kind of amazed her how easily the three of them settled in together. No doubt there would be bumps in the road, but this felt right.

She'd always miss Dave. But this was a new chapter. And she hadn't been happy since he died.

However, Issy was still insisting that she use dictation. Which was ridiculous since her hands were all healed. But Issy wasn't here right now...so...

She started typing. Oh, that felt so much better. It just felt wrong speaking the words out loud. She typed, not watching the time. She was deep in a scene when a loud throat being cleared startled her. She glanced up into Issy's angry eyes.

"Uh-oh."

"Uh-oh is right." He pointed down at her. "What was the deal with starting work again?"

"No more than four hours of work at a time."

"That's right. Which is why I came looking for you as your four hours are now up. What was the other rule?"

"That I had to use dictation."

"And what are you doing?"

"Typing." She bit her lip.

"Over here." He pointed at the carpet in front of him. She jumped up and practically raced over.

"Hands." He held his out for her to put hers into them. He turned them over, studying them. "They're swollen."

Only a little bit.

"Into the corner of the living room. Pants and panties down, ass poking out. Go. Now!"

He landed a sharp smack on her ass. She started then rushed into the living room and got into position. She blushed at the sight she must make with her naked ass pointing out, her nose pressed against the corner. She heard Issy moving around in the living room, but he didn't say anything.

Then she heard the front door open. Oh God, was Archer home?

"Well, that's a sight I didn't expect to greet me," Archer said calmly. He'd been working long hours, often not getting home until she was asleep, although he always helped Issy when she woke up in the night, and couldn't get back to sleep.

But he hadn't seen her much in Little space. And he certainly hadn't seen her standing in the corner, with her bottom on display and her pants down around her ankles.

"Someone decided dictation was too hard and that she was going to type instead, when she was told not to. We'll be adding a frown to your chart, baby doll. You're definitely going to be choosing something from the punishment jar soon."

Thank God he'd left that at home.

"Very naughty," Archer agreed. "I take it she's about to get that delicious ass reddened?"

Drat. There went any hope he'd be on her side.

"She certainly is. Caley, come over here."

She turned, glancing over at Archer with embarrassment as she shuffled her way across the room, her pants and panties around her ankles.

"That seems dangerous." Archer came over and crouched in front of her. "Hold onto me and lift your foot."

She placed her hands lightly on his shoulders and lifted one foot. He drew off her pants and panties. Then he did the same with the other foot.

He stood and winked at her.

"Come here, baby doll."

She glanced over to find Issy sitting on the sofa. He patted his lap. "Lie over Daddy's lap."

She positioned herself over his lap so her legs and torso rested on the sofa on either side of his thighs. Then to her surprise, Archer sat next to them. He lightly grabbed hold of her hands, inspecting them.

"They're swollen."

"Yep, same as her ass is about to be." Issy landed a smack to her bottom, making her cry out. Then another one. He wasn't messing around. "You disobeyed, Daddy, little one. That was very naughty. You need to learn how to use dictation. Or you're going to do real damage to your hands."

His hand landed over and over again on her ass. Archer continued to lightly massage her hands. Her legs kicked against the sofa as her ass burned.

"Daddy! Daddy, stop!" She couldn't stop from slipping into Little space, despite Archer's presence.

"Not yet, baby doll."

Slap! Smack! Issy continued to spank her firmly, his pace fast and hard. Finally, she succumbed to her punishment, lying over Issy's lap, sobbing breathlessly, her tears creating a wet patch on the sofa.

"From now on, are you going to listen when Daddy gives you an order?" Issy asked sternly, he was now massaging her poor bottom gently.

"Yes, Daddy. I promise."

"Good Girl."

He flipped her over, holding her on his lap and rocking her slightly. She buried her face in his chest.

"Can I get anything for her?" Archer asked quietly.

"Can you get Bumbly and her snuggly? She needs a bottle too; she missed her afternoon snack and I didn't want to interrupt her. Although I see now that I should have."

A bottle? In front of Archer?

"Shh," Issy told her quietly, obviously feeling her tense. "He's part of this. He doesn't have to be your Daddy, but he has to be okay with all of this. And I can tell you that he is."

She hoped so. Archer returned with her snuggly, Bumbly and a pair of fuzzy socks. They were yellow and black stripped and her favorite. He handed her Bumbly and her snuggly before slipping her socks on.

She thought she probably looked a bit silly dressed in a T-shirt and a pair of socks with a red ass. Then he surprised her by grabbing some tissues and wiping her face.

"Blow," he commanded.

She blew her nose. He moved to the kitchen and started preparing a bottle with her special nutritional shake. He knew how to do that?

"Besides," Issy told her in a quiet voice, "I think he has more of a Daddy side than he knows."

Archer returned with her bottle and Issy leaned her back. She shifted around to get comfortable on her hot ass as he held the nipple up to her mouth. She sucked on it, watching Archer move around. But every so often he'd look over at them.

Was that a hint of longing in his eyes?

"Right, I'm going to start dinner. Archer, you want to sit with Caley and keep her company?"

That wasn't half obvious. But she refrained from rolling her eyes at Issy as he stood with the empty bottle taking it up to the kitchen. She attempted to pull her T-shirt down to cover her butt as Archer moved over to sit next to her.

"Can I put my pants back on?"

"Nope," Issy said cheerfully.

She stuck her tongue out at him as he turned his back.

"Uh-uh, poppet. I saw that." Archer bopped her gently on the nose as she gave him an innocent look. Drat, she'd forgotten he was there.

"What did she do?" Issy asked.

She looked up at Archer with beseeching eyes. He shook his head. "Don't think you can play one of us off against the other."

He sat on the couch and settled her in against him. He picked her snuggly off the floor, where it had fallen and handed it to her. She gave him a shy smile, bringing the piece of material up to her nose to rub it back and forth. Then she slipped her thumb into her mouth as Archer relaxed back and turned on the T.V.

"She stuck her tongue out at you."

"Did she just," Issy drawled. "Well, I'll have to find something to do with that tongue later."

She blushed as Archer chuckled.

"Cat got your tongue now, poppet?"

She shrugged, not taking her thumb from her mouth.

"What do you want to watch?" he asked.

She glanced up at him, he looked tired.

"We can watch the news," she offered.

He stared down at her. "I don't think so. Nothing on the news for a Little girl to watch." He settled on a popular cartoon and she snuggled in against him.

She could get used to this.

35

"I cannot believe Hunter wants me to go on some weekend training course for his newest hires," Doc muttered irritably.

She sat on the bed, watching him pack. He was frowning. She felt sorry for everyone going on this overnight training course. Issy was not in the best of moods.

"Why does he need a doctor?" she asked, bringing her legs up to her chest and wrapping her arms around them. "Is it dangerous?"

"Knowing Hunter, possibly."

Her eyes widened.

He sighed and leaned over to flick her nose. "Don't stress, baby doll. All I'll be doing is sitting on the sidelines, bored out of my brains until someone injures themselves."

She bit her lip. She didn't like the idea of him leaving, but he owed Hunter a favor. He had to go. He didn't exactly have an excuse not to.

"Now, while I'm gone, I still expect you to follow your rules.

And keep typing down to a minimum, understand?" Issy gave her a firm look.

She nodded.

"No working too long and no stressing about me."

She nodded again.

"Hey, I'll be here, remember?" Archer said, walking into the room. He had a cup of coffee in his hand. "I'm perfectly capable of taking care of her."

Issy grunted. "Only reason I agreed to this favor."

Archer looked into his bag. "Man, that is a lot of protein bars."

"Probably all I'll be eating this weekend. Who knows how clean this place will be? Or who will be doing the cooking? I could end up with food poisoning and die."

Caley took in a sharp breath and Issy winced.

"Good one," Archer told him.

"Sorry, baby doll." He leaned over and kissed her. "You know I'm exaggerating. I'm just in a grump because I don't want to leave you." He lifted his duffel bag and turned to Archer, picking up a piece of paper off the bedside table and handing it to him. "I've written out a list for her care. Rules are on the back."

Archer gave him an exasperated look. "I've got this. It's two nights. What could happen?"

Issy grumbled something under his breath about fire and hospitals. She blushed. His phone rang and he answered it.

"Yeah, yeah, I'm coming. What? You're fucking kidding! I'm not happy about this. Fucking fine."

He ended the call with a scowl. "They're downstairs in a fucking van waiting for me. Apparently, we're going somewhere with patchy reception so don't worry if you don't hear from me. I'll be back sometime tomorrow afternoon." As he spoke, he moved to the front door. Then he stopped and turned, opening his arms.

She dove into them, wrapping herself around him. He hugged

her tight. Then he kissed the top of her head. "Gonna miss you, baby doll."

"Miss you too."

"Do as Archer says. Make sure he takes care of you. He messes up, you tell me, and I'll beat him up for you when I get back. I can do it. I've got more muscle."

Archer just snorted and set his empty cup down on the kitchen counter.

Issy finally let her go and stepped out without a backward glance. As the door shut, she felt Archer sweep his arms around her.

"Hmm, I have you all to myself now. Whatever shall we do?"

She laughed as he swept her up into his arms.

ARCHER CARRIED his precious bundle into the bedroom. Christ, he couldn't believe she was here with him. That she was his.

His and Issy's. But that didn't mean his bond with her was less. Far from it. He was sharing her with the only other person in this life he truly loved.

He set her down on her feet by the bed. He knew part of the reason Issy said yes to this weekend was because he wanted to give them some time alone. And he appreciated that.

More than he could say.

"Don't you have to get to the office?" she asked as he set her down by the bed. He had a few things to do this afternoon and then he was pretty much done.

"I have a bit of time." Enough time for some play. He sat on the bed. "Strip for me."

He watched her eyes flare open with arousal. His cock was hard, pressed against his pants. Fuck, he wanted her. All he'd been able to think about for weeks was her.

And now she's yours.

She slowly stripped off her clothes, folding each item neatly until she was dressed just in panties and a bra.

"Keep going," he growled.

She pulled off her bra, displaying her beautiful breasts. "Offer one to me."

After a momentary look of confusion, she stepped forward between his open legs and cupped one breast, offering it up to his mouth. He suckled on it until she was groaning, little whimpers coming from her lips.

"So beautiful," he told her. "Panties off now then I want you to find your position." He hadn't had time for much play with her. He'd been too busy trying to wrap up his life here. But he was determined to take advantage of his time alone with her. After today, he had the whole weekend free to play with her.

And there was something important he needed to discuss with her.

He stood and walked around her as she knelt on the floor, her legs spread, her pussy on display.

"So gorgeous." He stood behind her then, wrapped his hands in her hair and tugged her head back. Leaning down, he ravished her mouth.

When he drew back, her eyelids were heavy-lidded, her lips swollen, her cheeks flushed. He removed his hand from her hair.

"Stand and then bend over, show me your ass and pussy."

Her eyes widened slightly but she stood without argument. Her obedience fucking did something to him. Satisfaction filled him.

She bent over and he ran his hand over her firm ass cheek. Then he slapped it. He did love seeing his hand print on her ass.

Neanderthal.

"Spread your legs."

She widened her feet and he got a glimpse at that perfect

pussy. Reaching out, he ran a finger down her lips. Wet. Hot. Delicious.

Bending down, he bit one cheek and she let out a small cry.

"One day soon, I'm taking this ass, love. And fuck, it will be so good. Right now, though I want to feel your pussy squeezing around me."

He wished he had time to truly play with her. To tease it out.

Later.

He ran his hand over her bottom, slapping the other cheek. Damn, he wasn't going to last long with all this deliciousness on display.

"Get on the bed. Hands behind your head. Legs bent, feet flat on the mattress, thighs spread."

"Yes, Sir."

Hell. Yes.

As she got into position, he stripped off his clothes. He grabbed his cock, running his hand up and down it, squeezing the base, knowing he needed to calm down a bit.

"Oh. Wow," she muttered.

He had to grin. "Like what you see, love?" He moved his hand up the shaft again.

"Yes. Yes, Sir. Please, can I touch?"

He shook his head. "Not right now. Right now, I need to taste you. I need to fuck you."

He grabbed a condom from the bedside table and rolled it on. He moved between her open legs then dived into her pussy, his tongue working her clit then fucking her with shallow thrusts. He heard that hitch in her breath, felt her tense and knew she was close.

He drew back.

She let out a pained cry. "No! Go back! I was close."

"I know, love. That's why I drew back."

He teased her again. Tortured her up to the edge then pulled back. Her cry was loud. A wail.

"Nooo. That's so mean."

With a grin, he flicked her clit. Softly. Gently. Her small whimpers made his cock weep with pre-cum. Fuck. He was torturing himself. When he couldn't wait much longer, he took her up and over the edge. Her cries of release filled the room as he drove himself deep inside her.

Her passage clenched down around him, nearly making him come on the first thrust.

Fuck. That would be embarrassing. He took a moment, breathed in deep. Found his center.

"Wrap your legs around me, love. Hold on tight."

"Always, Sir. Always."

It didn't take long until he shattered, his roar of release erupting from him as he came, collapsing on top of her, his heart racing, sweat coating his skin. She ran her hands up and down his back until he managed to find the energy to roll to his side.

"Christ, I can't move. I need to get up. Shower. Get ready," he muttered.

"Ooh, yes. Shower sex."

He huffed out a laugh. "Love, you're gonna kill me."

SHE FELT nervous as she walked into the reception area. Archer had planned on coming home to get her before they went out to dinner, but he'd called earlier to say he was running late and he'd send a car for her.

First time she'd ever had a town car sent for her. She smoothed down her teal-colored dress. She hoped it was good enough for wherever they were going.

She wasn't used to fancy dinners. But it was what Archer liked.

And she wanted to give him what he liked. Especially, since he wouldn't have as much opportunity for nice dinners out when they were at Sanctuary.

His PA looked up as she approached. What was her name again? Susan, that was it. She barely recognized her as the same woman at the BDSM club the other night. She felt slightly awkward about the whole thing.

"Yes?" the other woman said coldly.

"I'm here to meet Archer," she replied, taken aback. "We're going out for dinner."

Susan looked her up and down and the look in her eyes said that she didn't approve of what Caley wore.

Something inside her started to shrivel. Then she reminded herself that she didn't care what this woman thought. She was nothing to her. Caley tilted her chin up.

"He'll be out soon." Susan stood. Then leaned over her desk. "You know you won't last, right?"

She blinked at the other woman. "Excuse me?"

"I know you've been chasing him. Getting injured so he'd come rushing to you was a good play. Seems it worked. For now."

She thought Caley got injured on purpose? Who the hell did that?

"You didn't forget to give him that message, did you?" she asked as it all clicked. "You purposefully didn't give it to him."

Susan sniffed. "I've known Archer a long time. Women never last. They come and go quickly, but I've always remained. He'll realize he's slumming it and come back."

She had a crush on him. Something like pity stirred inside Caley. "He's quit his job. He's moving away. He's not coming back."

Susan narrowed her gaze. "You are delusional, aren't you? My dear, you're not going to hold onto him. He's only with you because of his brother. I know what you are."

"What I am?" Okay, that pity was disappearing. Fast.

"I know you're a Little." She sneered at Caley. "Heard Hunter Black say it to his wife."

A gut punch. She sucked in a breath. Susan's disdain was clear. Which was odd when she was a sub herself. Somehow, she thought it would make the other woman less judgmental about Caley's needs and desires.

"Archer doesn't need someone like you. He's not into that," she spat out. "And look at you, you're hardly his type. You're a country bumpkin when he's style and class. All I have to do is wait you out and he'll come crawling back to me."

Her mouth was dry. Her heartbeat going too fast. Part of her wanted to run and hide. Part of her agreed with the other woman.

Except...he came for her when she was injured. He sat by her side all night. Held her through her nightmares. He wanted her. He loved her. Just a few hours ago, he'd made love to her.

And he wasn't ashamed or disgusted by her Little.

So why should Caley be? She thrust her shoulders back. "That's where you're wrong. I am exactly who Archer wants. How long has he known you?"

"Years," Susan said proudly.

"Years. And yet he's never once made a move on you, right? He's known me for less than two months and he's moving halfway across the country for me."

Susan flinched. Caley felt a bit bad, but the other woman started it.

"I could ruin you. I could ruin his career. Tell everyone about the three of you. About what you are."

"We're all consenting adults."

"Do you think people care? They'll think you're perverted. You'll ruin him."

"Go ahead," a deep voice said from behind Susan. She paled.

Caley jumped and looked over to see Archer standing there. How had she not noticed him? How much had he heard?

"W-what?" Susan asked.

"You can try to ruin my career. Although I doubt you will. People would actually have to care what you said. Thing is, though, at my new job nobody will care about the muttering of a disgruntled, bitchy personal assistant." Archer moved around Susan to stand by Caley. He pulled her in against him. "I am glad to learn about your true nature before I left, Susan. I'll be sure to let Hunter know about your opinion of Littles. And your loose tongue outside the club."

Susan flinched then her gaze narrowed. "You care! You can't not care! When you come back—"

"I'm not coming back," he replied. "Goodbye, Susan. I hope to never see you again." He drew Caley against him, his arm firmly around her waist and turned them towards the door.

"Your parents will care!" she spat out. "They'll want to know."

"Good Lord, I'm a grown man and she thinks I care about what my parents think?" he said loudly to Caley, winking down at her. The door closed on Susan's sputtering.

He led her towards the elevator.

"Good girl," he murmured quietly. "Not too much further. Just hold it together."

The elevator dinged open and he stepped inside, drawing her with him. He tapped the B for basement and then once the doors were closed, she collapsed against him.

"Caley, baby, I'm so sorry." He ran his hand up and down her back. "You're safe. I have you. You're safe."

She knew she was safe. She always was with him. Why was he saying that?

Maybe because you're shaking.

Oh, right.

"Caley? Talk to me, love. You're not crying, are you?"

She buried her face against his chest.

"Baby, it's all right. Just hold it together. You're safe. I'm not going to let anything happen to you. Papa's here."

She tensed. Papa?

Something tickled at the back of her mind. She'd thought it was a dream, though. She leaned back to look up at him. "Papa?"

Red filled his cheeks. "Didn't mean to blurt that out like that."

"I heard you call yourself that. At the hospital. But I thought it was part of my dream."

He ran his hand over her hair. "It wasn't. Umm, can we table that for the moment and go back to what happened. Are you all right? You're not upset?"

"I'm not upset. I'm fucking livid." She'd get back to the Papa stuff soon. "That...that bitch!"

She was vaguely aware of his eyes widening.

"How dare she! Who does she think she is? Where does she get off threatening to tell your parents! I ought to go back there and kick her ass!"

Suddenly, she realized how quiet and still he was. She froze. Had she said the wrong thing? Then he shocked her by throwing his head back and laughing.

"Hey! What's so funny?"

He wiped the tears off his cheeks. "Forgive me. It's just...I was expecting you to freak out not threaten to go kick Susan's ass."

Her cheeks grew red. "Sorry."

"Hey, you have nothing to be sorry about." He reached out and tipped up her chin. "You have every right to be mad. And I think in this case, anger is good. A few months ago, how do you think you would have reacted?"

She thought that over as the elevator opened and he took her hand, leading her to his car. He opened the passenger door, even doing up her seatbelt.

When he started up the car, she turned to him. "I might have frozen. Or panicked. Felt ashamed or scared. I did kind of feel like that. But then it turned to anger over her threats. She made me so mad."

He grabbed hold of her thigh. "That's why I'm so proud of you. You didn't let what she said to you make you spiral back to how *they* made you feel."

"I didn't, did I?"

"I'm proud of you, baby."

Happiness filled her. Then she frowned as she thought about Susan's threats. "Are you worried? Do you think she'll tell your parents about us? About me?"

Anxiety stirred at the thought of what his parents would think. Would they disown him like they had Issy?

He stopped at a light and looked over at her. "I don't care if she does."

"Are you sure?" She nibbled at her lower lip.

He reached out to free her lip. "I'm very sure. If they react badly then that's their issue, not mine. However, I think it's better that I tell them myself."

She nodded. She was glad she didn't have to have that conversation. And she was worried about his relationship with his parents. But he was right. She couldn't control their reactions.

"You are the most important thing in my life, Caley. If they can't accept you or Isaac being in my life then I don't need them in mine. I'm not some young kid. I know what I want. Now that I have you, nothing is taking you from me."

She let the last of her worries flitter away. He moved forward as the light went green.

"So where's dinner? And am I dressed all right?"

"You know what? I don't think I feel like going out for dinner anymore. What say we get some drive-through, go home and you can show me what exactly is under that very sexy dress?"

"I'd say that sounds perfect."

36

Caley listened to his heart beat as she lay against his chest. She felt sated. Tired. Slightly sore, because boy, someone seemed to be trying out every position in the Kama Sutra tonight.

But so happy she could melt.

"I have something for you," he murmured.

Did it have something to do with him calling himself Papa in the elevator earlier? "You do?"

He wiggled out from under her and moved towards the wardrobe. She ogled his amazing ass for a moment.

"But Archer, you've given me so much already." Some of which went up in flames in her cabin. She still hadn't heard from the fire marshal about the fire.

"You deserve so much more."

He turned with a large, wrapped box in his hands. He walked back, setting it down on the bed in front of her. It was quite large and she moved onto her knees to tear into the paper. Archer chuckled as bits of paper went everywhere.

"Issy would have a fit at this."

She just grinned. Then she lifted the lid of the box, surprised by the coloring book and pens inside. The coloring book wasn't an adult one, but rather a child's one with pictures of animals on the front. The pens were scented. She drew them out, setting them on the bed.

"Archer, these are so cute."

"Glad you like it. Keep going."

She looked again, pulling out an over-sized pacifier that was obviously for an adult. She blushed slightly. Was this his way of saying he was okay with her Little? She already knew that.

"That's to stop you from sucking your thumb."

She pouted slightly at that.

The next thing she drew out was a tube of bubbles. Ooh fun! She guessed she'd have to wait until Daddy returned to blow them, though.

The last thing was a nightie. It was soft, teal-colored and across the front were the words,

Papa's little girl

She sucked in a breath. Then she looked up at him as she held the nightie to her chest. "Archer?"

He cleared his throat and shuffled his weight back and forth. She'd never seen him look so nervous. "I...I never thought I was a Daddy Dom. Didn't think that was my thing. Until I met you. Then something came awake inside me. I tried to push it aside. But it kept building and building. I want to be your Daddy, little girl. Except, I figured two Daddies might be confusing. So will you accept me as your Papa?"

"You don't have to do this," she whispered.

"I know that. I'm not doing this because I have to. No, that's not right." He sat on the bed, facing her. "I'm doing this because it's what I want. It's a big part of who you are. And I need to give that to you. But I know you could get that from Issy and I'm not doing it because I think I have to in order to be equal in your heart."

"You're both equal in my heart."

He smiled gently, reaching over to squeeze her leg. "And I'm so grateful for that. I'm doing this because it feels right. I've loved you, perhaps since the moment I met you. This part of me, it wasn't an instant change, it's not something I'm jumping into. It's something I want and desire. To be your Papa. So, will you have me?"

She threw herself into his arms. "Yes, yes, yes!"

He laughed, pulling her onto his lap and squeezing her tight. "Well, thank God for that. Now, you might have to be patient with me. I don't have a lot of practice."

"You can have all the practice with me you need, Papa." She dropped her head back and he kissed her lips lightly.

"Does this mean I can play with the bubbles now!" she squealed.

"I don't think so, poppet. It's bedtime not playtime. And Daddy left me a list of instructions for your care. I'm already in trouble for not putting you to bed on time."

She pouted. Drat. She had a feeling it wasn't going to take him long at all to work out this Daddy stuff.

ARCHER FINISHED WASHING the suds off her breasts, trying not to let the sight stir him.

Well, not too much.

He was only human after all. But he knew she was exhausted. He'd kept her up too late. He'd need to put her down for a nap tomorrow.

It still surprised him how much satisfaction he got at the thought of taking care of her like that.

"Right, stand up, poppet." He grabbed a towel and wrapped it around her before lifting her out of the bath. He then dried her off thoroughly.

"Can I sleep in my new nightie, Papa?" she asked with a big yawn. She wiped at her eyes.

That was damn adorable.

He didn't know if he'd be this way with anyone else or if it was just Caley.

Didn't matter since there was never going to be anyone else for him.

"Of course you can, poppet."

Once she was dry, he picked her up and carried her, naked, out into the bedroom where he set her on the bed.

"Lay back, poppet, and I'll put your panties on."

She lay back tiredly, reaching for snuggly and pulling the piece of material close. Her thumb went into her mouth and he reached over and grabbed the pacifier he'd bought her. She pouted a bit but opened her mouth and took it.

Yep. Adorable.

He put clean panties on her, then sat her up to put her nightie on. Another wave of satisfaction. Funny, he was more used to taking clothes off women than dressing them.

But then, no one was like Caley.

He set a pillow on the floor. "Sit there, poppet. I'll get your hairbrush and braid your hair. Then I'll give you a bottle and put you to bed."

She removed the pacifier. "Yes, Papa."

She sat on the floor between his legs and he brushed out her hair. When it was tamed, he started to braid it.

"You're good at this, Papa."

"Oh, yeah?"

"Uh-huh. Don't tell Daddy, but he tugs too hard."

Archer had to grin at that. It was maybe a bit childish, but he liked that he was better at something than Issy when it came to her care.

"Right, let's get you into bed, poppet. I'll make your bottle."

"Umm..." She stood then hesitated.

"What is it?" He stood as well, staring down at her.

"I gots to do my teeth and go potty first," she whispered.

He shook his head. "Sorry, poppet, of course you do. Remember, I'm new to this stuff. I'm going to forget things. If you need something, you have to tell me, all right?"

"Okay, Papa."

"Good girl. Go do what you need to, I'll meet you back here."

When he returned with her bottle, she was lying on her side rubbing snuggly against her nose. The pacifier sat on the nightstand.

"Uh-uh, you're to use your pacifier, poppet. I catch you sucking your thumb instead and you'll find yourself over my knee."

She gave him big, puppy dog eyes but he kept his face stern. Finally she sighed and removed her thumb. "Okay, Papa."

He lay on the bed next to her, pulling her into his chest and feeding her the bottle.

Yeah. He could really get used to this.

SHE WOKE WITH A GASP. Sweat coated her skin and she was shivering. She looked around, disorientated. Where was she? What was going on?

Finally, her brain clicked into gear and her memory returned. She was in Archer's penthouse apartment.

He'd done pretty well at getting her settled and off to sleep. She'd wondered if she would have a nightmare after that run-in with Susan. Damn it. She pushed the covers back quietly and stood. Unfortunately, she didn't think she would be going back to sleep anytime soon. She walked into the living room, to stare out the big window at the twinkling lights of Dallas.

"Love? What are you doing?"

His sleep-roughened voice startled her and she turned, looking into the bedroom. He'd left the bathroom light on and she could see him climbing out of the huge bed.

"Sorry. I didn't mean to wake you. I had a nightmare. You should go back to sleep."

He walked towards her then swept her up in his arms and carried her over to the sofa. He settled on the sofa. "What was your nightmare about?"

She shuddered. "I can't remember, I think that confrontation with Susan stirred things up in my mind."

He hugged her against him. "I'm sorry, love."

"It's not your fault she's a bitch who got fixated on you." She leaned back. "You should go back to sleep. I'm going to stay up for a bit."

"No, you're not," he said.

"I don't think I'll be able to sleep."

"What's the rule when you wake up at night, Caley?" he asked. His voice was so calm that for a moment she missed the hint of steel.

She straightened her back. Uh-oh. "Umm, I'm to wake you or Issy up. But—"

"Did you wake me up?"

"No. But—"

"What happens when you break a rule, Caley?"

She shifted around on his lap. "But—"

"No buts," he said sternly. "What happens?"

"I get punished."

"Did you think that just because Issy wasn't here that the rules didn't apply?"

"No," she whispered.

"So how do you think I should punish you?"

"Time-out?"

"I don't think so."

Standing, he carried her into the bathroom. He set her down in front of the counter.

"Pull off your panties and nightie. Grasp hold of the edge of the counter then lean right over, spread those legs."

He picked up her hairbrush.

Oh hell. She was in trouble.

She stripped off her clothes and got into position. "Couldn't we talk about this?"

"What do you want to talk about?" he asked calmly.

Standing, she turned. She looked around for something to say to delay the inevitable. "Umm."

He raised an eyebrow. "Are you stalling?"

Her shoulders slumped. "Maybe."

He shook his head.

"You need a reminder of what happens when you break the rules. This is about your care. I want you to know you can come to me. About anything. Issy isn't the only one who can take care of you."

There was a hint of something in his voice. Hurt? Vulnerability. She wasn't used to hearing that from him. He always seemed so confident.

She took a step forward and wrapped her arms around his waist.

"I know I can come to you with anything," she told him. "You keep me grounded. You're the person I go to when I need advice. You're my sounding-board, my calm, my Archie. My Papa. And I love you with all my heart."

He leaned in and kissed her. When he drew back, his face was lighter and there was a small smile on his face. That disappeared as he pointed at her.

"In position. Now."

She turned around and leaned over with her hands grasping the counter. There was no getting out of this now. The first smack of the hairbrush made her cry out. The second had her shifting on her feet.

"Stay still, little one. You don't want me to have to repeat any of these."

No, she definitely did not want that.

Two more landed and tears dripped down her face. Then a sob broke free. By the time he reached eight smacks, her ass was on fire.

Another two, one to each cheek and then he put the hairbrush down before she found herself lifted and turned, being cradled against Archer's chest. He carried her into the bedroom and lay on his back with her sprawled over him.

She sobbed into his chest, completely soaking through his pajama top.

"Easy, baby. Hush, now, you're going to make yourself ill. Shh. It's all right, baby. Christ, did I hit you too hard? Caley, talk to me."

She became aware of the worry in his voice and forced herself to stop sobbing.

He rolled them both so they were on their sides, facing one another then he leaned over her to grab a tissue, wiping her up.

"Sorry. Sorry," she said hastily.

"Was I too harsh?"

She shook her head. "It wasn't the spanking. Or not just that. I think I needed the physical pain to let go of some of the pain inside me."

"Ahh, it was a cathartic cry." He pulled her close and she settled her face against his chest with a hiccup.

He rubbed his hand up and down her back and just held her until she'd settled. A yawn took her by surprise.

"Hmm, maybe instead of pleasuring you when you can't sleep, we should just be spanking you."

She stiffened. "I prefer the orgasms."

He chuckled then he lightly pressed her back so she was lying on her back. "What if you could have both?"

She raised her eyebrows. "I don't usually get pleasure after punishment."

"I'll make an exception," he told her as he moved between her legs and spread them wide before pushing up her nightie, "just this once."

Her breath stuttered as he swiped his tongue along her slit then swirled it around her clit.

Well, if he wanted to make an exception then who was she to argue?

37

"I'm home!" Doc stepped into the apartment, setting his bag down by the door to take care of later. There was something more important he needed to do first.

And that was feel his girl's arms around him.

Caley glanced up from where she was kneeling at the coffee table. She had a coloring book and pens in front of her. But as soon as she saw him, she dropped her pen and raced towards him.

"Daddy! I missed you!"

She jumped into his arms and he held her tight. He carried her to the sofa and sat with her on his lap. He didn't want to let her go.

"I missed you, baby doll."

He noticed she was wearing clothes he'd never seen before. Some tights with pictures of dachshunds on them and a T-shirt dress with Princess written across the chest.

Seemed someone had taken her shopping. And let her Little loose.

"Don't go away again," she demanded, waggling her finger at him.

His lips twitched. "Believe me, I'll try not to. Definitely won't be going anywhere with Hunter Black again. That guy is cranky."

She broke out into giggles.

"Hey! What's so funny?"

"It's just you complaining about someone else being cranky. Your nickname is Dr. Cranky, Daddy."

He growled. "Well, he's crankier than me. And he can't cook for shit. And the lodge where we were staying was filthy. Spent half my time cleaning it."

"Poor Daddy." She patted his cheek lightly.

"Yes, feel sympathy for me. I missed you the entire time. I need cuddles and kisses to make up for it."

She laid kisses all over his face then hugged him tight. "Want to see my coloring?"

"Of course."

She wiggled off his lap and held up the book that had been sitting on the coffee table.

He glanced at the picture. "That's gorgeous. Where'd you get the coloring book from, baby doll?"

He hadn't seen it before, either.

"Papa bought it and the pens for me! He also took me shopping yesterday for new clothes." She got up and did a twirl, nearly tripping over her own feet.

Archer jumped up and grabbed her, steadying her as she giggled. "Whoops."

"Steady, poppet. We don't want you getting hurt." Archer spoke calmly but with a note of command. Then he picked their girl up, sitting with her on his lap.

The look of happiness on his brother's face made Doc smile in response. Fuck. This felt so right. Coming back to the two of them was coming home.

"Papa?" he asked.

Archer shrugged. "Figured having two daddies was a bit confusing."

"Well, it's about damn time," Doc muttered to him.

Archer just rolled his eyes.

"Come back and give Daddy more cuddles, baby doll," he commanded. "He's had you all weekend."

She bounced back over to him with a giggle as Archer just smiled. She plopped down on his lap.

"Tell me about your weekend."

She proceeded to go through their shopping trip, playing with bubbles, and the fact that Papa went through a drive-through instead of some fancy, stuffy restaurant.

"Fast food, huh?" Doc raised his eyebrows at his brother.

Archer shrugged. "It's okay once in a while, right? Poppet, you're leaving a few things out."

She hunched her shoulders. "I didn't want to talk about that."

"Caley," Archer said warningly.

Okay, now he really had to know. He grabbed her chin, turning her face up to his. "What happened?"

"Papa spanked me." Her lower lip poked out adorably.

"Did he just? Why is that?"

"'Cause I woke up and didn't wake him."

Doc shook his head. "Well, then, sounds like you deserved it."

She sniffled pathetically.

"You know that Daddy would have spanked you for that as well. You have rules and both Daddy and Papa are going to make sure you follow them."

She sighed. Long and loud.

"That's not all," Archer said with a frown. "Susan, my ex-personal assistant spat some vile at Caley." His brother proceeded to tell him about the bitch from hell and everything she'd said.

When he was finished, Doc turned to look down at Caley. "You wanted to kick her ass?"

"Well. Yeah. She made me mad."

He grinned. "That's my girl." He stretched. "I need sleep. And decent food. And then I need to go home. Who's with me?"

"Me!" Caley stuck her hand up in the air, waving it around.

"Me too. I am more than ready to go home."

SHE MOANED as Archer circled her nipple with his tongue. Issy moved down her stomach, kissing along it until he reached her mound.

Pushing her legs apart, he lay on his stomach between them, spreading her pussy lips to lick at her juices. She clenched down on the huge plug in her ass that Issy had inserted earlier after her bath.

And she'd hoped that tonight was the night. The night they were going to take her together.

They'd been leading up to this, increasing the size of her plugs over the time they'd been here in Dallas.

But enough was enough.

She wanted to know what it was like to have them both inside her at the same time.

Issy lapped at her clit as Archer moved his mouth from her nipples to her mouth. He kissed her. She felt her arousal peaking.

He drew back, staring down at her. "God, you're beautiful."

She smiled up at him. Then she groaned as Issy flicked her clit. "Please!"

"Not yet, love. Not until we're inside you. Then you can come."

She pouted. That wasn't fair.

"Issy, she's ready," Archer said. He reached over for some condoms, handing one to his brother.

Issy moved so he was lying on his back on the bed. "Come here, girl."

"Crouch over him on all fours so I can pull the plug out," Archer commanded.

She straddled Issy and he placed his hand around the back of her neck, pulling her towards him so he could kiss her. She felt Archer spreading her ass cheeks then tugging on the plug. He drew it gently out. She moaned quietly and then Issy let her go. He grasped hold of his cock, guiding it inside her. She sighed with enjoyment as he filled her.

She placed her hands on his muscular chest as she moved up and down his thick shaft.

"God, you feel so good!"

"Fuck, yes." His jaw clenched, hunger filling his face. "Hurry the fuck up, Archer. I'm not going to last long. She's sucking on me."

"I'm coming," Archer grumbled. He pressed on her back and she lay against Issy. He held her hips as she felt Archer put more lube on her back passage. Then his cock nudged up against her back hole.

"Deep breath in, Caley," Issy told her. "That's it, now out. Relax."

As she let her breath out, Archer started pushing his way inside her. It stung and for a moment she worried it was too much. That she couldn't take him. But he paused, letting her adjust and Issy drew her lips against his, kissing her, distracting her.

Archer drove forward. Until he was fully seated inside her. Both of them filling her.

"All right, love?" Archer asked from above her.

She was surrounded by them, filled by them and she felt so right, so good, she could barely breathe.

"Yes. Move. Please."

"Doesn't have to ask me twice," Issy muttered.

Archer slid back as Issy drove her down on him. Then Archer pushed inside her ass again. God, it felt so good. It wasn't long until she was writhing between them. Archer groaned above her. "She feels amazing. So tight. So hot."

"Tell me about it, brother."

"Less talking, more making Caley come," she demanded.

They both stalled. No. No, no, no.

"She's sassy," Archer said.

"Bossy." Issy gave her a stern look.

"Remind me to spank her. After," Archer grunted.

"With pleasure."

Archer reached around and slipped his hand between their bodies, toying with her clit. She cried out, clenching down around them.

"Fuck!" Issy grabbed her hips, holding her as he pounded inside her. Archer held still for the moment, concentrating on her pleasure.

"Come, love," he said quietly.

"Come. Now," Issy demanded.

And, ever obedient, she obeyed. She came with a loud cry, spiraling up and up then falling with a crash. She heard Issy swear as he gave a final thrust. Then Archer moved faster, harder until he roared with his own release.

They both rolled, keeping her sandwiched between them as they lay on their sides.

She never wanted to leave.

Then Issy sat up and shuffled off the bed.

"Noo," she groaned. "Archer, make him come back to bed."

Issy reached over to drag her out as well. She let out a yell of surprise as he tossed her over his shoulder and slapped her ass. "We've got a long journey home. I want to get an early start. Especially now that Archer has added on a detour."

They were leaving Dallas today, driving back to Sanctuary in Archer's car. Doc had been teasing him about what he was going to do with a city car in the country.

When she'd asked about bringing her own truck down to the ranch, both men had just glared at her. She'd figure it out. With a bit of work she was certain her truck could get up to a high enough standard for them to let her drive it.

Maybe.

Archer sighed. "It's not that I want to go talk to them. But I think I have to."

Issy just grunted. "Well, you're not going alone."

"Issy, you don't have to come talk to them with me, you can wait at a hotel with Caley."

"We're family, aren't we?" Issy said abruptly.

"Yeah," Archer replied huskily. "We're family."

"Then I'm coming with you. We do this together."

"I'm coming too," she said, trying to wiggle off Issy's shoulder. He slapped her ass again.

"You are not," Issy barked.

"Absolutely not," Archer agreed.

They were ganging up on her. She sighed. She had a feeling this would be her life from now on.

And she couldn't be happier.

SHE SHIFTED around on her seat nervously as they drove through the Chicago suburbs. It had taken a couple of long days of driving to get here. Issy was relentless in his desire to get home. She thought it was mostly because he hated staying in hotels and eating out.

"Poppet, do you need to go potty?" Archer asked her.

Oh hell. For a man who hadn't been certain he was a Daddy Dom, he sure caught on quickly. Her face was bright red as he turned in the front seat to look at her.

"No, Papa."

"You're moving around like you do. Daddy can find a toilet."

"Told you we shouldn't have let her drink that giant coffee this morning," Issy grumbled.

"Stopping for a few minutes isn't going to add anything onto our journey, you old grump," Archer replied.

She giggled quietly.

"What's so funny?" Issy asked from the driver's seat.

"Nothing, Daddy," she said sweetly. "I'm okay, I don't need the toilet."

"If you don't need the potty why can't you sit still?" Archer asked.

Damn it. Couldn't he leave this alone?

"Maybe it's because someone was mean and spanked me last night," she muttered.

"That's because someone was naughty and wasn't using her pacifier," Archer reminded her.

"I think that spankings shouldn't be allowed on a road trip," she said sulkily. She'd already tried this argument before and lost.

"I'm starting to think that someone needs a nap," Issy said. "Maybe we should stop at a hotel for the night and go to their house tomorrow."

Their house. Not his house. She bit her lip. She knew Issy was so grouchy because he was nervous. From the look Archer shot his brother, she could tell he'd worked that out as well.

"You don't have to go in, Issy. I'm happy to go alone."

"We've already had this argument," Issy replied.

They pulled down a tree-lined street. The houses here were all large, set on big lots. Easy to tell that it was a wealthy neighborhood. This is where they'd grown up? She looked around curiously. Issy pulled into a circular driveway and parked in front of a gray stone house. She peered up at the house. It seemed so cold. So dark. She couldn't imagine two small boys living here.

"I still think I should come in," she said.

Both men turned to give her incredulous looks.

"You're not coming, girl," Issy said strictly.

"But—"

"No way in hell, love," Archer agreed.

"I don't want you near those vipers," Issy told her. "But I also think this is something that Archer and I need to do. Alone."

That silenced any arguments. She got it. And truthfully, she was a bit relieved.

"It's not that we're ashamed of you or hiding you away, love," Archer said worriedly. "It's just something..."

"The two of you have to do. It's all right. Really."

"Stay in the car," Issy barked orders. "Lock the doors. Do not move. No matter what. Got me? I come back and you are gone and you will not sit down for a week."

"I'll be here. I promise."

They each gave her a long look. Issy's full of heat and fire. Archer's calm and steadying.

Then they left and she took in a deep breath to try to calm her nerves. If she felt this bad, she could only imagine how they were feeling.

Doc tried not to let the memories swamp him. Remembering the last time he'd been in this cold, sterile house. Nothing much had changed. They waited at the door for Archer's knock to be answered. When the door slid open, there stood his mother.

She had changed in some ways. She seemed smaller. Her hair was fully gray now. And there was a fragility to her that hadn't been there before. But in other ways, she was still the same. The polite smile that never filled her eyes. Tailored, expensive clothes that were flattering yet boring at the same time.

"Archer, this is a surprise, you should have called, dear. We'd have had your room prepared."

Issy snorted, unable to stop himself. Her gaze turned to him as though she'd just noticed him, when he was sure she'd spotted him as soon as he stepped out of Archer's car.

"Isaac. Why are you here? Archer, why would you bring...him?"

Archer sucked in a breath. "Mother, Issy is my brother."

She sniffed. "You will refrain from using that ridiculous nickname in my house."

Doc waited for his brother's agreement. Instead Archer stiffened.

"Then I suppose I'll just say what I came to say from out here."

His mother rocked back on her heels.

"Agatha, who is here?" Their father moved into the foyer. "Archer? What are you doing standing out there? Come in."

"And what about Isaac? Is he welcome?" Archer sniped.

"Isaac made his bed," their father said coldly.

"You lied to me," Archer said to them. "You told me that he left. That he didn't want to be part of the family anymore."

"He did leave," their mother said. "He had a choice."

"Reform or leave," Issy said dryly. "That was my choice, huh, mother?"

"That stuff you were watching was sick," his mother hissed. "Imagine if anyone found out."

And that was the heart of it. What other people thought.

"They haven't changed," he said to Archer. "They never will."

Archer nodded his face cold. "I just came to tell you that I quit my job in Dallas. I'm moving in with Issy. We're sharing a beautiful, darling woman who you will never, ever meet. Not only is she my sub, but she's my Little girl as well as Issy's."

His mother's mouth dropped open. "This...this isn't happening!"

"It is," Archer replied. "I came to tell you as a courtesy since my assistant was threatening to call you herself. Although from your shock, I can see she hasn't."

"Harold!" his mother yelled.

"This...this is preposterous," his father blustered. He turned to Doc. "This is your fault. This is your doing."

"Yes!" His mother took up the cry, her face twisted and nasty as she stared up at him. "This is you."

Archer stepped back and took hold of his arm, pulling him away. "Actually, it's not. This is what I want. I want to share this gorgeous, wonderful woman with my brother. I want to be her Papa with Issy as her Daddy. And from your reactions, you'll never accept that. It would be best if you didn't call me."

With that parting shot, Archer led him away. Their mother called after them, but they both ignored her.

"I'm driving this time," Archer said, opening the driver's side.

Issy got into the back with Caley instead.

"What is it? Are you okay? Issy? Archer?" she asked worriedly.

He slid into the middle seat and pulled her against him. He took in her scent as she surrounded him with her love. There was silence for a long moment.

"I take it that it didn't go well," she said quietly.

"No worse than expected, love," Archer told her calmly.

"You didn't have to do that," he told his brother. "Cut yourself off from them like that for me."

"I didn't do it for you," Archer said. He pulled over to the side of the road. Then he got out and opened the back door. Caley undid her belt and they both moved over so Archer could climb in. They held her between them, surrounding her.

"I did it for us. They think you two aren't good enough for them, but they have it the wrong way around. They're not good enough for you. And I won't have that poison in our lives."

Doc sighed. Thank fuck.

"I love this, you know," she said quietly. "The three of us together. It just feels right."

He kissed the top of her head. "You know when I said I didn't believe in happy-ever-after's?"

"Yes," she said slowly.

"I think I've changed my mind."

She dug her face into his chest with a happy sigh.

"Take us home, Archie," she demanded.

"Gladly."

"And try not to crash this time, huh?" Issy said.

"You crash one vehicle and you never hear the end of it," Archer grumbled as Caley giggled.

Doc just smiled. If Archer had never crashed then they likely wouldn't have met Caley and if they hadn't met Caley, well, he wouldn't have everything he'd ever wanted and never thought he'd have.

His love. His Little. His brother.

EPILOGUE

"**D**o I gots to, Papa?" She gave Archer her best pout, using her biggest eyes as she pleaded with him.

She was dressed in a pair of leggings and a sweater dress with a picture of a dachshund on the front. Archer had bought it for her during their shopping trip before leaving Dallas. Archer had braided her hair for her this morning and she was wearing a pair of bumblebee slippers that Issy had bought.

They'd been back at Sanctuary for a week now and things had never been better. She knew they'd have some ups and downs. But she also knew that this is where she was supposed to be.

Soon after they arrived, Caley had gotten a call from the fire marshal about her house. Apparently, it had been the heat pack she'd put in the microwave for her hands. She'd left it in there to go say goodbye to Dave and forgotten about it. She was still kicking herself for being so careless, even though Issy and Archer had reassured her often that it was an accident.

She couldn't get back the things she lost, but she knew she wouldn't ever forget Dave. And in the summer, they all planned to go back there, and maybe camp for a while.

She wasn't sure how Archer was going to do with camping, but they'd see. They just needed to ensure he had his coffee. Especially in the mornings when he could almost be as cranky as Issy before his first caffeine hit.

He was constantly surprising her, though. He'd really taken to this Daddy Dom stuff. Maybe more than she'd expected he would. Which sometimes didn't bode well for her ability to sit comfortably. Neither man let her get away with much.

They were getting into a rhythm. She was working less, but still getting plenty done and when she wasn't working, at least one of them was always around. To play with her as Little Caley or as big Caley.

Things would be perfect. Or they would be, if she just had a way of getting rid of the damn punishment jar.

"Yes, Caley Jane, you do," Archer said sternly. "And if you keep procrastinating, you'll be choosing two punishments. You're probably owed that many anyway."

"Good idea, brother," Issy said, moving up to stand beside him, with his arms crossed over his chest.

Uh-oh. Okay, so maybe she should just get this over with.

She shoved her hand in the big jar and pulled a piece of paper out, handing it over to Archer who held out his hand. He looked at it then passed it to Issy who grinned.

For a man who had barely smiled when she first met him, he sure did smile a lot now.

"My favorite. Someone's getting ginger up her butt," Issy said.

"What! No! Papa!" She turned to Archer as Issy strode off to the kitchen with a whistle. They'd decided to expand the cabin so that both she and Archer had office space and she could have the second bedroom as a playroom. When she'd offered to pay for it, though, both of them had acted like she had mortally insulted them. Then she'd had to have a talk with Issy about how, no, she wasn't broke, she just wasn't very good at the day-to-day details which is why her cabin had been falling down.

Issy had been shocked. And a bit upset she hadn't told him. He was still asking to read her books. Even though he now knew her pen name, he hadn't peeked because he said he wanted her to be okay with him reading them first.

Well, she had something planned for him there...

"I'm sorry, poppet. But you have far more frowny faces than smiley faces. By rights, this is actually several weeks' worth of frowns so you should just be grateful that it's a bit of figging and some corner time and not a good strapping on top of it."

Her mouth dropped open. Okay, yeah, she should shut up now.

Quit while you're ahead, Caley.

Issy returned with a piece of ginger in a plastic bag. It was two fingers, but only one had been peeled. She guessed that was the bit that went in her ass while the other bit was used as a handle.

Holy. Crap.

"And here is a piece I prepared earlier. You know, just in case."

"Aww," Archer said. "Isn't he so happy?"

"Nothing like a figging in the morning to set the day off right."

She dropped her lower lip. Archer reached out and tapped it. "Don't worry, poppet. If you're a good girl and take your figging well then Daddy and I have a present for you."

A present? What sort of present?

"What is it? Can I see it now?" She danced up on her tiptoes.

"Nope," Issy said. "Right now, you need to strip off your leggings and panties then get on your back on the couch."

On her back? She looked to Archer who nodded.

She swallowed nervously but did as she'd been ordered. She even took the time to fold her leggings and put them down neatly with her panties. But that was more to procrastinate than because she wanted to be tidy.

Finally, she lay on the couch.

"Archer, if you will?" Issy said as he opened up the bag.

Archer knelt down next to her. "Legs up against your chest, poppet."

What? Oh God. She raised her legs up until she was in the diaper position. Archer placed an arm across the back of them, pinning them in place. Issy sat on the couch and pulled out the ginger plug, holding it up.

"It's beautiful work if I do say so myself." He held the non-skinned end then he parted her ass cheeks.

"Here we go, poppet. Just relax. It's not that big. You've definitely taken bigger." Archer winked at her, reminding her of the other night when she'd taken him there.

He was right. The ginger slipped in easily. It wasn't that long or thick and she didn't really feel much of anything. All right, maybe it was all hype and there wasn't much of a sting.

Then Issy slapped his hand down on her ass.

"Ow!" she cried out, clenching down on the piece of ginger.

Oh. Crap. Her asshole started to sting as the ginger released its juices. Issy continued to spank her, making her clench on the ginger more.

"It stings! Ouch! Daddy, stop spanking me! It's making it worse!"

"It's meant to be a punishment, poppet," Archer told her. "It's supposed to sting."

"Got to remind you that any time you disobey, there are consequences," Issy added.

"You're so precious to us, nothing can happen to you."

Issy applied more spanks to her ass until she couldn't decide what hurt more. The spanking or the figging.

Either way, she knew she didn't want to repeat this in a hurry.

Slap! Smack! Ouch! Crap! Tears dripped out of her eyes as he continued to spank her until her ass was throbbing on the outside and stinging on the inside.

Issy stopped spanking her. He rubbed her bottom for a moment, checking out his handiwork before he drew the ginger slowly out of her bottom. "I'll take care of this. You take care of her."

"With pleasure," Archer said. He studied her ass. "Now, that is a very red bottom. Bet it stings, huh?"

She pouted. "That was mean, Papa."

"Poor poppet," he crooned, dropping her legs. "Need a cuddle?"

She nodded and he rearranged them so he was sitting on the sofa with her straddling his lap. He rubbed his hand up and down her back.

"A red bottom and a stinging asshole. Maybe next week you'll try not to be so naughty huh?"

"I'll try, Papa."

Issy returned, sitting next to Archer and she turned her face towards him. He leaned in and kissed her lips gently, his hand resting on her lower back.

"So what did you think of your first figging, baby doll?" Issy asked.

"I think that I am throwing out every piece of ginger in the house."

Issy shook his head. "That sort of talk will just end with you over the kitchen table and my belt being applied to your ass."

Eek!

"I didn't mean it! I love ginger. It's the best."

Both men burst into laughter.

"What do you think, brother?" Archer asked. "Shall we give her our present now?"

"Present?" She sat up and looked at them both. "What present?"

Issy frowned. "Don't think she should be rewarded after being punished."

"Hmm. You are right." Archer rubbed at his chin.

"Please, please, please," she begged.

"She is pretty cute, though," Archer said. His eyes were twinkling with laughter.

Issy sighed. "It sets a bad precedent."

"How about just this once?"

"You're lucky your Papa is such a softie," Issy told her. But she could see the amusement in his gaze. "Baby doll, you wait here and we'll go get it."

Archer slid her off the sofa. "Hands over your eyes and wait right here." He waggled his finger for good measure. "We'll be back in minute."

What were they getting? What could it be? The suspense almost killed her and it wasn't until she heard them walk back in that she remembered to cover her eyes.

"Daddy! Papa! What is it? What's my present?"

"Keep those eyes covered," Issy warned.

She felt someone brush her left side then another against her right side. They each grabbed hold of a hand and pulled them off her eyes.

"Open your eyes, poppet," Archer commanded.

She opened her eyes, blinking, unable to work out what she was looking at for a start. Then it hit her. It was a small house. Similar to the ones that Dave had made for her, only...

Wonky.

Very wonky.

The overhang of the roof was longer on one side than the other. Then she realized that one wall was actually shorter than the other. The windows weren't cut evenly, giving it an even more lopsided appearance. It had been painted pink with white shutters, except some of the shutters were bigger than others.

"She doesn't like it," Archer said. "I told you we should have just bought one."

"It doesn't mean as much," Issy argued back. "Anyone can buy one. We made her one."

"It's terrible, though. It's going to break as soon as she touches it. It's not nearly as good as Dave's train set."

Her heart stuttered. Tears filled her eyes, blurring her vision. "You made this for me?"

Archer took hold of her left hand. "Yes, poppet. But you don't have to play with it if you don't want to. It's probably a hazard anyway."

"And I thought I was meant to be the negative one," Issy snapped. "It won't fall apart. Look at the back."

He turned it to show the open back, which had two levels and was painted a plain white. "We haven't had a chance to make any people for it. This has been taking up our spare time."

"When did you have time?" she asked in amazement.

"We found some time every day," Archer told her. "While one of us kept you entertained, the other one would sneak off to work on it." He gave it a skeptical look. "Still think it's not safe."

Issy turned it back around then he gave the roof a thump. "It's solid."

A shutter fell off onto the floor. He reached down and quickly scooped it up, placing it in his pocket. "Archer did that one."

"I did not!"

She started giggling. And then she wasn't laughing, she was crying.

"Shit! She's crying." Issy leaped for her but Archer pulled her up into his arms first, carrying her to the sofa.

"Shh, poppet. It's okay. If you don't want to play with it, you don't have to." Archer sat, holding her tightly on his lap.

Issy crouched in front of her. He rubbed his hand up and down her back. "We know it's not as good as Dave's train set that he made. We didn't make it to replace that. But we just thought... maybe you would like something to play with that we made for you. Look."

He moved back and picking up the house, tilted it so she could see underneath.

For Caley
From Daddy and Papa who love her very much.

She sobbed, burying her face in Archer's chest.

"Shit, Archer, what do we do?"

"Take it away," Archer told him. "Get it out of her sight."

"No, Daddy, don't!" She jumped out of Archer's lap and raced over to the small house, hugging it. Carefully. "I love it."

"Then why did you cry?" Issy asked.

"It just...it's amazing. And special. And I can't believe you guys did this for me. Thank you!" She jumped at Issy, hugging him tight before moving to Archer, giving him a squeeze. "Thank you so much. I'm so lucky."

"Nope," Issy told her, moving up behind her so she was wrapped up in their embrace.

"What he means is that we're the lucky ones," Archer told her.

"Christ. I hate when he does that," Issy grumbled.

She giggled.

She waited until later that night to give them their present.

She sat between them on the huge couch.

"What's this, poppet?" Archer grumbled. "You're not working tonight."

She cleared her throat. "Uhh, no. I thought you might like to read a bit of the book I'm working on. You'll probably want to wait until it's finished to read it all. But here's the beginning."

"Wait, I finally get to read a book you've written?" Issy asked, half turning towards her.

Heat filled her cheeks. "It's only fair. Since it's about the two of you."

She stared down at the opening words.

IF I'D KNOWN the thunderstorm was going to bring them to me, I wouldn't have been so scared. I would have known that my life was going to change. That nothing would ever be the same.

And I would have told myself that I never had to be frightened again.

They were going to heal me. Body and soul.

Because the two of them, they were going to be my saviors, my heroes, my protectors.

My Daddy and my Papa.

Printed in Great Britain
by Amazon

35807797R00218